the Trade

A novel by

KI STEPHENS

For all the people out there who were led to believe they're not enough.

Playlist

WHY	SABRINA CARPENTER	♥	2:51
LITTLE FREAK	HARRY STYLES	♥	3:22
SHE CALLS ME BACK	NOAH KAHAN	♥	4:04
PILLOWTALK	ZAYN	♥	3:23
STYLE	TAYLOR SWIFT	♥	3:51
BETTER	KHALID	♥	3:49
NOTICE ME	ROLE MODEL, BENEE	♥	3:12
YOU ARE ENOUGH	SLEEPING AT LAST	♥	3:00
POWER OVER ME	DERMOT KENNEDY	♥	3:27
MESS IT UP	GRACIE ABRAMS	♥	2:51
MORAL OF THE STORY	ASHE, NIALL HORAN	♥	3:19
BLAME'S ON ME	ALEXANDER STEWART	♥	2:18
PIECES	DYLAN CONRIQUE	♥	2:27
UNDRUNK	FLETCHER	♥	3:03
HOLD ME WHILE YOU WAIT	LEWIS CAPALDI	♥	3:26
A LITTLE BIT YOURS	JP SAXE	♥	3:46
FEEL LIKE SHIT	TATE MCRAE	♥	3:24
I MISS YOU, I'M SORRY	GRACIE ABRAMS	♥	2:48
KISS ME	SIXPENCE NONE THE RICHER	♥	3:29
THIS LOVE (TAYLOR'S VERSION)	TAYLOR SWIFT	♥	4:10

Chapter One
WEST

If I'm forced to spend another thirty seconds staring at this blank Word document, I might be tempted to bang my head against my desk. Repeatedly. I'm so sick of pretending like I'm cut out for all of this—my classes, my scholarship, my futile attempts at finishing this godforsaken essay.

I don't know how much longer I can play the dutiful college student, a D1 athlete who actually has his shit together outside of the locker room. The harsh reality? I'm not that guy, and I never will be.

But for now, this assignment will have to wait. There are only twenty minutes left on the clock before I'm due on the practice field, and I need to switch gears.

I don't have room to think about Greek mythology right now. Not when I'm meant to be throwing myself into our grueling two-hour practice schedule. And to top it all off, I'm still nursing a hamstring that's on the brink of tearing.

I tweaked it a few weeks back, and I don't want Coach to find out about it, especially considering my lackluster grades as of late. Not only would he lay into me about everything, but he could deny me the one thing I truly want—the singular ambition I've set my sights on for the past two years.

I plan to declare early for the draft.

It's becoming increasingly clear that I can't juggle being a college student and a potential pro athlete at the same time. Barely managing a C-plus average these past two years, hitting just the minimum grade point to hold on to my place on the team and, consequently, my full-ride scholarship.

It may sound like a breeze, but it's truly been a teeth-gritting struggle, and I'm more than aware that it's not a good look for anyone. I'm a negligent jock, a careless athlete, a fucking waste of potential.

I've heard it all before.

But damn it, I do try. Against all odds, I do. My learning disabilities might throw more hurdles in my way, but ultimately, others' opinions of me don't amount to shit. Because sooner rather than later, I'll be rubbing shoulders with the pros.

That is, provided I can get Coach Rodriguez on board.

By the time I've gritted my way through another tormenting round of RB drills and finished off with forty-yard sprints, I'm barely concealing my limp. I pull off my helmet, freeing my hair, now slick with sweat, as I work to shake off the exertion.

"Coach, can I have a minute?"

I struggle to maintain a normal gait as I jog up beside him. It may have been tense before, but now my hamstring's fucking killing me, cramping and throbbing with every step I take.

Coach Rodriguez pauses, a contrite expression on his face. "Don't think I didn't notice your leg out there, West."

"Just feeling tight." The lie carelessly slips from my lips as I tug at my clinging jersey, pulling it away from my neck. "I swear."

He gives me a wary look, eyes scanning my face before he speaks again. "Okay, you better foam roll and stretch tonight. I want you to take it easy."

"Yeah, of course. I'm planning on it."

"Did you need something else?"

"I was hoping we could set up a meeting to talk about the draft."

"No," he answers immediately.

"No?"

"We don't need to set up a meeting, son." He places one firm hand on my shoulder. "I already know my answer. It's gonna be a no from me."

His harsh words knock the wind right out of me. Two and half seasons on the field—exhausting myself physically, struggling academically, and always playing by the goddamn books—and yet this is my coach's response.

"We can't even discuss this?"

"No, we can't," he says. "Give me another good year, get those grades up, and graduate with your scholarship. You can declare once you've secured your degree. Just like pretty much every other senior on the team."

"Sir—"

"That's my recommendation. Take it or leave it, but just know you won't have the support of your coach if you decide to go against this." His gaze is somber but steadfast. "Understood?"

I clench my jaw, holding back the sudden urge to flash him both middle fingers and yell out a big Fuck You.

"Understood." I give him a tight half-smile, turning on my heel to catch up with my teammate. I don't know what I expected, but it sure as hell wasn't that. He didn't even give me the slightest shred of a chance.

"Cam!" I call, hands cupped around my jaw as I nod toward the bleachers.

Camden Scott is one big motherfucker. He's a linebacker for the team. Huge, intimidating, and one of my best friends. The man absolutely loves playing the game, but he has no plans to go pro. He'd rather study biomedical engineering for the rest of his life.

According to Cam, only about five percent of physical science jobs are held by Black men. And my best friend since freshman year, well, he's determined to contribute to the stat. In his words, he plans to become a goddamn engineer, a biomedical pioneer, and a PhD candidate in the next few years. All of the above, if he can swing it.

"Hey, man," he shouts back, shoving his helmet inside a Dayton U duffel. "Are you heading to the showers?"

"Nah, I'm just gonna shower back at the house."

"Then let's get the hell out of here." He swings himself over the divider, coming up beside me to exit the field.

We slowly make our way past the endless rows of bleachers, eventually crossing in front of the Intramural Training Building.

"So, what were you talking to Rodriguez about?" he finally asks, effectively breaking my brooding silence.

"He doesn't want me declaring early."

"Fuck, man. I'm sorry."

"It's just bullshit. He wouldn't even—"

"West! Hey!" I'm cut off by the sound of a familiar voice, tiny feet pattering on the pavement as she runs to catch up with us. I manage to stifle a groan, running my fingers through my sweat-damp hair before I turn to greet her.

"Cass," I grind out, forcing my lips to curve into a smile.

My eyes flicker across her uniform. Tight cheer skirt. Long tan legs. Tiny little waist. Yeah, Cassidy Viotto is hot as hell, but I'm really not in the mood for all this right now.

"Did you want to come over to my place tonight?" she asks, that fake sultry tone slipping into her high-pitched voice. She bats her thick lashes at me, biting down on those full lips of hers.

"It was a brutal practice, Cass." I sigh, rubbing at the back of my neck. "I'm tired, gonna hit the hay early."

She rolls her eyes, glancing quickly at Cam before leaning in close. She makes sure her lips graze my ear as she whispers, "I could do that thing with my tongue you like."

Fuck if I can help it, but blood immediately rushes to places it shouldn't. Maybe a night with Cassidy *would* be a good distraction from this bullshit with Coach, after all.

"Uh . . . I mean—"

Wait, no. Think with your upstairs brain, West. You want to be alone tonight, relaxing at home after a long steaming shower. Besides, she hooked up with your teammate less than a week ago. Not that I really give a shit, but it does kind of ruin the appeal.

"No, you know what? I said I'm tired, Cass." I work to keep the irritation from my voice. "Maybe another time."

"Well, if you're tired . . ." She places her palm against my chest, stroking her slender fingers down my jersey. "We could just, like, talk or something."

The fuck? I glance at Cam, shaking my head before pulling Cassidy to the side. She may be overly forward, bordering on stalk-erish, but I'm not about to embarrass her in front of my teammate.

Once we're a good few feet away, I open my mouth to ask, "What are you trying to do?"

"What do you mean?" She crosses her arms over her chest. "Why'd you bring me over here?"

"So we can have a private conversation. You want me to come over to *talk*? That's not what this is, Cassidy."

"Oh my God." She blows out a heated breath, perching both hands on her hips. "You're acting like I asked you on a date, West. I just said *talk*. Friends can talk."

"They can. Little problem, we're not friends."

"Oh, come on."

"No, seriously, Cass." I shrug off her advances for the second time. "We hardly talked before you brought me home that first night."

"Well, we could start now," she insists, stomping her foot with a dramatic flair.

"I don't think so. I'm not trying to confuse things."

"Confuse things?" she shrieks. "We can't even talk? Trust me, I'm not that desperate." Her eyes narrow as she pushes a thick strand of hair behind her ear. "Besides, you talk to O'Connor all the time."

And there it is. The fucking jealousy that always flares its ugly head. Sure, I occasionally talk to her cheer teammate Shannon O'Connor, the redheaded spitfire who's been on my mind since freshman year.

"Right, and there's the difference. I'm not *fucking* O'Connor."

Her shoulders straighten, spine stiff. "Yeah, but you want to."

Yeah, okay, well . . . she's got me there. Shannon's not only one of the hottest girls I've ever seen, but she's also a goddamn sweetheart. I'd be lying if I outright denied the accusation.

"Don't know what you want me to say to that."

Yeah, sure. It's an asshole comment to make to the girl you've been sleeping with, but I'm not gonna stand here and play games with her. Not right now, at least, when my head's still reeling from that conversation with Coach.

"Wow, West." She scoffs, and it grates on something soft inside my brain. "I thought you were different, but you're just like all the rest of your asshole teammates."

"Please, Cassidy, don't act like you would've been interested in the first place if I wasn't a fucking football player."

"I guess that's where I went wrong," she shouts, no longer caring that we have an audience. "You're all just a bunch of . . . slutty, little fuckboys, aren't you?"

"Seriously?" I raise both brows. "Is that why you had Miller's cock in your mouth last weekend?"

"What?" she asks, voice low and eyes wide.

"Yeah, think I didn't know about that?"

"More like I thought you wouldn't care." She flicks her hair over her shoulders, that evil little gleam returning to her gaze. "We're not together, remember?"

"Now you're onto something."

"Oh, fuck you, West."

"You certainly won't be anymore."

With a huff, she pivots away from me, her back straight as she strides toward the Intramural building. Exhaling a deep, resigned breath, I shuffle my way back to where Cam is waiting for me.

"What the hell was that about?" he asks, raising a skeptical brow.

"Fuck if I know." I shrug, devoid of the energy to explain myself. "But I'm definitely done with her."

"That's probably good." He hikes his duffel bag up over his shoulder. "She has those wild eyes, you know." I snort a laugh, giving him a quick dig with my elbow as we continue up the hill. "No, I'm serious. I've always thought so. I never understood why you went for her in the first place."

"She was there," I admit.

And isn't that the cold hard truth of it. *She was there.* Practically threw herself at me a few months ago, not that I have any right to complain about it. In fact, I was all for it at the time. Unfortunately, Cassidy's attitude got really old, really fast.

"Damn." He gives me a tight-lipped wince. "Glowing review."

"What can I say, man? I've got too much shit going on to work for it. She made things a little bit easier on me. That's all."

"Sure, I get it." He pats me on the bicep. "But you probably ruined your one shot of ever hooking up with Shannon."

"Why do you say that?"

"They're teammates, man." He gives me a lopsided grin. "You know, there is that whole girl code thing."

"They're not really that close."

"They live together, dude."

"Yeah, true," I say with a careless half shrug. "But I heard Shan's trying to move out at the end of semester—says she's getting too old for the drama of it all."

"There you go, man. You can wait until spring term to shoot your shot, then."

"I don't know. I'm not really trying to date."

"Who said anything about dating?"

"I don't know, Shan's cool . . . I just don't know if she'd be down for a fuck-buddy situation." Because at this point, that's about the only thing I can manage. Between the team, my slipping grades, maintaining my scholarship, and my chance at the draft, there's just too much hanging in the air for me right now.

It's not that I'm against dating in general. But seriously, who has the fucking time for it all?

"Might as well try. She's smoking hot."

"Ridiculously hot, man." I mull it over for another beat. "You know what? Maybe I will give it a shot. If the opportunity presents itself."

He grins wide and gives me one sharp pat to the back. "Atta boy."

Yeah, to hell with it. A potential night sharing the sheets with Shannon O'Connor? Only a saint with an iron will could pass up that offer.

Chapter Two

I'M down on my knees for the fifth time this week.

No matter how hard I scrub, the nail polish won't come off the carpet in my spare room. I've tried every little home remedy, from hair spray to vinegar to good old-fashioned acetone, and nothing seems to work.

My brother, Mica, should be doing this work for me. He's the one who wanted me to find a roommate in the first place. According to his twisted big-brother logic, it's not "safe or practical" for a twenty-one-year-old woman to live alone in the city.

Under normal circumstances, I'd tell Mica it's not safe or practical for him to tell me what to do. But considering he's paid for my housing for the last three years, I guess I have to suck it up and listen to reason.

"Ace," I chirp his nickname into the phone. "I can't get this fucking stain out. No one's gonna want to live in this room."

"Then I'll get the carpets redone, Lili." He gives me an exasperated sigh. "It's not a big deal."

My brother has always called me Lili, and I've returned the favor by calling him Ace. We traded these nicknames as kids, creating an unspoken bond, a secret language meant just for us.

We're the Jennings siblings—Jade Lilianna and Mica Aciano— our names inspired by gems and plants. Growing up, we were quite the formidable duo, far closer than most siblings of the opposite sex. And our parents always insisted that we were their perfect, little angel children.

While some might see me as mildly angelic, my brother's quite the opposite. It's a whole different story with him . . . and that's putting it mildly.

Mica has always been a wild child. He's a rule breaker, while I'm more straight-laced. He's a cocky player, while I'm the girl who usually plays it safe. He's a cornerback in the NFL, while I'm a . . . college journalist.

We're opposites, but we fit together like no one else.

"I probably won't find someone in the middle of the term, anyway." I shrug, pinning my cell phone against one shoulder. "You can have the carpets replaced during the break."

"Lili," he warns. "I want someone in there by spring term . . . at the latest."

"Yes, Father."

"I'm serious, Lil. I don't like you living alone, especially near all those drunk losers at your school."

"You think living with another girl is going to protect me?"

"I think there's safety in numbers, no matter what. Your room-mate would be around if you don't come home."

"Can't you just come stay with me after the season ends?" I ask the question even though I know the answer. It just doesn't make sense for Mica to live with me near Dayton. For many reasons, one being that his football team, the Bobcats, is constantly on the road traveling.

"You know how busy my schedule is, even in the off-season," he says, "I'd barely have time to be there."

"You'll still visit, though, right?"

I swear, every year, I spend less and less time with my brother. If he's not busy playing the game, he's training. If he's not training, he's in the gym. All other gaps and crevices are filled by his avid social calendar or, should I say, his endless string of one-night stands.

Yes. It's gross to think of my brother in that way, but it's just the honest truth. I doubt he'll ever settle down with one woman. He's not exactly a sleazeball, but he's no patron saint when it comes to his football groupies.

Come to think of it, I haven't seen him seriously date anyone since high school . . . and that was nearly ten years ago.

"You know I will, as much as I can," he promises.

"Okay."

"Just at least start the roommate search, okay? That's all I ask."

"Fine."

"Fine?" He lets out a hearty laugh. "You know, you're stubborn as hell."

"You're the stubborn one."

Because if it were up to me, I wouldn't even bother with all this roommate bullshit. I'm fine on my own. In fact, I prefer it. I'd never have to worry about leaving a dish in the sink, or bringing a date home, or cleaning nail polish off this damn carpet.

It's simple, uncomplicated, and quiet—just how I happen to like things.

"I swear it will be good for you. Trust me," he adds. "But hey, Lili, I really gotta get going. Practice starts in ten."

"Okay." I blow out a sigh. "Bye, Ace. Love you."

"Love you," he murmurs back.

I end the call, quickly scrolling over to my Instagram feed. I may have agreed to officially start the roommate search, but that doesn't mean I have to put in any actual effort. Swiping open a new story, I type out a quick message: *looking for female roommate to share two-bedroom apartment—preferably Dayton U student*

I'm certain Mica will catch sight of my post, and I can only hope he's appeased by my half-hearted effort. With that little task checked off my list, I turn my attention to my reflection in the mirror, fluffing my wayward curls. I make a mental note to give myself a break once in a while, take a deep breath, and recite my daily affirmations. Then I sweep my laptop into my bag and take one last look around my apartment before I make my way to campus.

As I push through the hive of students, the crisp morning air brings a welcome flush to my cheeks. The Hayworth Building, my daily destination and the home of the university newsroom, stands tall, grand yet familiar, amidst the flurry of activity.

Stepping inside, the hum of a newsroom in full swing greets me —a symphony of keyboards clacking, people chatting, and the subtle rustle of newsprint. It's a chaotic melody, but one I've come to find comfort in.

With a nod to some of the other reporters, I maneuver through the disorganization toward my small haven in the corner. It's cluttered, personalized with scribbled notes and discarded coffee cups. It's a far cry from glamorous, but it's my chaos, my home within these four dingy walls.

It's not long before my editor, Garrett, ambles over to my desk. His disheveled hair, five-o'clock shadow, and the hint of an almost smile give him a boy-next-door charm, a stark contrast to the authority he attempts to carry in our newsroom.

"Jade," he says, punctuated by a casual salute. "I have a fresh piece for you. Student Union, meeting tonight, budget cuts. I want you there."

While the topic isn't exactly the Super Bowl of news, I accept it, knowing every story, no matter how small, has its own merit. At least, that's what I've been telling myself for the past three years. It's the only way I've been able to survive Garrett's misogynistic attitude.

For some reason, the man doesn't think I have enough experience to be a sports reporter. Yet, Jeremy, Liam, and Dante were apparently born with the right credentials . . . as if their ability to write a quality article is quantified by the tiny male appendages between their legs.

I don't even need to be in charge of the sports section or to be taken off student life altogether. That's not what I'm asking for. All I want is a chance to cover a few Dayton U football games. Honestly, I have the experience because I practically grew up on the sport myself.

Not to mention my brother's a goddamn NFL player . . . not that I'll ever use that truth to my advantage. I shouldn't have to stoop to that level, especially not for the chauvinistic Garrett Warners of the world.

"Got it," I hiss between gritted teeth. "I'll get the scoop on the student body's reaction."

As he walks away, I nestle into my chair with a sigh, preparing for the mission ahead. This isn't the adrenaline rush of a sports story, but it's my assignment, my responsibility. And I'm going to give it my all, despite my distinct lack of interest in the subject matter.

Hours later, during a quick break from drafting potential interview questions, my phone buzzes with an unexpected message. Shannon—a lifeguard from Sunshine Ranch, the camp I counseled at over the summer—has just sent me a text.

> SHANNON
>
> hey girl! I saw your IG story. I'm looking to move out of my place at the end of next month. would that be do-able? I think we'd have fun living together!

This girl, with her fiery red hair and infectious optimism, had become a summer friend, bonded over shared experience and empathy. Her little brother was recently diagnosed with muscular dystrophy, while my dad has battled with multiple sclerosis ever since I can remember.

We've seen the same kind of pain in the ones we love, and it brought us closer, creating an unexpected friendship.

JADE

> that works! I'll send over some details, but the room is all yours if you want it

Her response pops up before I can even manage to lock my phone.

SHANNON

> yay! I'm so in!

So, I suppose that's all settled, then. Shannon O'Connor is going to be my new roommate for spring term. While I'm relieved that the situation has worked itself out, I can't help but feel a pang of unease in the pit of my stomach.

Shannon will undoubtedly bring her spark into my quiet world, shaking up my routine in ways I can't even begin to imagine. It's not the calm and collected life I envisioned, but maybe, with a bit of self-convincing, I could see this as the plot twist my story needs.

Chapter Three
WEST

I'm a third-year student retaking Foundations of English Literature during his second semester. If that wasn't bad enough, the fact that I need a writing tutor really cements the whole thing.

I'm officially a fuckup, and I can't even afford to pay the guy properly.

Thankfully, my new tutor accepts currency in the form of dining hall points and coffee cart pastries. I realize it's a brand-new level of pathetic, but I'm willing to exploit my athletic scholarship to the fullest degree.

While the cashier rings up a few cherry tarts and a cheese croissant for Mr. Tutor, my eyes drift to the girl standing beside me. She idly scrolls through her phone, and I take a second to check her out.

She's tall, leggy, with glowy skin and braided hair. Now, I'm not usually the type to ogle girls in public, but *damn*.

"Hey, I'm West." I pause for a beat, waiting for her to glance up and meet my gaze. "I don't think I've seen you at the Grind before."

"Not interested," she immediately fires back.

Well, okay, then. I guess I can appreciate that response. She seems like a girl who knows exactly what she wants and exactly what she doesn't. It's no skin off my back.

I mean, it's not every day that someone turns me down. I may not be the sharpest tool in the shed, but I know that most women find me decently attractive. Either they're primarily interested in my looks . . . or they just want me because I play football.

"Hey, man. Great last season!" I tilt my head toward the sound of the unfamiliar male voice, stiffening as he punctuates the compliment with a sharp pat to my shoulder. "You know, you guys deserved to beat the Ospreys this year."

"Thanks, man." I nod, holding back a grimace. "We had a great time out there, but I'm definitely looking forward to a rematch next season."

"Hell yeah, dude."

I suppress a wince as he grabs his to-go cup and turns to leave. While it's nice to be appreciated by a fellow student, I'm not sure why they always feel the need to put their hands on me in some way or another. I've suffered through more than enough random pats on the back, fist bumps, high fives, and the occasional chest stroking to top it all off.

It's a bit invasive, excessive, even for a guy like me who thrives on physical affection.

"So, you're on the football team." The leggy brunette slides her phone into her back pocket, giving me a blatant once-over.

"I am." I blink, put off by her sudden change in interest.

It's ridiculous, but I suppose I should know the score by now. I wouldn't say this campus is necessarily riddled with jersey chasers, but there's a select few who always manage to make their presence known—girls who are only interested in the potential money, fame, and popularity that comes with bagging an athlete.

I usually wouldn't complain, but today, it's just kind of pissing me off.

"My name's Aaliyah," she says, her voice sickly sweet. "Would you want to grab coffee sometime?"

"You know, I think I'll pass."

She scoffs. I hold back an eye roll. Then I happily swipe my pastries off the counter without another word and head toward the library. Balancing my snack haul with expert finesse, I stroll across the quad to make my way over to North Campus.

It's undoubtedly my favorite place to study. Mostly because there are no arbitrary rules about not talking, or not eating, or not . . . breathing the right fucking way. Somehow, I don't think I could survive an entire study session with my mouth closed.

Once I'm inside, I glance around in search of Mr. Tutor. I'm still a few minutes early, but if I'm lucky, I might just spot those familiar Coke-bottle glasses of his. Instead, I'm pleasantly surprised by the sight of my favorite redhead.

As soon as Shannon catches my eye, she waves me over with a wide grin. The seat beside her is empty, but an unfamiliar girl sits across from her at the same table. Books and notes are spread out evenly between them.

I slide in beside O'Connor, wrapping an arm around the back of her chair as she turns to face me. "Hey there," I say, lips curving up. "It's been a while."

"Sure has." The smile on her face is pretty, poised, and polite as I drink her in.

"I haven't seen you since last term," I say. "I heard you found a new apartment."

"I did. Actually, this is my new roommate, Jade." She gestures across me to her study partner. "She's also a junior this year."

"Hi." Her roommate gives me a small wave and a tiny smile, so I take a moment to soak in her appearance. She has shoulder-length chocolate curls with sun-kissed skin. The top half of her body is mostly hidden beneath a baggy sweatshirt. I suppose she has a cute face—heart-shaped with these big, bold brows—but nothing else about her features really stands out to me.

At least, not when she's sitting across from O'Connor.

"This is my friend West," Shannon says, completing the introduction. "You know what? I totally didn't even think of this before, but he's actually on the football team here at Dayton."

I give her an odd look before nodding my confirmation.

"Jade's a huge football fan," Shannon says. "She's got posters of the Bobcats all over the apartment. Did you know, her br—"

"Shan," Jade interrupts, shaking her head, eyes wide, as if to convey some secret signal.

"Anyway." Shannon awkwardly clears her throat. "Well, yeah, sorry . . . um, what I was trying to say is that Jade loves football."

Right. I'm sure Jade really *loves* football, just like every other supposed superfan at this damn school. In fact, I bet she's been to each and every game just for pure love of the sport.

"So, you've seen me out on the field before?" I ask, trying to mask my skepticism.

"Maybe." Jade shrugs, squinting her eyes to study my face. "What's your last name?"

"Uh, it's Westman-Cooke."

She cocks one brow. "Your name is *West* Westman?"

"No," I snort out my denial. "West's a nickname."

"Right." She pulls her bottom lip between her teeth, a sudden look of concentration on her face. "So, what's your first name, Westman-Cooke?"

"Theodore . . . uh, Theo."

"Oh, that's a nice name." She gives me an easy smile, but I can already tell another question sits on the tip of her tongue, so I wave a dismissive hand.

"Does everyone call you West, or is it mainly a teammate thing?"

"Everyone."

"Right." She purses her lips, nods once. "Makes sense. So, what position do you play, West?"

This fucking girl and her endless stream of questions. "Running back."

"You any good, then?"

"I'm on a full-ride scholarship at a D1 school." The corner of my mouth quirks up into a cocky grin. "You tell me."

"Good argument." Her brow lifts again. "Any plans to join the NFL?"

"Yes," I say, working over the muscles of my jaw.

"Thinking about declaring early?"

She fires off these questions like they mean absolutely nothing. Like I haven't spent the last two months agonizing over the prospect . . . as if Coach didn't think the notion was just some big fucking joke to everyone but me.

I turn my attention back to the redheaded cheerleader beside me. The girl I came over to talk to in the first place . . . before I got sidetracked by this nosy little mouse. Yeah, that's what she reminds me of—a squeaky mouse who can't be bothered to mind her own business.

I grit my teeth, fighting back my rising temper. Little mouse *is* Shannon's friend, after all. "Where'd you even find this girl, Shan?"

"I told you." Shannon narrows her eyes, clearly put out by my sour attitude. "She's my new roommate."

Right. Mousy's just her roommate, not her friend.

"Must be nice living with a jersey chaser," I half-heartedly mutter.

"Excuse me?" The three syllables hit like a strong wind that blows through the room, freezing everything in its path. I turn back to Jade, her dark eyes sparked with a flare of annoyance, cheeks flushed with indignation. "Sorry, Shannon," she stammers, obviously flustered, "I just remembered . . . I need to go find a book for class."

She doesn't wait for any sort of response, pushing her chair back with a loud, grating scrape against the linoleum floor. With a flicker of her dark curls, she disappears among the bookshelves, leaving an uneasy silence in her wake.

"Why are you being so rude?" Shannon's voice jolts me out of my trancelike state. She punctuates her words with a light shove against my shoulder, a playful gesture that contradicts the serious undertone of her words.

"You're right." I sigh, rubbing at my temples. "I'm sorry, I'm not in the best mood."

She pauses for a moment, her lips pursed in a thoughtful line. Then, with a good-natured roll of her eyes, she waves me off. "You don't need to apologize to me," she says, effectively shutting down any lingering awkwardness.

"Yeah." I bite down on the inside of my cheek, nibbling on the soft flesh. "I guess I wasn't really expecting an interview in the library."

"That's actually kind of funny," she says with a giggle, lip twitching as she struggles to contain her laughter. "Jade's a reporter for the *Daily*. She probably just got herself into interviewer mode without even thinking about it."

"Yeah? Well, shit . . . now I really feel like a dick."

"You should," she insists, pinning me with a harsh glare. "Jade's really cool. Actually, now that I think about it, you guys kind of have a lot in common."

"I'm sure we do." I shift course, pushing aside the flare of guilt burning in my stomach. "So, you finally did it, huh? Moved out of the Spirit House once and for all?"

Her face brightens. "Yes. It feels so good to be free."

"Free of Cassidy, you mean?"

She laughs again, folding her arms tightly across her chest. "Cass is fine, West."

"Sure she is."

"You know, you never told me your side of things. You and I have talked a few times since you two broke up, but you never actually mentioned what happened."

"I didn't *break up* with Cass," I clarify. "We were never together."

"Oh, that's not what she told people."

"What exactly did she tell people?"

"She said you wanted to be exclusive, but she didn't." A sweet smirk twists her expression. "Then you got angry and called her a slut in front of the whole football team."

"God, Shan." I give her a humorless snort. "I think you know me better than that. I mean, come on . . . you really believed that bullshit for the past two months?"

"Not really."

"Look . . . we were never really together," I adamantly repeat. "Cassidy was also hooking up with other guys on the team, you know? I told her I knew about it . . . but I was trying to have a private conversation. She was the one who started shouting at me in front of Cam. Which, by the way, he was the only other guy around us at the time. *Whole team*, my ass."

"That sounds a little more reasonable." She smiles, and a cute little dimple appears on her left cheek.

"Honestly, Shan?"

"What? You never gave me the lowdown."

"It's kind of an unspoken rule—don't talk about hookups with the girl you're interested in."

"West . . ."

"Shannon," I counter.

"You're not *interested* in me."

"I'm not?" Surprise laces my words, edged with silent laughter.

"I know you, West," she says. "I know the type of girl you usually go for, and it's not me."

"Yeah, no, you're definitely my type," I insist, running a ragged hand through my hair. "I think you're just about everyone's type."

I let my gaze wander, unabashed, tracing the contours of her body. She's undeniably attractive. Gifted with curves in the right places, her skin is a smooth canvas scattered with cute little freckles. And her lips, pouty and inviting, punctuate her soft features perfectly.

"Ohh, I see." Her giggle is lighthearted, a faint blush filling her cheeks. "So, when you say you're interested . . . you mean you want to sleep with me."

I raise both brows.

"West . . . we're *friends*."

"Yeah." I manage to stifle a full-fledged grin. "And I'd like to stay friends."

"*And* you'd like to sleep with me."

"Shannon."

"Cass would kill me," she argues.

"And?"

"And . . . it's not gonna happen."

She shifts in her seat, clearly off-put by my sudden forward approach. She's not a shy person by any means, but I doubt sweet Shannon is used to blatant propositions like this one.

"Okay, if that's your final answer."

"That's my answer for the foreseeable future."

I lift one shoulder. "Still friends, then?"

"Of course." A snort of disbelief escapes her, letting me know that I haven't overstepped my boundaries yet. Hell, maybe she'd actually be interested if it weren't for the whole Cass thing. Or maybe she'd be interested if I just gave it a little more time.

"Fair enough," I say, glancing at the clock behind her head. "I need to head to a meeting with my tutor, but can you tell your new roommate sorry for me?"

"You can just tell her yourself next time you see her."

"Yeah, alright, then."

"Later, West." She gives me a shy smile, tugs her lower lip between her teeth, and a soft heat rises from the base of her neck all the way to the apples of her cheeks.

Well, there you have it. She may be saying she's not interested, but her body language—not to mention that sweet, simmering blush—just taught me two crucial things. First, the door isn't fully closed on a night with O'Connor. And second, if I want a real shot, I better find a way to make things right with her squeaky little mouse of a roommate.

Chapter Four
JADE

IT TURNS out rooming with someone isn't exactly the nightmare I imagined it to be.

On the contrary, these past few weeks of cohabitating with Shannon have morphed into something unexpectedly great. We spend our evenings cooking meals, our heads buried in books during study sessions, and our weekend nights filled with gossiping about her teammates.

She has this uncanny knack for sensing when I need solitude, and she's also obsessively neat. Truthfully, it's like living through some unscripted reality TV show—entertaining, unexpected, and oddly comforting.

Unfortunately, it also means that Mica was right all along, as per usual.

"Jade!" Shannon's chipper voice echoes from the living room. "Pizza before the library?"

The two of us recently stumbled upon this hidden spot on campus called the Vault. It's an underground pizza place filled with late-night activities—improv shows, poetry slams, and open mics. The food never disappoints, even when the entertainment isn't quite up to par.

Ever since the first day we stumbled inside, the place has etched a permanent spot in our Thursday afternoon routine—a few slices followed by a diligent study session at the North Campus Library.

Except for today, Shannon's bowing out on the latter. Apparently, she needs to attend a team meeting for something called "Spring Spirit Night," which leaves me to face the library solo.

I don't mind the lack of company, though. All the more if it means steering clear of Shannon's less-than-savory friends.

Honestly, the whole thing makes zero sense to me. How does someone like Shannon O'Connor, a girl who's all sunshine and butterflies, end up associating with a guy like Theodore Westman-Cooke?

Shannon continues to defend him, claims he's "not usually like that." But he acted like I was invisible that day in the library. No, it was worse than that—he outright labeled me a jersey chaser. As if I'd ever spare a second glance for someone so self-absorbed.

Dismissing the thought, I make a mental checklist of what I'll need for today's session, cram a few books into my bag, and head to the living room. The moment I step inside, Shannon's amused gaze flits across my outfit.

Lips twitching with repressed laughter, she asks, "Lucky sweatshirt again?"

"Of course."

It may be silly, but I love this old, ratty scrap of fabric as if it were my own child. Mica gifted it to me the summer before my first semester of college. He wore it to his last round of finals, earning himself a perfect 4.0 GPA. And now, I'm fortunate enough to have that same luck rub off on me.

I wear it nearly every time I study and never forget to put it on for my exams. It seems inconsequential, really, but it's like my brain can't seem to absorb information without it. There's something about the familiar weight of the worn fabric on my shoulders, the way the material has softened with time, that feels like an old friend cheering me on.

"You do realize it's over seventy degrees outside?"

"Sure do," I chirp, slinging my backpack over one shoulder.

She shakes her head, a warm-hearted smile lighting up her features. "You and your superstitions."

"It's not superstition, Shan," I insist. "It's basically a proven science."

"I guess I shouldn't judge before trying it myself."

"Exactly my point." I return her easy smile. "You ready to go?"

As soon as we reach the Vault, I make a beeline for the counter, stomach rumbling with anticipation. Their pizza is a far cry from the usual, bland campus food we have here, especially considering my usual order—cheese with pineapple and jalapeño on top. I know it sounds odd, but it's actually the most delicious combination of sweet and spicy.

"So, you excited for your date this weekend?" Shannon asks, patiently waiting for me to finish chewing. It's only been about thirty seconds so far, but I've already managed to stuff half a slice inside my mouth.

"Eh." I give her a shrug. "Not really."

I've already been out with this guy, Fred Tomlin, and he wasn't anything to write home about. He's a Ceramic Arts major, so I thought he might actually be interesting. Or, at the very least . . . that he'd be good with his hands.

Instead, I almost fell asleep while he was going down on me.

"Why are you going out with him again, then?"

"I guess I'm hoping the sex is better this time around."

"Jade!" She scolds me like a child, swiftly glancing around to ensure our conversation hasn't turned into public entertainment.

"What?"

"You know, I think that's your problem," she begins in a hushed tone, leaning in closer. "You keep going out with these guys you have no real interest in. The sex is bound to be blah."

"Yeah, maybe you're right."

My heavy sigh fills the air. It's true; I've always played it safe, choosing the steady, dependable types instead of the riskier ones. Not that they're bad guys, overall, but there's been an undeniable void there, an element of passion that always seems to be missing.

"So, maybe it's time to expand your horizons," she says. "Try out a different type for once."

"What else is there?" I groan, rubbing my temples in frustration. "I've gone on dates with a bio major, an art major, engineering, philosophy, etcetera." I tap each finger as I list them off. "I've tasted every flavor by now, Shan."

Her lips curve into a sly smile, green eyes glinting with mischief. "You're missing a very important category here. You know, you can't just knock out all of Dayton's athletic department without even giving them a chance."

"Gag me," I say with a derisive snort.

"They would if you wanted."

"Oh, my God."

"No, seriously, if you're bored of your sex life . . . maybe try things out with an athlete." She gives me an earnest nod. "I can introduce you to some."

"Oh, you mean like your friend from the library?"

"He's not as bad as you make him out to be, Jade. But no, there are plenty of other guys who'd be interested."

"I don't know, Shan." I drag my lower lip between my teeth, contemplating. "I don't see you going on dates with any of these *sex god* athletes of yours."

"That's because I'm not looking for the same thing you are. I think I want a real relationship this time around."

"Then maybe we can trade. You set me up with an athlete, and then you go out with Freddy this weekend."

"Ew." She reaches across the table to smack me, one swift slap to the shoulder. "I'm not going out with a guy you've already slept with."

"What's wrong with that?"

"We live together . . . I mean, there's this little thing called boundaries."

"Suit yourself, then."

"Just go on your date with Fred," she says. "Then I'll put some more thought into who I might set you up with next."

I huff out a resigned "Fine."

"Yeah, it will be fine. But hey, look, I gotta get going," she says, gaze stuck on her phone, the unexpected urgency of her meeting written all over her face.

"Alright," I mumble through a mouthful of pizza, the spice still tingling on my tongue. I give my fingers a quick lick before waving her off. "See you later."

She calls out a hasty "Good luck at the library!" as she races up the stairs.

Left alone, I turn my attention to the remnants of our meal. I gather our trash, tossing Shannon's discarded crusts into the compost bin. She may be obsessively neat about our apartment, but she always seems to leave a mess behind her everywhere else.

With the table clean, I sling my backpack onto my shoulder, letting out a resigned sigh. The serene quiet of North Campus is my next stop—along with a daunting pile of assignments waiting for me.

An hour into my solo study session, I've barely chipped away at my study guide for Mass Media Law. The table in front of me is buried under a wild landscape of textbooks, notebooks, colorful sticky notes, highlighters, and pens.

This may look like a hot mess to an outsider, but to me, it's the opposite. The more chaotic my physical space is, the more organized my mind becomes. The visual clutter, in a strange, unexplainable way, helps me compartmentalize and sort my thoughts, untangling the knots inside my head.

Unfortunately, my concentration shatters at the sound of a familiar male voice calling my name. I raise my head to the sound, my gaze finding its way to the arrogant face attached to it.

"Um, hello?" I question, my confusion rising at the sight of West amidst my carefully orchestrated chaos. Of all the people, why did it have to be him disturbing my peace?

"Hey, it's, uh, West?" He furrows his brow, scratching at the back of his neck. "We met the other day."

A flat "Yes" slips from my lips, my face unreadable. "I recall."

"Right." He tightly grips one strap of his backpack, fingers drumming against the worn material. "Well, I just wanted to apologize to you for being a jackass then."

I raise a skeptical brow. "Really?"

"Really," he confirms, sincerity lacing his voice. "I wasn't in the best headspace that day, and I just . . . well, something you mentioned kind of set me off, I guess."

My lips quirk up into a teasing smile. "Are you saying that my nonstop questioning offended you, Theo?"

"West," he corrects swiftly. "And yeah, I guess. Something like that."

With a playful tap of my pen against my chin, I prod him further. "Which question was it exactly?"

He brushes it off with a curt "Not important."

"If you say so."

"You know, all those questions . . . Shan told me you're a reporter," he says, veering the conversation off course. "Must be kinda hard to turn it off, yeah?"

"I am," I say, leaning back in my chair. "And I guess it is, sometimes. Sometimes it's just my natural curiosity."

His features twist into a smug grin, echoing my words from the previous day. "So, you any good, then?"

"Well, I recently wrote a riveting article on the new residence hall. I'm sure you read that one, just as soon as you picked up the last issue of the *Dayton Daily*."

His smirk broadens, amusement sparkling in his eyes. "Ah, must have skipped right over it. I'll have to scrounge up my copy again."

"I'm sure you could find one in a recycling bin somewhere."

"Come on, Jade." His laughter fills the air, bright and surprising, an ember kindling in his eyes. "Not everything you write is complete garbage, I'm sure."

"Contrary to popular belief, Theo, it kind of is," I counter, keeping my voice low. "The day I get to write about something truly interesting . . . well, that's gonna be a cold day in Hell."

"It's West," he corrects me again with an indulgent smile. "And what is it that you want to write about?"

"Not important."

His grin spreads wider. "Aw, come on. I'll show you mine if you show me yours."

"Fine." I sigh, my hands clasped on the table, a silent signal of surrender. "I'd like to write for the sports section, but my editor is against the idea. Honestly, I just wanted to cover, like, one of your games last season."

His brows shoot up. "You want to write about football?"

"Yes," I say, my voice laced with dry sarcasm. "But apparently, I'm not qualified, just because I'm not part of some good ol' boys club."

His scoff is indignant, his expression morphing into disbelief. "Your editor doesn't think you can write about football just because you're a woman?"

"Don't act all surprised. I saw your reaction when Shan mentioned I'm a football fan."

He winces, a twinge of guilt crossing his face. "You're right. That was part of my shitty mood . . . not that I'm making excuses."

I wave him off, working to keep my tone neutral. "Go on."

He rubs the back of his neck again. "You wouldn't believe how many girls lie about being some big fan of mine. It gets old pretty fast."

"Oh yeah." A snort escapes me. "Must be utterly exhausting, having all these gorgeous women falling all over you."

He looks straight into my eyes, sincerity etched into his features. "It is when it's not genuine . . . when it's not about me at all. I could be any random guy on the team, so long as I'm a football player."

Something strange coils inside my gut. A pang of . . . what? Some sort of sympathy that surprises me, considering the awful impression he's made so far. I pause, taking the opportunity to truly soak in his features.

Tall, strong jawline, dark hair. Toned, tan arms. Not to mention those hands. And his eyes, they're a deep caramel brown, a sweet concoction of butter and brown sugar. He's a good-looking guy, no doubt about that. And he might have a decent personality . . . when he's not acting like an arrogant dick for no good reason.

I clear my throat, an attempt to regain my composure. "Well, I definitely don't operate that way."

He presses on. "So, you've never had a crush on a Dayton football player?"

"Not a chance."

"An NFL player, then?"

". . . Maybe," I finally relent. It's not as if I can help it. Some of the guys on my brother's team are just . . . well, there's really no words to describe the physique of a pro football player.

His smirk returns in full force. "I knew it. Come on, Jade. Who's your dream man?"

"I think I've overshared enough."

He raises a thick brow, a teasing smile playing on his lips. "You can tell me some other time, then."

"I don't think so."

"We'll see," he dismisses my protest with a casual wave of his hand.

"Whatever. All I'm saying is that I'm not a jersey chaser."

"Nah, I suppose you aren't." He gives me a genuine smile, a flicker of understanding in his eyes. "I shouldn't have jumped to conclusions."

"You definitely shouldn't have," I say. "And now it's your turn. Pay up."

He blinks in confusion. "Huh?"

"You promised to show me yours."

A slow, cocky smile stretches across his face. "I did, didn't I?"

I narrow my eyes. "It's only fair play."

"Alright." He sighs, collecting his thoughts. "When you asked me about declaring for the draft . . . Well, that's a touchy subject for me right now. Coach won't let me declare early. I approached him about it multiple times last term, and he wouldn't even entertain the idea."

"Why would you want to declare early? I mean, I'm sure you're a decent player, but don't you want to graduate?"

A shrug of his broad shoulders, a brief flicker of bitterness in his eyes. "School's never really been my thing."

"Wow," I sigh, understanding dawning on me. "That's a tough break."

"Yeah?"

"Yeah," I say, shrugging in turn. "Were you expecting me to say something else?"

"Just figured . . . you know, I might get another lecture about the importance of finishing my degree, especially from a girl like you."

"A girl like me, huh?"

"Oh, come on." His smirk returns in full force. "You're a good girl. Aren't you, Jade? Studious. Straight-laced. Serious."

An amused snort escapes me, eyes rolling at his stereotype. "I don't think you actually know a thing about me."

"Maybe not." He leans in, a challenge simmering in his gaze. "But maybe I'd like to."

An unpleasant snort squeaks out of me. "Yeah, those lines don't work on me."

"You think that's a line?"

"Oh, come on." I huff, exasperation lacing my tone. "You're not a good guy. Are you, Theo?"

"You could find out."

"Maybe I don't want to." I shake my head, pulling out my phone to check the time. "And maybe you've overstayed your welcome. I came here to study. Is there some other reason why you're here?"

He stands, tapping the back of my chair twice with his knuckles. "Just to study. So, I'm going to go do that now. See you around, Jade."

I wave him off, a mild twinge of amusement tugging at my lips. "See you."

Despite myself, my gaze lingers on him as he saunters away, an unexpected flutter stirring in my chest. Okay, so he may not be the world's biggest jerk, but that cockiness of his could certainly do with a reality check. It's unfortunate—and somewhat frustrating— how he seems utterly convinced of his own self-importance.

And as I watch him disappear into the crowd, I force myself to shake my head, brushing off the inexplicable warmth that's somehow crept its way into my cheeks.

Chapter Five
WEST

WELL, fucking hell.

That sure looks like another failing grade to me. I turned in my first-ever English Lit paper on Monday, and I've already fumbled the bag. I thought this tutor bullshit was supposed to be helping, but clearly, I need to bump up my efforts here.

With a resigned sigh, I sling my backpack over my shoulder, scrambling up to the front as my classmates shuffle out of the lecture hall.

"Professor, I was wondering if you had a spare minute?"

She glances up from her spot at the podium, readjusting her glasses before giving me a tight smile. "What can I do for you, Theodore?"

I clear my throat, nervously stuffing my hands into my front pockets. "I had a question about the grade I received on my paper."

"You know, all students must earn their grade in my class. Athletes aren't given any special permissions or leeway. Now that it's the off-season, you should be able to put in a little more effort."

Well, goddamn, that was mighty presumptuous of her. I've certainly never asked anyone for special treatment. My 2.3 GPA should be more than enough proof of that.

Besides, I worked my ass off on this paper. My tutor and I spent countless hours analyzing and discussing the assigned text. We worked on it until late into the night, making sure every point was well articulated, and the structure was sound.

I normally wouldn't be shocked by a shitty grade, but this time around, it just feels like a slap to the fucking face.

"I completely understand." I gulp back my frustration. "I'm not asking for leeway, but is there any other feedback you could give me?"

"Yes." She nods, tidying her papers into a neat stack. "Properly cite your sources, and check for grammatical errors."

"That's fair. I did have my tutor look over—"

"Theodore, if you have any further questions, you'll need to schedule a time to meet with me during my office hours." She slams her folder closed, clearly indicating my dismissal.

"Of course," I say through gritted teeth. "Thank you for your time, Professor."

"Very well, Theodore. Remember, my office hours are posted on the syllabus. Make sure to email me in advance to set up an appointment," she says dismissively, her gaze already shifting to the exit.

Biting back a harsh retort, I turn on my heel and stalk out of the lecture hall before her. It's one thing to be struggling; it's another entirely to be dismissed so easily by the person who's supposed to help you learn.

I run a ragged hand through my hair in frustration. If I'm going to pass this class, I need to figure out what the hell I'm doing wrong. I've got the drive; I just need the direction.

And it's clear as day that I'm not going to get that from Professor Hartman.

"I need a fucking beer," I mutter to myself, making a beeline for my favorite off-campus bar. If I'm going to spend the rest of my day staring at a red-inked English paper, I might as well have a cold one in my hand.

. . .

I TRUDGE BACK to my off-campus house, a dark cloud of frustration and dread following me like a bad omen. The potential implications of failing another assignment crawl through my mind, threatening my dreams—scholarship, football, first-round draft pick —they all hang in the balance.

"Hey, man." Cam's deep voice cuts through my brooding.

The two of us have been sharing this house since last year, along with Daniel Moreno, another linebacker for the team. Danny is good company, but he spends most of his time at his girlfriend's place these days.

My gaze finds Cam lounged on our living room couch, legs nonchalantly thrown over the coffee table, a laptop balancing precariously on one thigh.

"Hmph." I return the greeting with a grunt, hardly managing to conceal my irritation.

"Why do you look like someone ran over your cat?" he asks, not looking up from his screen.

Wordlessly, I stride toward him, flinging my marked paper onto his lap, the damning F atop the page all but screaming failure.

"Two weeks into the term, and I'm already tanking," I grumble, a bitter edge to my voice.

"Easy, man," he says, his eyes briefly scanning the paper before placing it on the coffee table. "There's still plenty of time to pull up your grade."

I scoff. "Right. Maybe if I sit next to you long enough, some of your genius will rub off on me."

His smirk is instant. "So, you want me to rub off on you?"

Rolling my eyes, I raise my middle finger in response. "Fuck off."

"Nah, I'm pretty comfortable here, thank you very much," he drawls, stretching both arms over the back of the couch with a smirk.

Sighing, I flop down beside him, trying to brush off my annoyance. "What are you even working on?"

"Coach put me on the planning committee for the Spring Banquet," he says nonchalantly, still engrossed in his screen.

My brow shoots up. "The fuck? Why did he ask your sorry ass?"

"I have the highest GPA on the team." He shrugs, scrolling through web pages without a care. "Coach thinks I can handle the extra stress of party planning."

"That's gotta suck. What's the theme this year?"

"Danny wants to go with Vegas." He rolls his eyes at the absurdity. "I was thinking something simpler. Black and white or . . . fire and ice. That's kinda sexy, right?"

My laughter escapes before I can manage to hold it back. "Banquets aren't fucking sexy."

"Speak for yourself," he snaps, feigning offense.

"And the Trade?"

The Trade's a sort of tradition for the Dayton football players. Every year, the upperclassmen secretly agree to swap dates at the Spring Banquet. It's mostly harmless—guys with girlfriends can opt out, but they must state an "off-limits rule," or their girls are fair game.

It's our little secret, a game with only two rules—take someone else's date home, and don't speak a word of it to anyone outside the team.

The reward for pulling off a successful trade is well worth the effort. Last year, only eight players managed to score a touchdown, so to say. As underclassmen, Cam and I had the dubious honor of cleaning their gear for an entire season.

This year, it's finally our turn to step up to the plate.

"Of course Trade's still on." He clasps his hands together with an eager grin. "You think Elliot's gonna lock down his girl before then?"

"Fuck no."

Our starting quarterback, Noah Elliot, has been chasing after the same girl for the past two years. She's definitely pulling his chain at this point, but the guy seems blissfully unaware. I'm sure he'll tell us all she's off-limits anyway.

He tilts his head, eyes keen. "Do you know who you're taking?"

"Doesn't really matter, does it?" I murmur, gazing off into space. "She's not gonna be mine at the end of the night anyway."

"Well," he says smugly. "I was thinking I might help my man out."

"What do you mean?"

"I could ask Shannon for you." His expression is downright gleeful. "Make it sort of a group thing so she doesn't feel like shit for going home with you at the end of the night."

Now that gets my attention. "Not a bad idea."

"On one condition." He raises an expectant brow. "You've got to take someone good for me. Let's make it a fair trade."

"And who do you want?"

"Another cheerleader?" he proposes. "Might make the whole thing a bit easier on Shan."

"I don't know, man." I pause for a beat, contemplating the repercussions. "Those girls already know the score with me. They'd probably get pissed if I asked them to the banquet and then went home with Shan anyway."

"Makes sense." He shrugs. "She have any other hot friends?"

My mind immediately drifts to Jade. The first time we met, she didn't strike me as someone I'd consider hot. After our second run-in in the library, I've seriously re-evaluated that thought.

Jade definitely has a pretty face. She's funny, too. Witty and sharp.

Hot? Now that's harder to say, especially with that baggy sweatshirt of hers. The worn-out thing is probably three sizes too big and looks like she snagged it from her dad's wardrobe or some-thing. I can't quite make out what she's hiding beneath it.

But even still, there's something about her that sparks my curiosity. A mystery I find myself wanting to solve.

"I mean, there's her new roommate," I suggest, mulling it over. "Jade something. She's cute . . . probably single. Plus, I doubt she'd give a shit what I did at the end of the night."

He shoots me a grin. "Think she'd go for me?"

"Who wouldn't, man?" I nudge him with my elbow, his broad smile growing even wider. "Brains and brawn combined."

"Alright." He chuckles, looking pleased. "I'm game."

"Sounds like the perfect trade."

I tip my head back, propping my feet up on the coffee table next to Cam's. If I was waiting for the right opportunity, well . . . I can't help the fact that this one fell straight into my lap.

And who am I to argue with fate?

Chapter Six

DRENCHED clothes droop from our shower rod like unwanted houseplants, the water pooling beside my feet and soaking my toes through my socks.

Two nights ago, the dryer in our apartment decided to retire early, leaving Shannon and me to resort to this unsightly temporary solution. But sadly, the novelty of our makeshift clothesline is quickly wearing thin.

And now, all I want is to take a shower without tossing my sopping-wet T-shirts on the cold tile floor.

As I mull over my new morning routine, my phone chimes incessantly from the bedside table. The culprit? My big brother, Mica.

> **ACE**
> Apple Pay - $500

Rolling my eyes, I immediately shoot the money back. He's been trying to fund a new dryer since ours quit on us, but accepting his money just feels wrong. I'd rather not exploit his generosity any more than I already have. I mean, he already covers more than my fair share of the apartment's rent.

Before I can contemplate further, Mica's name flashes on my screen once more. This time, he's chosen a more direct approach—a phone call.

"Stop sending back the money, Lili." My brother's demanding voice elicits another eye roll.

"Stop giving me money," I insist. "I'm just gonna start saving up for a new dryer. In the meantime, we can just hang our clothes up or go to the laundromat."

"That's unacceptable."

"What?" I laugh incredulously. "What do you mean 'unacceptable'?"

"What if I need to do laundry when I visit next month? I can't just twiddle my thumbs waiting for my clothes to air dry."

His words jolt me, and a knot forms in my stomach. "Wait, are you serious?"

"As a heart attack."

"You're really coming to visit?" The corners of my mouth lift into an automatic smile.

"How does three weeks from Saturday sound?"

"Um, incredible!" I nearly shriek, unable to contain my excitement. "Wait, you didn't tell Mom and Dad yet, did you?"

"Not yet." A hesitation lingers in his voice, stretching the silence a second too long. "Why?"

I groan, foreseeing the familial tsunami his visit might trigger. "You know Mom's gonna want to come, too."

"Are you suggesting we don't tell them?"

"I mean, we'll tell them . . . but maybe just at the last minute." I can't help the sly grin that pulls at my lips. "You know, so Mom can't possibly book a flight in time."

"Lili the liar! I can't believe my ears."

"Come on, Ace. It's been ages since I last saw you, and you know how they can be."

"I'm just messing with you. Of course I want to spend the weekend just with us," he assures me, his voice softening. "I need my little-sis bonding time."

"Then we're in agreement." My grin stretches wide. "We'll just tell them it was a spur-of-the-moment decision."

"Fine by me."

Usually, my brother has his own room when he comes to visit me at Dayton. We stay up all night eating junk food and watching our old favorite movies. With Shannon around, I guess that changes things.

"Now that I finally have a roommate, you're gonna have to sleep on the couch."

"Also fine by me. I'm just glad you actually listened to me for once," he teases. "How is that going, by the way?"

"It's actually great," I confess, voice muffled as if I'm admitting to a crime. "Shannon is an awesome roommate."

"Well, I'm glad it worked out," he says gently. "I won't even say 'I told you so.'"

"Good." I chuckle. "Oh, and you have to promise me you won't flirt with Shannon when you're here."

Shannon's the quintessential girl my brother would go for—tall, confident, effortlessly pretty, and a cheerleader to boot. I couldn't tell you why, but it's like all straight football players are biologically wired to want them.

"That depends . . . what does she look like?"

"She's beautiful, so don't even try it," I warn.

"Oh, come on, Lili." He draws out my name. "Isn't she like . . . your age?"

"Yeah, and you're only twenty-six," I remind him. "Dating a college junior wouldn't exactly make you a cradle robber."

"I mean, I guess. But, like, you're my baby sister. It's weird as hell to even think about."

"Good, then it won't be a problem."

He snorts, the indignation clear in his voice. "I promise I'll be on my best behavior."

"You'd better," I fire back. "Also, don't think I didn't see that

TMZ post this morning. Are you actually dating that Instagram model?"

"No, I wouldn't say that we're dating," he says, a note of smug satisfaction in his voice. "But we did have some fun together last night."

"Ugh, ew!"

"Hey, don't ask ridiculous questions if you don't want ridiculous answers."

I groan again, my face contorting with displeasure. "I'm hanging up now."

"I love you, Lil. I'll see you in three weeks."

"Three weeks," I echo. "Love you, too."

After flinging my phone onto the bed, I'm left wearing an irrepressible smile. I soak in the happy thoughts before disentangling my clothing from the shower. Seems like I'll have to bite the bullet and get a new dryer after all.

It may be ridiculous, but I should have just accepted the money from the start.

One way or another, I need to accept that Mica Jennings, NFL pro and star cornerback, always gets what he wants.

OUR USUAL LITTLE study nook is cluttered with an hour's worth of academic chaos. Shannon's calculus assignments sit neatly stacked beside my strewn-about textbooks and notes. And as the last slivers of sunset slant through the high windows, the contrast between our study habits couldn't be starker.

Lost in a sea of torts and constitutional principles, the sound of West's voice jolts me back to reality. He stands, arms crossed, with a teasing grin on his face. "Hey, you two. If I didn't know any better, I'd say you girls were stalking me."

The sight of him here, amidst the quiet rustle of turning pages and the murmur of low conversations, is disarming. I blink at him, my mind still tangled in my studies.

Shannon giggles in response to his taunt, pushing a strand of honey-red hair behind one ear. "Didn't you just get here? Besides, we always come here on Thursday afternoons. It's tradition."

"Well, isn't that just the perfect coincidence?" West's grin widens. "I meet my tutor here on Thursdays."

"Tutor?" My curiosity is piqued.

"Yeah—for English Lit."

"With Professor Hartman?" My question hangs between us. Memories of late-night paper writing and intense class discussions come flooding back. Despite her reputation for being a hard-ass, Professor Hartman's class was where my passion for writing took root.

West sighs, looking almost defeated. "That's the one."

"Cool," I say, albeit a bit awkwardly. "I took that course freshman year."

He lets out a surprised snort. "So did I. We must have had class together and didn't even realize it."

Caught off guard, I say, "I guess so. So, you're retaking it now?"

"Yeah, unfortunately, I failed the first time around," he confesses, looking even more deflated.

Shannon, ever the empath, reaches out to pat his arm. "I guess it's good you found a tutor."

West grimaces. "Yeah, except he bailed on me today. We have an assignment due on Monday, and our next session isn't for another week. So, basically, I'm screwed."

"That sucks," Shannon murmurs sympathetically.

Noticing my quietness, West turns to face me. His eyes, filled with a mixture of desperation and hope, meet mine. "You're a writer, Jade. Could you take a look at my paper?"

"Oh, um, I don't know that I really have time for that." I mean, I have an exam in Mass Media Law tomorrow, another article due for the *Daily*, and then there's my third date with Freddy. Normally, I wouldn't mind helping someone out with editing, but I'm honestly kind of swamped.

Undeterred, he says, "I'll pay you. I mean, I can't really pay you, but . . . what about coffee? I'll bring you coffee from the Grind . . . every day for a week if you help me out."

Well, I do love coffee. And I'm kind of strapped for spare cash at the moment, so it's not like I can afford to buy my own lattes on campus. "Yeah, okay," I finally relent. "Maybe I could swing it."

His response is a whoop of joy. "Yes! Thank you!"

I quickly interject, "But I can't do it right now. I have an exam in the morning, and I need to finish this study guide."

"That's fine," West concedes, his fingers combing through his disheveled hair. His lips curve into a small, appreciative smile. "How about after your exam tomorrow?"

"Yeah, sure," I say, returning the smile, the tension in his posture easing. "We could just meet up here again, say around two o'clock?"

He nods, relieved. "Okay, perfect—give me your phone."

I rummage through my bag, retrieving the device and handing it over to him. His fingers fly over the screen, entering his contact information before passing it back. "Just text me if you need to bail or something."

"I won't bail," I assure him, our eyes meeting for a brief moment. And there's that warm caramel again, something strangely comforting in the intensity of his gaze.

"I'm serious." He meets my incredulous stare with a look that's both earnest and grateful. "You're really saving my life here, Jade."

I roll my eyes, suppressing a full-blown smile. "So dramatic," I say, sliding my phone back into my bag.

His gaze flickers to Shannon, a soft smile gracing his features. "Shan, it was great to see you again." He reaches out, giving her shoulder a light, friendly squeeze. "Jade, see you tomorrow."

He saunters away, his presence slowly fading into the hum of the library. Impassively, I turn my attention back to my study guide, dutifully highlighting the section on intellectual property.

A few minutes pass, and now I'm squirming in my seat. I can tell that someone is staring at me, so I lift my eyes from my notes to meet Shannon's questioning gaze.

"What?" I ask, a hint of defensiveness edging into my voice.

A mischievous glint twinkles in her eyes. "You know, West's a good guy, Jade. But he's definitely a player."

I frown. "And why are you telling me this?"

With a shrug and a cryptic smile, she says, "No reason."

Suspicion creeps in. "Shan, are you trying to imply something?"

"No, not at all. I was just observing."

My mind whirls to catch up. "Wait, do you like him, Shan?"

"Nah, we're just friends. He did kind of hit on me the other week, but I'm sure he does that with everyone."

"So, you don't want to sleep with him, then?" I ask, working to read her dubious expression.

"I don't *not* want to," she confesses with a slight blush. "But I'm looking for something more serious right now, and West isn't the guy for that."

"Yeah, I get that."

The guy definitely seems like the hit-it-and-quit-it type, not that there's anything inherently wrong with that. If Shannon's not interested in a one-night stand, then she's right—she probably shouldn't go for a guy like West.

"So, um, do *you* want to sleep with him?"

Grinning, I echo her words. "Well, I don't not want to."

"Jade!" Her eyes widen comically, a playful smirk curling her lips.

"I'm joking, Shan." I can't help but laugh at her reaction. "I barely know him. He's *your* friend. He seems decent, but he also comes across as a bit too cocky for me."

"Well, if you ever decided to go there, I wouldn't mind."

I raise a brow. "Yeah?"

She nods, her green eyes twinkling with amusement. "West is totally fair game."

"Good to know," I say, unable to hold back a full-on chuckle. "But remember, you still owe me that official athlete introduction. West doesn't count."

She rolls her eyes, gently tapping my hand in mock annoyance. "Patience, Jade."

"Hmm," I muse, looking back at my study guide, "I'm not really a patient person."

Her laughter echoes in the quiet library. "Yes, I think I'm starting to see that."

Chapter Seven

WEST

THIS ESSAY IS pure fucking nonsense. An unmitigated disaster, really.

My attempt to express my thoughts has resulted in an unfathomable sea of words, and I'm drowning without my usual tutor. The syntax, grammar, and overall sentence structure—they're all a mess. The one salvation I've managed is ensuring my sources have been cited correctly this time.

At least, I think I did them correctly.

My gaze lands on Jade as her eyes skitter across my laptop screen. She takes a thoughtful pause, rhythmically tapping her pen against the table's surface.

"Theo," she starts with a reassuring smile. "You've got some fantastic ideas here. Your writing mechanics, however, could use a little bit of polishing."

"West," I correct her yet again. "And yeah, I'm listening. Go ahead."

"Alright, here." She extends her hand, her finger landing on the first paragraph on the screen. "This sentence is a run-on. You've got two distinct ideas here, jammed together. You've attempted to link them with commas, but now you've created a comma splice."

"And that's a bad thing?"

"Correct," she says. "You want to separate those sentences into two independent clauses."

"Okay, so just replace the comma with a period, then?"

"You could technically do that, but you'd still have two separate ideas here. You could always split up the sentence and then move the second half down further in the paragraph."

"Yeah, okay," I say. "That makes sense."

She pushes the laptop toward me. "Do you want to try to fix up your intro, and then we can go over it together?"

"I can handle the actual editing part later," I say, waving her off.

She gives me a small, uncertain nod, drawing the laptop back toward her. Her gaze darts across the screen, critically evaluating the rest of the paragraph. "Right here in this section" —she points out, her finger hovering over the concluding sentences—"the definition of your thesis isn't clear enough. I get the gist of what you're aiming for, but it needs tightening."

"Alright," I say, making a mental note of it.

"You might want to consider eliminating this portion and weaving it into your final sentence."

"Got it."

She pushes the laptop back my way. "Here, why don't you try it out?"

"No, really, I'll remember your feedback and implement it later," I reassure her, pushing back gently.

"But it'd be a lot easier if you just edit as we go."

"Nah, it's fine. I've got this."

"Theo," she presses on, concern lacing her voice. "This will just simplify the process for both of us."

"I said I've got it," I snap, my tone sharper than intended. "I can damn well remember your pointers outside of these four walls."

"Okay," she says, nostrils flaring in a silent display of frustration. "That's your choice, then, but I think I should probably leave."

Rising with deliberation from her chair, she hoists her backpack over one shoulder, her posture rigid. Her head is tilted downward, a few rebellious curls falling forward to partially obscure her face.

Jesus Christ. Why is it that I'm always putting my foot in my goddamn mouth around this girl?

"Wait, Jade," I call out, reaching out to gently hold her wrist, desperation coloring my tone. "I didn't mean to snap. Please, don't go."

Her gaze drops to my hand, confusion evident as she stammers, "I—I don't understand. Do you want my help or not?"

"Yes, I do, I truly do," I rush to say. "I actually *need* your help."

"Then why aren't you following my advice?"

"I, uh, I can't just edit my writing spontaneously like that," I explain awkwardly. "I use dictation software to write my papers."

Her confusion deepens. "What?"

"Dictation software," I repeat. "It's a speech-to-text tool for my computer. I voice my thoughts, and it types them out for me to edit later."

"Oh." The realization dawns on her, and she sighs, her shoulder sagging as she slides her bag off. "I see."

My voice is barely a whisper as I confess, "I'm dyslexic and, uh, dysgraphic, if you're familiar with either?"

She sinks back into the chair beside me. "Yeah, a little bit."

"Well, it affects my reading and writing, but also . . . my fine motor skills, among other things," I continue, offering her a lopsided, self-deprecating grin. "I kind of hit the jackpot, I guess."

"And you don't receive any accommodations from Professor Hartman?"

"Not really." I give a disappointed shrug. "At the college level, it somehow ends up being at the discretion of the professor, even when it's legally not supposed to be. I did receive help during grade school, but things have changed. I even tried to explain my situation to Hartman during freshman year. It didn't go well, and I ended up failing her class."

"That's fucked-up," she says, indignation flaming in her dark eyes.

"Yeah, so I've stopped trying to explain. To her and probably most of the faculty, I'm just a lazy, entitled athlete."

Her voice is soft as she asks, "Why do you think that?"

"Because she practically said it to my face," I say, grimacing at the memory. "She told me to 'put in more effort,' that I won't receive special treatment just because I'm an athlete."

"Theo . . ."

I scoff, attempting to lighten the heavy conversation. "I don't blame her. Most people just see a brainless jock when they look at me. And the sad part is, I can't even prove them wrong. I mean, I can barely fucking read as it is."

"But you have a learning disability," she counters passionately. "You're not brainless, careless, or any other negative adjective you've been taught to ascribe to yourself."

A bitter laugh escapes my lips, even as a heavy sinking feeling settles in my chest. She's wrong. I might put in the effort, but I'm destined to fail at the end of the day.

"You're not," she insists, her tone laced with conviction. "I already told you—you have some genuinely great ideas in this paper. If Professor Hartman can't take a moment to read between the lines, then she's the one who's ignorant."

"Damn." My lip twitches as I force back a smile. "Okay then."

"I'm serious," she says, thick brows knit together. "No one should make you feel less than for something like this." She taps her pen against the table a few more times. "You know what, I think you need your own personal mantra."

"Mantra?" I parrot, confusion lacing my voice.

"Yeah, like a phrase or saying you repeat to yourself every morning when you stare at your reflection. A positive affirmation, you could call it." She nudges the laptop away, swiveling in her chair to face me directly. "I have one I've been using for the last few months."

"Yeah?" I smirk, a spark of curiosity igniting. "And what might your mantra be?"

"Okay, here it goes . . ." She clasps both hands together, a serious expression clouding her features. "My name's Jade, and I'm a force to be reckoned with."

A burst of laughter shoots out of me. "That's it? That's what you say to yourself?"

"Mhm," she says, an infectious grin lighting up her face. "Every single morning. Want me to come up with one for you?" she proposes with a twinkle in her eyes. "How about . . . My name's Theo, and I'm smart as hell."

A snort escapes me before I can contain it. "You want me to say that to myself in front of a mirror?"

"It works, I swear," she says, tone full of conviction.

"Yeah, that's not happening."

"Suit yourself. Just know you're missing out."

"I think I'll live."

"Alright, your loss. But I do have another suggestion for your paper." She turns away from me now, her gaze laser focused on my laptop. "What if, at least for this one, we talk about the changes, and then I'll just edit it for you?"

"Isn't that, like . . . academic dishonesty?" I ask, not that I actually give a shit.

I'm certain Jade's the type of person who would care, though, and I don't want her to compromise her integrity for something as minor as this.

"No," she says firmly. "I won't change anything unless we both agree on it."

"Yeah, okay then."

Her smile blossoms, reaching her eyes as she extends her hand for a solid shake. "Then we have a deal."

We work through the paper for a few more hours, carefully passing my laptop back and forth. Jade explains where to make corrections, and we rework each paragraph together. Somehow, when all is said and done, she's helped twist my words into something I can be proud of.

"This is actually quite good," she praises, a hint of admiration in her voice. "It's solidly in the C+ or B- range."

As she leans over to retrieve her bag, my gaze instinctively follows her movements. Unfortunately, she's donned that oversized sweatshirt again. But today, her hair's casually gathered into this half-up, half-down style, a few curls escaping to frame her face.

Up close, I can spot this tiny spattering of freckles across the bridge of her nose. Plus, a heart-shaped beauty mark right above her top lip. It's cute, charming, a unique little feature that's caught my attention.

In a way, it's almost strange that I didn't notice it before today.

"Jade," I say, a certain tentativeness edging into my voice. "Before we head out, can I ask you something?"

She turns her gaze to meet mine, her brown eyes sparkling with curiosity. "What's up?"

"Alright, I promise I'm not trying to be a jerk, but why do you always wear that sweatshirt?"

Her laughter fills the room, surprising me with its soft, sweet undertone. She glances down at the faded fabric. "Oh, this old thing? It's kind of ugly, I know, but it's also my good-luck charm."

This piques my interest. "What do you mean?"

She reclines in her chair, her fingers tapping a steady rhythm on the table. There's a distant look in her eyes, as if she's recalling some cherished memory. "I wear this sweatshirt when I study and during all my exams," she says, her voice trailing into a comfortable silence. "It's a small thing, but it helps me focus."

"And what makes it so lucky?"

"It's a hand-me-down from my brother," she says, her tone laced with affection. "He's incredibly smart. I always joked that wearing his sweatshirt might somehow make his genius rub off on me or something like that."

"No shit? I just said the same thing to a friend of mine the other day." A chuckle bubbles up from my throat, my amusement spilling over. "So, obviously, you think it worked."

She nods emphatically, a triumphant grin stretching across her face. "I know it did. I wore it for all my freshman exams, and to my surprise, I aced them."

My laughter grows louder, the absurdity of her belief tickling something in the pit of my stomach. "Don't you think you're giving the sweatshirt a little too much credit?"

Her expression turns stern, her conviction evident in her voice. "No, Theo. I know very well that it wasn't the sweatshirt that aced my exams. But it did give me the confidence I needed. It made me feel like I could conquer anything."

My grin doesn't falter. "Alright, that does make sense. But why wear it while you study, too?"

"Do you know about the principle of generalization?" she asks, tilting her head slightly.

"Yeah, I think so."

"That's all it is, basically. If you recreate the conditions in which you studied, it's easier to recall the material later."

Her words are met with another bout of teasing laughter. "Sounds a little far-fetched to me."

"No, Theo. It's *science*."

"Okay, I'll take your word for it." I shake my head, chuckling. "I'm just relieved you're not wearing it because it belongs to a boyfriend or something."

"Nah, I don't have a boyfriend."

The words bounce around in my mind, the implications slowly sinking in. "No?"

"Nope," she affirms, her tone bright as she pushes away from the table. Well, there you have it. My opportunity has just presented itself.

Deciding to seize the moment, I start my next question just as she's slipping on her backpack. "Can I ask you something else real quick?"

A warm smile graces her features as she faces me, her cheeks flushing a soft shade of pink. "Is this one gonna be about my jeans?"

"No, you dork," I tease, gathering up my belongings. "I was wondering if you knew about the Spring Banquet?"

"Your team banquet?"

"Yeah, that one." Together, we make our way toward the library exit, our conversation continuing as we navigate the stacks of books.

"Who doesn't?" she says, an undertone of amusement in her voice. "Just another chance for football players to get drunk and give themselves trophies, right?"

"Oh, I see. So, you've never secretly wished you could attend?"

"That's ridiculous."

"Yeah, and what if you went as my date this year? Would that be ridiculous?" I ask, nudging her with my elbow.

She freezes midstep, her wide eyes meeting mine. "What?"

"Yeah," I confirm, a reassuring smile tugging at the corners of my mouth. "The banquet's at the end of next month. Would you come with me? Just as friends, of course."

She eyes me skeptically, her brow arching in question. "As friends? We barely know each other."

"I mean, we've hung out, like, four times now. Doesn't that count as a start?"

"We ran into each other in the library a couple of times, and I helped you with your paper. I'd hardly call that hanging out."

"You got me there."

Her gaze narrows as she considers my proposition. "So, why ask me, then?"

"I'd rather not risk taking another jersey chaser," I explain, hoping my fractured attempt at honesty might convince her. "Besides, my roommate's already asked Shan. We could make it a double date."

She pauses outside the library doors, her teeth sinking into her bottom lip as she mulls over my words. "I'll think about it," she finally decides.

"Wow, Jade," I say, pretending to nurse a wounded ego. "You sure know how to deflate a guy's confidence."

"You said you were asking as a friend!"

"We are friends, then?"

"Yeah, Theo. Sure, we're friends."

"I prefer West, but I'll take what I can get," I say, nudging her lightly. "Just think about the banquet and text me your decision, okay?"

"Okay."

"Thanks again for your help with the paper," I say, tapping her backpack lightly. "I'll see you in the morning."

"The morning?"

"Yeah, I promised you coffee every day for a week, remember? Just send me your address, and I'll be there."

Her eyes widen in surprise. "Really?"

"It's only fair play. I owe you."

"Okay, but just don't show up before 9:00 a.m."

"Wouldn't fuckin' dream of it."

We take a few steps apart, and she waves me off with a tiny furrow in her brow. Then, with her soft laughter echoing in my ears, I walk away from the library and from her, my mind still buzzing.

Spending time with this girl—with her quirky, little rituals and her penchant for calling me on my bullshit—well, I have to admit, it's like a breath of fresh fucking air.

Chapter Eight

JADE

IT'S BEEN AN EXHAUSTING DAY.

Just this morning, I sat through a grueling exam on defamation and criminal liability. Then I spent the first half of the afternoon writing an article about campus budget cuts, followed by three hours in the library editing West's paper.

Now, I'm sitting through one of the most boring dates I've ever been on.

I almost bailed on this date with Fred, but I hoped there might be a redeeming payoff at the end—a physical release I've been craving, especially after a taxing day like this. Is that an asshole thing to admit? Probably. But do I care? Not in the slightest.

Fred isn't captivating by any stretch of the imagination. He knows it; I certainly know it. So, at the end of the day, can't a girl just try to get laid?

"—yeah, so I started off with just one forty-pound bottle of propane," he drones on about his pottery project, seemingly oblivious to my rapidly diminishing interest. "But after about three firings, the bottle ran out, and I had to rush to the store to get a refill."

My eyes threaten to glaze over as I murmur a few noncommittal "mhms" and "ohhs," feigning interest.

"Very cool."

"Yeah, and they don't actually refill the bottles there—they just give you a new bottle. So, after a couple times of doing this, I just decided to get myself a second bottle."

I force my eyes to stay open, nodding absent-mindedly. "Awesome."

"Would you two like to split the check?" our server asks as she clears the plates from our table.

"Yes, please," I say simultaneously as Fred responds with a polite, "No, thank you."

I shake my head, giving him a wry smile. "It's fine, actually. I'd like to split the bill."

He agrees with a nod, handing over his credit card along with mine to the server. As she leaves, Fred, seemingly unstoppable, returns to his story. I groan internally.

Once the server returns, I take the opportunity to change the pace. "Hey, do you wanna head back to my apartment?

He cocks a brow, taken aback. "You don't want to see the movie anymore?"

"I'd rather skip it," I say, attempting a seductive tone.

"Really? I heard this film was supposed to be pretty good. Charlize Theron is one of my favorite actresses and—"

"Fred." I reach out to brush his arm lightly, interrupting him. "I'd rather skip it so that we can hook up."

"Oh?" He clears the sudden lump that seems to be stuck in his throat. "Yes. Definitely. Let's go."

When we reach my apartment, I unlock the door, grateful that Shannon offered to stay over at a friend's for the night, giving me the house to myself. Or rather, giving Fred and me the house.

As we step inside, my guest meticulously removes his shoes, placing them neatly near the door. "Thank you for inviting me over."

I offer him a half-smile. "Of course."

After several long, awkward seconds pass by, his hesitance is apparent. Taking the initiative, I grab his hand and guide him toward my room.

Once we're tucked inside, he sits tentatively on the edge of my bed. I position myself, straddling him with a knee on either side of his thighs. But the silence is heavy as his arms hang limply by his sides.

I lean in, my voice soft yet firm. "You can touch me, you know?"

He wraps an arm around my waist, nervously pulling me closer. I lean back in to kiss him. His lips are gentle and warm, but the kiss doesn't spark anything inside of me.

It's nice, though. It's fine.

I trail my kisses down his neck, nipping softly against his pulse point. Within seconds, he pulls back.

"Sorry, could you not kiss me there?" he asks. "I don't want to risk a hickey."

"Oh," I murmur, disappointed but understanding. "Sure."

We lie down together on the bed, and I run my fingers through his hair, lightly tugging at the silky strands, bringing our mouths together in a hungry kiss.

"Not so rough," he whispers against my lips.

Oh. My. God. I change course, writhing against him instead. His hands, seemingly encouraged by my movements, tenderly map out the curves of my body. Sitting upright, I strip away my top and swiftly unhook my bra.

Focusing on him now, I make short work of his shirt, my fingers moving toward the button on his jeans next. But his hand intercepts mine.

"Hold on," he says, voice straining with desire. "Let me take care of you first."

Surprised, but certainly not against it, I relax while he explores even lower. One hand moves to rest against my hip as he drags my shorts down, his trembling fingers trailing across my flushed skin.

"Is this fine?" he asks, uncertainty tinging his voice.

I offer back a breathy confirmation. "Mhm."

His fingers, though still shaky, slowly make their way toward my center, awkwardly exploring until one finally ventures inside me. Then he begins a tentative dance, moving it in and out, side to side.

The sensation is . . . strange. Oddly reminiscent of my last visit to the gynecologist.

"You okay?" he checks in, concern shadowing his face.

"Yep, maybe just—" I pause for a moment, carefully guiding his hand until it settles over my favorite spot. "Try right there."

"Yeah, okay," he complies willingly, his touch tracing slow circles around my clit.

"Yeah, that's good."

Leaning into his touch, my nose nudges against his chest. As soon as my lips graze his skin, however, his movements stop.

"That's a little distracting," he says. "Try not to kiss me while I'm doing this."

"Um, okay," I consent, but already, I can feel his fingers wander away from the promised land.

Oh, Jesus Christ. With my eyes squeezed shut, I realize I'm left with only one option. Yes, God help me, I'm going to fake an orgasm for this guy. I hold off a few more seconds before releasing a series of breathy moans.

"Did you come?" he asks, eyes heavy-lidded as he gazes down at me. His tongue darts out to wet his lips, as if he found pleasure in watching my little . . . performance just now.

"Uh-huh," I mutter in response, hastily pulling my shorts back up.

Shifting onto my side, I trace a light path across his firm abdomen. "Did you want me to return the favor?"

"No, thank you." *Wait, what?* "I just liked watching you."

Well, I'm certainly not going to beg the guy to let me blow him. "Okay."

"Do you want me to leave now?"

"Uh, no?" I say, although I would've preferred if he'd never come over in the first place.

"Okay, cool." He seems relieved, nodding as he rolls over to retrieve his T-shirt. "Can I stay the night, then?"

"Sure . . ." I manage to whisper out, baffled.

In a haze, I ease off the bed and wander to my bathroom. I swiftly clean myself up. And when I return, I find Fred already deep in slumber, my bedcovers wrapped snugly around his lower body.

Well, it appears we're going to sleep now. Together. As if this encounter could possibly get any more awkward.

THE NEXT MORNING, I'm woken up by a loud knock on my apartment door.

I roll over, cringing when I collide with the Fred-shaped lump beside me. Last night was probably one of the worst nights of sleep I've ever had. Not only does Fred snore, but he also turned my bed into a fucking furnace.

Regrettably, our date ended with me both sweaty and exhausted . . . and not in an enjoyable way. My shirt sticks to my skin as I slide out of bed. I take a few moments to adjust it, trying to conceal the strip of exposed skin peeking above my shorts.

As I swing open the front door, the realization hits me that it's well past nine in the morning.

"Oh, hey, Theo." My greeting is laced with anxiety as I subconsciously tug at my bottom lip. God, I must look like a hot mess. "Sorry, I forgot you were coming by."

"Uh . . . hey," he says, his expression filled with confusion. "Where's your sweatshirt?"

"Huh?" My gaze drops to my chest, puzzled.

"Your . . . lucky sweatshirt," he clarifies, his nostrils flaring. "You're not wearing it."

"Oh?" I raise a brow. "Yeah . . . I mean, it's not like I actually live in the thing."

"Right." His jaw tightens, his face glowing with an unreadable expression. "Of course not."

"Right." I return his odd gaze. "So, are you just gonna stare at me, or did you have something else you wanted to say?"

"Fuck, uh, sorry." He rubs at the back of his neck, eyes flickering nervously across my face. "No, I just wanted to come by and bring you the coffee. Iced soy latte, right?"

"Mhm." I reach out, gratefully accepting the chilled drink from his outstretched hand. "Thank you."

"Sure," he manages in a husky voice.

"Yeah, okay." I shuffle in place, my gaze instinctively drifting toward my bedroom. "Well, not sure if you were hoping to say 'hi' or something, but Shan isn't home right now."

"Nah, I just—"

"Jade?" Fred's voice, laced with concern, cuts through the quiet between us, emanating from down the hallway.

A wave of tension washes over me, my body going rigid as I find myself locked in a staring contest with West. His smirk leaves no room for misinterpretation.

"Who was *that*?"

"Ugh," I groan, an involuntary reaction. "No one."

"Wait," he interjects, propping himself against the door frame. "Is there a guy in your room, Jade?"

"Unfortunately, yes." I pinch my eyes shut. "Yes, there is."

"Damn, is he—"

"Jade, everything okay out there?" Fred calls out again, his voice reverberating through the living room.

"Oh my God. I wish he would just leave already," I mumble

under my breath, massaging my temples, utterly drained from the previous night's sleepless ordeal. I place a pleading hand on West's shoulder. "Wait . . . could you maybe help me get rid of him?"

He winces. "Uh, I don't think that's a good idea."

"Oh, come on, please?" I quietly plead. "Look, if you help me with this, I'll um . . ." My voice trails off, a desperate whisper. "I'll go to the banquet with you."

That perks him up. "For real?"

"Yes, I promise!"

"Fine." His eyes twinkle with mischief. "It's a deal. Tell me, do you ever want to see this guy again?"

"No, definitely not."

"Well, in that case . . ." He cups both hands around his mouth to project his voice. "What the fuck is going on here, Jade?"

"It's not what it looks like, I swear."

"Are you fucking kidding me?" West raises his voice even higher, his faux outrage echoing through the apartment. "After everything we've been through?"

I wince at the sound of Fred's hurried footsteps approaching from the bedroom. I don't have time to mentally prepare myself for the impending chaos. But, as they say, desperate times call for desperate measures.

A bewildered Fred appears from the hallway, confusion painting his features. "What's going on out here?" he asks, his gaze flicking between West and me. "Jade, who is this?"

Assuming a protective stance, West slips his arm around my waist, drawing me closer. "I'm Theo, her fucking boyfriend," he announces with a faux ferocity that's as convincing as it is comical. "Who the hell are you?"

Caught off guard, Fred stammers, "Uh, shit, man." His eyes dart to the floor as he shuffles toward the corner, hastily reaching for his shoes. "I'm sorry. I didn't know she had a boyfriend."

"Yeah, well, she does," West says, feigning a menacing tone. "So why don't you get the fuck out of here?"

"Yeah, yeah, definitely." The awkward shuffle becomes more pronounced as Fred maneuvers to put his shoes on and make his escape, all while avoiding eye contact. "I'm already gone."

West tactfully steps out of the doorway, making room for Fred's swift exit and pulling me along with him.

"Sorry, Freddy!" I call out, stifling a giggle. The man practically sprints toward the elevator, desperate to leave. When he's finally out of sight, I gently close the door behind him and press my forehead against the wood, cheeks flushing.

"Jade, come on," West exclaims, failing to hold back a hearty laugh. "Is that seriously the type of guy you're bringing home?"

I release a sigh, dropping my shoulders in resignation. "What? Fred's a nice guy."

"Mhm, yeah, nice." He snorts, a touch of amusement in his voice. "I think he just about pissed himself."

"I mean, to be fair, you *were* kind of scary."

His laughter bubbles up again, soft and low, and I suppress a shiver at the pleasant timbre of it. "Yeah?" He seems amused at the concept. "Good scary?"

I can't help the small smile that tugs at my lips. "To be honest, yes?"

"Hmm," he muses, drawing out the word with a slow, considering grin. "So that's what you're into, then?"

"What do you mean?"

"The whole jealousy thing? Do you like it when a guy is possessive over you?"

"I don't really know." His gaze continues to bore into me, making me shift uncomfortably. "I've never been with a guy like that."

"So, what, you've just been with a bunch of nice guys, then? Little Freddy clones?"

"Pretty much."

"Well, that must be fucking boring for you."

"Pretty much," I echo back, laughter escaping my lips.

"If you're actually bored, why do you keep going for guys like that?"

"I don't know, really." I chew on my lower lip, trying to come up with an answer that makes some sort of sense. "I guess it stops me from caring too much. Besides, that's the only type of guy that seems to go for me."

He raises both brows, clearly unconvinced. "I highly doubt that."

"Why?"

"Jade, you're cool and funny and smart. Not to mention your body is—" His gaze drops down to my hips, lingering there before slowly raking up my legs and then back to my eyes. "Well, you're really fucking hot."

Flustered, I manage to stammer out, "Right," as a blush spreads from my neck to my cheeks. "I am a force to be reckoned with, after all."

His grin broadens, amusement evident in his expression. "Yeah, and I'm smart as hell."

"Damn right," I say with a chuckle. "Well, er, anyway, thanks for the latte."

"Of course."

For a moment, I just look at him, a kind of mutual silence settling between us. But after a second, for whatever reason, I find the intensity of his gaze uncomfortable, and I'm compelled to break the silence. "You know, you don't actually have to bring me coffee every day."

He frowns at that, confusion lining his features. "A deal's a deal, Jade."

"Right, about that."

"What, you're seriously trying to back out of the banquet

already?" he teases, but there's a hint of genuine surprise in his tone.

"No." I shake my head, dismissing his suspicion. "I just want to make sure that it's just a casual thing. You know . . . a double roomie hangout."

"For sure, of course. Shan's date is actually a pretty cool guy." His voice slows a bit, as if he's carefully considering his next words. "I think you guys would get along."

"Yeah?" I ask. "What's his name?"

"Camden Scott."

"Wait, really, the linebacker Camden Scott? That guy is massive."

His jaw clenches slightly. "You know him?"

"I mean, I've just noticed him on the field. The guy's incredible. He's one of the best defensive players on your team."

He rolls his eyes, a playful smirk dancing on his lips. "Right, of course. So, you noticed Cam out on the field but not me?"

"Sorry!" I say, feeling a twinge of guilt. "I told you that I don't get to cover the football games. The *Daily* keeps me pretty busy with other stuff. But when I do make it, I mostly keep an eye on the defensive side."

His brows knit together. "And why's that?"

"Ah, um, because my brother's a cornerback."

"Oh?" He tilts his head. "I didn't realize your brother played football. Was he on a college team?"

"Mhm."

"Cool," he says, an approving nod following his words. "What school?"

"Solberg."

"Sweet, they have a good team. Did he ever think about going pro?"

I tense at the question. This is exactly why I didn't tell him about my brother in the first place. Knowing Mica's status always seems to change things for people. And with West, who wants to be drafted himself, I fear his shadow might eclipse our every conversation.

"Um, yeah, he did," I say, steering the discussion toward something neutral. "Hey, look, I actually have a really busy day today. I'm gonna go get ready, but thank you again for the coffee."

"Oh, yeah, sure," he says, offering me a warm smile. In a surprising move, he reaches out to tuck a stray curl behind my ear. "No problem."

A little startled, I clear my throat, stepping back. "And thanks for helping me with Fred."

"Anytime," he says, and I swear his gaze lingers on me a moment longer than necessary. "See ya, Jade."

"Bye, Theo," I say.

And then, as the door clicks shut, I linger there in the silence, my heartbeat echoing in the empty space, the heat of his unexpected touch burning against the shell of my ear.

Chapter Nine
WEST

It's been weeks . . . no, months since I've had a girl in my bed. Honestly, the last person I hooked up with must have been Cassidy fuckin' Viotto back during fall term. This has to be the longest dry spell I've had since freshman year.

No wonder I've been jerking it in the shower so often.

Leaning against the cold tiles, hot water streaming down my back, I close my eyes and clasp my hand around my cock. My thoughts wander off, straying toward some faceless porn star—large breasts, a fit body, and a cascade of silky hair confined to a ponytail.

But after a half-hearted stroke, my interest wanes out, my dick deflating on me.

Frustrated, I bite my lip, shifting my fantasy to the one I haven't dared to imagine—fiery red hair, a smattering of freckles, and a short cheerleading skirt. Encouraged, I give myself another stroke. Then another, tightening my grip along the base.

Well, fuck, this is definitely not going to work for me either.

Just as I'm about to resign myself to a failed attempt, a new fantasy works its way into my brain—images of a tiny heart-shaped birthmark, a pile of chocolate curls spilling out of a half bun, and a pair of long, tanned legs peeking out from striped pajama shorts.

Yeah, there it is. My hard-on immediately rebounds.

Tilting my forehead against the shower wall, I give in to the image of her standing in her apartment doorway, a tiny shirt clinging to her curves just so, offering a glimpse of her waist above the band of her shorts. She's smiling at me, saying my name, leading me back into her bedroom.

Now, it's her hand working me over, her mouth pressing to my neck. The pace quickens as she journeys from my neck to my jaw to my chest, biting softly at my shoulder before dropping to her knees in front of me. Those perfect lips whisper, "Theo," right before she wraps them around my cock, sending me over the edge.

"Fuuuck." I can't help but groan as I collapse against the cold shower tiles, panting, allowing my climax to wash down the drain. It takes me a few long moments to catch my breath before finally switching off the water.

Now, what the fuck was that all about? Seriously . . . I see the outline of Jade's tits for five seconds and she's already starring in my shower fantasies? This is a whole new level of pathetic.

Honestly, this probably only happened because I'm sex-deprived, and Jade's the most recent girl I've been around. Not to mention her body is fucking incredible, which I would've realized sooner if it weren't for that godforsaken hand-me-down sweatshirt.

I mean, I understand her reasons for wearing it better than most. But damn it. That thing, no matter how lucky it is, is truly a detriment to her and to the entire Dayton community.

So yeah, that's all this was. I was just surprised to see her wearing that tight little pajama set this morning and caught off guard by my sudden attraction to her. I'm sure, by the end of the week, the novelty will have worn off completely.

The next morning, I make a stop at the Grind before heading over to Jade's apartment. I stand outside her door for a full minute, steeling myself. If she's inside wearing that barely there outfit again, I'll just have to avert my fucking eyes this time.

After all, I've seen women wear much less . . . and with much more intention.

Drawing a deep breath, I force myself to knock on the door. It swings open to reveal a beaming Shannon, her cheerful greeting instantly easing my nerves. "Hey, West!"

Well, that's one problem solved.

"Oh, hey, Shan," I say, forcing a casual smile. "Good morning."

"Morning," she murmurs in return, her eyes lighting up with genuine warmth. "Jade just ran to the store. She said you might stop by while she was out." She steps aside, creating a clear path for me. "Do you want to come in?"

"Oh, yeah, sure." I nod, making my way inside, even as a strange sense of disappointment tugs at me.

Disappointment? No, it's just . . . well, surprise that Jade already left, especially since she knew I'd be coming over.

Shannon reaches for the iced latte in my hand. "Here," she offers. "I can stick this in the fridge for now."

"Alright. Will Jade be gone long?" I find myself asking, even as I wonder why I care so much.

"I don't think so," she reassures me, her gaze flicking toward the door. "She said she'd be right back."

She glides toward the fridge, her movements graceful and poised. And once she's placed the drink inside, she ushers us over to the living room couch. As I settle in beside her, my gaze falls on a pair of large posters on the wall—a framed image of the Bobcats' team mascot and a Superstars action poster from years ago.

Jade's favorite team, presumably. It's a bit random, but I suppose she must have grown up somewhere in the state.

"Awesome." I lean back, draping my arms over the back of the couch, as I force my attention back to Shannon. "I'll just wait until she gets back, then."

"Sure," she says, shifting to face me directly. Her expression turns curious as she asks, "Are you guys . . . So, you're actually friends now?"

"Yeah," I affirm quickly, "I'd say we're friends."

Her gaze flickers over my face, as if trying to determine the sincerity of my statement. "She told me you asked her to the banquet."

"Yeah, I did," I confirm, raising a brow. "I mean, I thought . . . you're going with Cam, right? It could be a good chance for all of us to hang out."

"That's true," she says, her wary gaze softening into a smile. "To be honest, I was kinda surprised he asked me."

"Why's that?" I probe, genuinely curious.

"Well . . . I thought you might ask me."

I swallow hard, a tinge of guilt washing over me. Okay, I had just insinuated I wanted to sleep with her a few weeks ago. Now my best friend is inviting her to the banquet while I'm here playing some juvenile game with her roommate.

"Oh, uh, yeah," I mumble, attempting to gather my thoughts. "Well, Cam and I both wanted to go with a friend this year. He thought of you first. You know how it is."

Her soft laughter fills the room, the sound easing some of the tension. "I am glad you're taking Jade, though."

"Yeah?"

"Yeah," she echoes. "She keeps going out with these complete duds. I've been trying to set her up with an athlete, but I'm not sure who to choose." She pauses, twirling a strand of honey-red hair between her fingers. "Maybe she'll meet someone at the banquet."

"Wait, are you serious?"

Shannon's been trying to set Jade up with a random athlete while I've been secretly maneuvering her toward Cam. I mean, simply to fulfill the terms of the Trade . . . not to actually date the fucker.

"What?"

"You're trying to set her up with someone?" I ask, my tone edged with a mix of disbelief and caution.

"Yeah." She shrugs, seemingly nonchalant about it all. "She's not usually into athletes, but we thought we'd give it a try."

My brain churns, slowly attempting to process this new piece of information. Well, it's unexpected, but I suppose it works in my favor after all.

"Right," I drawl, leaning back against the couch, my mind already spinning with possibilities. "Maybe I can help with that."

Inside, though, I'm not so sure. Despite my best efforts to ignore it, there's a twinge of something uncomfortable, something heavy and tight, stirring within me.

A teasing light gleams in her eyes as she drags one pert lip between her teeth. "What did you have in mind?"

Ignoring the bitter taste in my mouth, I press forward with my plan. "You two should come over next Saturday night," I suggest, a hint of urgency creeping into my voice. "A bunch of guys from the team will be streaming the UFC fight."

It's the perfect opportunity to nudge the Trade along, subtly but surely laying the groundwork.

"That's not a bad idea," she muses, a thoughtful crease forming between her brows. "I'll see what Jade thinks."

"Perfect," I say, winking at her as I lean back, my hands finding their place behind my head again. "Plus, that gives you and I the chance to spend more time together."

She rolls her eyes, though her lips curl into a coy smile. "West . . ."

My smirk widens at her reaction. "Oh, come on. You haven't actually been to my place before, have you? Some say that my bedroom's the best spot in the house."

"You're relentless," she says, though her giggles betray her amusement, a faint blush warming her pale face.

My gaze lingers on her rosy cheeks, tracing the constellation of freckles scattered across her skin. It's interesting, actually. Jade has freckles, too, a charming sprinkling across her nose and the apples of her cheeks. A stray thought, but it manages to wedge itself inside my mind, stirring an unexpected pang.

"Shan, you don't even—"

My attempt to flirt is cut off by the front door swinging open, and my attention immediately shifts to Jade. She's holding two paper bags full of groceries, her hair pulled up into a bun, loose tendrils framing her face. She's not clad in her tiny striped pajamas this time, but she still looks pretty fucking good.

"Hey!" Shannon calls out, then informs her, "West brought you another drink. It's in the fridge."

I give Shannon's knee two casual taps as a parting gesture before pushing off the couch to join Jade in the kitchen. "Hey, Jade."

"Hi." Her smile doesn't falter as she retrieves her coffee. "Thanks for the latte."

I quirk a brow at her. "Couldn't wait around for me this morning?"

"Time stops for no man."

"Right." I chuckle, my gaze lingering. "Same reason you shooed me out yesterday?"

"Something like that," she says, her lips closing around the straw of her coffee.

"Well," I say, clearing my throat, an unfamiliar awkwardness creeping in. "I wanted to make sure you actually got your drink. You know, gotta hold up my end of the bargain."

Her lips curve into a knowing smile. "Of course, it's only fair play."

"Exactly. Alright, I think I'm gonna head out now." I throw a glance over my shoulder toward her roommate. "Shan, thanks for the company."

"Bye, West!"

"Want to meet me on campus tomorrow?" Jade's question

steals my attention back. "You know, for the coffee? My first class is right near the quad."

"Sounds like a plan."

"Alright." She's opening the front door now, and I move to slip past her. "See ya, Theo."

And there it is . . . Theo. My given name escapes from her lips right before she closes the door on me, and it hits me like a punch straight to the gut.

Damn, now I'm standing in an empty hallway, sporting a semi, and those shower fantasies are springing to the forefront of my mind.

I shake my head, trying to clear it. Need to remember the fucking plan, the Trade.

You want Shan, you asshole, not her roommate. No, definitely not her—the one with the corny personal mantras and witty little comebacks. But a corner of my brain rebels at the thought, whispering, *Would it really be so terrible if you did want Jade?*

Wait, what am I thinking? Of course, it's fucking terrible, especially since I've spent the last few days trying to pawn her off on Cam—my best friend and goddamn roommate.

I just need to stick with the original game plan. I'm going to keep my head down, pass my fucking classes, maybe spend a night with Shan, and then get drafted. There's no time for other distractions.

Point. Blank. Period.

Chapter Ten
JADE

DESPITE THE EARLY MORNING CHILL, I've claimed a spot on the bench outside of Jones Hall, a laptop balanced precariously on one knee as I navigate through an email from my editor. His words, cryptic and ill-timed, are like a relentless echo in my head.

I must have read them at least a hundred times by now.

I squint at the glaring screen, the coffee in my stomach churning with a knot of disbelief and annoyance. It's laughable, really. Almost as if the universe is pulling some cruel prank on me. Or worse, Garrett Warner—the conceited man-child—has somehow tuned into a cosmic joke at my expense.

Sure, I should be grateful for this assignment. Hell, it's the first piece in ages that's sparked any semblance of excitement. But why did it have to be this specific story?

"Jade!"

The unexpected sound of West's voice cuts through my self-induced daze. His tone is warm yet slightly amused, and my heart inexplicably stutters in response.

I react on instinct, hastily snapping my laptop closed and shoving it into the safety of my bag, rising from the bench to greet him.

"Hey there." His lips curve into a cheeky grin, a lopsided tug that highlights the little indent in his right cheek. It's an attractive look on him, made even more so by his dark hair swept back to reveal his sharp features.

"Hey," I say, attempting to sound casual despite the hint of warmth blooming in my cheeks.

"Your morning coffee." He offers the promised drink, a swiping of his thumb across my wrist as he hands it over. A simple act, yet it sends my pulse fluttering.

"Thank you, Theo." I meet his gaze, daring him to comment.

"Oh, Lord." His lip curls in a teasing smirk. "When are you going to give it a rest?"

"Give what a rest, exactly?" I counter, a playful lilt to my voice. "Calling you by your name?"

He huffs a chuckle. "You're lucky I still owe you."

"Would you prefer I called you Teddy? Because I like that one, too."

"Hmm." He feigns deep thought, brow furrowing. "West is fine, thanks."

"But don't you get bored of everyone calling you the same thing?"

His gaze narrows slightly, the corners of his lips tugging up in an amused smile. "I don't know, do you?"

"Not everyone calls me Jade. Actually, my brother calls me Lili."

"Why's that?"

"It's a shortened version of my middle name, Lilianna."

He pauses, his gaze momentarily studying me. "Jade Lilianna, huh? You have a last name to go with it?"

"Wouldn't you like to know?" I ask, trying to suppress the small surge of apprehension that comes with his curiosity. If West knew my last name, he might easily connect the dots to my brother. And I'm not ready to reveal that part of my life to him just yet. So, for now, I'm more than happy to delay the inevitable.

"Ah, I see how it is." His grin widens, a playful glint in his eyes. "You know, if I really wanted to find out, I could just check your next byline."

"Hmm, you could. But that wouldn't be playing fair," I say, crossing my arms defensively. "Would it, Teddy?"

He groans in exasperation, his expression somewhere between amusement and annoyance. "Oh, sweet Christ."

"And yet, you're lucky I like Theo better."

He snorts a laugh. "Such a little dork."

"Such a little drama queen," I fire back, matching his playful tone. I pause for a moment, shifting the conversation. "By the way, about tomorrow—I was wondering if you could meet me in the afternoon instead?"

"Sure, whatever you need."

"Okay, cool." I pull out my phone and set a quick reminder for myself. "Meet at the library around two o'clock? I have a deadline coming up for the *Daily*, so I'm definitely gonna need an afternoon pick-me-up."

"Alright," he agrees, a hint of curiosity in his eyes. "So what groundbreaking article are you working on now?"

"Believe it or not, Garrett finally decided to throw me a bone this time."

"Garrett?" He tilts his head in question.

"Yeah, my editor. He assigned me a new piece on Immersive Arts."

"Oh . . . cool." He furrows his brow, then, "What does that mean exactly?"

"The art majors have decided to use our campus as their canvas," I explain, a flicker of enthusiasm kindling inside me. "There's this gruesome dead seal that they made out of ceramics. It's got, like, Coke cans and plastic bottles spilling out of its guts, but they placed him right in front of the eagle statue. I guess it's supposed to be a commentary on plastic in our oceans."

He shudders a bit, a look of revulsion briefly crossing his face. "That's . . . slightly disturbing."

I can't help but laugh at his reaction. "Yeah, but it's also kind of awesome, in its own way. You want to know the real kicker, though?"

"What's that?"

I sigh dramatically. "Remember Freddy?"

"How could I forget Mr. Pissed-My-Pants?"

"Well, he's the lead artist," I say, a pang of dread settling in my stomach. "Garrett just sent me the details this morning."

He blinks at me in surprise. "No shit?"

"None whatsoever. Irony's a bitch, isn't it?"

His eyes narrow, a sudden intensity in his gaze. "So, what, you have to go interview the guy now?"

"Actually, I already emailed him the interview questions. I know it's a cop-out, but fuck . . . I can't face him after the trauma we caused."

"Ruthless."

"Right?" I shake my head, a wry smile twisting my lips. "Anyway, I have to get to class. I'll see you at the library tomorrow?"

"For sure," he agrees, his voice low and soothing. "Would you mind if I stuck around to study?"

I purse my lips, teasing him. "The library's a public domain . . . but I don't really have time to help you edit another paper."

"Oh, come on," he says playfully, a spark of mischief in his eyes. "As if I'd trick you into helping me."

I raise a skeptical brow. "Don't act like you're so above shady tactics."

He momentarily sobers up, his expression thoughtful. "You know what, you're right." Then, a soft smirk slowly resurfaces on his lips. "If I want something from you, I'll just have to man up and ask for it."

His words catch me off guard, leaving a trail of confusion in their wake. "Um, okay, then," I stammer, fumbling to decipher his comment.

With an easy familiarity, he pats my bag before stepping away, a lingering warmth left in his wake. "I'll see you tomorrow, Jade."

"READ IT AND WEEP, BABY." West's voice breaks through the quiet hum of the library as he slams a stack of papers down on my table. The interruption is as unwelcome as it is jarring.

I blink up at him. "What is that?" I ask, cautiously edging toward the heap of papers.

His grin, spread wide across his face, could easily outshine the afternoon sunset. "Why don't you take a look, sweet cheeks?"

I scrunch up my nose in distaste, half-annoyed, half-amused. "First of all, ew. Second of all . . ." I divert my attention to the paper, scanning it quickly. Recognition hits, and I can't hold back a surprised laugh. "Holy shit."

"Do you see that?" His chest inflates with pride, a tangible energy emanating from him. "That's a fucking eighty-one."

"Wow, a solid B-." I can't help but mirror his excitement, tapping the papers as if to transfer some of the good fortune to myself. "Nice job, Theo."

He rewards my compliment with my signature iced latte, placing it on the table before sinking into the seat beside me. "This is the best grade I've ever gotten," he says, locking his gaze onto me. His hands grip the armrests on my chair, caging me in with his infectious joy. "Did you know that?"

"I didn't." I shake my head, grinning widely at his triumph. "But that's amazing."

"It is amazing," he says, an intensity in his eyes that I can't quite place. "And I owe it all to you, Jade. I'm so fucking happy right now I could kiss you."

A fluttering sensation rises in my chest at his words, my heart rate jolting. "Yeah?"

His gaze drops to my lips for a fraction of a second. "Fuck yeah."

"Well, if you want something from me, then why don't you just ask for it?" The words spill out before I can filter them, leaving us both startled.

He pauses, an awkward chuckle breaking the tension. "Wait, are you being serious?"

I steady my gaze, choosing to meet his challenge. "Are you?"

A furrow knots between his brows. "I—"

"It'd just be a congratulations kiss," I quickly backtrack, my words tumbling out. "Nothing serious."

He leans in. "Nothing serious?"

"Uh-huh."

His expression twists for a moment, an internal debate visible in his eyes. "I, uh—no, you know what? Why don't you give me one when I actually deserve it?"

"What do you mean?"

"If I can actually pass this course," he clarifies, his voice lower than before. "That's when I'll deserve a kiss from you."

I swallow the lump in my throat, trying to steady my pounding heart. "You think so?"

His answer is immediate and firm. "Yes." He stares me down, the intensity returning to his gaze, his proximity inching just a tad closer. "And don't think I won't come to collect."

Outwardly, I roll my eyes. Inwardly, I'm screaming. "So dramatic," I say, hoping my voice sounds steadier than I feel.

"Drink your latte, Jade." He smirks, finally releasing his hold on my chair. The warmth of his touch fades, leaving a strange sense of absence. "Besides, don't you have some big article to write about limp-dick Freddy?"

I shoot him a glare, my nerves rapidly shifting back to playful irritation. "You're so annoying."

His laughter fills the air, a deep, husky sound that sends a ripple of warmth right through me. "You're right." He turns away, pulling his laptop from his bag with renewed focus. "That's why I'm going to shut up and study now."

"Well, good, then," I huff.

"Yeah," he murmurs, his attention now divided between me and his laptop. "Good."

THE SUN DIPS well below the horizon by the time I finally leave the library, West's words still echoing in my mind. My thoughts are a chaotic whirlwind as I make my way back to the apartment, the scent of his cologne—something like sage and sandalwood—still lingering in the fabric of my sweater.

He'd been close today. Really close. Too fucking close if you ask me. I shudder at the memory, a strange sense of thrill tingling up my spine.

With my keys fumbling in my grasp, I storm into the apartment, my mind buzzing with thoughts I'm forcing myself to confront. "Shan," I groan, barging into her room without a second thought. "I have some really bad news."

Startled, she scrambles to sit up higher on her bed, eyes wide and alert. She pats the spot beside her. "What is it?"

The words taste like poison, but I push them out anyway. Flopping down next to her on the mattress, I admit, "I think I might have a teeny, tiny crush on West."

"What?" The corners of her mouth lift into a cheeky grin. "Are you sure?"

I let out a frustrated sigh, covering my face with my hands. "I don't know," I mumble from behind my fingers. "I think so? We were just studying in the library, and I kind of asked him . . . to ask me . . . to kiss him."

Her brow crinkles in confusion. "You asked him . . . to ask you?"

"Yes, I know, it sounds complicated," I say, dropping my hands and waving one dismissively. "We didn't actually end up kissing. But now I don't know what the fuck to do. This is silly, right?"

She shakes her head at me, her long hair swaying with the motion. "It's not silly. I told you West's a good guy. It's not so unfathomable that you'd have a crush on him."

"But I know guys like him. He's just like my brother, in a way," I say, falling back onto the bed with a huff. "And I've told you how Ace treats his girlfriends. He goes through them like they're disposable."

Her agreement is a small hum. She lies down next to me, our heads nearly touching on her pillow. "To be fair, I haven't really seen West with anyone for a while. Except . . ."

"What?"

"Well, he was being a little bit flirty with me on Sunday morning." She glances at me apologetically. "Before you came back with the groceries."

My heart sinks. "You think he's interested in you?"

She turns on her side, propping herself up on one elbow. "I think he wants to hook up, but I don't think he's interested in anything beyond that."

"Is that why he invited us over for the fight?"

"He did mention something about his bedroom, but that's kind of just . . . how he is. It was more of a setup for you. You know, to introduce you to some of the football players."

"So, you're saying West wants me to date one of his teammates?" My tone is incredulous, one brow quirked in disbelief.

"Maybe?" She hesitates, biting her lip. "I mean, that's what I was going for. I don't really know his game plan, to be honest."

"Well, shit."

"Why don't you just see how things go until Saturday?" she suggests. "If you think you're into him, that's cool with me. I definitely won't reciprocate his flirting."

"Honestly, I don't know how I feel," I admit, burying my face into her pillow. "It's like one second, he's a complete douchebag. Then the next second, he's being sweet and funny and charming. He's also ridiculously hot, so I think that's clouding my judgment."

"Take your time, Jade," she murmurs, placing a comforting hand on my shoulder. "Just . . . don't let him hurt you, and you'll be fine."

"Easier said than done," I say, pulling my face out of the pillow to look at her. I offer her a small, resigned smile. "Much easier."

As the night presses on, thoughts of West play on a never-ending loop. His smile, his laugh, the way he looked at me today in the library. It's all too much, too soon. And though I hate to admit it, I do have a crush on him.

It's too bad that a guy like West could undoubtedly turn my life upside down. I'm not sure I'm ready for it, but at the same time, I know I'm done with all the *nice guys*.

The guys who take me on sweet little dates and always say the right things. The guys who are supposedly generous in bed but have no fucking clue how to actually pay attention. The guys who are more than happy to take up space in my life but never in my mind, my body, or my heart.

Chapter Eleven
WEST

FOR THREE SOLID DAYS, there's been this gnawing thought inside my brain, this incessant drumming beat that's given me a headache. It may be ridiculous, but I've been wanting to kiss the shit out of Jade.

I know the idea is messed up, convoluted in a way.

Why did she have to throw that curveball at me in the library? It was mostly a joke. A comeback to my own proposition or some weird kind of "congratulations kiss." Whatever the hell that means. But did she have to smile like that when she said it?

"If you want something from me, then why don't you just ask for it?"

The girl knows how to use my own words against me, twisting them just to screw with my head.

Truthfully, I only said all that because I was feeling guilty. She called me out on my shady tactics, and she was fucking right about them. I've been manipulating the situation, tricking her into getting what I want.

And now, this Trade bullshit is grinding on my nerves, especially because I'm not sure if it's what I want anymore.

I mean, all this to win some silly competition? Yeah, sure, it's tradition. I remember, in painstaking detail, those long nights spent cleaning the seniors' sweaty practice gear. And I would love nothing more than to reap that reward for myself.

But what's the true cost-benefit analysis of this scenario? The costs: acting like a dick and keeping my distance from Jade. The benefits: free labor next season and a potential night spent with Shannon.

Is that what I really want?

Yeah, Shannon's smoking hot. Beautiful face, amazing body, and a personality that's just as sweet as she is pretty. Plus, I've been lusting after her ever since my first football game here at Dayton U.

I was running on an adrenaline high, and there she was—with her perfectly curled, honey-red hair, those faint little freckles, and that emerald-green cheer uniform. She was a breath of fresh air in a sea of unfamiliar faces. So, that night, I made it my mission to talk to her.

But then, in what would be the first of many drunken mistakes, I ended up with some random jersey chaser in my bed. Yeah, I've been a lust-driven fool since freshman year. I'm well aware.

But before now, if I'm being brutally honest, I didn't really care who got my dick wet. I was solely focused on getting drafted and finally going pro. Now, I want to get drafted, and I want to kiss the shit out of Jade.

So much so that I've spent the last few days avoiding her.

I've dropped off her coffee each morning but never stuck around to chat. I think she could tell something was up, especially when I stopped firing off snarky comments and downright ignored her attempts to rile me up.

"Thank you so much, Teddy," she said this morning, her last-ditch effort to get me to crack. I mean, seriously? Fucking Teddy? Of all the convoluted nicknames to call me, Teddy is what she comes up with.

I much prefer Theo.

But I simply flashed her a fleeting grin, handed over her iced latte, and turned on my heel. Today was the last day of our deal anyway, so I guess things just got easier for me.

Except . . . she and Shan are coming to our house tomorrow

night. Because, like the clown I am, I invited them over to watch the UFC fight. And now, I have to spend my time setting up my roommate with the girl I can't stop thinking about.

There's something seriously wrong with me, isn't there?

THE NEXT NIGHT, I'm running on a live wire by the time Jade and Shannon finally arrive. The fight is already cued up on the flat-screen while a dozen of my teammates cram around our living room couch.

Thankfully, the ratio is somewhat evened out by a few of their girlfriends who came along. Not perfect, but it'll do.

"Ladies, come on in." Cam's booming voice greets them at the front door.

"Hey, Cam!" Shannon bounces back. "This is my roommate, Jade."

I force myself up from the couch, making my way toward them at the entryway. As they turn to greet me, my heart stumbles, my throat tightens, and my words lock up.

"Hey, Shan." I manage to force out a casual nod. Then, I swallow, tasting dust as I turn my attention to her roommate. "Hey, Jade."

Oh, fucking hell. Her low-cut shirt does nothing to hide her curves, and those skintight jeans might as well be painted on. Her dark hair cascades over her shoulders in a waterfall of chocolate curls and soft waves. I want to reach out, to touch her, to—no.

Snap the fuck out of it, West.

Suppressing the urge to let my eyes wander, I clear my throat, forcing my gaze to a neutral spot between the two girls. "Thanks for coming."

Jade gives me an appraising look, lips pressed into a thin line. Her gaze travels over my tensed posture, that knowing look piercing into my obvious discomfort.

"Can I get you girls something to drink?" Cam interrupts, his offer a welcome distraction.

Shannon politely declines, stating she's driving, while Jade opts for a beer.

As the girls join Cam in the kitchen, I retreat into the living room, mentally berating myself for acting like such a fucking dweeb. New mission for tonight—avoid Jade at all costs or risk making a complete fool out of myself.

Unfortunately, I fail my own mission within half an hour, finding some half-assed excuse to approach her. "Hey, you want another drink?" I ask, the words tumbling out before I can stop them.

"I'm all good," she says, flashing me a tight smile. She gestures to her beer, swishing it around in the bottle to show me that it's still nearly full. It's a polite dismissal, and it's certainly a blow to my ego.

"Alright." I manage to keep the disappointment out of my voice, giving her a curt nod as I retreat to the other side of the room, aiming for the cooler with a heavy heart. Despite my efforts to the contrary, I've somehow messed this all up, haven't I?

Remington Miller, one of our team's wide receivers, is rifling through the drinks as I approach. He lifts his head at my arrival. "Need another beer?"

"Yeah, man."

He pulls out a bottle and a can, flipping the latter over to me with ease. With a lean against the wall behind us, he rummages in his pocket, pulls out a key ring, and pops his cap off.

"So, how does Shan know that chick?" he asks between gulps.

"Jade's her roommate." I keep my response short, taking a sip of my own beer.

Miller's gaze follows mine, landing on the couches where Jade's currently standing. "Damn," he murmurs appreciatively, eyes glazing over. "She's pretty hot."

"She is," I echo, my voice more strained than I'd like.

"Those jeans really do wonders for her ass, don't they?" His offhand comment rubs me the wrong way, but I keep quiet, unwilling to answer him. He may be acting like a degenerate, but he's not necessarily wrong in his claims.

I allow myself another quick glance at Jade. She's leaning against the armrest of the couch now, that perky round ass of hers on full display. Her laughter bubbles up from a joke Cam must've just told, and it feels like a sucker punch straight to the gut.

My gaze slides across her frame, from the cute crinkle in her nose down to the sweet curve of her hips. Then it's back up to her face, and I'm no longer just looking; I'm full-on fantasizing.

She presses those perfect pouty lips to her beer bottle, tipping her head back for a long drink, and I can't help but picture that same mouth wrapped around the length of me.

The muscles in her throat tense as she swallows the beer, her tongue darting out to catch a little dribble on the rim. But it's not the neck of the bottle she's licking. No, now it's her tongue licking from the base of my dick all the way to the tip.

Oh man, this is not the fucking time or place for this shit.

As I shift on my feet, my focus turns to subtly adjusting the hard-on straining against my jeans. Thankfully, Miller's attention has already wandered elsewhere.

A few hours pass, and I've somehow managed not to make a complete fool of myself. In fact, I've barely even glanced in Jade's direction the entire night. She seems to have cozied up to Cam well enough, which just kind of pisses me off.

So, when the moment finally comes for the girls to head out, my heart kicks into high gear. I hadn't planned on saying goodbye—didn't want to risk getting sucked back into her orbit—but, as if on autopilot, I find myself joining them at the door.

"Thanks for having us," Shannon gushes, her words blanketed in her typical enthusiasm.

"Yeah, it was fun," Jade chimes in, her smile so genuine it fully shatters my resolve.

"Anytime," I say, my eyes fixed on the contours of her face. As she turns to follow behind her roommate, my hand extends almost of its own volition, gently swiping the side of her arm. "Have a safe drive."

Her eyes widen before she gives me a tight nod, lips curling into a subdued smile. "Will do."

Once the final echoes of the night have faded and the last of the guests have cleared out, I beeline to my roommate. My mouth opens, and I blurt out the first thing that crosses my mind. "Trade's off."

"What?" His tone is shocked, confusion pulling at his brows as he stares up at me.

"The Trade's off the fucking table, as in, I'm not trading Jade. She's officially off-limits," I say, my tone brooking no argument. "And you can repeat that to anyone who might give a shit."

He flashes me a dubious look. "Are you joking?"

"Does it look like I'm joking?"

"Alright, dude." He holds up both hands in a pacifying gesture. "I got it, okay? Jade's off-limits."

My nostrils flare in triumph. "Good. I'm glad we're clear."

"You do realize that pretty much destroys any hope I had of pulling off a trade, right?" He folds his arms across his broad chest. "Shan wouldn't willingly go home with anyone other than you. She'd feel too guilty."

"You're right, she wouldn't," I concede. "And that's not my problem."

His sigh is almost painful, a gravelly groan rumbling deep in his throat. "Fine, but you're cleaning my gear for at least two weeks next season."

"Fine. Whatever you want."

He shoves me lightly with one hand. "So, you like her, huh?"

"What?" I play ignorant, rubbing my shoulder dramatically.

"You like Jade . . . enough to call dibs on her," he reiterates. "You planning on asking her out?"

"I don't fucking know, man." A sigh slips past my lips. "Even if I wanted to, I barely have time to breathe right now. My grades are in the fucking toilet, there's training camp this summer, and next season is gonna be hell before the draft."

"Your call. But remember, if you don't make a move, someone else will. And that's not even considering the banquet," he adds, a crease forming between his brows. "You weren't the only one checking her out tonight."

A tight knot forms in my stomach, a dark cloud of dread casting a shadow over me. "Who?"

"Miller was asking around, trying to find out if she's single."

"That little fucker. He was running his mouth about how hot she is earlier."

"Can you blame him?" He lets out a disbelieving laugh. "She is hot."

"I'm well aware," I snap, the heat rising in my voice.

"Dude, cool down." He claps me on the shoulder, but his attempt to soothe does little to calm the frustration bubbling inside me. "Just think about what you really want."

"Alright." I manage to swallow past the knot in my throat. "I will."

Later that night, as I'm lying in my bed—restless, unsettled—Cam's words continue to echo in my mind. He's got a point. If I don't make a move on Jade, it's only a matter of time before someone else does.

But would it even make a difference if I did? Who's to say she'd be interested in a screw-up like me? A jock with subpar grades, a guy who's got no business being with someone like her.

Despite my doubts, I grab my phone and fire off a quick text, truly testing the limits of my mental stability.

WEST

hey, so miller thinks ur hot

JADE

nice

WEST

what do u think?

JADE

I guess I'm pretty hot, ya

WEST

. . .

JADE

which one was he again?

WEST

green hat

JADE

yeah, he's cute

WEST

cool.

should I give him ur # then?

JADE

if u want

WEST

alright

JADE

goodnight theo

WEST

goodnight

Chapter Twelve

JADE

CRUSHES, I've decided, are a curse. A painful, gut-twisting, heart-wrenching curse. They swoop in, make you feel all giddy and hopeful, and then smack you down with the brutal weight of rejection.

West clearly isn't interested in me whatsoever. In fact, he's so uninterested that he's trying to pawn me off on his teammates, like some used car he's tired of driving or a beat-up piece of furniture he's left out on his front lawn.

I mean, Miller? Yeah, I suppose he was cute, but I caught him staring at my ass more than a handful of times. Meanwhile, West, who had managed to whip up this whirlwind of emotions inside me, barely glanced in my direction the entire night.

His behavior was nothing like the friendly, teasing dynamic we've been nurturing recently. So, what on earth made me think there was something more between us? Why did I fool myself into believing that our banter in the library was anything more than that? Just harmless, inconsequential flirting.

Clearly, I need to recalibrate my romance radar.

Oh well, there are plenty of other interested guys to choose from, those who won't just shove me off onto their friends. I was probably being naive about the two of us, anyway, but reality has a knack for crushing those illusions.

If anything real had developed between us, it would have

fizzled out sooner rather than later, leaving nothing but a weird vibe and one less . . . friend to hang out with.

Because that's what we are. Friends. It snuck up on me quicker than I expected, but I've become a little bit attached to him. To us. West is someone I look forward to spending time with, someone I enjoy teasing and being teased by. Especially when I call him Theo, a name that he pretends to despise, but I can tell he kind of likes it.

That cheeky little spark in his eyes is anything but subtle.

But none of that matters now because he doesn't want me back, and I have to accept that. So, I'm good with being just friends. And hell, maybe I will hook up with Miller if that's what he wants from me. He is an athlete, after all, and I did make a promise to try one on for size.

Thursday sneaks up on me, and now it's been exactly five days since I last spoke to West. No word, no text, no casual bump-into-you-at-the-library type deal. Nothing at all. And now that I think about it, it's been radio silence from his pal Miller, too.

What the hell's going on with them?

A nagging curiosity, woven with an unpleasant twinge of disappointment, picks at the edges of my mind. But I shrug it off and take matters into my own hands.

"Hey, Shan," I call, striding into her bedroom without so much as a knock. The room smells of vanilla and strawberries—her signature scents—and there's a soft glow emanating from the lamp beside her desk.

There's also another girl lounging on her bed, feet kicked up against the wall, engrossed in scrolling through her phone. I recognize her as Emmy, one of Shannon's teammates. Her ash-blonde hair is tied up in a half knot, and she's wearing this dark shade of lipstick that contrasts her pale skin.

"Hey, sorry to interrupt," I say, offering her a tiny wave before turning back to my roommate. "Er, Shan, do you have a minute to talk about Miller?"

"What's up? He still hasn't texted you?" she asks, brows arching in surprise.

"Nope," I say as I flop onto the edge of her bed.

Emmy perks up from her spot beside me. "Are you talking about *Remi* Miller?"

"Yeah," I confirm. "Do you know anything about him?"

She wrinkles her nose. "Well, I know he's a wide receiver, but he also dated one of our teammates last year. From what I heard, it was quite the dramafest."

"What kind of drama?" I ask.

"I think there was cheating involved, but I'm not exactly sure."

"Ah, okay. I suppose that's good to know."

"God, it's always something with these guys," Shannon groans. "So, does this mean you've officially moved on from . . . you-know-who?"

"There was never anything to move on from, Shan," I say, trying to shrug off the heaviness. "He's just not interested."

She swivels in her chair to face me. "He seemed out of sorts the other night, don't you think? Maybe he was just having an off day?"

"Yeah, maybe." The words leave my mouth, but I remain unconvinced. It's pointless to continue wondering what's going inside that head of his. Instead, I steer the conversation in a new direction. "Are you still up for the Vault later?"

Her face falls. "Oh, I totally forgot to tell you. We have another meeting for Spirit Night."

I push down a pang of disappointment. "No problem."

"Sorry, Jade."

"It's all good," I say, waving off her concern. I honestly don't mind going places alone. Sometimes, the quiet solitude is more comforting than company. Still, Shannon's presence has a way of making things feel lighter.

She gives me a soft, sympathetic smile. "You probably work better alone, anyway."

My lips curve into a smirk. "Only in the bedroom."

"Oh, my God." Shannon smacks a hand across her forehead, rubbing it down the side of her cheek. "See, we have to find someone better suited to your needs."

"Very true."

The room fills with our shared laughter, and the lingering traces of disappointment and confusion seem less overwhelming. I'm thankful for the comfort Shannon provides, for the friendship that's blossomed between us.

She's quickly becoming my go-to person, a confidante, and, in a lot of ways, my anchor. There's only one other person who still takes precedence.

On principle, Mica will always be my first and closest friend. But there are certain topics that are strictly off-limits between us— my love life, my solo sex life, and any potentially graphic details about an athlete's performance in bed, to name a few.

He's the overprotective type, and I can practically hear his threats to the male species on my behalf. But despite his overbearing nature, I wouldn't have him any other way.

LATER THAT AFTERNOON, I settle into the North Campus Library, a place that's become almost as familiar as my own bedroom. I've claimed a table as my private workspace—books splayed open in chaotic order, pens and highlighters to my right, my torn-up notebook on my left. My laptop's placed precariously at the center, screen glowing in the dim light.

Finally, I can put this dead seal article to rest. It was interesting, to say the least, but it's a mental image I'm eager to forget. And

Garrett, being the annoying person he is, promptly found another mundane piece for me to cover—the missing bricks in the middle of campus.

Yes, bricks. I can't decide whether to laugh or groan.

In the midst of contemplating this thrilling topic, something unfamiliar nudges my attention. Raising my eyes from the screen, I find West sliding into the seat beside me.

"I thought you'd be here today," he says, an air of nonchalance in his tone. He gives a quick look around, then turns back to me. "Where's your study buddy?"

"Cheer stuff," I say, my voice relaxed, a casual lift of my shoulder accompanying the words.

"Ah, gotcha." He cocks his head slightly, eyeing me with a playful glint. "I'm not meeting with my tutor for a couple of hours. Mind if I join you for a bit?"

"Go ahead."

Without another word, he wraps his fingers around my armrest. Slowly, with an unsettling intimacy, he swivels me around to face him, the legs of the chair grating against the linoleum floor.

His caramel eyes lock onto mine, his tone low, sincere. "How have you been? I haven't seen you since Saturday."

"I've been good." I force out the words, working to keep the tremor out of my voice. His gaze lingers on me, and there's a wild fluttering in the pit of my stomach. I nibble on my lower lip, hoping to ground myself with the mild sting. "Speaking of Saturday, your boy never called me."

I throw the statement out there like bait, waiting to gauge his reaction. But his expression morphs into one of confusion. He blinks, genuinely caught off guard. "My boy?"

"Miller, right?"

His features relax into recognition. "Oh, right." His broad shoulders lean back against the chair, arms folding over his chest in an unconscious defense. "Probably because I never actually gave him your number."

My brain sputters to a halt, words struggling to piece together. "What? Then why ask me if you could?"

A hint of a smirk crosses his face. "Shan told me you wanted to try dating an athlete. I was trying to help you out, but then I changed my mind."

My pulse quickens. There's something new in his gaze, a secret I can't quite decipher. "Why?"

"I realized that Miller's actually a fucking douchebag," he drawls, his smirk deepening. "Just because you want to date an athlete doesn't mean you should go for one who only wants up your skirt."

His words hang in the air between us, and I let out a snort of incredulous laughter. "Is there any other kind?"

He blinks at me as though trying to communicate a message I'm not quite receiving. "Is that a serious question?"

"Yes?"

"Of course there's another kind," he grumbles, barely meeting my gaze. "There are nice guys out there who just so happen to be athletes."

"Oh, please." I scoff at his defense. "We've gone over this. I'm so tired of nice guys."

He narrows his eyes, a challenge flickering in their depths. "Why's that?"

"You know who was a nice guy? Fred Tomlin," I insist, my voice rising with frustration. "You know who else were nice guys? My last two ex-boyfriends. Want to know what they all had in common?"

He leans back in his chair, amusement softening the sharp edges of his features. "I'm sure you're gonna tell me either way."

"They were all terribly boring, terribly self-involved, and equally as terrible in bed."

His chuckle is short-lived. "Jesus, Jade."

"What? I'm serious," I say, defensive and exasperated. "At first, I thought it was just me. Like, I don't know, I'm a tough nut to crack or something. But no, I can get myself off just fine alone."

His brows shoot up in surprise, but he remains silent, waiting for me to continue.

I plow ahead, ignoring the heat creeping up my neck. "You know exactly what I mean," I say, more for my benefit than his. "That's the whole reason Shan suggested the athlete thing in the first place. We all know your reputation."

His surprise ebbs, replaced by a stern gaze. He leans forward slightly. "So, what then, you just want to be with a guy who can get you off?"

"I guess." My own words wobble, and I'm acutely aware of the blush flooding my cheeks. "I don't know, I thought maybe . . . for a second, I wanted a relationship. But maybe that's not what I need right now."

"Oh?" The muscles in his neck twitch. "So, what, you just want a fuck buddy?"

"Would that be so terrible?"

"You can do what you want. But it's certainly not gonna be with fucking Remington Miller, that's for damn sure."

"What about your roommate, Cam?" I suggest. "He seemed kind of interested."

"Fuck no."

I can't help but groan at his stubbornness. "Are you just gonna veto everyone?"

He glares at me, his jaw firmly set. "Yes, Jade. If anyone's gonna get you off, it's gonna be me."

"What?" I manage to squeak out, my heart pounding in my ears.

He takes a moment, licking his lips before locking his gaze on mine. "You heard me."

"You want to . . ."

"Fuck yeah, I want to."

I struggle to catch my breath, the weight of his words hanging heavy in the air between us. "I don't think we can be . . . fuck buddies, Theo. We're already friends and"—I gesture to the table beside us—"study partners. It would be too messy."

His response is immediate, almost automatic. "I can keep my shit in separate boxes."

I shake my head, my brain buzzing with a whirlwind of thoughts. "Yeah, well, I can't," I admit. "Mixing sex and friendship and . . . whatever else. It's too confusing."

The look on his face shifts from frustration to hurt. "So, you want to fuck somebody you don't even know?"

"I'm not sure. I'm still trying to figure out what I want, okay?"

"Sure, Jade. Whatever."

His dismissive attitude stings, and I can't help but challenge him. "So now you're mad that I won't fuck you?"

He flinches but quickly regains his composure. "No, I'm not." His shoulders slump a little, a tiny wisp of air pushing between his full lips. It's a careful mix between a sigh and a shallow exhale, as if he needs just one extra breath of time to calculate a response. "Trust me, I'm not. I just . . . I want you to be careful. It's your body, you do what you want with it."

"Yeah, okay."

With that, he pushes on the armrest of my chair, forcibly turning me back to face the desk. But before I can fully resume my work, his low voice stops me.

"Just—just don't go for Miller, okay?" His plea is earnest, his gaze intense.

"Okay," I say with a sigh. "I won't."

Chapter Thirteen
WEST

I'M AN ASSHOLE.

I mean, seriously. What kind of dipshit says those kinds of things to the girl he likes?

If anyone's gonna get you off, it's gonna be me.

What I should have said is this: "No, Jade, you don't need a fuck buddy. I like you. I want you. I'll fuck you so good that you won't even remember your own name."

But it's clear that I'm not what she wants. She'd rather pursue a no-strings-attached fling who can rock her world in the bedroom. According to her, our friendship would only complicate things.

Well, fuck our friendship.

No, wait. I want our friendship. I want to make her laugh, make her smile, make her call me by those goofy fucking nicknames. I want to spend time with her. I want to keep figuring out what makes her tick. I also want to kiss her and then take her to my bed.

Actually . . . I just want Jade in any form I can get her.

She's driving me wild, and she doesn't even know it. She says she's willing to give things a try with Miller, with Cam, with any other fucking athlete at this school. And I know I'm not a damn saint, but the thought of her with anyone else? It's like a slow, painful churning inside my gut.

I want to be her first choice and not just because she thinks I can scratch her itch. I want her to see me, to want me, as a man who's developing real feelings for her and not just some athlete who can show her a good time.

But it's obvious she doesn't see me the same way. Or maybe she just doesn't want to.

Whatever it is, I need to stop before I ruin everything. But as I look at her, engrossed in her work and wearing that cute little frown, I can't help but think I've already screwed up my one and only chance.

I've let my feelings cloud my judgment. I mean, offering myself up as her fuck buddy? Who the hell does that? And yet, I did it. I did it because the idea of her with another man is unbearable.

She says she can't mix friendship with sex, but I can't help but wonder if I could change her mind. Could I make her want me enough that she'd risk the confusion?

Or maybe I should respect her decision and back off. Stick to being her friend and pretend that her words haven't left a gaping hole inside my chest.

THE NEXT NIGHT, my teammates and I hit up Lucky's, one of our favorite bars near campus. The place is typically packed to the brim with student athletes, a veritable playground for the physically gifted. That, coupled with the jersey chasers who have a knack for being everywhere but where I want them, often makes for an interesting night.

Yet, tonight, the allure of Lucky's seems to have lost its shine. I'm not really in the spirit to party, if I'm being honest. I'd rather be trapped in the fucking library of all places.

But social obligations have a way of forcing your hand, so here I am, celebrating our quarterback's birthday.

Noah Elliot, the big man himself, is the first one amongst us to hit the twenty-two mark. He red-shirted his freshman year, meaning he didn't compete against other teams. This gave him a shot at five academic years with four full seasons on the field.

"Happy birthday, Elliot." Sliding into the vacant seat next to him at the high table, I give him a firm clap on his shoulder.

"Thanks, man." His nod comes with a clink of beer bottles, the glass cool and slick against mine.

"Let's get you laid tonight." The suggestion, laced with an unsettling amount of enthusiasm, comes from Conor McNair. Wide receiver and resident dickwad of the team, he has a knack for opening his mouth before engaging his brain.

"Dude, you know he's with Steph," I say, irritation seeping into my tone. McNair often has his head in the clouds, but this is a low blow, even for him.

"That true, QB?" His eyes seek Noah's, curiosity flaring in them. "You finally lock that shit down?"

"We're not official," Noah mumbles, his shoulders deflating slightly. His gaze finds a fascinating spot on the table, avoiding our prying eyes. "But I'm not looking to score with anyone else."

McNair, finding no fun in this revelation, huffs in disapproval. "Suit yourself. More pussy for me." With a graceless shove, he rises from his chair, the grating metal echoing in my ears as he saunters over to the bar, leaving Noah and me in relative peace.

"What's going on with that, anyway?" I ask, curiosity getting the better of me. Noah and Steph have been dancing around each other for a while, but the delicate dynamics between them remain a mystery to everyone else. "Is Steph still stringing you along?"

"No, man." He sighs, his voice heavy with emotion. "It's not like that. She's been burned one too many times, so we're taking things slow."

"Burned?" I parrot back.

"She's been, uh . . . hurt by guys before," he clarifies. His expression is a painful mixture of regret and anger. I can tell that something serious is lurking in the shadows of his girl's past—something that's shaken Noah to his core.

"Oh fuck, dude," I blurt, my eyes widening. "I'm sorry."

"Yeah, thanks," he mutters, his voice hoarse. "I just . . . I love Steph. The idea of being with another girl doesn't even cross my mind."

"I get it," I say. I wish I could provide more solace than a cliché statement, but empathy has never been my strong suit.

His brows shoot up. "You get it?"

"I mean, I don't . . . get it," I quickly backtrack. "But I can understand how you feel . . . in a hypothetical sort of way."

"Yeah, well." He shrugs noncommittally, an indifferent smile tugging at the corners of his mouth. "It's both a blessing and a curse."

"Right," I say, because it's the only thing I can think of in the moment.

"Right," he agrees, and we clink our beers together again. It's our silent pact, a show of solidarity.

A COUPLE of hazy hours later, I'm staggering back home, flanked by both my roommates. It's a strange sensation because, as far as I can recall, I've only had a handful of beers. Yet, my balance feels off, and the world around me is a blurry mess.

My bed beckons, promising a soft haven from the spinning room. I make a beeline for it, an odd sense of anticipation churning in my stomach.

But the moment my head makes contact with the plush pillow, the harsh light of my phone screen slices through the darkness. A new text notification flashes across the screen, and I pick it up to find a message from Jade.

JADE

hey. your friend miller just DMd me

WEST

did u respond?

JADE

ya, asked if he was DTF

My mind is a whirlpool of thoughts, each one worse than the last. In an irrational move, my fingers fly over the phone screen, dialing her number. I can't think straight right now. The only thing running through my head is her voice, her laughter, her presence.

"Hello?"

"Please tell me you're just fucking with me?" I practically growl into the phone, my fingers digging into the soft material of the mattress. The jealousy rears its ugly head again, a gnawing sensation in my gut.

"No." She snorts, clearly amused. "He really did DM me."

"Jade." My voice drops, a warning tinge to it.

Her laughter trickles through the line, a sweet melody that somehow softens the edges of my irritation. "Of course I'm fucking with you. I didn't actually respond. You told me not to go for him, and I won't."

The tension finally dissipates, a soft sigh of relief escaping my lips. "You're evil."

"Maybe I just like screwing with you."

"And what if I screw with you back?" I ask, unable to help the grin that tugs at my lips.

"Well . . . that would only be fair play."

"You better watch your back, then."

"So dramatic." I can almost see her rolling her eyes, an affectionate smile playing on her lips. "Okay, I'm officially getting into bed now."

"That's fine," I say, though my chest tightens at the thought of ending the conversation. "I'm actually in bed, too."

A soft rustling sound filters through the phone. "I mean . . . I'm about to go to sleep, Theo."

"Oh." The word falls from my lips, the alcohol in my system encouraging a boldness I wouldn't usually possess. "Well, before you do, could I ask you something?"

"Sure, what's up?"

Well, here goes nothing. "I've just been wondering, you know —since the other day, just . . . what made them so terrible?"

"Huh?"

"You said the sex was terrible," I echo, my voice carrying an unwelcome strain. "With your exes and . . . Freddy. Why?"

"Oh, um, I don't know, really." There's a long pause in which I can almost hear her mind whirring, and I nearly regret the question. "I guess it was just boring."

"Boring?" The word echoes in my mind. I can't imagine being bored during sex, especially with someone like Jade.

"Yeah, I was just bored of what we were doing. Or, I don't know, maybe we just weren't compatible in the bedroom."

"Yeah?" I swallow hard, a knot forming in my throat. "They didn't turn you on?"

"No, it's not that," she insists, and the words bring a tiny sense of relief. "I mean, I wanted to have sex with them. I was always into it at first."

Oh God, why did I ask her this? My jaw involuntarily clenches. Please, tell me more about how much you wanted to fuck other guys. "At first?" I manage to squeeze the words out, my throat dry.

"Mhm, but then we'd get to the good stuff, and it would just be . . . blah."

"Blah?" The confusion is evident in my voice. I can't understand it, the idea of her not enjoying it, not when she's so vibrant and full of life.

"I don't know," she says, her voice dropping, embarrassment making her words tremble. "I guess, just . . . my body didn't respond to it or something. I mean, the way they were doing it anyway."

A slow burn of curiosity begins to take root in the pit of my stomach. "So, how would you want it done, then?" My voice comes out lower than I intended, but I blame it on the alcohol, the hour, the intimacy of our conversation.

"What?"

"I think you heard me," I say, trying to keep my voice steady, suppressing the rising wave of desire.

She stutters, then falls silent, and I rush to ease her discomfort. "Fuck, sorry," I say quickly, my free hand furiously running over my forehead. "You don't have to tell me if it makes you uncomfortable."

"No, I mean." Her voice trails off, then comes back stronger. "It's not a big deal, right?"

"Right," I agree, but the conviction is missing. *You're about to tell me what you like in bed, Jade. This is a huge fucking deal.*

"Okay," she says, her voice tinged with a vulnerability that draws me in further. "Well, first off, there'd be lots of touching. Oh, and kissing—lots of kissing."

"Good start," I say, my heart pounding against my ribs.

She snorts. "Yeah."

"Where?" My teeth sink into my bottom lip, the taste of my own anticipation filling my mouth.

"The kissing?" she clarifies, and I murmur my agreement. "Oh, um, I guess I'd want him to start with my lips. Then maybe . . . move to my neck."

"How would he kiss you?"

"He would probably . . . use his tongue," she whispers, her voice low and shy. "Um—maybe suck on my neck just a little bit, but not enough to leave a mark. Then he might . . . move down a little further."

"How much further?"

"Down past my collarbone." She sucks in a breath, the sound making my chest tighten. "He would—he'd kiss me there, too."

"Would he take off your shirt?" I press, my words a threadbare whisper in the quiet darkness of my room.

"Yes."

"Are you in your bed when he does this?"

"I am," she says, her voice a soft murmur in my ear. And there she goes again—more fucking rustling.

"Under your covers?" My voice is a rough hush, a strange tightness constricting my throat.

"Mhm," she breathes out. "And he's—he's on top of me. He takes off my shirt, and he . . . licks his way down to my nipples."

"Yeah? He probably pops one into his mouth, doesn't he? Sucks on it?"

"Mhm," she moans, but it's a quiet, barely there sound that somehow amplifies my desire.

"Maybe he uses his teeth," I suggest, my voice sinking into a low rumble. "Just to lightly nip."

"He does, and I—I really like that." She shifts in her bed, and I can picture her perfectly. "I press my legs together as he does it, just trying to get . . . a little bit of friction."

"Jade," I call out to her, my voice a low warning.

"Uh-huh?" A breathless question.

"Are you wearing those little striped pajama shorts?"

"Uh-huh." A breathless answer, the rustling growing louder as my imagination runs wild. Because now I know, without a doubt, she's touching herself under the covers.

"He really wants to touch you. Will you let him?"

"Yes, Theo," she manages to squeak out. "I mean, he—he can touch me."

The floodgates open, and there's no turning back. The image of her body under my touch, the sound of her gasps and moans, drives me to the edge. "He pulls those little shorts down over your hips, pressing his thumb to your clit."

"Oh," she sighs. "That feels . . . that's good."

"Yeah?" I ask, my own hand finding its way down, the sensation mirroring the picture in my mind. "Then he strokes your pussy nice and slow before slipping one finger inside."

"Mmm, that's really good." The approval in her voice is all the encouragement I need.

"He's pumping his fingers in and out, and you start bucking your hips." My movements match my words as I imagine my fingers inside of her. "You're—you're fucking his hand, Jade."

"Oh fuck," she breathes out, the words half moan, half gasp. "I want—I want him inside me."

My heart slams against my ribs. "He is inside you, baby."

"I want his dick . . . I want his dick inside me," she clarifies, the words punctuated by shallow, rapid breaths. "I want to—" Another breathless gasp. "—be fucked."

"Jesus," I whisper, and the vision of her body writhing under mine sets me on fire. I can imagine her flushed skin, her chest heaving, her fingers clutching the sheets in ecstasy.

Her little cries of pleasure echo in my ear, the sounds driving me to the brink. And when she finally lets out a cry of release, I know she's reaching her climax. The mental image of her coming unravels me.

"Fucking hell," I groan, my own release pulsing through me in powerful waves.

Panting, I hastily discard my phone, collapsing back onto my pillow, my mind a whirlwind of sensations. We just . . . inadvertently had phone sex. And it was the best damn thing I'd ever experienced.

"Jade?" I manage to gasp out, fumbling to retrieve my cell phone.

But all I'm met with is silence. She just . . . hung up.

Chapter Fourteen
JADE

Holy shit. Holy shit. Holy shit.

The phrase reverberates in my head, a three-beat litany of stunned disbelief, an echo of shock that shivers through my entire body.

Last night, I had phone sex with West. The sentence still sounds absurd when I say it in my head, too surreal to be true. The raw intimacy of it all, the whispered words that slipped so easily over the line and broke down barriers we'd carefully kept in place.

We got each other off, lost in a tangle of sighs and gasps that soaked through the air between us. And then . . . I just hung up.

God, what was I even supposed to say after something like that? A weak "Thank you?" that would somehow trivialize it all? Or maybe I should have tried for calm, cool, and collected, brushed it off with an airy "Oh, oops, I guess we just got carried away!"

But the memory of his voice, husky and raw with desire, floods back into my mind. I mean, why did he have to sound so fucking hot on the phone? That voice. Those words. Just thinking about it now is making me wet, a steady thrum of desire that I can't ignore.

This is bad. This is really fucking bad.

I'd already made up my mind about him before this happened. I thought I had wrestled my crush into submission, had trampled it down until it was nothing more than a distant echo of feelings. But then he had to go and say all that shit at the library.

The memory of it still burns, a sharp-edged reminder of how

easily he can unravel me. Oh God. He offered to be my fuck buddy, and I declined, the words coming out automatically, serving as a defensive shield.

After fight night, I'd allowed myself to believe that he didn't want me. The rejection was a bitter pill to swallow but also a comforting lie that I let myself believe. Now, in the stark light of day, I know he wants me. He's made that very clear, his words echoing through my mind, hot and insistent. But it's the way he wants me that's the problem.

West just wants to "get up my skirt," which is exactly what he accused Miller of.

A bitter taste lingers in my mouth as I think about the truth of it all. I mean, he flirts with Shan, his words casual and easy as if they mean nothing at all. Then he flirts with me, his gaze burning into me as if I'm the only person in the world.

And then he probably flirts with any other girl with a pulse, spreading his attention around like it's free for the taking.

God, it's like some silly little game to him, and I'm just one of the players. Yeah. Nothing real is going to happen between us. I have to keep reminding myself of that, have to keep that reality firmly in front of me.

I have a crush on him, and God help me, I want to sleep with him.

But that's not what I need right now. I was supposed to find someone else to cure my sexual boredom, to spark some excitement into the monotony of my life. But instead, I went and made things ten times worse.

I want to write this off as a onetime lapse in judgment, a moment of lost control that I can brush off and move past. But instead, it's become a gnawing reminder of the attraction between us.

And now, I'm stuck in a vortex of conflicting feelings, caught between what I want and what I know is best for me.

. . .

I'm still in bed, the sheets twisted around my body, when a cautious knock breaks through the early morning quiet. I have a sneaking suspicion that West is the culprit, especially since my phone's been turned off since our call ended last night.

Internally, I'm in chaos. Panic swells in my chest, making my heart pound and my thoughts scramble. But externally, I strive for composure, raking my fingers through my sleep-tousled hair and hastily scrubbing at the mascara smudges under my eyes.

When I finally muster up the courage to open the door, my suspicion morphs into an undeniable reality. West is here. And God, he looks just as deliciously sinful as he sounded over the phone.

His broad shoulders fill the doorframe, stretching the fabric of his long-sleeved Henley T-shirt to its limit. His dark hair, unstyled today, falls around his face in a sexy, just-rolled-out-of-bed kind of way. His face is perfect, from his strong, angular jawline to his tanned complexion.

But as usual, it's those eyes that reel me in—they're the color of warm honey swirled with molten caramel, and they're looking at me with an intensity that racks through me.

"Jade," he greets in a voice that's all gravel and raw emotion. His gaze sweeps across my face, as though he's trying to memorize each tiny detail. "Can I come in?"

"Sure," I manage to breathe out, my voice barely audible. I step aside, gesturing for him to enter.

"You look good." His gaze flicks across my body, a swift, head-to-toe examination that somehow feels more intimate than the events of last night. "Really good."

"Um," I stutter, taken aback by the compliment. I shift on my feet, awkwardly rocking back on my heels. "Thank you," I say, but the words come out sounding more like a question than a confident response.

He raises one dark brow, an amused smirk playing on his lips.

"Look, about last night—"

"We don't need to talk about it."

"I think we do," he says firmly.

I glance back down the hallway, eyes flitting nervously toward Shannon's closed bedroom door. "Okay, but let's talk in my room," I say. "Shan's home."

Without giving myself the time to second-guess, I grab hold of his hand. The warmth of his skin startles me as I tug him behind me. But as soon as my door shuts, the energy in the room changes. The air grows heavy, thick with unspoken words that crackle between us like static electricity, charged and unpredictable.

"Jade," he rasps, voice low.

He steps forward, his fingertips lightly grazing the side of my arm. The sensation startles me, and I'm hyperaware of every point of contact. He moves another small step forward, and instinctively, I retreat a timid step back.

It's a dance of sorts—forward, back, forward, back—until my back is flush against the cool wall, my breath hitching in my throat.

"Wait," I murmur, a plea or a protest, I'm not sure. His strong hand cups my cheek gently, his other settling on my hip, grounding me. As he leans in, my resolve weakens. "We shouldn't do this," I murmur, even though every fiber of my being is crying out otherwise.

"Why not?" His breath ghosts over my lips, the scent of mint mixed with something distinctly him.

"I know we both got carried away on the phone last night," I say, my voice barely above a whisper. "But I'm not just looking for a fun time, West."

His grip on me loosens, his brows furrowing as he steps back, creating a much-needed space between us. "It's Theo," he mutters, the soft rumble of his voice betraying a hint of frustration. "And who the fuck said that's what I'm looking for?"

His words hang in the air between us, an unexpected challenge. He's so close yet so far—close enough to touch, to feel his breath on my skin, but far enough that I can't decipher the thoughts swirling behind those captivating eyes.

"Nobody needed to spell it out for me," I insist, my voice wobbling with vulnerability. "And I'm sorry if I gave the wrong impression."

"Jade—"

"No, let me say this," I interrupt, lifting a hand to halt his words. "I think—no, I know I like you. And I can't just . . . I can't have casual sex with someone I have feelings for."

His brows knit together. "I don't want casual sex," he says, voice laden with confusion.

I gulp down the knot in my throat. "You . . . you don't?"

"No," he says firmly. "That's not what keeps me up at night—the thought of fucking you."

Suspicion flickers in my eyes, and I cross my arms defensively. His choice of words sounds like a red flag, but he's quick to clarify.

"Sure, I think about that a lot," he confesses, a faint blush heating his cheeks. "Probably more than I should. But there's more to it. I think about your sense of humor, how fucking funny you are." He closes the distance between us, invading my space again, reaching up to tuck a stray curl behind my ear. His hand lingers, fingers softly tracing the curve of my jawline. "I think about your wit, your sharp comebacks, the way your eyes light up when you smile or laugh. I think about how being around you makes me feel, like I'm not just some aimless jock, adrift in a sea of expectations."

His words send a warm wave of butterflies straight to my stomach. I lean into his touch, his large hand cradling my face. He draws a shaky breath before continuing. "You make me feel like I matter, like I'm more than just a football player."

"I do?"

"Fuck yeah, you do." He grins, a genuine, heart-stopping smile.

"I like you, Jade. I don't want to be just a fuck buddy to you. I want more with you."

My heart leaps in my chest, a smile spreading across my face. "I want that, too."

He perks up at my response, a spark igniting in his eyes. "Yeah?"

"Yes," I confirm, my voice steady and confident. "Spending time with you makes me happy, too. You make me feel good."

"Good," he murmurs, nodding slowly. "Does that mean I can kiss you now?"

At my eager "yes," he's leaning in again. Our lips meet in a tender kiss that hits me like a bolt of electricity. The initial touch is soft, exploratory, but the spark it ignites is anything but gentle.

Then my lips part, and the kiss deepens. His mouth claims mine with a raw intensity that leaves me breathless, our lips crushing, bruising together. He teases my bottom lip between his teeth, his tongue slipping past to taste me.

The cool wall presses against my back, acting as a stark contrast to the solid warmth of his body. Moving from my jaw, his hand traces a searing path down to my waist, his strong fingers pulling our bodies closer.

A low, involuntary moan escapes me as my hips move against his. He pulls back a fraction, his gaze sweeping over my face, my lips, my body in a hungry appraisal.

"You're so fucking hot," he groans.

Heat floods through me. The feeling of his hardness pressing against me makes me clench my thighs together, desire coursing in my veins. So, I reach down to fumble with the button on his jeans.

"Hold on," he rasps, catching my hands in his. "I don't—fuck, I can't believe I'm saying this, but . . . we shouldn't rush this."

His words send my mind reeling. "Sorry, what?" I pant, confused and off-balance.

"I want to show you that I really want this. You," he says,

running his thumb gently across my bottom lip. "Us."

"What do you mean?"

"Jade," he says, voice rough with emotion, gaze locked onto mine. "Let me take you out on a proper date first."

I let his words settle, pausing for a few moments, my heart thudding erratically in my chest. "Theo Westman-Cooke," I tease, the corners of my lips tugging up into a knowing smirk. "Are you trying to woo me right now?"

"Hell yeah, I am."

"Wow," I finally manage, my mind reeling. "Okay . . . so, no sex until we go on a real date?"

"That's the deal."

My eyes flit down to the obvious bulge in his jeans. "Hmm," I drawl, pretending to consider the proposal. "Can I at least blow you first?"

His gasp is almost comical, and his voice comes out husky and choked with surprise. "Fuck, seriously?"

"Seriously." I pull my lower lip between my teeth, an attempt at seduction. "I've been thinking about it nonstop since last night."

"Oh, sweet Christ," he groans, his head falling back as he tries to rein in his desire.

I bite back a triumphant smile, playing coy. "Is that a yes?"

His eyes snap open, and he almost stutters as he says, "Uh . . . I mean, no. A deal's a deal." His eyes flicker with regret. "No sex, period. Including oral."

Shaking my head, I break into laughter. "You're such a prude."

"And you're such a little tease," he counters, his voice rich with affection.

Clearing my throat, I busy myself with straightening my disheveled clothing, turning the conversation to safer waters. "So, you want to just . . . hang out, then?"

"We could watch a movie?"

"Sure," I readily agree, pointing a thumb over my shoulder to the bed behind him. "Hop on, and I'll set it up."

I rummage through my backpack for my laptop. As I turn back to him, I find he's already sprawled out on my bed, his hands clasped behind his head in a picture of casual ease.

"So," he starts, drawing out the word with a teasing lilt. He gestures vaguely around the room. "The Bobcats, huh?"

Caught off guard, I falter. "Oh . . . yeah." I shrug, attempting to sound casual. "They're a great team."

His brow quirks. "Did you grow up around here?"

"Nope, Washington."

"Hmm, okay," he says, skepticism etched in his voice. "So, you just have a thing for Mica Jennings, then? That's your dream man?"

I suppress a gag at his assumption. "Ew, definitely not."

"Oh, really?" He arches a brow, a challenging gleam in his eyes. His gaze sweeps across the room, taking in my odd choice of decor. "You say 'ew,' yet you have his posters plastered all over your room."

"He's one of the best cornerbacks in the NFL," I defend, my tone light.

"Right," he says, cocking a brow, voice brimming with humor. "And you totally wouldn't sleep with him if you had the chance."

The suggestion sends shocked laughter spilling out of me. "Oh, my God, no." I crinkle my nose, swallowing down the bile in my throat. "Don't make me puke."

"What?" he asks, eyes widening. "I mean, he's not my type. But you can't deny the guy's objectively good-looking."

"Well, yeah, he's handsome," I admit, wincing slightly. "But he's also my brother."

"Your . . . brother?"

"Mhmm," I confirm slowly, carefully gauging his reaction.

The stunned silence stretches on for a moment before he finally manages to speak. "Mica Jennings is . . . your brother."

"Yep."

"Holy shit," he breathes out. "So—Jade Jennings, huh?"

I study his expression as it shifts through various emotions—from surprise, to confusion, to something I can't quite pinpoint. With a twinge of anxiety, I finally ask, "Are you mad?"

"No, definitely not," he rushes to assure me, his voice filled with sincerity. "I'm just . . . shocked. Why didn't you mention this before?"

"I didn't want you to treat me any differently," I say, my voice quiet. "I mean, I didn't want to spend all of our time together talking about my brother. Been there, done that."

He gives me a sympathetic smile. "Has that happened to you before?"

"So many times."

His expression hardens. "That's shitty, Jade."

"I know," I say, a wave of resignation washing over me. "But it is what it is."

"I mean, damn, you're related to Mica Jennings," he mutters, mulling it over. "The man's a legend, but . . . that doesn't change how I see you. It changes nothing."

"Okay," I murmur.

"Jade . . ." His voice is soft, soothing, and I focus on him. "I know you weren't trying to lie to me. I just needed a moment to wrap my head around it. You just wanted to see where things went before bringing it up."

"Exactly."

His subsequent sigh is one of disbelief, amusement tinged with fondness. "Well, shit. Now I feel like an even bigger jerk for calling you a jersey chaser."

"It's fine." I wave him off, chuckling at his self-deprecating tone. "Well, not fine. But I've moved past it."

"That's good," he says, eyes twinkling with mischief. "But I should probably keep making it up to you, though."

Raising a playful eyebrow, I challenge him, "Oh? And how are you going to do that?"

His lips curl into a confident smile. "I guess you'll find out after our date."

"Yeah, I'm counting on it."

Chapter Fifteen

WEST

I DIDN'T REALIZE it could be like this.

That sharing a bed with a girl, with no intentions other than to spend time together, could feel so fucking satisfying. It's not just good, it's intoxicating.

And Jade—she's fucking flawless.

She embodies all the qualities I could ever want in a woman. Her humor never fails to make me laugh, her sarcasm is refreshingly honest, and her passion is infectious. She's determined, a hard worker who refuses to give up.

And God, is she sexy. To the point where it's a challenge not to be perpetually turned on around her.

The strange thing is, when we first met, I don't think I truly appreciated what was in front of me. Now I know, without a doubt, she's the most stunning thing I've ever seen.

Of course, there's no denying the physical desire between us. I'd be lying if I said I wasn't dying to taste every inch of her. This morning, I wanted nothing more than to press her against the wall, shove her panties to the side, and slide my aching cock between those perfect, sun-kissed thighs.

But I didn't, despite the undeniable fact that we both wanted it.

I have to admit this is all new territory for me. Doing things properly with a girl, taking the time to build a genuine connection —it's unfamiliar ground.

But with Jade, I want it all. I want the deep, meaningful conversations, the excitement of dating, the inevitable clashes that come with two strong personalities. And then, once all of that's in place, I'd very much like to fuck her until she can't remember her own name.

But it's true, I want that underlying foundation to be there between us. I crave the emotional connection, the depth that stems from truly knowing one another. Because this time around, I'm not just in it for the thrill. This time . . . I want something that's built to last.

By the time I leave Jade's apartment, the digital clock on my car dashboard reads just a few minutes past two in the afternoon. I'm in a mad rush, with only a few hours left to map out our date.

"Bro, I need your help," I call out, pounding a quick rhythm on Cam's bedroom door.

When he finally swings it open, he's standing there in nothing but a towel slung low on his hips, a toothbrush poking out from the corner of his mouth. He squints at me, a single brow arched in silent query.

"You just now getting up?" I venture to ask, working to suppress my smirk.

He removes the toothbrush from his mouth and holds up a finger, signaling for me to wait. After a moment, he reappears wearing a pair of worn-in boxers.

"I went back out after we hit Lucky's," he says, a trace of a sheepish grin playing on his lips. "A couple of us ended up at Dante's Nightclub."

"Ah, got it," I say, nodding my understanding. A night at Dante's can definitely take its toll. "Anyway, I'm taking Jade out on a date tonight."

His brows shoot up, skepticism etched across his features.

"Really?" I return his doubt with a definitive nod. "Alright, then. Atta boy."

"Yeah, thanks." I clap my hands together, determination coiling in my stomach. "I need your advice, though. Where should I take her? I'm not exactly an expert in this whole dating arena."

He levels me with a dubious look. "You've never been on a date before?"

"I've been on dates," I clarify, "but I never really cared about the details—where we went, what we did. They were more of a stepping stone to . . . other activities, if you get my meaning."

His eyes narrow for a moment before realization dawns. "And this isn't?"

"Fuck no, it isn't," I say, my tone dead serious. "I want her to enjoy herself, to remember this night."

"Right, so what's she into?"

"Well, she's a football fan, studious, a writer." I mention the tidbits I've gathered about her. "Also, a huge fan of *New Girl*. We just binged a few episodes this morning."

"She seems down-to-earth. Relaxed." He rubs his neck in contemplation. "Maybe a chill spot like a diner or sports bar? Maybe follow it up with something fun, like putt-putt golf or batting cages?"

"Camden Scott," I drawl, a grin spreading across my face. "You're a certified genius."

"Yeah, yeah." He dismisses me with a wave, a smug smile taking over his features. "Just add it to the list."

"Appreciate it, man. I'll keep you posted on how it pans out."

He tosses me a casual salute. "Good luck tonight."

As I retreat to my room, my stomach contracts with an uneasy feeling. No, wait, it's more like . . . a slow fluttering in my gut.

God forbid, I think I'm actually nervous for tonight.

I can't remember the last time I felt like this about a girl. It must've been when I was sixteen. The sensation, surprisingly, is invigorating. It's a spark of change, a different rhythm in my predictable life.

Whatever it is—this uneasiness, this thrill—all I know is that I really fucking like it.

Hours melt into late afternoon, and Jade and I are setting up at the batting cages. I gave her a few options, and this is what she picked. Honestly, she seemed pretty fucking stoked about the idea herself.

It's a good thing my girl is so easy to please.

I sit back on the metallic bleachers, my legs stretched out, one foot propped atop the other. My gaze is drawn to Jade, who stands poised by the plate. She looks so fucking cute in that oversized helmet, wearing nothing else but her tiny little T-shirt and shorts. Her dark curls cascade down her back, kissing the soft curve of her spine.

As she shifts her weight, digging her heels into the artificial turf, the muscles of her calves tighten. The sight sends an unfamiliar pang shooting through my chest, only to settle lower—a sudden, gut-clenching pull that stirs beneath my belt.

I'm eager to wrap her curls around my fist, to slide my hands up her legs, to touch the soft place between her thighs. Every little piece of her seems to be calling my name. I nearly jolt out of my seat a moment later, her body perfectly pivoting as she makes contact with the ball.

"Oh, God," I groan involuntarily. "This was a seriously bad idea."

Her gaze flickers to me, her face a picture of adorable confusion. "Why?"

"Watching you swing that bat . . . well, it's a huge fucking turn-on."

She looks back at me, a flicker of a knowing smile playing on her lips. "So, watching me do this—" She swings again, the sound of the crack ricocheting through the air. "—makes you hard?"

"Jade, everything you do makes me hard."

She drops the bat, leveling me with a seductive stare. "Theo."

"Uh-huh," I choke out.

"We should go back to my place now."

I laugh, shaking my head at her bold proposition. "Hang on. Aren't we supposed to have a proper date first?"

"But this was a proper date," she argues, her tone playful. "I picked up a bat, hit some balls. Had an absolute blast." Her smile is cheeky and utterly convincing. "Now, I'm ready for the next part."

"But we didn't even have dinner yet," I point out, my voice almost a whine.

She waves her phone with a triumphant flourish. "That's what takeout and modern technology are for."

I tilt my head back, staring up at the sky as I contemplate my next move. "Fuck it, you win. Let's get out of here."

Her sigh of relief is almost comical. "Thank God."

She takes me by the hand as we run to my car, laughing and stumbling in our haste to get home. I wrap an arm around her waist. She brushes her fingers against my hips, my shoulder, my bicep as she clings on for dear life.

Every soft touch sends a jolt of anticipation straight to my head, stopping for just a lightning-quick moment inside my heart. The engine rumbles to life, and her hand finds a comfortable spot on top of my thigh. While lust courses through my veins, there's a deeper warmth that settles around me now.

I know it's still early days, but I can truly see myself falling for this girl.

It's more than just wanting her. It's the little things—her soft smiles, the spark in her eyes when she talks about her favorite show, the way she handled that fucking baseball bat. The easy intimacy we've built from spending just a few short moments together.

I'd thought this kind of realization would send me into a tail-spin, but instead, it's like reaching a calming oasis. Despite the weight of what I'm feeling, there's a reassuring sense of rightness to it.

The drive back feels quicker than expected, and soon we're parked outside her apartment. She gives my hand a gentle squeeze, a silent promise of what's to come.

"Home sweet home," I murmur past the gravel in my throat.

Her gaze meets mine, filled with expectation and desire. And there's an open invitation there, too—an offer to dive deeper, to truly understand the girl who's turned my world on its head.

And damn, am I ready for it.

By the time we make it up to her floor, the anticipation is nearly eating me alive. She unlocks her front door with shaky hands, dragging me down the hallway and into her bedroom.

"Shan's not home tonight," she whispers in my ear, a subtle tremor in her voice.

Her words barely register before I have her pinned against the wall, my fingers threading gently through her hair. I'm kissing her before I can think, my mouth seeking hers with a hunger I can't control.

Oh God, the taste of her is so fucking good.

Her soft lips brush against mine, our tongues gently stroking one another. My grip tightens in her hair as I deepen the kiss, reveling in the soft heat of her mouth. And when she bites down on my lip, it's almost too much.

I pull back, letting out a groan as I trail my hands over the sweet curve of her breasts, her hips, her ass. She rocks against me, seeking friction, seeking release, as she presses her heat into my thigh.

As my fingers slide under the hem of her T-shirt, I look for a sign of approval in her eyes. The moment she nods, I peel the fabric off her, revealing the lacy white bra underneath. The sight of it against her flushed skin is more intoxicating than any drink I've ever had.

She arches her back off the wall, reaching behind with one arm to unclasp the hook. I stifle a groan as she shrugs the tiny, delicate straps away from her shoulders.

Oh, *fuck*.

My mouth waters at the sight of her perfect tits. Barely more than a handful, her plump teardrops are marked by rosy, red nipples. Goddamn, the real thing is so much better than the fantasy inside my head. I reach up to cup them with both hands, gently squeezing until she's moaning beneath me.

Then, I lower my hands, fingers hooked into the waistband of her shorts. "Can I?"

"Please," she rasps, inching forward to attach her lips to my neck.

At her request, the scrap of fabric joins the growing pile of clothes on the floor. And when my own shirt follows suit, there's an undeniable look of appreciation in her eyes.

"Mmm," she hums, her gaze roving over me like a physical touch. "You're so damn hot."

She presses her thumbs through my belt loops, tugging me back against her. There's a thin layer of sweat beading on my forehead. My heart beats wildly in my chest as she unfastens the button on my jeans, yanks at the zipper, and drags them down over my hips.

"I want you inside me," she breathes out, her gaze falling to the bulge straining against my boxers.

"Let me taste you first," I demand, and her breath catches in her throat.

Before she has a chance to respond, I sink down to my knees and pull her panties down along with me. The sight of her laid bare to me—slick and wet—nearly makes me lose control.

"Jade, your pussy's fucking perfect."

Her response is swallowed by a gasp as I bury my face between her thighs, flattening my tongue against her slit. She moans, soft and breathy, while I slowly lick my way back to her clit. And when I press my lips around the sensitive bud, she cries out in pleasure.

Her fingers rake through my hair, and she rocks against my mouth. I thrust one finger inside of her. Then two. She's impossibly tight, and hot, and so fucking wet. I pump inside of her, and I can't help but imagine my pulsing cock pushing into that perfect heat.

Instead, I focus my attention on her clit, sucking until I sense the unmistakable signs of an impending orgasm. I pull my fingers away but keep up the pressure with my mouth, aiding her through the surge of her release.

She sinks back against the wall, panting and spent, riding out the tidal wave of pleasure I've given her.

"That was so fucking hot," I tell her, my voice a rough whisper against her slick skin.

She simply hums in agreement, her eyes heavy with satisfaction, chest rising rapidly while she catches her breath.

"Need a minute?" I chuckle, brushing a stray hair from her face, pulling her against me.

"Uh-huh."

"Take your time, baby." I press a kiss to her forehead. "We have all night."

Chapter Sixteen

Oh God, West has a magical tongue.

I can honestly say that no man has ever made me orgasm like that in my life. The way he makes me convulse with pleasure—it's unparalleled. A sort of primal release that rocks me to my very core, leaving my legs trembling and my heart pounding relentlessly against my ribcage.

He's fucking incredible.

And don't get me started on the visuals. The sight of him, his head buried between my thighs, is enough to send another shock wave of pleasure right through my electrified nerves.

To be honest, my pussy's still pulsing, even as I sag against him now.

"Jade." He laughs softly, a quiet rumble that vibrates against my skin. His nose nuzzles into the crook of my neck, sending an unexpected jolt of pleasure skittering down my spine. "Let me take you to bed."

"Mmkay," I lazily murmur, lost in the afterglow. His hands move to the backs of my thighs, hitching them around his waist as he picks me up with effortless strength.

He carries me to the bed, his steps confident and measured. When he sets me down, my legs feel like they're made of lead, heavy and uncooperative as they dangle off the edge of the mattress. A haze of lust and satisfaction muddles my thoughts, and for a moment, I revel in the feeling.

"I love your tongue," I manage to say, craning my neck to meet his gaze directly.

His chuckle is low and rough, a sound that sends a flutter of excitement spiraling deep within my core. The reaction is so intense that I press my thighs together instinctively, seeking some form of relief.

"You really know how to stroke a guy's ego," he says, an amused glint dancing in his eyes.

"Mm, I do," I say, returning his playful smirk. "Can I stroke something else now?"

"Jade, you can stroke whatever the hell you want."

That's all the encouragement I need.

I slide off the bed, settling on my knees in front of him. My eager hands frantically tug at the waistband of his boxers, rushing to expose him to my hungry gaze. His solid arousal springs free, a sight that does nothing to curb my own desire.

I stare up at him, eyes locked as I wrap my fingers around the base of his shaft. When I lean forward to take him in my mouth, he lets out a low groan of pleasure from the back of his throat. Then his head drops back, hands tightly grasping the edge of the bed, trembling as I lick and suck from base to tip.

"So. Fucking. Good," he pants, his fingers threading through my endless mess of sweat-damp curls.

The sound of his gravelly voice sends an achy pulse of need straight to my core. An involuntary hum of pleasure escapes my lips as I press my thighs together, the mix of pleasure and pain nearly unbearable.

His hips shoot off the edge of the bed, cock thrusting deeply into the back of my throat. "Fuuck." He inches back, breathing heavily. "Sorry."

In the next instant, he's pulling me up from my knees, a soft pop echoing in the room as my lips leave him.

"What?" I ask, heart pounding.

He stares into my eyes, chest heaving as he says, "I need to be inside you."

His rough hands grasp the back of my thighs again, lifting me in one swift movement. As soon as he gets us flipped around, I'm tossed like a weightless doll back onto the bed. His heavy torso twists, muscles heaving as he leans down to retrieve a condom from his pants pocket.

He carefully slides it onto his thick length, and my eyes are hooded, mouth watering at the sight.

"I want you," I tell him impatiently.

He smirks, crawling forward until his cock is nestled right against my throbbing core.

"I want you back," he says. His strong hands clasp around my wrists, pinning my arms above my head. Then he pushes inside me, the hard length of him sliding against my firm walls. "Oh God, baby. You feel so fucking good."

I arch my hips off the bed as he thrusts slowly, deliberately inside me. The sweet friction, combined with a deeper angle, has me shuddering with pleasure.

He leans forward to brush his lips against mine. Our mouths touch, and tease, and lick, and suck until we're both out of breath. He pulls back, groaning, as his fingers trail down the sides of my arms.

Cupping my breasts with both hands, he squeezes them gently, kneading them as he fucks into me.

"Your body drives me wild," he rasps.

Bracing himself against the bed, he presses one hand into the mattress beside my head. His other hand trails down between our joined bodies, his thumb circling against my clit.

"Oh, God," I gasp, wrapping my arms around him as another wave of pleasure hits me. With every deep thrust, my nails gently scrape against his back. And my hips, they rock against him, matching him thrust for thrust as he buries himself to the hilt.

"So . . . good," I moan, biting down on his shoulder to stop from crying out. My fingertips trail down the sides of his biceps, pressing and squeezing into the hard muscle as I attempt to gain control.

"Yeah?" he asks, voice filled with gravel. "You like that?"

"Mhm."

"Wrap your arms around my neck," he instructs, his voice a seductive command. I comply without hesitation, looping my arms securely around him as he secures my legs around his waist, drawing me in closer.

In a swift and unexpected movement, our positions are switched. I'm straddling him now, the soft sheets of the bed beneath me. His strong hands on my hips anchor me in place.

"Is this okay?" His voice is ragged, raw with need, yet he pauses, waiting for my confirmation.

My nod comes quickly, the eagerness to proceed mirrored in his eyes. As soon as he sees it, he grasps my hips, hoisting me upward before plunging me back down on him, fucking me on his cock. He moves inside me in a rhythm that's frantic yet controlled.

And though I'm on top, there's no mistaking his dominance.

As our bodies mercilessly slap together, I lean forward until our mouths meet in a hungry kiss. It's a wild mixture of tongues, lips, and teeth. Sloppy but so fucking good.

I lift up on my knees, slowing down the rhythm of our thrusts until I'm grinding against him, our hips undulating together in search of heated, unending friction.

He releases a deep groan against my mouth, and the sound of his pleasure pushes me right over the edge, my pussy spasming against his throbbing length. He's still kissing me when he starts to come, his release spilling into the condom inside me.

Before I completely collapse onto his chest, I lift my hips and slide him out of me, rolling onto my back. We're both breathing heavily now—panting—covered in a thin sheen of sweat from head to toe. The curls on my nape are damp from exertion, and my heart is out of control.

"That was—" I start, but the words seem to dissipate in the air, my brain still drenched in the hazy aftermath.

"Yeah," he says, his voice a ragged whisper, echoing my thoughts exactly. "It was."

"I'm gonna go clean up." By some miracle, I summon the energy to slip out of bed, tugging a loose T-shirt over my head. The walk to the bathroom is a shaky one, though, my legs wobbling beneath me like a newborn baby deer's.

Not to mention there's a dull aching sensation that throbs between my thighs, but I savor the way it feels.

By the time I stumble back toward my bed, West has already slipped his boxers on. He's leaning against the headrest, one arm perched around his neck, scrolling through his phone. And when he notices me approach, his dark, caramel eyes lift to meet mine. There's a warm glow in them, mirroring the one in my chest.

"Hey, gorgeous," he says, his gaze tracing over my silhouette with a hint of lingering heat. "What would you like to eat?"

"Pizza?"

"Pizza, it is," he says, his tone suggesting it was never up for debate. "What toppings do you want?"

"Oh, uh—" I hesitate, unsure of how to respond. "Get whatever you like."

"No, what do *you* like?"

"Okay, you asked for it." Sighing in feigned exasperation, I roll my eyes at him. "I like pineapple and jalapeño."

A brow arches on his forehead, a bemused expression sweeping across his features. "That's . . . devastating."

"So dramatic."

"I'll just order Hawaiian with jalapeño on one side," he says, his face softening into a teasing smile. "Sound good?"

"Yep."

As he dials in our order, I climb back into the bed, nestling against his side. The warm scent of him wraps around me as he drapes an arm over my shoulder, pulling me close against his chest. When he ends the call, he leans over to press a soft kiss onto my hair.

"You still owe me a real date," he reminds me, his voice a low murmur against the top of my head.

"You're just mad that I hit more balls than you."

"We weren't even there for half an hour." His chuckle is soft as his fingers dance along the curve of my shoulder. "But you're right. Where'd you learn to swing like that?"

"Ace taught me," I say proudly.

His brows knit together, eyes clouded with confusion. "Ace?"

"Oh, sorry, that's Mica's nickname. He calls me Lili, and I call him Ace," I explain, warmth filling me as I mention my brother. "It's short for his middle name, too."

"You guys are pretty close, huh?"

"Yeah, he's actually coming to stay with me next weekend."

"That's awesome."

"Yeah." I hesitate, biting my lip as I consider my next words. "Maybe you could come meet him? You know, if you're gonna be around."

"Are you sure?" His voice is laced with surprise, but the spark in his eyes betrays his interest.

"I mean, you guys have a lot in common," I say, hoping to put him at ease. "Plus, I thought it might be cool for you."

"That'd be really fucking cool for me," he says, his face splitting into a grin. "I'd get to meet an NFL player, but more importantly, a member of your family."

"Okay, I'll arrange it, then."

"Perfect."

"Do you have any siblings of your own?" I ask, tracing my fingertips across the hard planes of his abdomen.

"Only child."

"Hmm," I murmur, trying to imagine his life without siblings. "What was that like?"

"Kind of dull, actually. I didn't exactly love the alone time, especially after my parents divorced when I was pretty young."

"That sucks," I say sympathetically. "It must have been tough."

"Yeah, but I'm stronger for it," he says, a hint of self-deprecation lightening his tone. "You know, independence and all that shit."

"And your parents now? Are you close?"

"Dad's been out of the picture for a long time," he says, his voice hardening slightly. "My mom's great, though."

"What's she like?" I ask, eager to learn more about him.

"She's sweet, hardworking, honest. She really tried to fill both roles," he says, a hint of fondness creeping into his voice. "She cried so much when she found out about Dayton."

"Was she sad that you were leaving?"

"No," he says, a soft chuckle escaping him. "She was just really proud that I made it to college, especially with a scholarship."

"She sounds really supportive." I tilt my head up, leaning in to place a chaste kiss against his jawline.

"Yeah, she is. What about your parents?"

"They're great, too. Very supportive of my brother and me," I tell him. "My dad actually has MS, though, so he has a lot of health problems. He's always tired and in pain, that sort of thing."

"Damn, that's—I can't imagine how tough that must be."

"Some days are better than others, but he finds ways to cope."

"That's good," he says, brushing a lock of hair from my face with gentle fingers. "It's clear you care a lot about your family."

"I do," I admit, my voice barely above a whisper. "I'm planning to spend some time with them this summer, back in Washington."

"Oh yeah?" he asks, his body stiffening slightly beneath me.

"Mhm," I confirm, my voice equally quiet. "You'll be at training camp, right?"

"Right." His jaw is set in a tight line. "I guess we'll both be pretty busy, then."

"Yeah." A wave of unease washes over me at the thought of a long-distance summer. I know it's still a few months away, but these feelings between us are still so new. Does West even see us lasting that long? Or would he cut me loose for the summer, regardless?

Admittedly, it might simplify matters for both of us. He could devote his undivided attention to football, and I could pour my energy into supporting my family. He says he wants more with me now, but who's to say that doesn't have an expiration date?

Still, we have an immediate future to look forward to. His team banquet is just around the corner next month. But beyond that, spring term will be closing its curtains in a matter of five weeks. So, I suppose we have the present, and that's what truly matters.

"Are you lost in your thoughts, Jade?" he asks, a hint of amusement coloring his tone.

"A little," I admit, a small smile playing on my lips. "Can I tell you something?"

His brow furrows. "What's up?"

"I like you," I tell him for the second time, fingers clutching at the firm ridges of his waist, anchoring me in place.

"And I like you," he says, tapping the end of my nose, a grin tugging at his lips. "You little dork."

Chapter Seventeen
WEST

Tonight will mark the first full night I've spent with a girl—actually lying in bed, cuddling, and talking after sleeping together—and I can't shake off this strange mix of guilt and exhilaration.

It might sound like I'm bragging or, even worse, complaining, but I'm not trying to. I've always been wary about what messages I might unintentionally send. The last time I was truly emotionally invested in a girl was back in the early days of high school.

Since then, everything's been more or less . . . shallow. So, why pretend otherwise?

Straight-up honesty has been my game. No messing around, no beating around the bush, and definitely no painting illusions of something more significant. My prior relationships, if you can even call them that, were just a string of . . . well, casual sexual encounters. From the moment I set foot on Dayton's campus, that's how it's been.

Until Jade, that is.

And now, I'm more than grateful that I have her. We've barely known each other for a month, yet she's already claimed a significant space in my life.

It's not like I don't have enough on my plate already—football, classes, my scholarship, and the looming draft. But there's an undeniable, irresistible urge to include her in that list of priorities too.

If I want this to work, if I want us to be something more than a passing phase, then I need to carve out time for her. For us. For this new, uncharted territory of what seems like an actual grown-up relationship.

For me, it's the first of its kind.

In the stillness of the night, my brain working in overdrive, I sense her stirring beside me. The gentle rustle of the sheets is the only sound that breaks the silence. She snuggles up against me, nuzzling her nose into the welcoming crook of my neck.

"Jade," I whisper, stroking the back of her hair.

She responds with a sleepy "Mhmm," but the drowsiness doesn't linger for long. Now, she's pressing gentle kisses against my neck, and the soft, barely there touch of her lips elicits a low rasp from the depths of my chest.

"What are you doing?" I manage to ask through the thickening haze of desire.

She doesn't bother with a verbal response. Instead, she continues to trail kisses from my neck to my jawline, peppering them until she's nipping at my earlobe. Her thigh moves to nestle between my legs as she rocks her hips against me.

I wrap my fingers around her waist to pull her closer. Our hips press together—my hard length against her soft core—and I can feel the warm, heavy pulsing of her desire as she whispers, "I want you," into my ear.

In a coordinated flurry of motion, I grab the stash of condoms on her nightstand. Rolling one on, I nudge her panties aside and slowly push my cock inside of her. This time, we fuck nice and slow.

In the morning, I take her again in front of the bathroom mirror. She's tying her hair up when she starts reciting that corny little mantra of hers. So, I bend her over the counter and slide into her from behind. She's just as tight, and wet, and needy as she was the first time.

Well, fuck me.

I didn't realize that's what spending the night could entail. I mean, we talked for hours about our family, ate pizza in bed, and then she asked me the big question: "Theo, do you want to stay over tonight?"

"Hell yeah," came my instant response. No need to mull it over, not even a second thought about it.

And I suppose that's the difference right there. There's no need to pretend, no room for ambiguity. I want her—all of her, every single part. I can't seem to get enough of her, physically or mentally.

Even when I'm finally back home on Sunday afternoon, attempting to study for my Greek Mythology midterm.

"God, I'm a fucking dipshit," I groan, my forehead meeting the cool surface of our dining table.

"Tell me something I don't know," Cam calls, a grin playing on his lips as he fishes out a couple of Gatorades from the bottom of the fridge.

"You're a dick," I say as he tosses one over.

"Again—tell me something I don't know," he echoes, sinking into the chair next to me.

I let out a huff, running a hand through my hair in frustration. "Okay, what I'm trying to say is—I've been drilling the wrong fucking material into my head for the past two hours."

"No shit?"

"Yeah, man. I've been diving into Unit 4 when we're only on 3.8 right now," I say, the stress of the situation settling in. "No wonder none of this shit rings a bell."

"That sucks."

"Yeah, it does." I rub my temples in frustration. "Especially since I put off studying to spend more time with Jade."

A flicker of understanding crosses his features. "Shit, was it at least worth it?"

"Yeah. It was . . . really good."

"What'd you guys end up doing?"

I pause for a moment, my lips curving into a twisted smirk. "Oh, uh . . . batting cages," I say, my mind replaying the rest of our night in vivid detail. "It was cool."

"Sweet, I've been wanting to go for a while. Maybe we could make it a group thing?" He glances up at me, enthusiasm filling his voice. "You know, invite Shan and the others?"

"Oh, yeah. Sure, man," I say, a noncommittal shrug rolling off my shoulders. My mind's still too full of Jade to truly engage in the idea.

His eyes narrow at me, his playfulness replaced with a piercing gaze. "Yeah, alright."

"What?"

"You're really not into Shan anymore?" he asks, a single brow raised in blatant doubt. "Not even a tiny bit?"

"Nah, man." The truth of my words sits heavily in the air. "I'm all about Jade now."

As I say it, I'm hit by a sharp pang of regret. The thought of willingly allowing Cam, or anyone else on the team, to have a shot with Jade—well, it's ridiculous. Laughable, even.

"Seriously? You've known her for what, a month?" He sounds cautious, almost wary. "You've been mooning over Shan for three fucking years, dude."

"Think of it this way," I say, my gaze steady on him. "If I really wanted to be with Shan, I would've made an actual move by now."

And that's the crux of it. I had plenty of opportunities, countless moments where I could have made a real, true effort with Shannon. But something always stopped me. There was always a barrier, an invisible line I never wanted to cross.

With Jade, though, it was different. I was like a river drawn to the sea—I wanted her, and I pursued her without hesitation. That has to count for something, right?

"True," he concedes after a moment, a thoughtful look crossing his features. "I mean, I thought you just 'didn't have time to date.'"

"Yeah, but I can make time," I assert, my voice firm. "For Jade, I'll make the time."

"You sure about that?"

Am I sure? I mull over his question. The school year is winding down, and summer looms over the horizon. Jade's planning to return to Washington, and I have a football training camp here. That inevitably means time apart.

But maybe that's not such a bad thing. Maybe the separation will be good for us. She'll have her family, and I'll be engrossed in training with my teammates. Granted, it's not the ideal situation for a new relationship, but at least it will offer us a chance to concentrate on our individual lives before we plunge into our senior year.

But that's assuming we're still . . . together by then. The thought sends a strange jolt through me. It's an uneasy possibility that I'd rather not entertain, yet I can't deny its existence.

Fucking hell, I sure hope we're still together.

"I don't know, man," I finally admit to Cam, allowing my confusion to bleed into my words. The whirlpool of thoughts distills into one simple, powerful sentiment. "But I'm sure as hell gonna try."

After all, there's no blueprint for this. There's no guaranteed path to ensuring we stay together through the summer or even the rest of the school year. It's new terrain, and all I can do is hope that my earnestness, my genuine feelings for Jade, will be enough.

Sure, it's a risk, but it's one I'm more than willing to take. For Jade, I would wager it all.

THE NEXT DAY ROLLS AROUND, and Jade and I are tucked away in a corner of the North Campus Library. She's neck-deep in her latest piece for the *Daily*, the sound of her tapping away on the keyboard mixing in with the hushed whispers around us.

Me, I'm in the audiobook world of Oedipus the King. But even as my ears are filled with ancient Greek tragedy, my mind has other plans.

More specifically, I'm distracted by thoughts of Jade's lips. The shape of them. The color. The feeling of them pressed against mine. And now, my gaze is drifting across every little detail of her face—from the scatter of freckles across her nose to the tiny birthmark above her top lip.

And that's when I land on something new: a small indentation, a soft dimple beneath her chin that I've never noticed before. I wonder if it's a scar.

If it is, how did it come to be? Did she fall off her childhood bike? Or maybe it's just a playful scratch from a family pet. But then again, do they even have a family pet?

The question bubbles up before I can stop it. "Jade?" I ask, a faint smile playing on my lips, breaking through her dedicated concentration.

"What's up?" She glances up from her laptop, a cute little crease settling between her brows.

"Do your parents have a dog?"

Her response is a snort—a sound I've grown quite fond of. "Now, there's an urgent question."

"Ah, come on," I coax, gently nudging her laptop aside to command her full attention. "Do they?"

"They don't." She pivots in her chair to face me, a teasing grin spreading across her face. "Why this sudden curiosity?"

"Just popped into my head."

Guided by impulse, I lean forward, my hand instinctively seeking hers. She flips her palm up, so I press my thumb into the center and give it a gentle squeeze, our fingers interweaving. It's simple and warm—a silent promise of comfort.

"Okay, I'll bite," she says. "Does your mom have a dog?"

"No, she doesn't." I break our hand hold, instead opting to rest mine gently on her knee.

"That's nice. I'm so glad I paused my work to have this extremely enlightening conversation."

My chest rumbles with a soft chuckle. "Apologies for the interruption."

Her eyes flit down to my hand resting on her knee, her smirk deepening. "I'm sure you are."

"You know, I read your article this morning," I say, my hand unconsciously trailing up her leg, drawing small, lazy circles on her legging-covered skin.

"You did? The one about the bricks?"

"That's the one."

"Wow," she says, her tone carrying a note of disbelief, the hint of a proud smile playing on her lips. "And?"

"I'll be honest, it was a little hard for me to get through," I say, my hand subtly continuing its journey up her leg. "I blame it partially on the dyslexia and partially on the subject matter, but damn, Jade—you're an incredible writer."

She snorts dismissively, her cheeks blooming with a soft pink hue. "Oh, please. It was a piece about literal bricks."

"Exactly," I counter, my touch growing bolder. "It was an article about bricks, and I was still into it."

"You're just saying that because I wrote it."

"No, I read it because you wrote it. I enjoyed it because you're fucking talented."

"Oh," she stammers, blush deepening, gaze drifting down to my hand on her thigh. "Stop doing that."

"I'll stop if you stop," I say, my smirk growing wider.

"Stop what?" Her eyes dart around the room nervously, ensuring we're not the center of anyone's attention.

"Stop making me want you."

She scoffs. "I'm just sitting here, minding my own business, working."

"True," I say, my voice lowering to a sultry whisper. "And I'm just sitting here, watching you work. It's not my fault you look so damn good . . . even when you're wearing that godforsaken sweatshirt."

Rolling her eyes, she shoves my hand away from her thigh. "You love this sweatshirt."

I chuckle, leaning back in my chair. "Well, it is growing on me. Just a little."

She shakes her head, the corners of her lips pulling up into a smile as she shifts back into work mode. I can't help but watch her for another moment, letting my eyes roam over her from head to toe, lingering on all my most-loved spots.

The sweater might be concealing her figure right now, but damn . . . I know what lies beneath the surface. Jade's body is a fucking masterpiece—her soft thighs, her supple hips, the gentle dip in her waist, the swell of her breasts, and that beautiful face of hers. She's filled with all my favorite curves, slopes, freckles, and marks.

But here's the real kicker: her body isn't even the most attractive part about her. Not for me. And not by a long shot.

Chapter Eighteen

THE PAST FIVE days were a blur of libraries, term papers, and far too much caffeine.

While West busied himself with catching up on his reading, I juggled my course assignments. Our first week of dating was far from romantic. But we decided to study together anyway, working to blend our relationship into our daily lives.

Honestly, it's nice to have a built-in study partner, albeit one who revels in distracting me. West has a knack for derailing my focus, be it by tracing an imaginary line on my thighs, fiddling with the ends of my hair, or sneaking in a quick kiss when I least expect it.

Yes, it's distracting, but it's also incredibly reassuring. It feels nice, being wanted so blatantly, so openly.

And West never misses an opportunity to compliment me. He showers me with praises, asserting that I have a "perfect fucking body." But it doesn't end there. He thinks I'm smart, funny, talented, and he ensures I know it. He feeds my ego, and I, shamelessly, lap it all up.

I know our relationship is still so fresh, but I like that there are no guessing games when it comes to his feelings. He's not pretending to be aloof, or cool, or coy. And that's probably my favorite thing about him—that he's unapologetically himself.

He's honest and straightforward. In my mind, he's the

complete fucking package. Actually, he's everything I never knew I needed.

Before West, I always avoided dating athletes, thanks to Mica's less-than-ideal dating habits. My brother, for all his good traits, is pretty lousy at being a boyfriend. Football is his world, and his relationships have always taken the back seat.

But Mica is just one guy, and his actions don't reflect every athlete. West is the proof of that.

Or at least, that's what I'm hoping.

When Friday night finally arrives, my heart is hammering with excitement. The sound of three loud knocks sends me vaulting off the couch and hurtling toward the door. As I wrench it open, the sight of my brother's familiar, broad grin smacks me with a sense of homey comfort.

"Ace!" I nearly shout, a surge of joy lighting up my features.

He envelops me in a fleeting hug, his laughter rumbling low in his chest. "Lil, you look so much older every time I see you."

"Congrats, you've got the basic concept of time down pat."

He steps inside, scoffing as he shrugs off his duffel bag. "You've changed, Lil. You're more . . . cynical. I suppose we have college to blame for that."

"Well, you definitely played a part in that evolution."

His gaze sweeps the living room, his grin broadening at the sight of my Bobcats posters plastered on the walls. He jabs me lightly with his elbow, a twinkle in his eyes. "I see your taste in decor hasn't evolved much, though."

"Hey, that's unfair," I argue, feigning offense. "Shannon's added her feminine touch to the place—plants, candles, and some other shit."

"So, she's giving you a crash course in being a girl, is she?"

I narrow my gaze, playfully swatting him. "You're insufferable."

His chuckle rings through the room. "But you missed me."

"Yeah, of course."

We sink onto the couch, taking a moment to simply sit in the familiarity of each other's company. His towering frame fits effortlessly into the space, his six-foot-five presence always commanding, always larger than life. Yet, in my apartment, he seems to blend in seamlessly.

"I'm happy I could swing by," he says. "I needed a weekend full of sibling bonding."

The prospect makes me chew on my lip, the tendrils of anxiety curling in my stomach. "Actually, about that . . . I recently started seeing someone."

"Okay, and?"

"I thought it'd be nice for you two to meet," I say, attempting to keep the apprehension from my voice.

He grunts, clearly unenthusiastic. "Why?"

"Because I genuinely like him. He's cool, and I have a hunch that you two would click."

"I highly doubt it."

"No, seriously. You and West share a lot of similarities."

"Mhmm," he drawls, voice dripping with skepticism. "I'm sure I have a ton in common with the asshole who's dating my sister."

"He's not an asshole," I counter defensively, then mumble under my breath, "At least, not all the time." And then louder, "He's a running back for Dayton."

His mocking expression slips, giving way to a more serious demeanor. "Lilianna, you're telling me your jock boyfriend wants to meet me? What a shocker."

"I don't appreciate the sarcasm," I snap, my fingers kneading the fabric of my jeans. "I know what you're thinking . . . but he wasn't aware we were related before we got together."

His response is a slow, contemplative drag of his hand over his face. "Alright, I'll reserve judgment if that's what you want."

"I want you to be supportive. He's coming to dinner with us tomorrow."

"Fine, I'll try." He heaves a heavy sigh. "You know I only want the best for you, right?"

"Yeah, I know," I say, my gaze softening. "But I also wish that—"

The sound of our front door rattling stops me midsentence. It swings open, and Shannon steps inside. There's a flash of fiery red hair that instantly draws my brother's attention. And then, there's her bare, freckled thighs peeking out from beneath her cheerleading uniform, the emerald green of the fabric a stark contrast to her pale skin.

As always, she manages to look put together and full of life.

"Hi," she greets us with a wave, her attention shifting to Mica. "I'm Shannon. You must be Jade's brother."

Mica rises from the couch, a fluid movement that contrasts sharply with his bulky frame. He strides over to Shannon, greets her with a firm handshake, and says, "Mica," his voice a shade deeper than it was earlier.

It's his "charming stranger" tone, one I've seen him use too many times to count.

At that, I jump to my feet and join them, casting a quick, pointed look at my brother, who answers it with a knowing smirk. "Shannon, you free tomorrow night?" he asks, brushing off my silent warning. "We'd love for you to join us for dinner."

I clamp my mouth shut, jaw clenched as I wait for her response.

"Sure!" Her tone is light and cheerful, unaware of the tension filling my body.

"Great." Mica grins, tossing her an unmistakable wink. A very deliberate, very infuriating wink.

. . .

The next morning, I'm up with the sun, despite the chaos swirling in my head. Shannon, being the absolute sweetheart she is, insisted on staying at a friend's house to allow Mica the comfort of her bed.

"Why would he sleep on the couch?" she'd asked, oblivious to the situation. "There's a perfectly good bed in my room."

Mica's petty antics are as predictable as they are irritating. Step One: Invite Shannon to dinner, knowing I'd feel cornered. Step Two: Dazzle her with his star-athlete charm, right in front of me. Step Three: God, I hope we never get to step three.

While I'm not particularly bothered by her joining us, it's obvious he invited her as a provocation. He's had a vendetta against every guy I've dated, stretching as far back as my first high school boyfriend, whom he had quite seriously threatened to castrate.

It's juvenile. It's chauvinistic. It's downright infuriating. And yet, it's also somewhat endearing. I know my brother cares for me, that he wants to protect me. But there's absolutely no reason for him to do so with West.

"Ace," I call, pounding on the door to Shannon's bedroom. "Get your ass out of bed. We're going to the farmer's market."

Predictably, he groans, "Shut up."

I count to five in my head, putting on my best "mom" voice. "Get up, or I'm coming in there."

Sure enough, Mica's out the door and ready to go in less than five minutes. With just a pair of jeans, a simple T-shirt, and a quick run of a comb through his hair, he somehow looks like he's walked straight out of a catalogue. It's annoying as hell.

We make it through the day relatively unscathed, but as we prep for our dinner, I find myself issuing the same warning to him over and over again—not to fuck with Shannon. After the sixth repetition, I can only hope he's taken it to heart.

"You know I'm serious," I say, my voice a hushed whisper.

"She's, like, my best friend. I don't want you screwing with her, even if you think it's harmless."

We're in my room, with him buttoning up his shirt and me trying to wriggle into my two-inch Manolo heels. Shannon's in the living room, ignorant of our conversation. And by my calculations, West should be at the restaurant already, waiting for us.

"I thought I was your best friend."

"You both are," I correct him, my voice firm. "Which is why your flirting doesn't amuse me."

"Okay, okay." He rolls his eyes in playful resignation. "Just make sure your running back keeps his hands to himself."

"Don't you worry about West. He's one of the good guys."

His laughter fills the room, an easy sound that temporarily calms my nerves. "Yeah, we're all good guys . . . until we're not."

"Who's the cynic now?"

"We both are," he says, mischief dancing in his dark eyes. "I just happen to know how guys think, that's all."

"Yeah, well . . . keep your guy-brain away from Shan, and we're golden."

He laughs again, though it doesn't give me the reassurance I'm hoping for.

"Ace . . ."

"Lil, I love you." He turns away from the mirror to pull me into a hug. "I'll be on my best behavior tonight."

His promise hangs in the air long after his words fade. I hold on to it, hoping against hope that he'll stick to it. For the sake of Shannon, West, and especially me.

For the past hour, Mica's been trying to uphold his promise, keeping his interactions with Shannon civil and merely polite. He initiates rounds of drinks, orders a handful of appetizers, even extends the courtesy to ask for West's preferences.

Yet the man in question is nowhere to be found. He's nearly an hour late, with not so much as a text or call to offer a lifeline.

And Mica, bless his heart, is holding it together, but the clench of his jaw and the darkness flashing in his eyes betray his anger. He's trying for my sake, and damn if that doesn't twist my insides in guilt.

Escaping our table, I step outside, the third time tonight, desperate for fresh air and a break from my brother's silent wrath. Phone pressed to my ear, I'm left again with the dial tone ringing in my ears, West's voicemail message practically imprinted on my mind.

"Hey, I'm so sorry." His voice, gruff and tinged with regret, startles me from my frustrated thoughts. Turning around, I'm met with an apologetic gaze.

I cross my arms, working to suppress the tremble in my voice as I shoot back, "What the hell, Theo?"

He tries to reach out, but the disappointment on my face must stop him. "We had a team meeting—it ran late. I accidentally left my phone at home."

A long sigh escapes my lips. Shit. It's not entirely his fault, and I know it. But a flicker of disappointment is hard to shake off. He could have planned better.

"You know, this is strike two with my brother, and you haven't even met yet."

"Strike two?"

I manage a small smile, attempting to lift the heavy mood. "The first strike was dating me."

His relief is evident as he takes a step forward, his movements slow and cautious as if he's scared I might bolt. Our fingers entwine, and his thumb rubs comforting circles on the back of my hand. "Jade . . . I feel like such a jackass. I'm sorry I'm late, and I'm sorry I left your brother waiting."

My sigh echoes the soft night. "It's a good thing Shan's here to play buffer."

He cocks a brow. "Shan's here?"

"Yeah, Ace invited her. I'll fill you in later."

We enter the restaurant together, his grip on my hand a silent promise of reassurance. Yet, as we step toward the entryway, he stops in his tracks. "Wait, Jade," he says, his voice a soft plea. When I turn to look at him, the intense sincerity in his gaze is enough to dampen my lingering frustration. "Will you forgive me?"

His question leaves me at a crossroads. I could choose to continue being frustrated, casting a further shadow on the night and hindering any hope of smoothing things over between Mica and West. Or I could opt for forgiveness and focus my energy on bridging the gap between them.

The answer bubbles up naturally. "I forgive you," I say, matching his sincerity. "It was a mistake. Unfortunate timing, but we all make them."

His sigh of relief wraps around me. He leans in, his lips meeting mine in a tender, apologetic caress. The kiss is brief, the kind of sweet that leaves your stomach fluttering in anticipation. "Now I need to go apologize to your brother."

"Oh, are you planning to kiss him, too?"

"Only if you think it'll help."

Chapter Nineteen

MICA JENNINGS IS one intimidating motherfucker.

He's huge, he's famous, and he's scary as hell. And as Jade and I approach their table, our hands interlocked, his intense gaze drills into my forehead, leaving a mark that lingers.

"So, this is my—" Jade shifts uncomfortably on her heels, pulling her hand from mine. "This is West."

"Mica," her brother fires back, jaw clenched.

Summoning up all my courage, I clear my throat and pull out a chair for Jade, a silent gesture of support. She takes her seat, and I settle down beside her, working to exude a sense of calm despite my nervous energy. "Sorry to keep you all waiting."

Mica scoffs dismissively, his voice dripping with sarcasm. "Yeah, it's been what, an hour?"

"Yeah, I know." I sigh, conceding my fault. "I'm sorry, our team meeting ran late tonight."

"Right," he grits out, his frustration barely contained. "And phones don't work in Dayton locker rooms?"

"Ace," Jade intervenes, palm settling on my knee.

"No, he's right," I say, my thumb stroking hers as I lean closer. "I forgot my phone, and I messed up. I knew this was important to Jade."

Jade's touch tightens, her fingers applying gentle pressure against the taut muscle in my leg. "It's okay because you're here now. Right, Mica?"

His guarded expression softens, broad chest deflating ever so slightly. "Right, sure. Let's just order."

"Thank you." I give him a grateful nod, appreciating the small victory. "Shan, it's good to see you."

"Hey, West," Shannon chimes in, her voice as warm as usual. "Glad you made it."

With the spotlight back on me, Mica refocuses his piercing gaze. "So, Lili tells me you're a running back."

A weighted pause lingers as I assess his agenda. It's clear where he's trying to steer the conversation. He's testing me, anticipating that I'll spend the night talking about myself, hoping for a connection through football, all while vying for the approval of an NFL player.

But tonight isn't about that.

Yes, I'm awestruck by the guy. He's undeniably one of the best cornerbacks in the league, and his talent as a defensive back is legendary. However, my primary focus is on the woman by my side —Jade, my girl, and her family.

I've already made enough mistakes tonight; I can't afford to lose sight of what truly matters.

"Yeah," I say, maintaining my composure and subtly steering the conversation. "That's right. But first, I need to graduate."

"Really?" Mica probes further, continuing his examination. "No plans for an early declaration?"

I wave off the suggestion, deflecting his attention. "Nah. You finished your degree, right? Jade mentioned your ridiculously high GPA in college."

"Oh, she did, did she?" Mica smirks, reclining in his chair. There's a flicker of amusement in his eyes now. "Well, I'll be damned, Lil."

Jade rolls her eyes playfully, failing to suppress a smile. "Oh, shut up. You know I think you're smart."

"She does," I say, seeking to boost the man's ego even further.

"She almost never takes off that hand-me-down sweatshirt you gave her."

"Really?" Mica chuckles, his tension dissipating like smoke in the wind. "Little Lili just loves me so much."

Jade snorts, attempting to hide her amusement but failing miserably. "You're full of yourself."

"I mean, he's not wrong," I chime in once again. "Actually, man, do you have any tips on becoming Jade's favorite person?"

"Oh, so you think you can just take over my spot?"

Leaning back in my seat, a sliver of tension finally rolls off my shoulders. "Well, I guess that's up to Jade."

"Yeah," he murmurs in response, a newfound ease in his voice. "Yeah, I guess it is."

With the arrival of our food, we indulge in another round of drinks. Jade sticks to a simple gin and tonic, while Shannon opts for a virgin margarita. As for me, I remind myself to pace my alcohol consumption, limiting myself to two drinks at most.

After that awkward first impression, the last thing I want is to stumble through the night, intoxicated in front of Jade's brother.

Surprisingly, the conversation steers clear of football altogether. It's a nice feeling knowing that our connection can go beyond the realm of sports. And as we eat, we talk about our favorite movies, reminisce about shit we got up to in high school, and the siblings delve into the nostalgia of growing up together.

Mica, it seems, was a rebel with a brain, his intelligence shining through even amidst his rule-breaking antics. On the other hand, Jade, though a rule-follower by nature, has always possessed an inner fire, a certain feistiness to her that can't be tamed.

"Lil, remember that time you fell in a ditch outside Mr. Grady's house?" Mica leans back in his chair, his beer bottle tipping slightly.

"It's hard to forget," Jade mutters, her voice laced with a mix of exasperation and fondness, a delicate burst of laughter escaping her lips.

"She didn't want us to call Mom and Dad," he says with a chuckle, his eyes flickering toward Shannon and me. "But I had to play the hero and rescue her with a rope from Dad's shed."

Jade folds her arms across her chest. "We weren't supposed to be playing there."

"Yeah, well." Mica snorts. "You're lucky I was there to save your life."

"You always exaggerate!" Jade scolds, a playful glint in her eyes. "You know, you and West are two dramatic peas in a pod."

I join in, embracing the lighthearted banter. "She likes to pretend I'm some kind of drama queen."

"We're drama *kings*, sis."

"Exactly," I say, lips curving into a wide grin.

"I don't know," Shannon says softly. "It sounds like a classic sibling adventure to me. You two have always had each other's backs."

Jade nods, a smile of gratitude forming on her lips. "Yeah, we may fight like cats and dogs, but when it matters, we're there for each other."

"That's the best part about family, isn't it?" Mica asks, clapping a hand against my shoulder. "No matter how much I might piss my sister off, we'll always have that unbreakable bond."

Jade's resounding laughter lights up her features, a rosy shade of pink flushing through her cheeks as she smiles. Beneath the table, her fingers tap against my knee, a silent invitation to thread our hands together.

And in that moment, an overwhelming sense of contentment washes over me. It feels so fucking good to see her happy like this—cheerful, relaxed—surrounded by people who care about her more than anything.

God, I can't wait for more of it.

. . .

A FEW HOURS LATER, we make a collective decision to call it a night. Stepping outside together, we huddle beneath the shelter of the restaurant's awning, seeking refuge from the pouring rain. Water cascades off the side of the building, forming puddles at our feet, as we prepare to part ways.

Mica's gaze drifts toward the parking lot before returning to his sister. "Why don't I go grab the car while you hang back with Shannon?"

Jade's voice is soft as she murmurs her agreement. "Sounds good."

Shannon adds her thanks. "Thank you, Mica."

Taking a step forward, I extend my hand toward him, hoping to bridge the gap between us. His gaze narrows as he gives me a quick once-over. After a tense moment that seems to stretch into eternity, the star cornerback finally takes a leap of faith, gripping my hand and shaking it twice.

"I'm glad we got to meet," I say sincerely, my words carrying the weight of appreciation. "Thanks for giving me a second chance."

"Sure." He shrugs, relaxing into his stiff posture. "You know, you're actually not a huge asshole."

"I'll take that as a compliment."

"Coming from my brother," Jade interjects with a teasing tone, "that's pretty much a glowing review."

"It's true," Mica says, grin widening. "I'll catch you next time, man."

"Looking forward to it," I say, a genuine sense of anticipation coloring my words.

With one final nod, Mica races through the bustling parking lot, raindrops streaming down onto his flimsy baseball cap.

"That actually went super well, all things considered," Jade says, her voice filled with warmth. "I think you guys—"

"O'Connor!" Her words are cut off by the sound of an all-too-familiar female voice piercing through the rain-soaked air.

"Oh!" Shannon's attention quickly shifts toward the source. "Hey, Cassidy!"

"Hey, girl." Cassidy's voice resonates with cheer as she turns her gaze toward me. "Oh . . . and you're here with West."

"Hey," I mutter, giving her a stiff nod.

"Cassidy." Shannon pauses for a moment, glancing in Jade's direction before continuing. "This is my new roommate, Jade."

"Ohh, new roomie!" Cassidy claps her hands together with enthusiasm. "I used to live with O'Connor, too, from sophomore year until last term."

"Right, she told me about that," Jade says sweetly, extending a friendly hand. "It's nice to finally meet you."

"Mhm. So, are you two, like, on a date tonight?" Cassidy asks, her curiosity evident as she gestures toward me and Shannon.

"Yeah, Cass." I snort in amusement. "We're on a date, and Shan brought her roommate."

Cassidy's eyes narrow, a mischievous glint in her gaze. "He's kidding," Shannon rushes to say. "Um, actually, they're together now. West and Jade."

"Huh." Cassidy's tone drips with intrigue. "Really?"

"Yes, really," I say, my voice carrying an undertone of exasperation. Then, without hesitation, I wrap my arm around Jade's waist, pulling her gently against my side. A thin sheen of sweat forms on my brow as I brace myself for the ensuing conversation.

Cassidy gives me a sly look. "It's just . . . that's kind of ironic, isn't it?"

Jade tilts her head. "How so?"

"Well—" Cassidy twirls a strand of her hair between her fingers, her gaze piercing. "When I lived with O'Connor, West was dating me. But now that you're living with her, West is suddenly dating you."

"Oh," Jade says awkwardly, her confusion mingling with

obvious discomfort.

"O'Connor," Cassidy says, crossing her arms and leaning in. "What do you think about that?"

"I mean, it's just a coincidence," Shannon says with a shrug, attempting to diffuse the tension.

"Hmm, yeah," Cassidy drawls, her tone dripping with skepticism. "Such a funny coincidence, isn't it, West?"

I attempt to unclench my jaw as I respond, frustration simmering beneath the surface. Cassidy's words stir up memories that I'd rather forget. She knows full well the truth, that we were never together in the way she implies.

In fact, I'm fairly certain she was involved with half the team at the time. As for me, I've always been more of a one-woman kind of guy. One at a time, anyway.

Now, it's just one and only. And it's all the time if I can have it my way.

"Anyway, it was nice to see you guys," Cassidy says with a fake smile. "Daddy's waiting in the car, so I better get going."

"Good to meet you," Jade offers politely, her voice laced with a touch of relief.

"Yeah." Cassidy smirks, her words tinged with an undercurrent of bitterness. "It was great meeting you, Jane."

I wince inwardly as she walks away, her absence leaving an uncomfortable silence in its wake.

"Well then." Jade clears her throat, her tone a mix of curiosity and caution as she raises a brow.

Shannon steps in to apologize on behalf of her friend. "Sorry, she's not usually that . . . spiteful."

"Nah, I get it," Jade says, waving off her concern. "It's always hard to see your ex with someone new."

"She's not actually my ex," I say, frustration seeping into my voice, my tone defensive. I want to set the record straight, to ensure that Jade understands the truth.

Jade's response is measured, her gaze steady as it meets mine. "Well, she definitely lived with Shan. So, I guess that makes her an ex-roommate, at the very least."

Shannon chimes in, attempting to shed some light on the situation. "Yeah, she's probably just a little jealous."

Jade's eyes flicker toward me, seeking confirmation. "I'm assuming you didn't have a great breakup?"

I protest once more, my words carrying an undercurrent of exasperation. "We weren't together."

Jade's voice falls to a mumble. "Okay."

I lock eyes with her, desperate to bridge the gap. "Jade . . ."

She turns toward the street, a hint of tension in her stance. "Look, Ace just pulled up. We should really get going."

My spine stiffens at the thought of any lingering tension between us. "Are we fighting?"

"No, we're not," she reassures me, her voice gentle yet guarded. "It was just a weird moment, okay? No biggie."

"I just . . . I don't want there to be any doubt between us."

Jade's smile is tight-lipped, a touch of weariness visible. "Okay. We'll talk more tomorrow, then. After my brother leaves?"

I soften slightly, realizing the need to respect her boundaries. "Yeah, alright."

"It's okay, Theo." Pushing up onto her toes, she places a chaste kiss against my jaw. "I'll see you later."

"See you," I murmur in response, my eyes fixed on her as the two girls walk through the rain, pull open the car doors, and slip inside.

What Cassidy just implied . . . it's a twisted, fucked-up version of the truth. Yes, I asked Jade to the banquet with the intention of trading her, but it wasn't some desperate ploy to screw her over. Our relationship grew organically, and I regret ever entertaining the idea of the Trade.

As for Cassidy . . . sleeping with her as long as I did was a lapse of judgment, fueled only by physical attraction. But her opinion doesn't matter to me in the slightest.

What truly matters is what Jade thinks of me, her understanding of my intentions and emotions. I don't want her to doubt my feelings for her, nor do I want her to think I have lingering feelings for Shannon.

Because I don't. Honestly, I don't think I ever really did. Our connection was based on a spark of lust and friendship, nothing more. I twisted those nonexistent feelings into something they were never meant to be.

Fuck. Maybe I should just tell her about the Trade.

On one hand, complete transparency seems ideal. Jade would most likely understand, especially since I called things off early on. It would mean no more secrets between us, a chance to lay everything on the table.

But on the other hand, it would be a betrayal to my teammates. We made a pact not to disclose anything about our tradition, and going back on that promise could have serious consequences. The team could face backlash, and I would bear the brunt of the blame from Coach.

Worst of all, I could risk losing Jade.

And I can't fucking lose her.

Chapter Twenty

My MORNING with Mica was exactly what I needed. Just me and my brother making the most of our time together. We indulged in a breakfast of chocolate chip waffles, a treat that set a cheerful tone for the day. Full and happy, we decided to take a stroll around campus.

As we walked through the crowd of students, I brought him up to speed with my classes, shared about my recent work with the *Daily*, and vented a little bit more about Garrett fucking Warner.

Mica, of course, did his whole big-brother bit. Throwing around phrases like, "I'll knock some sense into that asshole." He also argued I should have a free pass to the Dayton football games, leveraging his status and all.

He doesn't understand it, though, the weight that comes with a famous sibling. Yes, his position could open doors for me, but the idea of riding his coattails, of relying on nepotism, isn't something I'm interested in.

Not to mention the incessant comparisons and expectations. Being "Mica's little sister" has always made me feel like I need to work twice as hard just to prove my own worth. But I'd rather fight my own battles, carve my own path for myself.

When evening came, it was time for Mica to head home. Our goodbye hug was tight, laced with promises of seeing each other again soon, especially since a trip to our parents' place is long overdue.

But now, with my brother gone, I'm left to untangle the events of last night. West, for starters, was a whole hour late to our dinner. Annoying, yes. Irresponsible, absolutely. But he'd apologized so much that even Mica seemed to have forgiven him.

The two of them getting along without any threats of bodily harm? I'll chalk that up as a win.

Then there was Cassidy. Bumping into her outside the restaurant was an unwelcome surprise. She'd suggested, not so subtly, that West was using me to get to Shannon, just like he'd used her.

Her words, her perspective, it doesn't fit with the West I know. If he wanted Shannon, he wouldn't tiptoe around it. And I know they've shared flirty exchanges in the past, but there's never been anything more than that between them.

Still, Cassidy's words are sowing tiny seeds of doubt, taking root in my mind. West has been nothing but open about his feelings for me, but what about his past with her?

Had he treated Cassidy the same way he treated me, only to shrug her off saying they "weren't together"? And would I be the next "not-ex" if things didn't work out?

We're still building trust, but we haven't defined our relationship yet. Dating? Seeing each other? Close friends with even closer benefits? It's all so muddled. And now, I'm teetering on the edge of sounding desperate, and that's not who I am. It's not who I want to be.

So, I have to face this head-on. Picking up my phone, I shoot West a text.

JADE

ace just left. can I come over?

WEST

yeah, of course. the boys aren't home rn

JADE

see u soon

WEST

XO

It takes me less than ten minutes to reach his house, and as soon as he opens the front door, I'm pulled into his embrace. His strong arms envelop me, offering a sense of comfort and security that I've come to crave.

"Jade," he starts, voice thick with emotion. There's an urgency in the way he grips me, pulling back to look me in the eyes. "About last night . . . I'm really sorry."

"Stop apologizing," I say, doing my best to lighten the mood. "I told you it's okay. My brother actually ended up liking you . . . he said he'd like to see you next time he's in town."

An incredulous look replaces the tension in his eyes. "Wow, really?" He laughs softly, his lips stretching into a warm grin that reaches his eyes. "That's fucking awesome."

"Yeah, so stop freaking out."

"I'm mostly freaking out because of Cass."

A hot prickling sensation creeps up the back of my neck, and I shift on my heels. "Yeah?"

"Look, I need to tell you—"

"Hey, I get what she was implying, and I know it's bullshit."

A flicker of surprise flashes across his face. "You do?" He scrutinizes me, eyes narrowed in suspicion.

"I mean, it doesn't even make sense," I push on, voicing the thoughts that had been eating at me. "Why would you fuck Shan's roommate just to get to her?"

His eyes widen, taken aback by my blunt words. "Jesus Christ, Jade."

"No, I'm serious. You said you didn't date Cassidy. So, I'm assuming you were just fucking her."

A grimace stretches across his face, a reaction to the harsh reality of the words hanging in the air between us. "We were sleeping together, yes," he admits reluctantly. "Nothing more."

"Okay, and with us . . . it's more?"

He gives me a dark look. "Is that a serious question?"

"Just answer."

"Of course it's more. I thought it was clear how I feel about you."

"I thought so, too."

His brow furrows. "Jade, you're the one who didn't call me your boyfriend last night. You know, when you introduced me to your brother?"

"Well . . . he was already mad. I didn't want to poke the bear. Also, I just—I didn't know."

He snorts, raising one dubious brow. "You didn't know?"

"Well, we've never used that particular word."

"Okay, well . . . we're using it now," he says, a slight edge to his voice. "I'm your fucking boyfriend. You're my fucking girlfriend."

"So, that means . . . we're exclusive?"

He gives me a pointed look. "Fuck yeah, we are."

"Okay. And Shan?"

"What about her?"

"I know Cassidy was just trying to stir the pot." My stomach's churning as I force out the question. "But you didn't have actual feelings for Shan, right?"

He pauses for a split second, then, "I didn't."

"I mean, I know you two were kind of flirty before, and she's—I mean, she's so beautiful."

"No, I didn't have real feelings for her. We flirted—there was nothing beyond that."

"So, you just wanted to fuck her, then?"

His brows skyrocket. "Jade."

"Just be honest."

"I used to be attracted to her, yes. But that changed when I started to have feelings for you."

Relief courses through my veins, washing away any lingering doubts. "So, you absolutely don't want to fuck Shannon anymore?"

He winces at my blunt choice of words. "Can you stop saying that?"

"Sorry, I don't know how else to put it."

He takes a deep breath, his eyes locking onto mine. "Look, I don't even see anyone else when you're in the room. When you're not there, I fucking wish you were. You're the only girl for me, Jade."

A wide smile stretches across my face, my cheeks warming, heart swelling. "Yeah?" I take a step toward him, pushing onto my tiptoes to bring my lips closer to his ear. "You should prove it, then."

His breath hitches. "What do you mean?"

"Prove that I'm the only girl for you," I say, my voice filled with a mix of challenge and desire. I bite my lip as I pull away from him. "Prove how much you want me and only me."

A spark ignites in his gaze, a flicker of intensity betraying his desire. "Oh? How can I prove it?"

"I think you know."

"Come here." His fingers curl around my wrist as he leads me down the hallway. With a swift motion, he yanks open the door to his bedroom, urging me inside. The moment we step over the threshold, he pushes me gently against the nearest wall. "You need me to prove how much I want you?"

"Mhm."

"Then take off your clothes," he demands, his voice low and rough with need.

A sense of urgency takes over as I frantically remove my sweater, unhooking my bra with practiced ease. The fabric of my jeans and panties slide down my legs, pooling on the floor beneath me.

His gaze roams hungrily over my exposed body. "God, I'm so fucking obsessed with you."

He lifts his own shirt over his head, the muscles in his abdomen bunching and rippling with every careful movement. Then he slowly inches toward me, backing me up until my legs are pressed against his dresser. His strong fingers wrap around my hips as he lifts me up and places me on the flat surface.

"Your gorgeous eyes, your pouty lips, that fucking heart-shaped birthmark." He unfastens his belt, sliding it through as he removes his jeans. "One look at you and I'm instantly hard."

"Theo," I whisper. "I need you to touch me now."

He moves to cup my breasts with a firm yet tender touch. Teasing my nipples, he rolls them between his fingers, eliciting a soft moan. Then, with a tilt of his head, he captures my mouth in a hungry kiss. Our lips meet, tongues tangling together.

The rough pads of his hands continue their exploration, teasing, stroking, driving me to the brink. And now I'm squirming against the hard surface of the dresser, aching for more, a warm pool of heat flooding my center.

"Your body is so fucking tight and sexy," he murmurs between kisses, fingers trailing down from my breasts to my waist. His words make me flush, a mix of pleasure and a tinge of insecurity creeping in. I've never considered myself to be sexy, not when I've always been more of the girl next door.

"Fuck, baby, your hips"—he groans, his hands squeezing them possessively—"your thighs. Every time I see you in the library, I can't help but imagine my head between them."

"Show me."

The words barely leave my lips before he's kneeling before me, his lips pressing tender kisses along the inside of my thigh, slowly inching closer to my core.

His movements are deliberate, unhurried, as he licks a slow, torturous path toward my center. A low groan escapes his lips as he pushes one finger inside me, his touch igniting a spark of pleasure that spreads through every nerve ending in my body.

"Fuck, Jade. You're so wet," he groans, his voice laced with desire. "So . . . tight."

With each deliberate thrust of his fingers, he delves deeper, stretching me, driving me closer to the edge. "That feels. . ." I trail off, unable to speak as his lips wrap around my clit, his tongue flicking and teasing.

The combination of his fingers and mouth sends me spiraling. Wave after wave of pleasure crashes over me, shattering me completely.

As I slowly come back to my senses, he stands up, his boxers discarded, his eyes locked onto mine. "I'm going to fuck you now."

"Please."

He slowly rolls on a condom. With gentle hands, he grips my hips and guides my body forward on the dresser, aligning my pulsing core with the head of his throbbing cock. Then he presses his hand flat against the wall behind my head, his gaze drilling into me with an intensity that sends shivers down my spine.

"Tell me you know," he whispers, his voice low and rough.

I gasp as he inches forward, the tip of him nudging at my entrance. "Know what?"

"That I want you and only you."

"I know."

"Good." With a firm grasp on my hips, he pulls me closer, impaling me with a single, punishing thrust that steals my breath away. The force of his movements rocks us together, the dresser scraping against the wall behind us.

Oh, God. He's almost brutal in the way he pounds into me. With every push and strike of his hips against mine, my fingers nearly slip out of place on the wooden edge.

"Theo," I moan, the sound a desperate plea for more.

This is unlike anything I've ever experienced before. It's rough and fast and all-consuming. Every stroke, every collision of our bodies, drives me wild. I let out another moan, but this time, it comes out more like a whimper.

"That's a good girl," he growls, his voice gravelly and commanding. "Take it."

With one last forceful thrust, he slides out of me, lifting me off the dresser and tossing me onto the bed. I'm on my stomach as he comes up behind me. His strong arms slide underneath my hips, jerking me onto my hands and knees.

My body shudders as his fingers trail up my spine. He threads them into the hair at the nape of my neck, pulling gently until my head tilts back, exposing the column of my throat.

"Tell me what you want," he says, lips grazing against my ear, breath hot on my skin.

"I want—I want you to fuck me."

He brushes my curls over one shoulder, his lips trailing from my ear down to my neck. A low moan escapes my lips as he nips and bites, marking me as his.

"How?" His hand snakes around my waist, trailing across my stomach until it reaches my throbbing clit. With skilled precision, he presses his thumb against the sensitive bud, circling it until I fall apart.

"Hard," I plead, breathless and desperate.

As soon as the word leaves my mouth, he removes his fingers from the tiny bundle of nerves. In a swift motion, his palm comes crashing down on my ass, the sound of the impact reverberating through the room. I gasp, shocked by the sting, but the pain mixes with pleasure as he slams his cock deep inside me.

"Oh!" I cry out.

He's pummeling my pussy now, dragging my hips against him with one arm. His other hand snakes up my body. Those long, calloused fingers wrap around my throat as he lightly squeezes, hauling me against him while he fucks into me.

A deep groan escapes his lips as he buries his face into the crook of my neck, his warm breath tickling my skin. The rhythm of his thrusts becomes more measured, more deliberate, as he seeks his release.

My walls flutter around him, tightening with every movement, signaling my own impending climax. And with a final, powerful thrust, he comes. My body quivers with the force of it, my fingers clutching onto the bedsheets.

A moment later, I collapse, completely spent and sated.

As we lie side by side, our bodies glistening with a sheen of sweat, his breath ragged, he rasps my name, breaking the silence.

I turn my head toward him, meeting his gaze with a mixture of bliss and contentment. "Hmm?"

"Don't ever doubt how I feel for you."

"Okay," I pant, heart stuttering. "I won't."

Chapter Twenty-One

THERE'S a distinct kind of magic being wrapped up in bed with Jade. Looking back at just a few weeks ago, this moment would've seemed like a far-fetched fantasy. But here we are, exactly where we're meant to be.

Her body finds solace in my arms, her chest rising and falling in rhythm with my own. I trace my fingers through her soft curls, stirring a sigh from her lips as she snuggles against me, her breasts pressed into my chest.

After drilling her on my dresser and, subsequently, my mattress—this all feels soft, and warm, and so fucking sweet. It's a feeling that I don't ever want to let go.

Jade stirs, stretching until she's balanced on her forearms beside me. Her voice breaks the silence, tinged with sleepiness. "What was your team meeting about anyway?"

I roll to my side to face her, my free hand tracing random patterns along her bare spine. "Coach scheduled a scrimmage for us against Coastal U," I say with a shrug. "It's in two weeks."

"Really? Have you ever done a spring scrimmage against an opponent?"

I shake my head. "This will be a first. The NCAA's finally allowing it. Plus, Coach Rodriguez thinks it will give us some perspective on how the team's doing. You know, prepare us for fall term."

She hums in understanding but doesn't miss a beat. "Except

Dayton hasn't been doing regular practices. And I heard Coastal has a really tight team this year."

"Exactly," I grumble, grimacing at the reminder. "Which is why we're doubling down for the next two weeks."

"Well, I'm sure you guys will kill it anyway." Her faith in me is endearing, yet another reason why I'm drawn to her.

I lift a shoulder, attempting to downplay it. "I mean, it's more so just for fun. But yeah, losing could definitely put a damper on the . . . banquet."

The word tastes bitter now, given the past implications. It was a moment of vulnerability when she asked me about Shan, and I should've just told her about the Trade. But it felt wrong to do it then, not when she was already grappling with her own insecurities.

Which are . . . hard for me to fathom because I'm fucking lost when it comes to this girl. It's like I'm disconnected from my own mind sometimes, just wandering around until I can get my next fix of her.

Her eyes narrow, picking up on my hesitation. "That's the following weekend, right?"

"Yeah," I manage to say, forcing a casual half-smile. "You know, we always do awards and stuff. I think another loss might rain on our parade."

Her smirk is teasing, playful. "I guess you better win, then."

"I guess so," I say with a lighthearted chuckle, my fingers tracing over the smooth planes of her back. "You think you could make some time to watch me play?"

"Hmm, I don't know." She feigns contemplation. "I guess I could try and pencil you in."

An idea forms, and I act on it. "Wait," I say, my hand stilling. "What if you asked to cover the game for the *Daily*?"

"What?"

"Yeah, tell Garrett you have some interviews lined up already. It's just a scrimmage, so maybe he'd be down to give you a shot."

She lunges forward to hug me. "Theo! That's such a great idea."

My heart lightens at her enthusiasm. "Yeah?"

"Yes! I'm definitely gonna ask him. I mean, there's no way he could have already assigned the piece to someone else. You just found out about it last night, and you're on the team."

"Fair point." I grin, proud of my suggestion.

"God, see, this is why I date you." Her hand traces a path down to my arm, gripping my bicep.

"Oh, so that's the reason?"

She laughs, giving me a gentle squeeze. "Well, that and you're great in bed."

"Damn right. Speaking of . . ." I slide my hand over the curve of her hip, a smirk playing on my lips.

"You're trying to wear me out, aren't you?"

"I'm just trying to prepare us both for another weeklong drought. I'm gonna be at practice almost every night."

Her playful demeanor fades, replaced by a soft pout. "I really won't be seeing you much, will I?"

I cup her cheek, my thumb tracing her jawline. "Don't worry, we'll make time."

"Promise?"

My answer is sealed with a kiss, soft and reassuring. "I will if you will."

"Okay." Her smile returns. "Then it's a deal."

THE FOLLOWING DAY, the sinking feeling of mediocrity sets in as I receive my assignment back from Professor Hartman. A bright red "72%" glares at me from the top of the page. It's a clear sign that Jade's tutoring sessions hold more weight than my regular tutor.

Fucking pathetic if you ask me.

As we gear up for afternoon practice, Cam crunches the numbers for me. I'll need a 75% on the written exam to keep my overall GPA intact. And I don't have much faith in myself to achieve that. One fuckup has become my Everest, and now I'm standing at the foot of it, unsure of how to scale my way to the top.

I slip my jersey over my head as I pose the million-dollar question to Cam. "How am I gonna make time to study these next couple of weeks?"

"I can pull some late nights," he offers. "Help you after practice."

I dismiss him with a wave, appreciating his offer but refusing it all the same. "Nah, man, you got your own shit. And you might be the smartest motherfucker I know, but writing? Not your thing."

As I deflect, his mind works in overdrive. "What about Jade?" he asks. "She helped you out before, right?"

"Yeah," I say, conjuring up images of her intense focus, the softness in her voice as she pored over my essay. "But she's swamped with her own stuff."

"You should just ask her."

"I don't know." There's a strange tightening in my chest at his suggestion. I don't want to push her to help me, to make her feel obligated. "I don't want her to think I'm asking too much."

"That's what relationships are for."

I glance at him, skeptical. "You sure?"

"Yeah, man. If she doesn't have time to help, then she'll tell you. It's all about give-and-take with the person you're dating."

I take a moment to assess my best friend, appreciating his genuine concern. Objectively, he's a good-looking guy, intelligent, and seems to know a hell of a lot about relationships. "Why don't you have a girlfriend again?"

He chuckles, a light sound that breaks the tension. "Too busy giving out free dating advice."

"Well, thanks, man." I thump his back in gratitude. "In some twisted way, you're the reason Jade and I got together."

"You mean because of the Trade?"

"Yeah, you know . . . I thought about telling her the other day," I confess, my voice tinged with apprehension. "I was actually—"

"Wait, are you fucking serious?"

I shift uncomfortably, my gaze fixed on the ground. "I mean," I say sheepishly, "Jade wouldn't tell anyone."

"Dude, are you using your brain at all?" He runs a hand through his hair, frustration twisting his features. "She would definitely tell someone. You know Coach would be livid if he found out, right? Like, half of us would be benched for the season."

"I know," I say, grinding my teeth together. "But Jade's not spiteful like that."

He lets out a disbelieving snort. "Right. And again, you've known her for what . . . a little over a month? Think with your head and not with your dick, man."

"Oh, fuck off," I snap, my jaw clenched tightly. "I didn't tell her, so stop acting like I killed somebody just for thinking about it."

"I'm sorry," he says, his tone softening. "I'm just trying to look out for the team right now. I know you like this girl, but you gotta think rationally here."

"It's not about that. It's about the fact that my girlfriend straight-up asked me if I had feelings for another girl last night."

His brows shoot up. "She asked if you had feelings for Shannon?"

"Yeah, and I told her I never did," I say, a mixture of guilt and uncertainty swirling inside me. "I mean, that's the honest truth. I fully realize that now. But still, part of me feels like I'm lying to her."

"You're not lying," he insists, his voice firm. "You're just . . . not telling."

"Same shit. It's a lie by omission."

He places a heavy hand on my shoulder, a gesture of both support and reassurance. "Dude, trust me when I say this—nothing good can come from telling her about the Trade."

I pause, his words sinking in. I can't deny the truth behind his advice. What good could possibly come out of telling her about this —something that could potentially disrupt not only our relationship but also my entire team's dynamics?

It's a big risk, with very little reward.

"No," I finally say, rubbing my temples to ease the building tension. "I guess you're right."

"I know it sounds harsh, but it's all gonna be over in a few weeks," he assures me, his voice filled with empathy. "Besides, you called that shit off before you even got together. You're not doing anything wrong, man."

"Alright."

"Alright, then." He gives me a stiff nod, reaching for his cleats. "Swear you won't lose your mind over this?"

"Cam, seriously, fuck off," I repeat, my words clipped. "I'm not swearing shit. I said I won't tell her, and I won't."

"Okay, I'm fucking off now." He holds both hands up in mock defense. "I know you got this."

"Sure," I grumble, grabbing my gear and following Cam out the door. We toss our things into the back of his Jeep and climb in. I slide into the passenger seat and dial up the radio, a feeble attempt to drown out the disquiet in my mind.

Despite Cam's supportive words, my guilt remains. I've tried to rationalize this, to convince myself that I've done nothing wrong. Yet, the facts are the facts—I'm a fucking liar at the end of the day. I've manipulated the truth, and there's a weight to that reality, a heavy certainty that my actions will come back to bite me in the ass.

Chapter Twenty-Two
JADE

I HAVE TO SAY, I'm one lucky girl to have West in my life.

When he initially let slip about the scrimmage, it didn't even cross my mind to consider writing an article for the *Daily*. Or, more accurately, to wheedle my editor into giving me the assignment. But now, by some quirk of fate, I have the clear advantage.

I'm sure I'll be the first to break the news to Garrett. And while I'm still not a huge fan of leveraging personal connections, in this instance, it's less about nepotism and more about a lucky break. It's not like I'm going to prance around, flaunting my relationship.

In fact, I'd rather Garrett, and by extension, the rest of the *Daily*'s staff, remain oblivious to my personal life.

Usually, our article assignments are divvied up on Tuesdays, making Mondays in the newsroom as lively as a graveyard. Naturally, Garrett is almost always lurking around doing who knows what. Sometimes, when I traipse in after regular hours, I find him hunched over his desk, just sitting there in the dark like some . . . creepy little bat in a cave.

I wouldn't put it past him to be roosting in the rafters.

Bracing myself, I inhale deeply, squaring my shoulders as I sidle up to his fortress of a desk. "Hey, Garrett," I say, injecting as much warmth into my voice as I can muster.

"Jade." His acknowledgment is as stiff as his posture, his eyes barely flicking up from his scattered workspace.

"I was hoping to talk to you about a concept for the next issue."

My voice wavers, prompting me to clear my throat, an awkward sound echoing in the near-silent room.

Honestly, there's zero reason to feel intimidated by Garrett fucking Warner. He's nothing more than a chauvinistic busybody with the attention span of a goldfish. Still, in his clutches, he holds the fate of my journalism career.

"I'm listening," he murmurs, his fingers idly shuffling through the heap of papers in front of him, eyes still glued to his desk.

"Okay, well, I'm not sure if it's hit your radar yet . . . but the football team is preparing for a spring scrimmage against Coastal. It'll be their first against an opponent, and the game is next weekend."

That certainly grabs his attention. His head snaps up, eyes narrowed in curiosity.

"How did you get wind of this?"

"Let's just say I have an inside source."

"Who?"

I give him an odd look. "Does it matter?"

He just stares at me, his gaze unblinking, waiting for me to give him the details. So, I invent an excuse, a half-truth, that's a little easier for both of us to swallow. "My, um, roommate is a cheerleader."

"Ah, I see. Well, thank you for the scoop. I'll notify the sports team," he says, jotting down a quick note on his cluttered calendar. "I don't think I've given Liam a new piece yet."

My spine stiffens. "Actually, I was hoping to write the article myself."

His response is a burst of laughter, only cut short when he catches sight of my stone-faced expression. "Jade, you're not a sports reporter."

"Yeah, but you know that I'd like to be," I counter, my voice tightening as my fingers dig into my thigh. "I've drafted pieces on the games before; you just never considered them worthy of printing."

"Those were backups, Jade. I didn't even have time to go through them. You're aware of the number of reporters we have on staff."

My fingers curl tightly against my palm, nostrils flaring as I tamp down my disappointment. "Right. Silly me."

"Look . . . this is an important piece. I don't have the time or patience to make it your training ground."

I cross my arms defensively. "You wouldn't even know about the scrimmage if it weren't for me."

"Seriously? I would've found out in a day or two. Besides, I've already assigned you another article."

"So, give that one to Liam," I say, flustered. "I'll take the scrimmage, and he can take whatever the hell you wanted me to write."

His jaw twitches. "This is ridiculous. Now you're just being emotional."

"Emotional?" My shoulders sag, the fight draining out of me. "You know what, that's just fine. Liam can write about the football team again. I'll just write about the parking lot outside of Haggerty Hall or maybe the new turnstiles in the arts building."

He levels me with an impatient stare, glancing pointedly at the stack of papers on his desk. "Great idea, Jade. I knew you'd understand."

I whirl around, my heels clicking against the floor as I stalk away from his desk and out of the newsroom. By the time I finally reach class, I can feel the sting of frustrated tears pricking at my eyes.

Why did I even bother to try?

Steeling myself, I blink away the welling tears. I know I'm fighting an uphill battle here, but God, I'll be damned if I let this be the end of it.

. . .

MY WEEK HAS OFFICIALLY devolved into a trash pile. Between the constant demands of class, relentless studying sessions in the library, and the mundane task of writing the most uninspired article of my journalistic career, I'm fucking exhausted.

And Garrett, as usual, is partially to blame for this mess. He must have a deep-rooted hatred for me or just for female reporters in general. It certainly feels like this is his idea of a cruel joke, him assigning me a story about the new turnstiles.

Really? Fucking turnstiles?

At this point, I'm ready to tear my hair out. The library's brimming with anxious students all cramming for midterm exams. It's so chaotic, so nerve-racking, I could probably start screaming and nobody would bat an eye.

"Jade." The timbre of West's unexpected voice hits me like a warm caress. "I can't believe I actually caught you in time."

He slides into the chair behind me, his strong hands enclosing my tense shoulders. I practically melt into my seat as he starts to knead the stiffness out, his touch familiar and comforting.

"I was just about to leave," I murmur, craning my neck to look up at him.

"No." He frowns, bending to plant a quick kiss on my lips. "I've got two hours until practice."

"I know, but I promised Shan I'd be home by three."

"I've barely seen you all week. Can't you stay just one more hour?"

"Don't you have to study for your Lit exam?" I ask, my smile tender. "I'll only distract you."

"Maybe you could help me study? I mean, I understand if you're too busy with your own stuff. You don't need to if—"

"Theo," I cut in, grinning at his flustered ramblings. "I can stay and help. But just for an hour, okay?"

As the hour trickles away, it feels like we've barely made a dent in the material. West's dedication to his studies is clear, but he has a tougher time grasping certain concepts, especially when it comes to writing assignments.

"Damn," he groans, slamming his book shut with finality. "I'll never be able to learn all this shit."

"Hey, you can do this." I place a comforting hand on his knee. "I can help you study more this weekend."

He swivels in his seat to face me, toying with a loose curl of my hair. "I don't want to study this weekend," he grumbles. "I want to take you out."

"We can go out after your exam. Plus, once the scrimmage is over, you'll have a lot more free time."

"Yeah, I guess so."

"Besides, the banquet is the following weekend," I say cheerfully. "That's kind of like a date. We get to dress up and eat a fancy dinner together."

He stares at me for a long moment, his brow furrowed as he searches my face.

"What?" I laugh, puzzled by his intensity.

He gives his head a slight shake. "You're just so fucking beautiful."

"Theo."

"No, I mean it," he insists, his hand reaching up to tuck the stray curl behind my ear. "I can't believe I wasn't falling at your feet the first time we met."

I snort in response. "You mean, when you rolled your eyes at me and called me a jersey chaser?"

"Yeah." He nods solemnly, a tense line forming along his jaw. "Exactly. I was such a goddamn fool back then."

"That was only, what, six weeks ago?"

"Yeah, and a lot can change in six weeks." He rises from his seat, pulling my chair away from the table. "I need your help with one more thing before you leave."

Before I can ask, he's pulling me to my feet and leading me to the furthest corner of the library, where we sneak in behind towering stacks of books.

"Theo, what are you—"

He interrupts me by seizing my face in his hands and capturing my lips with his own. His kisses are hot and insistent, heavy with unspoken yearning. In seconds, he maneuvers me against the bookshelves, his body pressing me into the cold metal.

"It's so hard to resist you," he confesses in a husky whisper, his mouth trailing down to the sensitive skin of my neck.

He teases me with his teeth before latching on to suck at my pulse point. His hands roam over my body in a dance of desire— from my waist to my hips to my ass. He's kneading me, setting me on fire with each caress.

"Damn, I want you," he breathes against my skin.

My breath hitches in my throat, and his tongue invades my mouth, tasting and teasing me. He wedges a thick thigh between my legs, and I can't stop the instinctive roll of my hips against him.

The pressure is intoxicating.

I feel the telltale pulse of my arousal against him, matching the hardness straining in his jeans. And now, I'm gasping for air, desperate little sounds threatening to spill from my lips. My core aches, empty and needy, a heady warmth pooling inside me.

Fuck. I might just come from this alone.

"Did you find it?" a male voice rings out, emanating from a few shelves over.

My eyes snap wide open. I push against West's chest, trying to put some distance between us.

"I think it's another aisle over," a female voice responds.

I glance up at West, working to regain control over my erratic breathing. He's grinning down at me, running a hand through his hair to tame it.

"That was hot," he murmurs, his grin widening.

I can't help but grin back, my heartbeat still racing with the thrill of nearly being caught.

"Shut up," I whisper back, lightly swatting his chest.

"Make me," he says, that smug smile still firmly in place.

"You're insufferable."

"And you're a dork," he teases back. "Let's get out of here before we get caught by some unsuspecting librarian."

"After you," I say, gesturing toward the end of the aisle.

His grin softens into a warm smile as he laces his fingers with mine. "We'll go together," he decides.

Chapter Twenty-Three

THE WEEKEND TURNS into a marathon of brain-crushing studying.

Between running endless drills on the field and immersing myself in the world of Victorian prose, I hardly see Jade. Even when we're together, we're drowning in books on her couch instead of drowning in each other.

By the time Thursday comes around, fatigue has claimed my body and mind both. Tomorrow looms like a dark cloud, the dreaded day of my Lit exam, but at least this will all be over then. I'm done living and breathing nothing but English literature and the damp scent of the field.

The grind is brutal, and whether it'll pay off is anyone's guess.

Jade's engrossed in her own notes as I stretch my legs out and cross my ankles beside her. The weight of my textbook drops onto the coffee table like lead, an echo of my own exhaustion. "Hey, Jade?" I call out, letting my head fall back against the couch.

She makes a quiet sound, her eyes never leaving her notebook. "Yeah?"

A dry chuckle crawls up my throat as I close my eyes. "Do you think you'll still be into me when I fail this class, lose my scholarship, and get kicked out of Dayton?"

Without missing a beat, she tosses back, "You'd still have a slim chance of getting drafted. So yeah, I think I would."

"Wow."

Her notebook snaps shut, and her warm hands cup my face, forcing me to meet her gaze. Her touch grounds me, an anchor in my sea of worries. "Theo, you're not gonna fail."

I'm drawn in by the conviction in her voice, the way her fingers gently trace the edges of my jaw. "What makes you so confident?"

"Well, first of all, because I believe in you." The hint of a smile dances in her eyes, her hands slipping from my face to my lap. "And second, because you're gonna be wearing my sweatshirt tomorrow."

My gut clenches. "Sorry?"

She wrinkles her nose in response, a touch defensive. "I know you think it's goofy. But you should really give it a shot."

A sensation I can only describe as pure, unadulterated warmth spreads in my chest at her words. The fact that she's willing to share her cherished good-luck charm with me isn't goofy at all. It's . . . really fucking special, actually.

As my surprise fades, my mind grasps at words, trying to express my appreciation. "Jade—"

"Please, for me?" She pushes out her bottom lip. "At the very least, you'll be comfortable for your test. Plus, it'll probably smell like me."

My heart thuds against my chest. "You'd trust me with your magical sweatshirt?"

"Again, not magic . . . *science*. But yes, I trust you."

A million reservations flood my mind. "What if I accidentally stain it, or lose it, or . . . something? I feel like it's just too fucking precious for me."

Her eye roll is accompanied by a playful scoff. "Oh, my God, there you go again with the dramatics. You can take care of a damn sweatshirt, Theo."

"Okay, yeah. You're right." I suppress a smile, the corners of my mouth twitching. "I want to wear it."

Her eyes brighten. "You do?"

"Of course. I've seen what that thing can do for others."

A pleased sigh slips from her as her grip on my knee tightens in satisfaction. "I knew you'd come to the dark side sooner or later."

"You've definitely turned me." I brush my thumb against her soft shoulder, tracing the edge of her collarbone.

An excited twinkle lights up her eyes as she pulls back. "Ah, you should really put it on now. Then I can take a picture and send it to Ace."

"Yeah, no. That's where I draw the line."

She bats her lashes at me, tugging at my resolve with a pretty pout. "Please, for me?"

"No amount of begging is gonna work on me."

"Hmm, what about a hand job, then?"

"Oh, sweet Christ," I sputter, choking on my own saliva.

"Is that a no?"

"You want to take a picture of me to send to your brother . . . in exchange for sexual favors?"

"I mean, when you put it like that . . . yes?"

"Sex is not currency, Jade."

Her laughter echoes around the room, her eyes gleaming with unapologetic delight. "Aw yeah, I forgot. Sex is sacred to you, isn't it?"

"It is when it's with you," I tell her, my words laced with sincerity.

The grin on her face spreads wide and bright. "God, you're corny."

"And you like it."

"Nahh, but I do like *you*. So much."

Her words wash over me, sparking an affectionate glow in my chest. "And I like you . . . enough to let you take a picture of me in that ratty-ass sweatshirt. For free," I clarify, plucking at the end of her curls. "No handy necessary."

She slides closer to me now, her hand inching even further up my thigh. "Mm, you're so generous," she coos, her fingers toying with the waistband of my sweats. "So thoughtful. And oh, so—" Her voice drops to a sultry whisper, her hand slipping beneath my boxers. "—dramatic."

Oh, fuck.

Her delicate fingers envelop me, a perfect contrast to the raw heat pooling in my gut. She moves, her touch fluid, heavy over the ridges and contours of my cock. A primitive groan slips past my gritted teeth as she cradles my aching balls in her free hand.

My hips jerk upward instinctively, seeking more of the friction. "Ah, shit," I gasp, my composure slipping as she teases the sensitive underside of my shaft with a flick of her nail.

God bless my girlfriend; I don't think a hand job has ever felt this good.

In a matter of minutes, I'm completely undone. I mean, full-on groaning, rocking my hips into her hand as she moves beside me. And then, she pulls my boxers down and takes me into her mouth. The sudden shift in sensation, the heat, the pressure—it's enough to make my world spin.

When I finally come, my cock is buried deep inside her throat.

I'm still catching my breath as she swipes her thumb across her bottom lip. "You owe me a picture," she says simply.

"You can have a hundred pictures," I mumble. "Whatever you want."

"Mm, I like the sound of that."

She leans back, plucking her discarded journal off the coffee table. With a casual flick of her wrist, she starts writing again, as if that little interruption never even happened.

It's in this moment, panting and spent on her couch, that I'm once again reminded how un-fucking-believable my girlfriend is. Not to be dramatic, but I think I'm the luckiest bastard that's ever lived.

. . .

YESTERDAY WAS FINALLY the day of reckoning.

I tackled that exam with everything inside of me and, by the end, felt as though I had, if not hit a home run, at least managed a decent hit. It wasn't so much the content itself that posed a challenge—Jade and I had drilled that thoroughly—but the translation of thoughts into words, the articulation of arguments under time pressure that really tested me.

But I took a deep breath, did my best, and now all that's left is to let the chips fall where they may. Or maybe, to let Jade's magical sweatshirt do its thing.

Ah, that sweatshirt. When I pulled it over my head, I felt a surge of belief so strong I could almost see the A+ on my test paper. Okay, maybe it wasn't just the sweatshirt but the entire sentiment it represented: Jade's faith in me.

Her words of encouragement, her unflinching belief in my potential—they were like an adrenaline shot straight to my heart.

Empowered by her belief, I felt invincible . . . which is why I find myself knocking on her door now, halfway into my gear for the upcoming scrimmage. She greets me there, a picture of adorable confusion, her cheeks flushed, my loaner jersey hanging off her body.

"Hey, what are you doing here?"

"I wanted to come see you before the game," I say, shifting on my feet, holding up her sweatshirt. "And also, I wanted to return this."

Accepting it from my hands, she balls the fabric up against her chest. "Thank you, babe."

I knit my brows together. "Are you okay?"

"Yeah, I'm just . . . frustrated. I'm trying to finish this fucking article before the game, but I keep wishing I could write about that instead."

I grab her hand, wrapping my fingers around hers. "Jade, if you want it bad enough, we'll make it happen."

Her lips pout as she asks, "How?"

"I'll kick Garrett's ass, that's how." I can't help but smile at her shocked expression. "No, but seriously. Stand your ground. Write about the scrimmage anyway. Get interviews that outshine Liam's. Keep proving yourself. Any good editor would recognize your talent."

"You think so?"

"Jade, you're an incredible writer, passionate about the game. You've told me repeatedly that you believe in me. Well, I believe in you, too. I know you can show Garrett what you're capable of."

"Thank you." She gives me a genuine smile, a light squeeze to my hand. "I love how you always go after what you want, no matter what anyone else thinks."

Barely suppressing a smirk, I cock a brow. "Oh, is that what I do?"

"Yes, you're like the most straightforward person I know. If I didn't know you better, I'd probably think you were just a cocky asshole. But I know it's not like that."

There's a grin playing on my lips, uncontrollable, drawn out by her admission. "Yeah? What's it like, then?"

"Honest," she says simply, her dark eyes locked onto mine. "I guess you're just . . . honest. It's a huge turn-on for me."

The sentiment, so genuine and sweet, hits me like a physical blow, leaving me breathless. "My . . . honesty is a turn-on?" I manage to choke out.

"Yes. I think that's the main reason why I never went for athletes before you. I was always worried they'd just try to play games."

"Oh." I swallow hard, fighting back the urge to wince. "You weren't worried about that with me?"

"Actually, I was at first," she confesses, eyes downcast, a touch of reservation in her tone. "I've seen the way Ace treated girls all my life. Family comes first for him, then football, and then his teammates. He can barely make time to date, so when he does, he likes to keep things interesting. Meaning . . . he tends to string girls along and act like they're disposable."

She stares up at me, trust and reassurance reflected in her eyes. "I thought you might treat me the same way if we gave things a shot. But time and again, you've shown me I have nothing to worry about."

I feel like I've been hit by a fucking truck. This entire time, she's been seeing me as the most honest guy in her life, when I've been hiding the truth of the Trade from her. I can't let this lie continue a second longer. I owe her that much.

"Jade—" I begin, bracing myself.

"I know, I'm sorry for placing my doubts on you right before the game. But I do trust you now, okay?" Her words are like a salve to my conscience, but they also deepen my guilt. "Besides, you're about to go kick ass against Coastal."

The scrimmage. Right. I blink, the sudden reminder shoving me back into reality. There's no time for confession now, but that doesn't mean it won't happen. It has to.

"I'll be looking for you in the stands," I tell her, my voice slightly choked.

"I'll be there to cheer you on, front and center."

I'm taken aback by the promise in her voice, and it further cements my resolution. After the game, I'll tell her everything. No secrets. No barriers between us.

"Jade," I say, my voice heavy with an emotion I can't quite place.

She looks at me, a crease between her brows, concern etching her features. "Yeah?"

"Thank you for believing in me, even when I don't deserve it."

Her frown deepens, confusion painting her beautiful face. "But you—"

"I gotta go now," I cut her off with a quick peck to the lips and check the time on my phone. There's a game to play, a crowd to wow, and a girl to prove myself to. "I'll see you after we win."

Chapter Twenty-Four
JADE

WEST'S WORDS linger in my mind, like a mantra of motivation, pushing me to claim what I deserve. If I want this opportunity badly enough, then I need to find a surefire way to make it happen.

The initial step? Convincing Garrett that I'm not someone who's easily dismissed. So, I pull up my resolve like battle armor.

I'll write a quality piece on this scrimmage, far better than any regurgitated stats Liam Kessler can produce. I've read his work, over and over again. His articles are about as uninspiring as a weather forecast, with no heart, no substance, and definitely no love for the game.

For God's sake, the man's a baseball fan.

A sudden surge of annoyance sweeps through me. How could I ever step back and watch someone undeserving claim my rightful place? But then again, maybe Liam isn't the real enemy here. Maybe he's just an unknowing pawn in Garrett's game.

Fingers trembling, I dial his number. "Hello? Warner speaking," he answers promptly, his voice the usual mix of professionalism and indifference.

"Hey, it's Jade."

"Jade," he repeats, no hint of emotion.

"Jennings," I quickly add, attempting to mask my growing apprehension.

"Yes," he says in a clipped tone. "I know who this is, Jade. I have caller ID."

Nice, we're off to a wonderful start already.

I clear my throat, square my shoulders, and plunge right ahead. "I'm just calling to let you know that I'm going to write a piece on the scrimmage tonight. I'm planning on interviewing some key players afterward, but I'll have it on your desk by Tuesday morning. If it's better than Liam's work, then I deserve to have it published."

His silence stretches long enough to ignite a flicker of doubt inside me. I pace the length of my living room, growing more desperate with each lingering second. "Garrett," I urge, "say something."

"I don't want you covering the game tonight," he finally speaks.

"But—"

"Liam will already be out there interviewing players. I don't want you two doubling up. Besides, I'm not choosing which article to publish after the fact. It would be a waste of time for you."

His words knock the wind out of me, but I scramble to regain my footing. "It's not a waste of time." I take a deep breath to calm my racing heart. "I'm trying to—"

"I have a different proposal for you."

A pause. I stop pacing. "Okay, go ahead."

"The football team is hosting a banquet next weekend. I want you to get a press pass and cover the event. It's still technically a student-life piece, so it's right in your ballpark. It'll also give you a good opportunity to interact with the team and mingle with the players. If you produce quality work, I'll consider you as a full-time reporter for the upcoming season."

My heart leaps at his offer. Is this real? An actual opportunity to prove myself? And at an event that I was already set to attend? This is . . . brilliant.

"Seriously?"

"Yes," he confirms, his tone unchanging. "Do you need me to contact the team to get you a pass?"

"No, I can handle it."

"Alright, then it's settled. Have a nice afternoon, Jade."

"Thank you, Garrett. You too."

I hang up, reeling, still in disbelief. Who would have thought it could be so simple? The good old Westman-Cooke method actually worked.

AN HOUR LATER, I meet up with Maya and Sophie, a couple of girls I know from the paper. We're not too close, but our paths have crossed enough over the years to form a casual friendship. And while we don't have much else in common, I enjoy how easygoing they are.

They're fun and flirty, and their infectious excitement is exactly what I need for the game tonight.

They're already waiting for me at the agreed-upon spot, their outfits proudly showcasing our school's colors—emerald green and gold. West has made sure I'm equally decked out. His jersey hangs off me, a sweet reminder of our commitment, and I can't help but feel all sorts of giddy inside.

"Hey, you two," I greet them, beaming. "Let's go grab our seats."

Maya's response is a quick, warm hug. "Jade! You look so cute."

An exchange of compliments follows as we link arms and navigate our way into the pulsing heart of the stadium. Even with kickoff forty-five minutes away, the stands are already brimming with anticipation.

It's our first spring scrimmage, and the football-starved students are eager to witness the action. A lump of excitement nestles in my stomach as well. I've always loved everything about the game—the energetic buzz, the fervor of the fans, the players' relentless drive, and now, the exhilaration of watching West play.

As we settle into our seats, my gaze combs over the crowd in search of his number. A thrill runs through me when I spot him on the sidelines. Decked out in his gear, he's a fucking sight to behold, his dark hair swept back, helmet gripped casually in one hand.

Sophie nudges me. "Found him?"

"Mhm," I confirm, a little breathless. I point him out right away. "He's there, number thirty-eight."

Maya's eyes light up. "Oh, I see him!" She then proceeds to cup her hands around her mouth and yell, *"Number thirty-eight! We love you!"*

The bold display earns us the attention of half the nearby crowd, but most importantly, West's. His gaze sweeps over the stands, eventually landing on us. A wide grin splits his face, and he salutes me, throwing in a wink for good measure.

Maya giggles. "See! Totally worth it."

"He's a hottie," Sophie sighs before quickly adding, "Sorry, that's your man."

I laugh, waving off her apology. "Don't be. I know he's hot."

We continue our lighthearted conversation, the kickoff approaching rapidly. My attention, however, keeps diverting to the field, drawn by the energy radiating from West. The game hasn't even started yet, and I'm already enthralled.

The opening announcements blare out, revealing that Coastal's won the coin toss. Predictably, they choose to receive, banking on their impressive offensive stats. The kickoff initiates a frenzied start to the game, the Ospreys putting up a solid offense, leading to an early touchdown and conversion.

Then it's our turn to strike back. It comes as no surprise that Coach Rodriguez called in Noah as the starting quarterback. A redshirt freshman who, over the years, has risen in ranks.

Noah's impressive out the gate, but his efforts aren't being matched by our receivers. A sequence of crucial drops on the third down disrupts our momentum, which leaves a window of opportunity wide open for the Ospreys.

Despite the odds, by halftime, we claw our way back to a tie, the scoreboard reading 14-14.

In need of a break, I let my friends know I'm headed to the restroom. I tug my jersey over my shorts, prepping to navigate through the crowd.

Sophie, eager to help, leans in and yells, "Do you want some company?"

"That's okay," I shout back. "I can find my way back if you stay here."

"Alright, text us if you get lost."

I slowly weave my way through the chaos around me. To my relief, the line for the women's restroom isn't too long yet. And after waiting a few minutes, I'm able to slip inside.

I slide my shorts down, getting comfortable in the confines of the small restroom stall. I had expected this to be a brief sanctuary of calm. But it's more like a hub of animated gossip instead, the whispers and giggles echoing in the tiled space.

"Oh my God, did you see Conor out there?" a female voice practically squeals in excitement.

"Are you kidding? He looks so fucking good," says her friend. "It's a shame he's not even playing tonight."

"Yeah, but you know who *is* playing?"

"Please don't tell me you're eyeing West again," the first voice cautions. "He's bad news, Cass."

My back stiffens involuntarily, a knot of unease growing in my stomach. Still, I remain silent, frozen in place while they carry on.

"He may be bad news," Cassidy's voice flows confidently, "but he's got some other skills that make it all worthwhile."

A pang of jealousy courses through me, sharpening my senses.

"Yeah, yeah," the first girl dismisses her with a knowing chuckle. "West is great in bed, but he'll also eat your heart out."

Cassidy's giggle grates on my nerves. "Who says I have a heart?"

"You know he's seeing someone else now, right?" a third voice chimes in, one I'm fairly certain belongs to Shannon's friend, Emmy, the sweet girl who warned me off Miller.

Heartened by her effort to stand up for me, I quickly zip up my shorts and emerge from the stall. I join them at the sink without a word, moving beside her to wash my hands.

As I glance up, Emmy's surprised reflection meets my gaze in the mirror.

"Cassidy," she softly chides, her gaze darting between me and her teammates. She looks almost apologetic, an uncomfortable tension settling on her features.

"What's the—?" Cassidy starts, but her friend cuts her off.

"*Jade*, hi," Emmy greets, attempting to defuse the situation with a small smile. "How are you?"

"I'm great, thanks," I say, returning her greeting with a forced half-smile of my own.

The third girl makes a small choking noise, her eyes darting back and forth between us. Cassidy's glance follows and then lands squarely on me, blatantly sizing me up. There's an awkward pause, but she doesn't immediately backpedal or apologize. Instead, she raises a brow, a smug grin stretching across her face.

"Hey, Jade. Didn't realize you were here." Her voice resonates within the small room, laced with feigned innocence that only amps up my irritation.

Emmy intervenes before I have the chance to respond, her tone soft yet firm. "Cass, we should probably get back to the team."

Ignoring her, Cassidy continues. "You still have your little thing going on with West, don't you? Isn't he just a beast on the field?"

Something inside me snaps at her tone. I'd let her comments slide earlier, but now, I can't hold my tongue any longer. "Yes, he's my *boyfriend*," I correct, meeting her gaze dead-on. "And he's incredible both on and off the field."

The bathroom descends into an uncomfortable silence, Cassidy's smirk faltering. The third friend looks at her shoes. Emmy, bless her heart, sends me an apologetic glance, to which I respond with a small, appreciative nod.

"Now, if you'll excuse me," I say, wiping my hands on a paper towel. "I'd rather not keep my friends waiting."

With that, I make a hasty exit, leaving them behind in the restroom. The whole encounter wasn't pleasant, but I'm proud of how I stood up for myself.

By the time I make it back to my seat, I've successfully managed to squash all the weird feelings they just stirred up. West is mine, and I'm his. And he's certainly not gonna "eat my heart out," as the girls would say.

Barely suppressing a grin, my gaze finds its way back to the game. Maybe it's my bias, but I can't tear my eyes away from West. His power as a running back is something to behold, his ability to weave through the defense and run the ball a testament to his talent.

And it's his claim on the field that serves as our ticket to shattering Coastal's defense.

With only nine minutes remaining in the game, Dayton secures the ball. They proceed to run it on all fifteen plays, which sets up our senior kicker for an easy field goal to close us off.

It's a 27-21 victory for Dayton, and the sounds of the crowd are ear-splitting.

As the student section rushes the field, I shove past the endless crowds of people until I make it all the way to my new favorite player. When I finally reach him, West's a vision of victory—sweat streaking down his face, black smudges marking his cheekbones.

He shouts my name from just a few paces away. I'm close enough to see his lips move, but it's loud enough that I can barely hear him.

"Jade!" he calls again.

I push past the last few stragglers standing between us. He's beaming at me now, his arms spread wide as I rush to meet him, his energy practically sparking against my skin.

"You were incredible!"

He tilts his head down, brushing our lips together. "Only because I had my good-luck charm in the stands."

I roll my eyes, but the grin on my face—the warm flush of heat on my cheeks—betrays me yet again. "So corny."

"Only for you, baby." He smirks, his gaze softening. "Only for you."

Then his lips are on mine, sealing his promise with a kiss that's anything but chaste. His strong arms pull me closer, pressing me against the armor of his chest as our mouths move in a rhythm all their own.

It's a rush, the way we fit so perfectly together. And nothing, not even the sounds of the cheering crowd, can drown out the thundering of his heartbeat against mine.

Chapter Twenty-Five
WEST

As I EMBRACE my girlfriend on the field, the adrenaline high slowly wears off.

We put on a good show and won the scrimmage, fighting tooth and nail to get that winning TD. But somehow, the taste of victory doesn't feel as sweet as it should. It's overshadowed by a gritting sense of guilt, an unease that prickles at the back of my mind.

The way that Jade's gazing up at me now, eyes so full of trust and pride, well . . . it's gonna hurt like hell when I ruin that.

The crowd gradually disperses, allowing our team to convene for a quick post-game debrief. Jade, understanding as always, waits patiently on the sidelines. Once the huddle breaks, I'm drawn back to her, craving her, crushing her against me like it's the last time I ever will.

Our moment is interrupted by Cam, his upbeat greeting breaking us apart. "Hey, you two," he says, giving me a hearty slap on the back.

"Hey, Cam," Jade says, pulling away from our embrace. Her bright smile returns, a stark contrast to the turmoil twisting inside me. "Congrats on the win."

"Thanks," he says. "You guys heading to the Cathouse?"

Jade gives him a puzzled look. "Cathouse?"

"Team house. Our QB lives there with a bunch of other guys from the O-line, and they're hosting an after-party. You guys coming?"

"Oh, uh . . ." I wring my hands together, keeping my gaze locked on my girlfriend. "I was hoping we could head back to our place instead."

Cam snorts, misinterpreting my meaning. "I think you can wait a few hours, man."

"Nah, just, uh—just to talk," I clarify, my voice unsteady, palms clammy, the tension seeping into my bones.

"We can *talk* later," Jade says with a cheeky smirk. "We should go celebrate your win."

"Okay, maybe we'll check it out for a bit," I say, a reluctant agreement. "Then you can come stay the night at my place."

"Do you think I could invite Sophie and Maya, too?"

"Absolutely," I say, the corners of my mouth lifting in an automatic smile. "Invite whoever you want, baby."

With that, she leaves me with a soft kiss on my jawline and a promise to meet me after my shower, making her way back to her friends.

"Dude," Cam drawls out the moment she's out of earshot. "Were you actually planning on skipping the party?"

I shrug, bending down to gather up my gear from the sidelines. "Yeah, I guess. Just not really feeling up to it tonight."

"Honestly?" He shakes his head, clearly baffled. "We just busted our asses to beat one of the best teams in the NCAA."

"Yeah," I say as I sling my duffel bag over one shoulder. "But it was still just a scrimmage."

His brows shoot up. "That doesn't sound like the West I know."

He's right. It's not. Because the West he knows is usually over the moon after every win, no matter how insignificant. But today, I'm a fucking stranger even to myself.

"I dunno." I sigh, rubbing a hand over my face, feeling the grime and sweat. "I guess I just wanted some alone time with Jade."

"Nah, I get it. You wanted to celebrate in private."

Not quite what I meant, but I just nod in response, letting him believe what he wants. "Yeah, sure."

"Well, I can make myself scarce if you want the place to yourself later on," he offers, already planning his exit strategy. "I'm sure Danny will be crashing at his girl's place like usual."

"That sounds good," I say, relief washing over me. This way, Jade and I can be alone when the storm inevitably hits. "Thanks, bro."

With a final salute, Cam heads off, leaving me standing in the echo of the crowd's cheers, panicking about how I'm going to make it through the next few hours.

An hour after parting ways, I meet Jade and her friends outside the Cathouse. Underneath the faint, flickering glow of the streetlight, I can make out their wide-eyed excitement. I take a moment to introduce myself to the two girls, trying to commit their names to memory before we all trudge inside.

The party is pretty fucking packed already, potent with the scent of sweat, alcohol, and loud music blaring from the speakers. Everywhere I look, there are bodies swaying to the beat, bottles being passed around, and people shouting over the loud music.

It seems like the whole team turned up tonight, along with their friends, dates, and the majority of the cheer squad. I haven't seen a party this wild since the end of last season, and honestly, I can't say I've missed it for a second.

"Is it always like this?" Jade asks, her voice a note above a whisper, eyes wide.

"Pretty much," I say, glancing around at the growing chaos. I spot some of my teammates in the crowd, their laughter ringing loud and clear above the music. Turning back to Jade, I ask, "Can I grab you girls a drink?"

Maya, the more outspoken one of the two, grins. "Actually, we're just gonna go explore. Which of your teammates are single?"

The question brings a chuckle from me. They're definitely here to have some fun. "Pretty much all of 'em, except Noah and my housemate, Danny. A couple of our linebackers have girls, but they'll be here tonight."

"Ohh, sounds like we've got options," she says, linking her arm with Sophie's and disappearing into the crowd.

With their departure, Jade and I are left standing on the outskirts of the party. I glance at her, one brow raised. "They seem . . . nice."

"Yeah, they're just thirsty. They're actually really sweet girls."

"That's good. I was—"

"Hey, West!" Some bouncing brunette cuts me off, nearly stumbling into me as she does. She's fumbling on her feet, her strappy heels slipping on the slick floor beneath us. Her voice is shrill and unfamiliar, but there's a telltale glimmer of recognition in her eyes.

"Hey," I awkwardly greet.

Wobbling, she steadies herself by clutching my shoulder, her fingers digging into the fabric of my T-shirt. "I just wanted to come say hi really quick," she slurs, pushing her stringy hair out of her face.

Recognition dawns on me. I know she's a junior on the cheer team, but I still can't put a name to the face. I decide to play it safe. "How's it going?" I ask, giving her a quick nod. "This is my girlfriend, Jade."

She turns, her eyes widening slightly. "Oh," she chirps, an odd mixture of surprise and disappointment washing over her. "Right, of course. I'll see you later, West."

"Who was that?" Jade asks, confusion knitting her brows.

"I think she's one of Shan's teammates." I give her an easy

smile, slinging one arm across her shoulders. "Come on, let's get you a drink."

We navigate our way through the crowd, our hands clasped tightly together. People I half recognize pat me on the back, their faces blurring in the dim lighting.

"Hey West, amazing run tonight!" another random girl shouts at me, her hand lingering on my chest a second too long. Along the way, we're stopped a few more times by some other women I fail to recognize. And, unfortunately, each unwelcome interaction seems to leave Jade quieter, her grip on my hand tightening.

When we finally reach the kitchen, it's so packed that we have to weave our way through, bodies pressing against us from all sides. But by some miracle, I finally manage to snag us a couple of beers.

"This is a little overboard," Jade murmurs, gaze sweeping over the crowd.

"Yeah, we don't have to stay long," I assure her, shouting over the noise. "I was actually hoping we could talk tonight."

"Sure." She shrugs, popping open her beer. It's like she's parched, downing the contents of the can in almost one go. A droplet of beer trickles down her chin, and she hastily wipes it away.

She looks so out of place here, so unlike the confident, relaxed woman I know. "Jade," I start, concern tightening my chest. "Is everything okay?"

"Everything's fine," she snaps, a bit too hastily.

There's something off about her behavior. Something about the way she's avoiding my eyes. "No, it's clearly not fine."

Grabbing hold of her hand, I lead her down the hallway, away from the blaring music and prying eyes. After a few seconds of searching, I push open the first door I see. It's a bathroom. Not the most ideal place, but it will have to do.

She glances around the small space, tossing her now empty beer into the trash bin. "Why are we in a bathroom, Theo?"

"So you can tell me what's going on," I say, placing my unopened can on the counter. "Everything was cool when we got here, and now, you're pissed off. Tell me what I did wrong so that I can fix it."

She crosses her arms over her chest, gaze falling to the floor. "You didn't do anything wrong."

Her sudden change in demeanor throws me off-balance. "Okay," I say slowly, unsure of where this is going. "What is it, then?"

"I'm just . . . how many girls have you slept with in this house?" she finally blurts out, cheeks flushing a deep shade of crimson.

I freeze. "Sorry? What?"

"Like, at least half of the girls here are acting like they know you. You know, in the biblical sense."

"Probably because half the girls here are on the cheer team."

The look she gives me is somewhere between frustration and confusion. She pulls away from me, her back pressed against the cold bathroom tiles.

"Right, that doesn't help." I grab her hand again, thumb tapping against her palm. "No, of course I haven't slept with anywhere near half the girls here. I barely even know most of them. They're just friendly with all the football players."

"Friendly, right."

I furrow my brows, studying her flushed expression. "Where is this coming from?"

"I overheard some girls talking about you at the stadium," she admits after a long pause. "And even Sophie made a comment about how hot you are. I wasn't expecting all these girls to be . . . doting over you tonight."

"What did they say?"

"Not much, honestly. But Cassidy was there talking about how good you are in bed."

And that's when it all clicks. Jade isn't used to dating athletes, and especially not a Dayton football player. We're treated like commodities here—good for one thing and one thing only.

"Ah, I see." I thread our fingers together. "So, this is about you being jealous."

"I'm not jealous," she counters hastily. I cock a brow at her, working to suppress my smirk. "Okay, I'm fucking jealous. I mean . . . it's so annoying. Why can't you just be ugly?"

I can't help but chuckle. "You want me to be ugly?"

"No, I just, I want you to be unappealing to the rest of the female population."

I release her hand, trailing my fingertips along the side of her arm. "You know there's no reason to be jealous."

"I know."

"I'm so fucking into you," I murmur, moving to her hips, pulling her closer. "Didn't we agree you wouldn't doubt that?"

"We did."

"Do you need me to remind you?" I boost her up so that she's sitting on the bathroom counter. "Because I'm more than willing to do so."

"Here?" she whispers, dragging her bottom lip between her teeth.

"No time like the present," I tell her, my hands moving up her thighs, stopping just at the hemline of her skirt. My voice is rougher than I'd intended, my own desire mirroring hers.

My focus narrows in on my girlfriend, her flushed face, her wide eyes, the way she's looking at me like I'm the only thing that matters. The loud thumping of the music fades into the background, replaced by the quickening of my heartbeat.

She tenses under my touch. "Someone will hear us."

"Not if you stay quiet." I slip my hand under her skirt, rubbing my thumb in circles on the bare skin of her inner thigh.

"Oh," she murmurs in response, eyes drifting shut. The sight is intoxicating, the pure vulnerability in that one sound, in the way she trusts me.

"I like this skirt on you," I say, bunching up the thin material.

She laughs, and it's a musical sound that sends a jolt of desire straight to my dick. "I'm sure you do."

My hand slides up higher on her thigh, resting right at the edge of her damp panties. "Do you want this?"

As soon as I hear her whispered "yes," I dip my fingers inside the lacy scrap of fabric. She's already wet, and warm, and waiting for me. So, I plunge one finger inside her tight core, stroking in and out at a lazy speed.

She leans forward on the counter, whimpering as I pump into her. Her palm gently cups my erection through my jeans, and my cock swells, a jolt of pleasure clenching in my gut.

"Hop off the counter," I say, voice husky and demanding.

I slip my finger out of her, grabbing her hips as she touches down onto the tile. My grasp on her body is rough as I flip her around to face the bathroom mirror, the front of her thighs pressing into the countertop.

"Bend over," I rasp.

As she gets into the position I want, I hastily undo the button on my jeans and yank them down over my hips. I bunch up her skirt the rest of the way, sliding her panties aside. After slipping a condom out of my pocket, I free my straining erection from my boxers and slowly push inside her.

"Brace yourself on the counter, baby," I demand, tangling my fingers into the hair at the nape of her neck.

She scrambles to grasp at the cold countertop, one hand gripping the edge while the other loops around the faucet. Once she's stable, I pound into her. The movement of my hips is wild and uncontrolled, a barely restrained force of lust and desire for the girl who completely owns me—body, mind, and soul.

A muffled moan escapes from her lips. "Good girl," I rasp. "Stay quiet."

Her pussy is pulsing around me, sucking me tightly inside of her with each forceful thrust. There's just something so fucking hot about the way she's struggling to keep quiet, those tiny little whimpers escaping her as we fuck.

"Theo," she squeaks out. "I'm going to—"

"Come for me, Jade," I urge, sliding in and out of her at a frantic pace. She's gasping now, her fingers slipping as she struggles to brace herself. It's not long before she collapses onto the counter, her core fluttering and pulsing around my cock as she comes.

My own release follows closely behind. And God, it feels so fucking good to spill inside of her. Once I pull out, I pinch off the condom and toss it in the trash. Then I tuck myself back into my jeans and yank Jade's skirt into place.

As soon as the haze of desire clears from my brain, I realize that I fucked up again. I was supposed to talk to her, confess to her, clear the air . . . but instead, I fucked her in the bathroom at a party.

What the hell is wrong with me?

She's staring into the mirror, breathing heavily as she runs her fingers through her hair. "That was . . . really good."

"It was," I say, but the words feel awkward, stiff, a stark contrast to the raw intimacy we just shared. "Uh, maybe we should just head back to my place now."

"Round two already?" she jokes, flipping around to face me. Her fingers curl around my shoulders, face flushed as she steadies herself against me.

"Actually, I wanted to talk to you. I have something I've been wanting to tell you."

"Oh! I actually have something I want to tell you, too."

"Okay, we can sort it out when we get to my place."

"Can I just tell you my news now? I'm really excited about it, and all I've been thinking about is sharing it with you."

"Of course."

"Garrett is letting me write a piece on the banquet," she reveals, the pride evident in her voice.

My mouth runs dry, heart clenching. "Our banquet?"

"Yeah, I called him after you left my apartment earlier. Told him I was going to write about the scrimmage anyway."

"Oh?"

"He ended up offering me this article instead—said if I did a good enough job, then he'd let me work sports next season."

My palms are sweating. "That's, uh, wow."

She gives me an odd look, brows furrowing. "I mean, I know it's just another boring puff piece . . . but maybe I could spice it up a little. You know, now that I have the inside scoop."

I swallow back a giant lump in my throat. Fuck, fuck, fuck. Yeah, she's got the inside scoop alright. If I tell her about the Trade, she'll have the fucking scoop of the year.

But I can't keep this shit inside me any longer. She thinks I'm straightforward, honest even. She thinks I'm worthy of being with her. How do I reconcile that with what I've been hiding?

So, I gather up my courage, but all that comes out is this: "That's great, Jade."

"Do you think you could get me an interview with Elliot?" she asks eagerly. "Everyone loves to hear from the QB. Oh, and maybe Cam would be a good option, too. You said he was part of the planning committee, right?"

With every excited word, my resolve crumbles a little more.

"Sure, of course," I say, but my voice betrays the anxiety I'm feeling.

"Wait, what's wrong?"

I shake my head, wiping my palms down the front of my jeans. "Nothing's wrong."

"I mean . . . I know that when you first invited me, it was more of a friendly group hangout. But now things have changed between us, so if you don't want me to be, like, working during the event or—"

"That's not it. I'm happy for you, baby. This is what you wanted."

"Yeah, it is," she says, her smile radiant as she wraps her arms around me. "Honestly, it works out so great. I was already planning on going with you, so it's, like, oddly perfect."

"Yeah," I mutter, the affirmation tasting bitter on my tongue. "Just perfect."

Chapter Twenty-Six

JADE

WEST HAS BEEN ACTING all shades of strange since yesterday afternoon. After our little bathroom tryst—where he bent me over, claimed me, left me breathless—he's been oddly silent, especially after I dropped the news about the article.

Back at his place, he plastered on a smile, brushing off my concerns with a casual, "I just need to sleep it off." He chalked it up to postgame fatigue, but there was a tension in his voice that gave me pause.

We slid into his bed together, my body finding its rightful place against him. He held me close, wrapping me up in his strong arms. But despite the comfort I felt, there was a rigidity to the way he held me. Something was gnawing at him, keeping him on edge.

His reassurances were earnest when I offered myself to him later, and he turned me down. "I want you. Always," he said, his voice a tender whisper against the shell of my ear. "I'm just too tired right now." But even though his words sounded sincere, they felt foreign.

His behavior was far from the West I'm used to. He's never turned down sex before, backed away from the raw connection that's always sparked between us.

Not to mention there was something he'd been wanting to "talk" about. He'd seemed eager, insistent even, about discussing something once we reached the privacy of his place. But once we were comfortably nestled into his bed, he conveniently forgot all about it.

And then there was this morning. Apparently, he was in a hurry to get back to his "studies," even though it's a fucking Sunday. His big exam is finally over, and so is the scrimmage.

He's been more than vocal about how much he missed me over the last couple of weeks, and now that he finally has some time on his hands, he's choosing to bury himself in his books. It doesn't add up.

Is he upset about the article? My jealousy? Or is there something else, an entirely different reason, lurking behind his strange demeanor?

If he would just communicate, tell me what's on his mind, I wouldn't be stuck playing this guessing game. But the West I'm dealing with right now is a mystery—a puzzle I'm desperately trying to solve, piece by confusing piece.

Lost in my head, the sound of the apartment door creaking open finally rips me back to reality. It's almost noon, and Shannon's just now making her way inside.

"Hey, Jade!" she says, her cheerful voice echoing off our thin walls. She flings her keys onto the kitchen counter and moves toward me, settling down on the couch.

"Hey," I say, kicking my feet onto the coffee table. "Did you stay at the Spirit House last night?"

"Yeah, we all got a little too sloppy," she says, a sheepish grin on her face. "Did you and West end up skipping the party?"

"Nah, we just dipped out a little early. He was . . . tired, I guess."

"What does *that* mean?"

"I don't know, honestly," I say, a sigh escaping me. "He's just been acting a little weird lately."

"Weird how?"

"Like . . . tense?" I shrug helplessly, running my fingers through my hair, anxiety knotting in my stomach. "We, um, we had sex at the party last night."

"At the party?" Her eyes blow wide. "Damn, okay."

I look down at my hands. "Yeah, weak moment on my part. West was getting all this attention, and I was feeling a little insecure."

"Okay, that tracks." Her face softens with sympathy. "Jersey chasers always pop up after a big win."

I groan, resting my head back on the couch. "It was definitely eye-opening."

"So, you think he's mad about that?" she asks, puzzled. "That you were feeling jealous?"

"I don't know, really. He might be upset about me writing an article on the banquet."

"Why would that upset him?"

"Maybe he just wants me to be there for *him* and not for myself."

My brow furrows at the realization. The banquet is a team event, after all. The premise of me attending should be to celebrate West and all his achievements, but somehow, I've made the night about myself.

"That doesn't really seem like West, though. Maybe he's just in a weird mood?"

"Yeah, maybe," I say, a sinking feeling creeping into my chest. "What are you wearing to the banquet, by the way?"

"Cam says it's black-and-white themed, so I'll probably pick a white dress out of my closet. I assume you'll be wearing black."

"Duh." I give her a tiny smile, my spirits lifting slightly. Aside from my favorite sweatshirt, most of my other wardrobe is black— it's practically my brand at this point. "Are you excited to go with Cam?"

"Yeah, I think it'll be fun. He's a good friend."

I nudge her with my elbow, waggling my brows. "A friend, huh?"

She snorts. "Yes, just a friend."

"So, you're not interested in anything more?" I ask, this time serious. "West says Cam's a relationship kind of guy. So, he must not be a total player."

"I figured, but I'm not really getting any vibes from him. I don't think he sees me that way."

"Shan, he'd be a fool not to." I shake my head, casting her a reassuring smile. "You're, like, everyone's type."

"That's sweet." She returns my smile, her eyes soft. "But I don't know, I don't think Cam's the guy for me. Guys our age just seem so immature."

"You're not wrong," I say, although West is my one and only exception. "Maybe we should find you an older guy, then? What about a *professor?*"

She visibly cringes, nose scrunching up. "Jesus. That'd be all sorts of fucked-up."

"Okay, maybe not a professor." I stretch my arms over the back of the couch, nudging her on the shoulder in the process. "How about a TA? They're totally fair game."

She gives me a noncommittal shrug. "We'll see what happens. I'm not focused on finding a relationship right now, anyways."

"Really? I thought you said that's what you wanted."

"I thought so, too." She bites her lip, lost in thought. "Maybe my priorities have changed."

"Well, if they have, just let me know if you need a wing-woman." Not that she would ever need someone else's help to secure a man. Shannon is the kind of girl who lights up the room, not only with her beauty but with her kindness and humor. She's clever, brave, and fiercely independent. Any man she chooses will be more than lucky to have her. "I got your back."

"Thanks, Jade. I know you do."

. . .

As THE DAYS PASS, they're filled with an unnerving silence from West. His brief texts and clipped calls offer no clue into his thoughts, only a continuous stream of vague commitments and "last-minute agenda items."

Whatever the hell that means.

And so, the days turn into a week. A week where the only substantial conversation we have revolves around the upcoming banquet—our outfits, the location, the expected attendees—anything but the thoughts trapped inside his head.

Even tonight, he insisted on helping Cam with the setting up, leaving Shannon and me to navigate our way to the banquet alone. It's not that we're helpless, but we did spend a ridiculous amount of time primping and preening for this event.

Shannon looks like a heavenly vision in white, her fiery red hair cascading in soft waves across an open back. My dress is a little more understated, black but still elegant and classic. It clings to my body in all the right places. And honestly, I'm excited for West to see me wearing it.

Admittedly, this is a much more refined version of me than he's used to. A touch fancier than my usual jeans and well-loved sweatshirt. But somehow, no matter what I'm wearing, West still finds me irresistible.

It's nearly six o'clock by the time Shannon and I pull up in front of the Gaia Hotel. Apparently, Cam picked this location because of the beautiful outdoor gardens. He called it a "welcome clash of green amongst a sea of black and white."

Seems he's taken the role of party planner quite seriously.

As Shannon hands the keys to the valet, I notice the guys waiting to greet us at the entrance. A few minutes of compliments ensue before Cam, on a mission, loops his arm through Shannon's and leads her through the grand double doors.

And now, it's just West and me—alone together for the first time since the scrimmage night.

"You're gorgeous," he breathes out, his gaze slowly dragging across my body.

"Thank you," I murmur. "You look great, too."

And he really, truly does.

His hair is swept back to one side, just lightly gelled in an effortless sort of way. He's wearing a nice tailored black suit, with a matching undershirt and tie. His sun-kissed skin and dark hair perfectly complement the all-black ensemble.

"Let's head inside," he says, offering his elbow. "Cam did a fucking awesome job setting this all up. You gotta see it."

I graze my fingertips along his thick forearm, gently wrapping my hand around him. "Hold on a sec."

He gives me a puzzled look. "What's up?"

"I just . . . I missed you this week."

"I missed you, too. I've been thinking about you nonstop."

My heart flutters. "You have?"

"Of course I have." He laughs softly, a hand moving to my waist. "You're always on my mind, Jade."

"And you're always on mine."

His grip tightens around my waist as he pulls me closer, his other hand cradling my jaw. He leans in, capturing my lips in a sweet yet passionate kiss. I lose myself in him, his taste, his touch, everything about this moment feels so right.

Finally, he pulls away, a devilish grin playing on his lips. "Okay, now that's settled, we can go inside."

DURING THE NEXT NINETY MINUTES, the banquet is a rush of tasty hors d'oeuvres, cocktails, and conversation. In between, I scribble a few quick notes, hoping it'll be enough to flesh out my article. Still, I'm not stressing too much over it—I trust in my ability to impress Garrett, and the interviews are sure to be the heart of the story anyway.

As we move on to dinner, West and I are nestled at a round table with three other couples. Shannon and Cam, of course, are part of our little congregation, along with Danny, another housemate of theirs, and his girlfriend, Sofia. The last couple consists of Shannon's friend Emmy and a third football player, whose name I can't quite recall.

We're all served a three-course dinner, which is absolutely delicious. In fact, everything about this night has been perfect so far. The entire time, I find myself showering Cam with compliments. The decor, the food, the seamless flow of events—he's really outdone himself.

As we scrape up the last morsels from our plates, Coach Rodriguez takes the stage. "Hi, everyone," he announces into the mic, his voice washing over the room. "Thank you all for coming out to celebrate the team. I thought we'd take advantage of everyone still being seated."

His words stir a wave of anticipation, conversations fade into a lull as all heads turn toward the stage. After expressing gratitude to our banquet planners, Cam and Vance, he delves into a series of awards, ranging from Outstanding Leadership to Best GPA to Most Improved Player.

And as he rattles off the names, I manage to recognize about half, thanks to the handful of games I've attended.

And then, the "Solid Rock" awards are announced. "This award goes out to the most solid, consistent, and dependable players of each position," Coach elaborates. The familiar names roll off his tongue—Noah Elliot, Theodore Westman-Cooke, Treyvon Johnson, Robert Graham, and Morgan Hughes.

West's fingers tighten around mine under the table, a silent signal before he strides up to the stage to collect his award. I join the applause, my heart thumping like a proud drum in my chest.

When he returns, I lean into his side, my words whispered for his ears only. "Congrats, baby. You deserve it."

He offers a soft "Thank you," his hand settling comfortably on my thigh.

Once the coach concludes, the banquet comes back to life with chatter, music, and the bar's renewed popularity. Most of our table companions scatter to grab drinks or join other groups.

"So, do you think you could introduce me to some of the other award winners?" I ask him, noting down the last few names. "I'd love to get an interview."

"Sure," he says, a touch of tension in his voice. "No problem."

Concern prickles at the back of my mind. "Is everything okay?" I ask, placing my journal back in my bag. "If I'm bothering you with my work, I can put it aside for a while."

He gently squeezes my knee. "Nothing you do bothers me, Jade."

While that may be true, something is clearly off with him. I can see it in the way he looks at the table, shoulders drooped. "Then what's wrong?"

"I'm just trying to get through this night."

"Get through it?" I wrinkle my nose. "You just won an award. I figured you'd be excited."

"No, it's not—" He's quiet for a moment, then, "I just—I need some air."

I offer him an understanding smile, rubbing his bicep gently. "We could go out to the gardens?"

He nods, rising from his chair. "Yeah, I'll be back in a minute."

"I could go with . . ." I trail off, bewildered as he rushes off alone. "Well, alrighty, then."

With West making his hasty exit, my focus shifts back to our table, where Emmy is sitting by herself, phone practically glued to her hand. "Hey, girl," I offer, trying to keep my tone light. "Where's your date?"

Her response is a soft sigh as she glances up from her screen. "He's over there, hitting it off with some other guy's date," she says with a roll of her eyes. I follow her gaze to find the man in question, making himself cozy with someone who is decidedly not Emmy.

"Oh, I see," I say carefully, studying her expression. "Are you two . . . together?"

She shakes her head, letting out a dry laugh. "Hardly know the guy. I came because Shannon told me she would be here, too. I mean, I don't mind him not sticking around . . . I halfway expected it, honestly. But what I didn't expect is for him to go flirt with everyone else."

My brows furrow in sympathy, a comforting reply half-formed on my lips when someone interrupts. "Hey, you're Jade, right?" The voice is masculine, familiar, but I can't place it immediately.

When I turn to the source, there's a random guy now filling West's vacated seat. "Oh, hey," I say, offering a polite smile. I glance back to Emmy, but her wandering date has already returned. "Yeah, I'm Jade. Have we met?"

The new guy grins, running a hand through his hair as he jogs my memory. "We watched a UFC fight together once. I'm Remi Miller."

Recognition flickers. "Oh, right. Green hat," I say, a hint of amusement in my voice.

"Huh?"

I wave his confusion away with a laugh. "Never mind. Enjoying the banquet?"

"Yeah, it's been great. My date's off having a chat with my teammates, and I saw you sitting here, so . . ."

Glancing around the table, I note that Emmy and her date have vacated as well. Miller and I are the last and only ones here. "West went to get some air."

"Ah, gotcha." He slings an arm over the back of my chair,

making himself comfortable. "So, heard you and Shannon are roommates."

"Yes, we are," I say cautiously. "She's awesome."

His interest seems genuine as he leans in closer. "How'd you guys meet?"

"At a camp last summer. We hit it off right away."

"That's cool," he says with a light chuckle. "Must be fun living together."

"We do have a good—" I'm cut off as he places a hand on my thigh, his fingers brushing against my knee. My words stutter to a halt as my skin prickles under his touch.

"Miller," I manage to force out, my voice icy cold.

He grins at me, leaning back in his chair. "Call me Remi."

"Remi," I snap, my frustration simmering. "You're aware that I'm here with West, right? We're a couple."

His smirk is infuriating, the grip on my knee tightening. "I doubt he'd mind."

"Well, I'm certain he would," I shoot back, pushing his hand away and sliding my chair back with a screech. Without another word, I stalk off, leaving Miller behind in my search for West.

God, what a fucking asshole.

I'm seething as I head outside, my mind a whirl of indignation. I mean, there are boundaries, aren't there? Isn't there some unspoken rule that you don't hit on a teammate's girlfriend? Apparently not at this damn banquet.

As I step into the quiet solitude of the garden, I hope West is done with his "air break." The last thing I want is to spend any more time alone at this party, especially with Miller lurking around like a little rat on the prowl.

Chapter Twenty-Seven
WEST

I CAN'T BELIEVE how ridiculous this whole situation feels. I've spent most of the past week stressed-out about this event, but it's just the same old banquet we have every year.

First comes the mindless mingling, then an over-the-top meal, followed by an endless string of awards. This year, I've managed to snag a "Solid Rock" award—my first ever. On any other day, I'd be drowning in a heady rush of pride, soaking up the validation. But right now, it doesn't even feel like a blip on my radar.

I'm too consumed by this silly ritual that's hovered over my head for weeks now. The fucking Trade. A tradition that once felt like a playful rite of passage, now morphing into a crushing burden. I wish I had been honest with Jade from the get-go. Maybe she'd have been pissed for a while, but we could've moved past it, together.

And now, the secret feels like a ton of steel, pressing down on me, threatening to break me under its weight.

"Your date's pretty hot, man." Conor McNair's smarmy voice interrupts my turmoil, forcing me to whip around.

"Damn right, she is," I snap, the words grinding out between clenched teeth. "And she's also off-limits."

"Yeah, I figured you'd already be locked into a trade with Cam." His smirk stretches wide across his face, his eyes glinting with an infuriating cockiness. I want to smack it right off him. "I can respect that."

"No, there's no trade," I say, my voice rigid with irritation. "Jade's my girlfriend."

"Oh?" He cocks a brow. "I mean, dude, everyone knows you've been after Shannon since freshman year. I just figured you'd be trading for her."

"Keep your goddamn voice down," I snarl.

And then, just as I'm about to lose my cool completely, Jade's voice floats in, filled with an undercurrent of worry. "Theo, there you are."

Spinning around, I lock eyes with her, hoping to hell she didn't overhear our conversation. "Jade," I say, trying to infuse some semblance of normalcy into my voice.

"Uh, I'm just gonna slip out of here," McNair mumbles, picking up on the tension. "Gotta get back to my date."

Once he's sauntered off, I turn back to Jade. "Did you hear any of that?" I ask, apprehension tingeing my words.

"No, why?"

I shake my head, dismissing the question. "No reason."

"Theo, I can tell something's off. You've been acting weird for days now."

"I know," I confess, exhaustion seeping into my bones. "I'm sorry."

She gives me a derisive snort. "That's all I get? An 'I'm sorry'?"

"I don't know," I mumble as I run a hand through my hair.

A frustrated sigh escapes her, and she gazes upward, pinching the bridge of her nose. "You know, when you ditched me just now . . . your friend Miller made a pass at me."

"What?" My anger surges back with a vengeance. Fucking Miller. He's a dead man.

"Yeah, he didn't even bother being subtle about it," she grumbles. "He was caressing my thigh and everything."

A flood of rage washes over me. "He what? He fucking touched you? Jesus Christ, didn't that dipshit get the fucking memo?"

"What memo?"

"That you're off-limits tonight."

Her eyes narrow. "Off-limits? I'm not property."

"I know that," I say defensively, my nostrils flaring in agitation. "But you're my girlfriend. My teammates should respect that."

"And what about the rest?" she demands, one brow cocked. "Should they feel free to just hit on every other girl here? Date or not?"

"That's not what I mean."

"Really?" Her gaze desperately searches mine. "Because your teammates seem to think there's no line they can't cross. Emmy's date was making moves on other girls right in front of her."

Damn it, my teammates could at least try to be more subtle. I bury my face in my hands, groaning. "Oh," I manage to mumble, feeling the weight of her stare.

"'Oh'?" she parrots, indignation coloring her voice. "Seriously, tell me what's going on with you. And while you're at it, clue me in on why your teammates are acting like predators on the prowl. Is this some sort of sick competition to see who can hook up with the most girls?"

I choke back a shallow breath. "No, it's not that . . . exactly."

Her eyes narrow even further, if that's possible, arms crossed tightly across her chest. "Theo, spill it."

"Look," I start, my hands clenching and unclenching with anxiety. "I've been meaning to tell you this, I really have. Way before we even arrived here tonight."

"Go on."

"The reason that I've been acting weird, the reason that the whole team's been behaving so oddly tonight . . . well, there's this tradition that we have," I manage to say, each word feeling like a betrayal.

"What kind of tradition?"

"It's this silly competition that the team has been doing for ages. The upperclassmen try to swap dates during the banquet every year. If you pull it off, newer recruits have to clean your gear for the next season. But I wasn't . . . I mean, I had no intention of trading *you*."

My confession hangs between us like a live wire, the air buzzing with tension. Jade just stands there, arms crossed, her deep brown eyes staring holes into me. She's silent. An uncomfortably long moment stretches between us, and I brace myself for the inevitable fallout.

"Right, okay," she says softly. The distance between us seems to grow with each heartbeat, as if the weight of my confession has physically pushed us apart. "You were planning on it, though. Weren't you? When you first asked me?"

The words stick in my throat like broken glass, and I swallow hard against them. "I was . . . only at the very start, I swear," I manage, my voice a pitiful whisper against the harsh truth. "I called it off the night you came over to watch the fight."

"So, before that, you were just gonna trade me with whoever . . . in hopes that you could screw some random girl?" Her tone is lower now, a whisper of barely contained fury.

"That's not . . . no," I blurt out, my hands stretching out toward her, yet too afraid to touch. "It wasn't going to be someone random."

"What do you mean? Then who—" The words choke off, her eyes widening with the realization. "No, seriously?"

"Jade, just hold on a second. Before you think—"

"This whole thing was a setup so that you could sleep with Shan?"

"No, not the whole thing," I stammer, panic wriggling in my gut. "Not even close."

"What the hell is wrong with you?" She takes a wary step back, body rigid, her words ringing in my ears.

"I'm sorry," I say, emotion thickening my voice. "I wasn't

thinking about how much I'd like you when I first invited you. It was supposed to be a casual thing. I thought we'd all trade dates at the end of the night and laugh about it later. I didn't know I'd feel this way about you."

She scoffs, the bitter edge in her voice slicing through me. "Yeah, you didn't think you could actually like someone like me, huh? Just a jersey chaser wearing an ugly hand-me-down sweatshirt. I mean, I'm certainly no Shannon O'Connor."

"No, Jade, you're perfect." My hand extends toward her, desperate to bridge the growing distance, but she evades it, stepping further away. "You're more than I could've ever hoped for."

"So why didn't you just tell me?" she challenges, her voice shaking. "You had so many opportunities to say something, and you didn't. I even asked you point-blank if you had feelings for Shan."

My stomach twists. "And I wasn't lying about that. I never had real feelings for her—it was just a . . . physical attraction. I was going to tell you about all of this, I swear. Cam warned me against it at first, but I made up my mind to tell you regardless."

She closes her eyes, rubbing at her forehead. "I think I'm missing the part where you actually told me."

"I was going to last weekend after the scrimmage," I confess, the words clawing their way past the lump in my throat. "But then there was the whole . . . article thing."

"Are you trying to say it was for my own good?" I can picture the gears working in her mind, attempting to rationalize this. "You wanted to make sure I wrote the article, but you thought I'd bail if you told me the truth. Is that it?"

I flinch, another wave of nausea threatening to break. "I, uh, well—"

"No," she interjects, the disappointment raw in her voice. "It wasn't about that, was it? This has always been about you. You didn't tell me because you thought I might write about it. You were worried I'd expose the team."

"I'm so sorry," I stammer, desperation seeping into my voice. The apology feels woefully inadequate, but I'm out of words.

Her jaw clenches, sorrow-filled eyes boring into me. "Do all your teammates know that you were planning to trade me?"

The question is a devastating blow, and I wince at the impact. "Jade."

"Great, so they all know." She throws her hands up in exasperation. "Glad to hear it. Do you think one of them would still fuck me, or am I just spoiled goods now?"

"Baby, fuck . . . can we please go back to my place and talk about this?" I'm begging now, my pride discarded at her feet. "Please?"

"I don't think I'm ready to leave just yet," she says, her eyes glistening with unshed tears yet her chin tilted in defiance. "I don't have enough content for my article."

The realization slams into me, and my heart plummets. "You aren't—" My voice breaks. "Are you seriously going to write about this in the *Daily*?"

"It's only fair play," she snaps, her eyes alight with a fire that sets my nerves on edge. "After all, you boys love the thrill of a competition. Let's see how you handle a real fallout."

Panic seizes me. "Jade, you can't do that. Coach will bench anyone who—"

"Oh, go fuck yourself, West." She cuts me off, venom dripping from her words. "I'm leaving. By myself. And don't worry about your precious team. I won't put this bullshit in my article."

Relief washes over me, but it's a hollow victory. The damage to us is already done, even if she spares the team. "Thank you," I manage to croak.

She snorts, her expression hardening. "Don't thank me. I'm not doing it for you. I'm doing it because I won't let you and your ridiculous tradition ruin my career. I'm not going to get kicked off the paper for trying to burn bridges with the team."

"Okay," I murmur, my gaze fixated on the ground. The taste of regret is heavy on my tongue. "Jade, I—"

"I never really knew you at all, did I?"

Her accusation stings. "You did," I insist, clinging to the remnants of what we had. "You do. Sometimes, I feel like you're the only person who really does."

"Well, that sucks for you because it's over. We're done."

"I know I fucked up." The confession is a weak counter to her conviction. "So badly. But just . . . please don't give up on what we have."

"You're a fucking liar, West." She swipes a hand over her eyes, smudging her mascara. "What we had was built on lies. And I'm done with it now, so let me go."

"Jade, please."

"I stood in front of you a week ago and told you how much I valued your honesty." Her voice wavers, unsteady and broken. "I told you I was afraid that you'd play games with me, and you said nothing."

"I know, I—"

But she's not done, her gaze shifting away from me and out to the gardens. "I can barely look at you right now, so I need to leave."

"Baby—"

"If you say one more word, I'm going to start screaming," she warns, her voice dangerously low. "I'm leaving now. Don't you dare think about following me."

And then she's gone, disappearing from my life as abruptly as she entered it. Her name catches in my throat. I can't go after her now, not when she's begged me to stay. So, I'm left alone, the taste of my regret lingering as a stark reminder of my mistakes.

I fucked up, so badly, and I lost her.

I lost everything.

Chapter Twenty-Eight

THE DAYTON FOOTBALL TEAM, in all its glory, is a cesspool of misogynistic jackasses. Heartbreakingly enough, this includes my boyfriend—well, ex-boyfriend now. My heart shatters all over again at the thought.

There's a bitter sort of humor in the situation. All that time I spent wringing my hands, worrying that West could end things between us this summer. As though our relationship had any hope of surviving the long haul.

What a joke.

How could it have possibly withstood the lies? All this time, West has been bending the truth to suit his needs—to protect himself, his precious team, and their revolting little game. He chose to safeguard them over honesty with me.

I mean, who in their right mind invents a game like that? Trading girls around like pieces of meat? The audacity of it all makes me sick to my stomach. Fuck the football team. And most importantly, fuck West.

The banquet invitation wasn't ever about wanting the company of a friend or worrying about jersey chasers. It was a carefully calculated move. And I only got swept up into it all because I'm Shannon's roommate.

I was simply a pawn to West—a matter of convenience to win the prize he really wanted. But then he caught feelings, and that screwed over his game plan.

I just wish he had mustered the courage to come clean with me earlier. Of course, I would have been livid. Let's not sugarcoat that. But I could have moved on, given enough time.

West wanted to be with Shannon before we got together. My roommate. My best friend. That's a bitter pill to swallow, but back then, he and I were strangers. Honesty from the start could have smoothed things over, made me come to terms with his past choice. But now, it's too little, too late.

He was given the chance to come clean, to reveal the truth of his own accord. Instead, he procrastinated, leaving it until I was on my knees begging for honesty. He waited until he had no other choice. And that sort of cowardice, it's not something I can easily forgive.

West lost my trust tonight, and with it, he lost me.

So here I am, parked alone at a high stool in the middle of Lucky's, a charming little bar nestled near campus. It's usually a buzzing hive for student athletes, but tonight, the banquet has conveniently cleared the place out.

Seems like no one else cares to drink alone, no one but me. Because God knows, I need the dull numbing effect that comes with a stiff drink. I grimly swallow another shot, the gin burning a trail down my throat.

Stumbling slightly, I pay my tab and manage to call myself an Uber. If I drink any more, I'm going to start crying, and I'm not sure my fragile heart can handle any more emotional damage tonight.

Once I'm home, I clumsily unlock my front door, stumbling over an unruly pile of shoes in the darkness of the entryway. The noise seems to echo, far louder than I would like. A moment later, Shannon, her silhouette lit by the hallway light, appears.

She's weary, her hair messy, and wrapped in a silky robe. Her sleep-dazed eyes land on me, and for a moment, there's a painful silence between us.

"Jade, hi," she says, her face flushing a soft pink.

"Oh, you're home," I mumble. My voice sounds small, shaky in the quiet of our apartment. "I'm sorry, did I wake you?"

"No, you didn't," she assures me, eyes wide. "I heard you and West left the banquet early. I . . . I thought you were spending the night at his place."

A shaky breath escapes me as my eyes well up with tears. "Yeah, well, we broke up instead."

"What?" she gasps, her expression a mix of shock and worry. "What happened?"

"God, Shan. He . . ." My voice trails off, faltering as a sudden noise interrupts me from the hallway. My brow furrows. "Wait, is there someone here? In your room?"

She blushes deeply, the red creeping up her cheeks as she admits, "Um, yeah," in a low voice. "Yes, someone's here."

"Oh, please don't tell me you're hooking up with Cam. Because—"

"No, it's not Cam," she interrupts me, her voice hurried, gaze shifting nervously toward the living room.

I follow the direction of her stare, my eyes landing on a small duffel nestled against our worn-out couch. A large, familiar grey luggage tag sporting a bright purple lily sits on the front of it, almost taunting me.

"Shan," I whisper, my heart pounding wildly in my chest. "Why is my brother's bag here?"

She seems to shrink back, her eyes wide with panic. "Look," she stammers, her words tumbling out in a rush. "I promise you . . . we didn't mean for this to happen."

The room spins around me. "Oh, you've gotta be fucking kidding me," I mutter, disbelief lacing my words.

Fueled by frustration, I stomp down the hallway and throw open her bedroom door. There he is—Mica, my half-naked brother, standing in the center of her room. His jeans hang low on his hips, his belt undone as he hastily pulls a shirt over his head, desperately trying to regain some sense of decency.

"Ace, what the fuck are you doing here?" I demand, my voice echoing off the walls.

"Lil, I, uh—" He glances up, and shame flickers in his eyes. "I came to surprise you."

My laughter is bitter and mirthless. "Well, color me surprised," I say, voice steady despite the turmoil raging inside me. "I told you not to mess with Shan, and you promised you wouldn't."

"I know, Lil," he says, his voice quiet, filled with regret. "I'm sorry, it was a mistake."

I cast a glance at Shannon. She's cowering behind the doorway now, her eyes fixated on the floor, unwilling or perhaps unable to meet my gaze.

I turn back to Mica, seething. "You need to get the hell out of our apartment."

"Can we talk about this like adults?"

"Get the fuck out!" I shout, my anger giving way to strength.

"Really, Lil?" He shakes his head, disappointment lacing his tone. "Because there are only two of us who pay rent here. And neither of them is you."

The words strike me right in the center of my chest. If it's possible for a heart to shatter into three distinct pieces, I swear that mine just did.

"Fuck you," I manage to spit out.

"Wait . . . shit." He sighs, rubbing at his temples. "I'm sorry, that didn't—"

"You know what? You're right," I cut in, my voice devoid of emotion. "I should leave so you two can fuck in peace."

I push past Shannon's doorway, my footsteps echoing through the otherwise silent apartment as I head in the direction of my bedroom.

"Jade, I'm so sorry," Shannon calls after me, her voice filled with regret. "He's right, it was just a careless mistake. It won't happen again."

They both follow me to my room, their apologies failing to make an impact as I kneel beside my dresser, haphazardly shoving my belongings into a duffel bag. There's no way I can stay here tonight . . . not after everything that's happened.

"Look, sis, I'm sorry," Mica insists again, desperation seeping in. "Just please stay."

"I really can't be here right now," I choke out, clumsily making my way back to the living room.

"Where are you going, then?" Mica asks, running a ragged hand through his hair. "To West's?"

"It's none of your business where I'm going," I snap back, my patience worn thin. "Now, if you'll excuse me."

I shove past them one last time, my grip tightening around the handle of my duffel bag as I step out into the cool night air. The door slams shut behind me, effectively cutting off any further attempts at apologies.

I'm officially out of patience, out of shits to give.

Once I reach the edge of our parking lot, I pull out my phone to call a cab. As the screen lights up, illuminating the darkened street, I blink my bleary, tear-soaked eyes and scroll through my contact list.

Where the hell am I going to stay tonight?

I dial Maya's number first. As soon as her laughter rings in my ear, competing against the loud bass of nightclub music, I know she's not available. Despite her chirpy invitation for me to join the party, that's not where I need to be at this moment.

Sophie, on the other hand, doesn't even pick up. A few Instagram posts later, I find out she's skipped town for the weekend, and a pang of loneliness echoes through me.

That only leaves me with a few other colleagues from the newspaper. Even as the thought crosses my mind, I wince. They aren't really close friends, just coworkers. The last thing I want is to share this heartbreak, this disgrace, with them.

The cab driver's voice interrupts my spiraling thoughts. "Do you have a destination?" he asks, looking at me through the rearview mirror.

I think for a moment, then blurt out the first place that comes to mind. "Can you take me on campus? To the Hayworth Building?"

It's a little past midnight when I finally stumble into the news-room, fumbling with my all-access pass as my hands tremble.

Inside, I'm greeted by a dark figure looming by the entrance. "God! You scared me," I gasp, clutching my chest. "What are you even doing here so late?"

Garrett, ever the diligent worker, merely shrugs. "I'm finishing up some editing for our next issue."

"In the middle of the night on a Saturday?"

"I work best at night," he grumbles, "Not that it's any of your business. Why are *you* here?"

I bristle at his question. "Is that any of *your* business?"

His eyes flicker down to my tear-streaked face. "You're crying in my newsroom, Jade," he points out bluntly. "I think you've made it my business."

I swipe at the fresh tears staining my cheeks, my face heating under his gaze. "It just—it seemed like a good spot to come and think," I admit, sounding pathetic even to my own ears.

"Think about what?"

I rub my forehead. "If this is going to be an interrogation . . . then I'm just gonna leave."

"No, it's fine." He shoots me a strange look, then, "Stay. I won't ask you any more questions."

"Good, then."

"Good." His footsteps are heavy, following a deliberate step-by-step pattern as he trails over to his desk and takes a seat. He pulls a notebook from a mismatched stack, rifling through papers and jotting down notes.

"So, do you like . . . live here or something?" I ask, desperately needing to keep the conversation going, distracting myself from the reality of the situation.

He rolls his eyes, but there's a hint of amusement in his voice. "Oh, so you can ask me questions?"

"You're not the one crying."

He chuckles, shaking his head. "No, I don't live here. But I do live nearby, just off University Ave."

"Oh," I say, not sure where I'm going with this conversation. It's either small talk or a complete breakdown. I choose the former. "Those seem nice."

"They are."

"Do you—are you in a studio, or . . ."

"No, I live in a one-bedroom."

"Very cozy."

He tosses the notebook onto his desk, giving me his full attention. "Jade, did you need somewhere to stay tonight?"

I hesitate, then sigh, a slight nod of my head serving as my confession. "If you're offering."

A corner of his lip quirks up in a half-smile. "I thought you hated me."

"Oh, God, am I really that obvious?"

His brow lifts as he poses the question, "So, you do hate me?"

"I don't . . . hate you," I stammer. "It's just, I think you're kind of a little bit . . . sexist. But maybe we should wait on this conversation."

"I'm not gonna make you sleep on the streets just because you called me sexist."

Crossing my arms, I give him a defiant look. "I wouldn't be sleeping on the streets regardless."

"Fine," he says, an amused smirk playing on his lips. "Enlighten me anyway. Why do you think I'm sexist?"

"Uh, because you are," I snap back, frustration coloring my words. "You continuously refuse to let me write about football, always passing those pieces to the male reporters under the guise of them having 'more experience.' And Liam's articles?" I let out a huff of disbelief. "They're subpar at best."

Rising from my chair, I pace the room. "And let's not forget how you consistently assign me the most boring stories. You do realize no one wants to read about new cutlery or turnstiles or . . . bricks in red square, right? It's ridiculous!"

He leans back in his chair, barely containing his grin. "Jade, I assign you those articles because you're one of the best reporters we have."

"That doesn't even make sense," I splutter, caught off guard by his counterargument.

"Those topics are assigned to the *Daily* by the university. We're obliged to cover them. And I assign them to you because you have the knack for making even the most mundane interesting."

My pacing slows as his words sink in. "Oh."

"Yeah, oh."

"What about football, then? Why can't I cover that?"

"Because weekly sports coverage isn't that challenging," he says dismissively. "Any generic reporter could write those articles."

"That's the issue." I drag a weary hand down my face. "You just said any 'generic reporter' could write those pieces. Aren't we, as women, just as capable of regurgitating stats as male reporters?"

"Yeah, you are."

"What?"

"I said, yes . . . you are," he repeats, his gaze never leaving mine. "I didn't realize it was *this* important to you."

Frustration bubbles up inside me. "I've been practically begging to cover their games for years!"

"I know," he says simply. "I thought it was more of a passing interest."

"Garrett, I love football," I reiterate, gritting my teeth. "And I hate that all our sports coverage is handled by men."

"Then, I guess we'll have to fix it."

"We?"

"Look, Jade." He sighs heavily. "I'm in this room almost every night, working myself to the bone. Things can slip through the cracks. You see issues that I overlook. How about you help me fix them?"

His suggestion leaves me reeling. "Seriously?"

"Why not?" He shrugs, a devil-may-care attitude plastered on his face. "What do I have to lose?"

"Power, maybe?" I ask with a snort. "Control over your subordinates?"

"You really think I'm the villain, don't you?"

"Well, that depends. Are you going to let me sleep on the couch tonight, or is it the floor?"

"The floor," he fires back, grinning wide. "Definitely the floor."

Chapter Twenty-Nine
WEST

LAST NIGHT WAS ROUGH. I ditched the banquet and got shitfaced out of my mind. Then I collapsed onto my bed, alone, to toss and turn for the rest of the night.

Jade dumped me. She broke up with me and walked away, just as I fucking deserved. I should've known this was coming because what we had was too good to be true. And I fucked it all away from the very beginning.

If Jade gave me another chance, I'd move heaven and earth to win back her trust. I gave her the space she asked for last night, even though every fiber of my being screamed to beg for her forgiveness. To drop to my knees and plead.

I want her back. Hell, I need her back.

With the dawn comes a semblance of sobriety, enough to get my hungover self out of bed by nine. A shower helps, washing away last night's regrets, scrubbing clean the past month's mistakes until my skin is nearly raw. Cleaned up and dressed, I head straight to Jade's place.

If she tells me to get lost . . . if she says that this is over for good, then I'll have no choice but to respect that. But I'm not throwing in the towel just yet. Not until she gives the final verdict.

I take a deep breath, trying to steady the adrenaline coursing through me. I wipe my sweaty palms on my jeans, and with shaky resolve, I knock on her front door.

Shannon answers almost instantly.

"Oh, West," she says, disappointment clouding her face. "Good morning."

"Hey, Shan," I say, my voice tense, words shooting out like bullets. My gaze slips past her, scanning the apartment for Jade. "Could you maybe ask Jade if she'll see me? If she's up for it."

Her brows knit together, a soft sigh escaping her. "She's, uh—she's not home, West," she says, shifting uncomfortably on her feet. "I sort of assumed she'd be with you."

My heart jolts. "She didn't tell you about our breakup?"

She presses her lips into a flat line. "She did."

Disoriented, I struggle to find my footing in this conversation. "Okay, then," I manage, my voice heavy with confusion. "I guess I'll give it another shot later."

"No, you don't understand . . ." She trails off, a shadow crossing her face. "Jade didn't spend the night here."

"What do you mean? She didn't come back home last night?"

"No, she came home," she quickly clarifies. "But she didn't stay. She said she couldn't bear it here."

The world seems to tilt on its axis. "God." My hand skates across my forehead, pressing into the tension lines. "This is all on me."

"No, it's on me," she says, her eyes darkening with a sorrow I hadn't seen before. "I messed up big-time."

With a bitter chuckle, I stand a little straighter, my back going rigid. "Well, welcome to the club. What did you do?"

She seems to shrink, her eyes dropping to the floor. "I'd rather not get into it."

"Then can you at least tell me where she stayed last night?"

"I have no clue," she says, her voice dropping to an uneasy whisper. "She turned her phone off. Radio silence since then."

I swear under my breath. "She's . . . she's safe, right?"

"Jade can handle herself," she says, yet her voice carries a tremor. "But, yeah, I can't help but worry."

I draw in another slow, steadying breath, my mind tumbling into a dark place. Had she picked up a stranger from a bar? Or, worse, was she lying somewhere hurt and alone? My chest aches at the possibilities.

"Should we do something?" I ask, frustration gnawing at my edges.

Her eyes flit toward the living room. "Want to come in? Maybe wait for her?"

I stiffen, shaking my head. "It's probably best if we don't ambush her."

"You're right. I can always try—"

Her words are cut short by a derisive scoff. "You've gotta be kidding me."

I whirl around, coming face-to-face with Jade. She's strung out, twisted curls falling out of her loose ponytail. She's wearing mismatched pajamas, and her eyes tell a tale of a sleepless night, red-rimmed and shadowed. Yet, even in this disheveled state, she remains the most beautiful woman I've ever seen.

Her gaze is a storm, her steps purposeful as she maneuvers around me, entering her apartment like a force of nature.

"Jade," Shannon breathes out, relief evident. "We were so worried about you."

"We?" Jade scoffs, her laugh a bitter note in the air. "You mean, you and West? Or you and my brother?"

I blink, completely taken aback. "Your brother's here?"

"I don't know if he's still here," she fires back, her voice biting. "Shan, why don't you fill us in?"

Shannon shrinks, looking smaller than before. "He checked into a hotel right after you left."

"How sweet of him."

Shannon reaches out. "Jade, I'm so—"

"Look, I just can't right now," Jade cuts her off, shaking her head. She steps back, distancing herself physically and emotionally. "I get it, Shan. I know my brother; I know what he's like. This is what he does. I'm angry at you, sure, but I can't blame you for what happened."

My mind spins, pieces of the puzzle clicking into place. Last night was a fucking roller coaster for Jade, in more ways than one.

"When can we talk about this?" Shannon pleads, a hint of desperation in her voice.

"I don't know." Jade rakes a hand through her hair, her fingers tangling in the wild curls before yanking out the elastic. As she pulls her hair into a neat bun, she continues. "Maybe once I've had a chance to digest everything. Maybe when my ex-boyfriend isn't standing there, eavesdropping on every word between us."

"Fuck, I'm sorry," I stammer, the words lodging in my throat. "Do you want me to leave?"

Jade's eyes pin me in place, a piercing gaze that burns right through me. "Why don't you just say what you came here to say?"

In the background, Shannon clears her throat, a loud, awkward sound in the silence. "I'll, um—I'll just be in my room."

"Good idea," Jade says, her words pointed and crisp. She seems to be holding herself together by sheer force of will.

Once we're alone, my gaze traces the contours of Jade's face. She's a picture of devastation, a testament to a sleepless night. It's as if a hurricane swept through her and left only wreckage in its wake.

"Are you okay?" I ask, the words tasting bitter on my tongue.

She laughs, a harsh, grating sound. "Hell no, I'm not okay. I mean, fuck, did you use your context cues? Figure out what happened between Ace and Shan last night?"

"Yeah, I got that part," I manage to say, my voice a soothing contrast to her fiery outburst. "Where'd you end up staying?"

She crosses her arms, her body language defensive. "If that's what you wanna talk about, then fine. I stayed with Garrett."

"Your editor, Garrett? You hate that guy."

A smirk spreads across her face. "Not after last night."

"Wait, what are you saying? You didn't . . .?" I trail off, my eyes searching her face, desperate for a hint, a clue.

"Didn't what? Sleep with him?" she asks, her tone devoid of any warmth. "So what if I did?"

My mind reels. I can't believe it, can't rationalize it. Would she really go to him, of all people?

"If you did, then . . . fuck, Jade," I breathe out, blood pulsing behind my temples. "You dumped me, so I guess that's your right."

"So, if I tell you I slept with Garrett, then that's it? You'll let me go?"

"Fuck no, I won't," I say, my voice firm despite the knot in my stomach. "Even if you slept with Garrett, it doesn't change how I feel. I still want you back. But the thought of you turning to him of all people . . . it's driving me up the wall."

Her voice breaks, the façade crumbling. "What did you expect me to do? You broke my trust. And then, to come home and find Ace and Shan together . . . It's just too fucked-up."

"I can't even begin to imagine the hurt you're feeling right now. Lying to you was the worst mistake I've ever made. You mean everything to me, Jade."

Her posture deflates, crossed arms falling to her sides. "I just wish that you hadn't done it."

"I wish that, too."

She's silent for a moment, then, "Okay."

"You know, I used to think the Trade was just a silly tradition. When I was a freshman, it seemed like a rite of passage. But now, because of you, I see how wrong it was."

Her voice is thick, weighed down by hurt and exhaustion. "I'm glad you learned your lesson. It's just a little too late for us."

A pang of despair hits me. "Is there nothing I can do to earn back your trust?"

"Honestly, I don't know. But I know I can't look at you the same way anymore."

"If you tell me to leave you alone, then I'll respect that," I promise, working to keep my voice steady.

"I just need time, West," she says. "I don't know how much, and I can't say how long. I'm not saying we'll never get back together, but I know I need some time apart right now . . . without you showing up at my apartment unannounced."

"I can give you that."

She gestures toward the open doorway. "Then you should probably go."

I clench my fists, fighting the urge to reach out, to pull her close one more time. "Can I just say one more thing before I leave?"

"Sure," she murmurs, her voice barely audible.

"Jade, I'm so damn sorry that I hurt you." My voice is heavy with sincerity, the truth of my words ringing out in the empty space between us. "It's the last thing I ever wanted to do."

She stares at me for what feels like an eternity, her teeth worrying over her bottom lip. "I know that."

"And, fuck." I breathe out the word, my gaze roaming across her features, drinking her in. "I really hope, for Garrett's sake, that you didn't sleep with him last night. But if you did, just know that it doesn't change anything between us. I want you. I want all of you. And nothing you can do will change that."

She simply stares, lost for words as I ready myself to leave. I swallow the lump in my throat, reminding myself that if she doesn't want me to beg, I'll grant her the space she needs.

But Jade . . . she's it for me.

She was yesterday, she is today, and she will be tomorrow. No matter how long it takes, I know the two of us belong together. I knew it from the first moment my lips touched hers. This girl unhinges me, shatters me from the inside out, forces me to see the world differently.

And I know that she feels the same way about me; I've seen the look on her face every time we're together. Maybe, if I'm lucky enough, someday she'll look at me that way again.

Until then, I'll wait.

Chapter Thirty
JADE

I DIDN'T SLEEP with Garrett last night, nor would I ever.

The truth settles heavily in the vacant space of my mind, filling the silence like the echoes of a ghost. Restless and uneasy, I spent the night tossing and turning on his pull-out couch, in an apartment tainted with the lingering scent of his partner's cologne and the remnants of takeout containers.

So yeah, I let West think that something more happened between Garrett and me. I neither confirmed nor denied his assumptions because, truthfully, it's none of his damn business. And yet, despite my resolve, I can't deny the pang of regret that slices through me at the sight of his shocked expression, the hurt in his eyes.

I'm not intentionally trying to hurt him, not in a vindictive or spiteful sort of way. It's just that West no longer has the right to know certain things—when, where, and with whom I decide to have sex. Not that I can even fathom being with anyone else in the foreseeable future.

Moving on from West is going to be torture, especially because deep down, I know he still wants me, desires me in every way. And he does seem genuinely remorseful for what he's done.

But it doesn't change the harsh reality. West is a liar, a user, a manipulator. I need space from him, space to heal and breathe again. If only that space could also distance me from my roommate and my brother, the tangled web of their involvement.

In a twisted way, though, I understand that they're the crutch I'll need to lean on as I navigate through this chapter.

Mica royally fucked up, thinking with his dick instead of his head or his heart. But tomorrow morning, he'll be boarding a flight and leaving town, so today is our chance to mend the fences, to rebuild the trust that was shattered. That's the only reason I agreed to meet up with him for dinner.

"Hey!" Mica practically leaps up from his booth, his arms outstretched. I slide into the opposite seat, my body reflexively pulling away from his attempt at a comforting hug.

"Hi" is all I manage to muster.

His apology is quick, earnest. "I'm a dipshit and an asshole. What can I do to fix this?"

I sigh, my fingers drumming an anxious rhythm against my thigh. "Why'd you have to go there? Especially when I begged you not to?"

"I know I fucked up. The problem is . . . I wasn't even making a conscious decision to ignore your wishes. I'm not trying to make excuses, but it just fucking happened."

"How does that just happen? You tripped and fell into her bed?"

"That's not what I mean. Look, there was some . . . tension the first time I came to visit you. I know you didn't see it, but you left us alone together a handful of times."

"What?" I scoff incredulously. "So, during those five or ten minutes, you just had to fight the urge to jump each other's bones? Is that what you're trying to say?"

"Not exactly." His answer is vague, convoluted. "I don't know, sis. Have you ever felt this strong attraction to someone? Like fuck, you don't know where it comes from, but . . . for some reason, you just want that person."

My body reacts before I can stop it, a nervous shift in my seat at his question. "Uh—"

But he's quick to backpedal, his face crumpling. "Fuck, wait. Please don't answer that."

"So, you're saying you want to . . . be with Shan?"

"No." He adamantly shakes his head. "It was an intense physical attraction, but I never should have acted on it. Not when I knew it could affect our relationship."

"But you did it anyway."

"Yeah, I did," he concedes. "It was a mistake. I won't make the same one twice."

"Tell me that you didn't make any promises to Shan. If you hurt her, I'm not forgiving you so easily."

He shakes his head, a snort escaping him. "I didn't make any promises. Actually, there wasn't much . . . talking between us at all."

"Oh, ew." The thought of them together elicits another eye roll. "You know, I'm still really mad at you."

"I know," he says simply. "And Lil, I'm sorry about the rent comment. That was uncalled for."

"Yeah, it was. But I probably shouldn't have screamed in your face like that either."

He shrugs as if it was nothing. "I deserved it."

While his comment truly hurt my feelings, I suppose I could've held my tongue. We have a few unspoken rules between us, one of them being to never swear at each other or resort to hurtful phrases like "fuck you" and "I hate you."

But last night, Mica seemed to believe that breaking that rule was warranted, so I'll let it slide this time.

"True." I smirk, turning to the menu. "Just so you know, I'm ordering two dinners tonight. Maybe a lobster appetizer. Oh, and dessert. I'm definitely getting dessert."

He chuckles, relief washing over his face. "Get whatever you want. I doubt two dinners make up for what I did."

"Damn right, it doesn't," I confirm with a harsh laugh. "You're gonna be groveling for years, pal. Years."

"If that's what it takes."

As Mica's plane takes off, cool relief washes over me. Although we didn't part on an outright positive note, things are decidedly better than where we started.

Mica's my brother, my partner-in-crime, my confidant, and I love him fiercely. But that doesn't erase the fact that he betrayed me. While love might help pave a path to forgiveness, it isn't an instant cure for the raw wounds he inflicted.

I need time. Time to mend, to regain balance, to process.

And now, Shannon is another thorny issue I need to address. I told her that I don't blame her for falling into Mica's well-laid trap. After all, he's a football superstar in his prime, effortlessly charming, and unfairly handsome. How could I hold that against her?

But in a way, I still do. There's a simmering resentment there, an unpleasant undercurrent to the hurt. She should've known better. We're roommates, close friends. She should've realized that getting involved with my brother crosses an invisible line for me. It wasn't just about them—it was about the trust we had, the mutual respect. And now, that's been irrevocably shattered, leaving me to pick up the pieces.

It seems that everyone is hell-bent on crossing my boundaries, on spinning my life into chaos. The painful reminders are everywhere, forcing me to constantly reevaluate my relationships—with my brother, with Shannon, and especially with West.

Still, I have my professional duties to fulfill. My unfinished article on the banquet demands attention, and thanks to my impulsive midnight chat with Garrett, I've secured coverage of all of next season's football games. It should be thrilling, but instead, it holds the promise of constant, painful reminders of West's betrayal.

To make things easier on everyone, I've decided to conduct only two interviews about the banquet. One with Noah Elliot, the starting quarterback, and the other with Vance Donahue, the other mastermind behind the event. I simply can't bring myself to stomach an interview with Cam or anyone else from the football team. But life and, more importantly, my job have to go on.

Over the following week and a half, I skillfully navigate around any potential confrontations with Shannon or West. I exchange the library for the newsroom, immersing myself in my assignments.

Garrett and I work in harmony, laboring long hours to devise a fairer, more balanced system. The effort is significant, but he willingly agrees to all my suggestions as long as I spearhead the changes.

As a team, Garrett and I click in a way that's undeniable. We complement each other's strengths and work seamlessly together. A part of me can't help but wonder what could've been if we had found this rhythm years ago. But dwelling on what-ifs won't change the present circumstances.

One morning, after another late-night working session, I decide to break away from the routine and pick up some coffee. It's high time I return the favor to Garrett for all the in-office lattes he's made for me.

Stepping into the bustling café, I join the line, ready to place our orders.

As I wait, the distinct sound of a throat clearing behind me sends a shiver down my spine. It's a sound I know all too well. I turn around slowly, my heart pounding a frenzied beat against my ribs.

Of course, it's West. A mix of emotions courses through me—fear, longing, resentment—all jumbled into a chaotic mess. His presence catches me off guard, reopening a wound that I'm trying desperately to heal.

He's breathtaking, as always, with his dark, tousled hair and deep caramel eyes. But upon closer inspection, there's an unmistakable hint of exhaustion etched into his features—dark circles under his eyes and a furrow to his brow. He looks worn, fragmented, and still, somehow, absolutely captivating.

The silence stretches on until it's West who breaks it. His murmured "Hey" falls between us, landing like honey on my bruised heart.

"Hi," I murmur.

A slight twitch of his lips produces a smile that's too gentle, too sweet. "I haven't seen you at the library in a while."

"Yeah," I breathe out. "I've been studying in the newsroom."

His expression shifts. There's an unspoken grief in his eyes, a flicker of regret as he asks, "Spending all your time with Garrett these days?"

I take a step back, creating some space between us. "Let's not go there,"

His gaze drops, and he audibly swallows. "Right. Of course."

I chew on the inside of my cheek, my heart pounding wildly in my chest. This encounter has stirred up emotions I thought I had buried. I need to regain control of the situation before it spirals out of hand. "Alright," I say, my tone guarded. "Well, this has been fun, but I've got to—"

"Can I just ask you one question?" he cuts me off, a nervous quirk in his brow.

"What?"

"Does he make you feel the way that I did?" he asks, voice low, an uncertain tone I've never heard from West before.

My heart fractures, splintering into the pieces I hastily patched together. "You mean used, lied to, and manipulated? No, I can't say that he does."

A flicker of sadness passes across his face, and the tiny flame in his eyes goes out. "Okay," he murmurs softly. "I'm glad you're happy, then."

And with that, he turns and walks away, leaving me standing there, my heart heavy with a bittersweet ache.

You know what? Fuck you, West. Because I'm not happy. Not without you.

Why did he have to go and ruin everything we had? Why did he have to betray my trust? For a fleeting moment, I allowed myself to believe that it was possible to have everything I ever wanted in a relationship.

And now, I'm left feeling lost, adrift in a sea of uncertainty. I don't know what I'm doing or where I'm going. His absence is a constant ache, a void I can't seem to fill. Part of me still yearns for him, for the connection we shared.

But I know I can't bring myself to trust him yet. Because right now, I can't even trust myself.

Chapter Thirty-One
WEST

THREE WEEKS.

It's been three soul-crushing, agonizingly long weeks since Jade left me, saying she needed time away. Time away from me and the mess I had unwittingly created.

Her parting words still echo in my ear. I try to imagine her healing, her moving forward, but the image only brings forth a wall of sharp, jagged pain. Three weeks of silence to me feels like three weeks of giving up.

But damn it, there's no way I'm giving up, not when it comes to her, to us. No way in hell.

I'm determined to give her all the space and time she needs, as much as it tears me apart. But how is she ever going to find forgiveness in this overwhelming silence? In this physical and emotional distance?

Especially with that smug, insufferable Garrett strutting around, standing where I once stood. Fuck that guy.

"West, get your sorry ass up." Cam's voice booms, bouncing off the walls of our cramped living room. "We're going to Lucky's tonight."

My limbs are heavy. Fatigue etches into every muscle fiber. I lazily stretch my arms across the back of the couch, sinking further into the worn-out cushions. "No, thanks, man."

"Dude." His voice carries a warning note. "We gotta get you back out there. I mean, you said it yourself—Jade's moved on."

My throat tightens at the reminder. "I know, Cam." My words are barely more than a whisper. I tilt my head back, staring at the ceiling as if it holds the answers. "But it's not over for me."

"Really?" His voice drips with disbelief. "Didn't she get with someone else like the same night you guys broke up?" He doesn't even attempt to veil his pity. "I'm sorry, but that's pretty brutal."

The reality of the breakup, the sheer force of it, slices through me. The dark abyss of that night at the banquet, of finding solace in the false cheeriness of alcohol, still lingers. The days after were no different—just another hangover punctuated by my broken spirit.

Damn it all . . . how would anyone react if the girl of their dreams dumped them and started sleeping with someone else? It was only natural that I sought oblivion, that I spilled my guts to my best friend in my drunken haze.

At first, Cam was a little pissed that I'd confided to Jade about the Trade. But his annoyance melted away into sympathy, understanding. He's been my rock, then and now. His personal mission: to drag me kicking and screaming out of this hell.

"She's still figuring out what she wants," I say, clinging onto this belief like a lifeline. "I'm just . . . I'm giving her space."

"Giving her space to figure shit out or giving her space to get with someone else?"

"Fuck, I don't know," I grumble, my voice heavy with frustration. "Both, I guess."

"Do you think she'd be all over this new guy if she wanted to work things out? Because I don't," he tells me, shaking his head. "So let Jade do Jade. You, on the other hand, need some help getting out of your funk."

A humorless snort escapes me. "And you think you can help me?"

"I think Lucky's can help you—the alcohol, the team, the jersey chasers. They can all help you."

"Fine, man," I say, exhaustion lacing my tone. "I'll go to Lucky's, but you need to forget about the girls."

His grin widens, triumphant. "Alright. Boys' night, then. I'll call the team and get the ball rolling."

"Whatever," I grumble, the bitter taste of defeat sitting heavy on my tongue.

With a groan, I force myself off the couch, attempting for the first time in weeks to look presentable. Whatever it takes to move past this feeling, this wretched, consuming sadness. Whatever it takes to mend my shattered heart.

By the time Cam and I have settled into a high table, nearly half of my teammates have already shown up. Sure, it's a typical Saturday night here, but God, it feels alien to me now, like I'm a stranger intruding on a secret gathering.

Especially when I take note of the swarm of girls circulating around us.

It's as though we've got some bright, glaring neon sign hanging over our heads, an irresistible beacon for every jersey chaser in the place.

Cradling my second beer of the night, I barely register the girl sliding into the spot beside me. The first thing that strikes me about her is her cropped black hair, sharp and fierce. It gives her an uncanny resemblance to a younger Zoë Kravitz.

The proximity, however, is not as appealing. She's so close I can feel her warmth seeping into me, and it's pretty fucking clear it's no accident.

A wide-eyed glance in Cam's direction pleads for help, but the bastard just winks back at me, thoroughly amused by my discomfort. Internally groaning, I inch away from the Zoë look-alike, a move that only prompts her to close the distance between us again.

The awkward dance continues until a throat clearing to my side saves me from the embarrassment.

It's our QB, Noah Elliot, whose voice cuts through the heavy din. "Look who just showed up." His head nods subtly toward the bar entrance.

My gaze follows his indication, my heart hitching as it falls on those unmistakable dark curls, that breathtaking face. Those long, tan legs on display beneath a tiny skirt are a painful reminder of what I've lost.

"So much for getting back out there tonight," Cam grumbles, the smugness from earlier replaced with a thin veil of sympathy.

"What the hell's she doing here?" My demand comes out strangled, a knot forming in my chest.

"Fuck if I know, man." He shrugs, looking as clueless as I feel. "You think Shan brought her?"

I strain to get a better look, recognizing the two girls who accompanied Jade to the scrimmage. "Nah, she's with some other friends."

"Just pretend like she's not here." Elliot's advice grates against my already fraying nerves.

Easier said than done. Even in the jam-packed bar, Jade's the only one I can see, the only one I want to see. Her presence seems to swallow the room, and memories flood in—tidal waves of recollection that threaten to drown me.

Her black attire, the cascade of curls down her back, the faint red lipstick accentuating her full lips . . . lips that I used to know by heart. Fuck, how I miss kissing her.

I know it's only a matter of time before she sees me, and the last thing I want is to be caught gawking like a lovesick fool. So, I tear my gaze away from her and back to my friends. I reach across the table and snatch Cam's beer, downing it in two quick gulps.

"The fuck, bro?" he exclaims, looking at his now-empty glass with an accusing glare.

"Go get another one," I bark, suddenly impatient. My wallet is in my hand before I can think twice about it, and I'm flicking my credit card at him.

Rolling his eyes, Cam pushes away from the table and ambles toward the bar. As he leaves, I can't help but let my gaze drift back to Jade. She's at the other end of the bar, clutching her cocktail in one hand, a radiant smile on her face as she absently twists a curl between her fingers.

As though drawn by the intensity of my scrutiny, Jade's head jerks up, her eyes meeting mine. A jolt of recognition fires between us, searing through my chest. In this moment, where it's just us, it feels as if time itself has stopped. There's a pulse, an energy, a live wire connecting us, causing every thought, every breath to escape me.

Then, out of nowhere, the spell is shattered . . . because Zoë's hand darts up to fuck with my hair. My senses return as a surge of annoyance pricks my skin.

Twisting toward her, I manage to withhold a grimace, her brazen familiarity irritating me. I catch her wrist, removing her hand. "What are you doing?" I ask, my words clipped, every ounce of my attention already aching to return to Jade.

Her lips twist into a pout. "Sorry, your hair was in your eyes."

"Sure it was," I say dryly, letting out an exasperated sigh. I can't help but cast a quick glance back to where Jade was standing, only to find that she's already melted away into the sea of bodies. A bitter curse slips past my lips.

My eyes frantically skim the room, my heart pounding wildly in my chest. They halt abruptly at the sight of Jade. She's sequestered some faceless man from the crowd and is now pulling him onto the dance floor.

Hell, no.

Ignoring the girl beside me, I make a beeline for the bar and order a shot of whiskey. I knock it back, my throat burning, my eyes never leaving Jade as she sways with the stranger. Her body moves against him, her arms coiling around his neck, the sight tearing at my insides.

"Bro, get it together," Cam warns, materializing next to me, his voice strained with concern. "You're making an ass out of yourself."

"Does it look like I give a fuck?" I snap, snatching his beer again.

He grumbles something about me drinking all his booze. "You brought me here," I remind him bitterly. "And now I have to watch Jade grinding with some asshole. I think it's the least you can do."

"Maybe it'll help if you stop acting like her stalker."

"I think she's just jealous," I mutter, more to myself than him.

"Sure, man," he says, shaking his head. "Just keep torturing yourself." With that, he gives me a harsh pat on my shoulder and makes his way back to our table.

As he walks away, I can't help but look back at Jade. She's whispering something into the guy's ear. Then she pulls away, prying his greedy hands off her. She slips out of his grasp and makes a beeline toward the restroom.

For a moment, I contemplate the consequences of following her. Yes, it would be an absolute stalker move. But a nagging voice in the back of my mind tells me she wants me to follow her. She's playing a game here, and I'm too far gone to not play along.

I take a deep breath, then set off after her, weaving through the crowd until I reach the empty corridor. Leaning against the wall, I try to look casual.

When Jade finally emerges from the restroom, her sigh tells me she isn't surprised to see me waiting.

"Very creepy, West," she says, her voice tinged with a mix of annoyance and something else I can't quite decipher.

"What are you doing here?" I find myself asking. It's not a great opener, I'll admit it, but it's the only thing that seems to make sense in this moment.

"Drinking, dancing," she deadpans. "What does it look like I'm doing?"

"You know what I mean. Why here at Lucky's? You know my boys are always here."

I take a step closer to her. She doesn't back away but raises a brow, clearly unimpressed. With a scoff, she says, "My bad. I didn't realize you and your *boys* owned the place."

"You sure about that?"

"Sophie and Maya wanted to come here, okay?" she finally admits, her voice a notch quieter. "They're on the prowl for athletes tonight."

Her explanation barely registers. All I can focus on is how close we are. She's wearing my favorite skirt, the one she wore the last time we were together—when I fucked her in the bathroom at the Cathouse. "And you definitely weren't hoping I'd be here."

"No," she argues, eyes defiant. "In fact, I was hoping you wouldn't be."

Her denial does nothing to dampen the spark between us. I smirk, my gaze locked on hers. "And you also didn't dance with that guy just 'cause you knew I was watching."

"I don't know what you mean."

"I know you, Jade," I tell her, voice low and sincere. "And I know how you get when you're jealous."

"Jealous?" She gives me a dramatic eye roll. "Please, like I would be jealous of that . . . girl. She can have you."

"I don't give a fuck about that girl," I say, my gaze steady. "I'd never touch her, not when I have you."

"You don't *have* me," she says, her words firm, but I can see the conflict in her eyes.

I take another step closer, backing her up until she's pressed against the wall, and her breath hitches in her throat. "I beg to differ."

"You're such an ass."

"And yet, you still want me." I barely register the words leaving my mouth, my fingers tugging at a loose curl. "Admit it."

A shudder courses through her as I bend closer. Her eyes, heavy with longing, stay fixated on mine, as if willing me to read the desires she's too guarded to voice.

"Maybe . . . maybe physically," she confesses, her voice catching in a way that suggests she's lying, and that scrap is just enough to give me hope. "But that's it."

"Yeah?" My voice drops to a husky whisper, the question on my tongue drenched in anticipation. "I can work with that."

She swallows hard, her eyes still half-lidded, staring up at me through a veil of longing and conflict. "I'm sure you can."

My fingertips trace her jawline. "Jade."

"I . . . *no.*" She shakes her head gently, gaze still glued to my lips. "This is a bad idea."

"If it's such a bad idea, then why is your hand on my chest?" I throw back at her. Each thud of my heart against her fingertips amplifies the raw, aching need coursing through me.

"Your hand's on my cheek!"

"Because I don't think this is a bad idea." I move another breath closer. "I think it's a great idea. I've been dying to kiss you ever since I saw you walk into this bar."

The second the words tumble out, her fingers clutch at my shirt, dragging my lips down to hers. The world shifts and narrows until there's only her—her taste, her touch, her scent consuming me whole. She kisses me with a kind of desperation that shatters my last shred of restraint.

My hand cups the back of her neck, and the other roams freely along her side. As I grip her hip and pull her against me, it feels as though I've finally come home. But then, she pulls away slightly, her breath heavy.

"We're not getting back together, you know?" she whispers.

My stomach drops, but I carry on kissing her anyway. If this is the last moment we'll have together, then I might as well take advantage of it.

Her arms are around my neck, my thigh wedged between her legs as I press her into the wall. The world outside this darkened hallway fades into a mere hum, the presence of others an afterthought against the draw of her body moving with mine.

My hands venture from her waist to her hips, and even though we're in a semi-public space, our actions border on indecent.

"Tell me this doesn't mean anything," she murmurs against my lips.

I respond by shifting my hands up, my palms coming to rest on the swell of her ass. A gasp slips from her as she instinctively wraps one leg around my thigh, her body rocking against me in sweet desperation. As I sneak my hand underneath her skirt, a soft sigh escapes her.

I break from the kiss, moving along her jaw, her cheek, until I reach the spot just below her earlobe. I let myself get lost in her, tracing my lips along her throat and marking her with my desire until she's whimpering beneath me.

"West, tell me," she manages to gasp.

"Lie to you?" I choke out, my voice ragged. "I promised I wouldn't do that again."

She goes still beneath me, eyes wide. She disentangles herself, the cool air suddenly stark against the heat of her body. "This was a mistake."

"Was it?" I challenge, a part of me unable to accept her denial. "It didn't feel like a mistake to me."

"Well, it was."

"Because of Garrett?"

She flinches, a visible sign of her discomfort. "*No.*"

I study her, my gaze tracing her body language—the deflated posture, the guarded look in her eyes, the reluctance in her voice. "There was never anything between you two, was there?"

"No," she finally admits, the word slipping out like a quiet sigh, her fingers nervously tugging her clothes back into place. "There wasn't."

"You just let me think there was," I say, the weight of my accusation hanging heavily between us. "For weeks."

"I don't owe you anything."

"You're right. You don't," I say, a heavy mixture of relief and indignation swirling in my gut. "But it's nice to know you haven't moved on."

"I . . . whatever."

I draw in a deep breath, readying myself for the inevitable heartache. "Tell me the truth . . . do you still want space from me? Because space is the last thing I want when it comes to you."

A heavy silence follows, the seconds stretching into a lifetime. "I'm not ready to forgive you, West."

"*Fuck*, I really wish you wouldn't call me that."

"What—your name?"

Her indifference punctures me. "You know, you're killing me tonight."

"I'm not intentionally trying to hurt you," she says, her voice softer now. "See, this is why we just shouldn't be around each other."

"That's so fucking false. I'd rather have you break my heart a hundred times over than spend another week without you."

Her eyes pinch shut at my confession. "Look—"

"No, I get it," I interrupt her. "You're still not ready. Just . . . go find your girls and have fun tonight. Dance with whoever you want. I'll mind my own fucking business."

With one last lingering look, I turn to leave, knowing that there's another stiff and solitary drink in my future.

"West," she calls after me. "I'm sorry."

I pause, my heart racing as I meet her eyes. "For what?"

"For kissing you tonight when I wasn't ready to."

With a bitter smile, I shake my head. "Don't apologize for going after what you want."

And when I finally leave her alone in that dark bathroom hallway, a cocktail of emotions surges through me, a chaotic symphony of heartbreak, hope, and resolve.

Jade hasn't moved on. Not in the slightest. And maybe, it's time for me to fight for her forgiveness, to fight for us, rather than stay drowning in my own self-pity.

Chapter Thirty-Two
JADE

LAST NIGHT WAS A TOTAL DISASTER. I shouldn't have let myself get anywhere near West, let alone share a kiss with him. The error wasn't just in that moment, though. It started when I allowed us to be alone in that dimly lit hallway, away from prying eyes.

He knew just where to place his hands, just how to touch me. He's an expert at pushing my buttons, at knowing exactly how to make me lose control. And he's infuriatingly good at it, too.

I won't lie. I did feel a sting of jealousy when I saw that pixie-haired girl sitting beside him. She was stunning and practically attached to his hip. She was running her fingers through his hair, attempting to mark her territory right there in front of me.

It was nothing but a petty, raw pang of envy, but it felt real.

It's not like I'm the only one who'd feel that way. No one wants to see their ex in the arms of someone else. But it's just that—a simple, involuntary reaction. Doesn't mean I'm looking to go back to him right away. It doesn't imply that his kiss magically glued together the pieces of my broken heart.

And it's even further from meaning that I'm able to trust him again.

He's done nothing to earn my forgiveness other than give me blanket apologies. I know I asked him to stay away, and he's done his part in respecting my wishes, but it's not enough to make me reconsider.

What really stings is not having anyone to share these feelings with. Sophie and Maya, my fair-weather friends, were too busy hooking up with West's pals last night.

Their initial advice? Fuck his best friend. Utterly useless. Still, I can't blame them—they were just looking for some fun. Besides, I've been avoiding spilling the real reason behind our split to anyone.

Not even to Shannon.

Instead, I've been keeping my distance, making excuses to stay out late, evading the issue for weeks. I want us to go back to being friends, to lean on her like I did before. Sure, she slept with my brother. It was a mistake, spurred by hormones, impulsiveness, and the classic Mica Jennings charm.

I could forgive her for that. I can see her regret, in the little notes she leaves me, in how she steps up with our shared duties, in how she gives me space when I need it. But my pride has been a barrier, stopping me from bridging the distance between us.

I know I'm blowing things out of proportion at this point. Mostly because I'm too scared to confront the reality of the situation, which is that I allowed myself to feel second rate. To let jealousy and comparison seep into my mind.

Because it hurts, so badly, thinking that West might have chosen Shannon, my friend and roommate, over me. Might have swapped me around like a playing card. And all of that just for one night with his gorgeous, redheaded, fairy dream girl. It was all before West and I were even a thing, but it still fucking stings.

So, when I found my brother in her room that night, it left me feeling like the second option all over again. The afterthought. It felt like my own sibling had chosen Shannon over me. But that's my issue, not hers. So, I need to let go of this bitterness, once and for all.

"Shan," I call, gently knocking on her bedroom door.

"Come in," she says cautiously.

I push open the door and step into her room, finding her

lounging on the bed. Her eyes meet mine, and I can sense the wariness in her gaze. "Hey . . . um, is everything okay?"

I offer a small smile, attempting to put her at ease. "I just wanted to talk. Are you . . . do you have time right now?"

"Absolutely." She shifts as she leans back against her headrest. Her eyes are earnest, her expression open. "Of course."

The simple affirmation prompts me to move. Quietly, I make my way toward her, awkwardly settling on the edge of her bed.

She draws in a slow, deep breath. "Where do I even start?"

"I guess . . . at the beginning?"

"Well," she says, her fingers playing anxiously with a strand of her hair. "There isn't much to it. You were there when I met your brother. There was a . . . a spark, I guess. Nothing big, just a little one. You were constantly leaving the dinner table to call West, so Mica and I . . . we flirted. Just harmless stuff."

"Were you planning on sleeping with him then?"

"God, no!" she assures me, fervently shaking her head. "It wasn't like that. It was just . . . the attention, I guess. Mica, your brother . . . he's larger than life. Tall, handsome, famous. Being noticed by someone like that is overwhelming."

"So, then, the night of the banquet?"

"I came home early from the event because of Cam—you know, he had to stay back to help with the cleanup. Mica was already on our couch when I walked in."

"Okay, that makes sense."

"I thought you were still staying with West. I told Mica you wouldn't be back until morning, assuming he'd call you right away to return. But he didn't. Instead, he suggested we watch a movie. One thing led to another, and we . . . ended up in my room."

"I think I've got the picture from there."

"I swear, Jade, it wasn't planned or anything," she rushes to clarify. "But I am truly, deeply sorry. I got caught up in the moment."

I meet her apology with a knowing look. "Believe me, I know what that feels like."

Her brow furrows. "You do?"

"Yeah, I may have kissed West at a bar last night."

"Oh, shit."

"It was a careless mistake. We were alone together, and . . . one thing led to another."

"Oh, Jade." Her eyes hold genuine concern as she asks, "Are you okay?"

"Not really," I say, honesty overriding my pride. I quickly steer the conversation back to her. "Shan, I want to tell you everything. But first, I need to ask—are you . . . are you still interested in my brother?"

"It was a onetime thing. Mica and I . . . we're not . . . we wouldn't be good together."

"Okay." Relief washes over me. "Then let's consider it water under the bridge. I'm sorry I didn't hear you out sooner. I just wasn't ready yet."

She dismisses me with a wave of her hand. "You don't have to apologize. I'm just glad we're finally talking about it."

"So am I."

"So, tell me what happened," she says, curiosity in her eyes. "Why did you guys break up? From the outside, it seemed like everything was going so well."

I guess it's my turn to be vulnerable. I swallow the lump in my throat before I ask, "Will you promise to keep what I'm about to tell you between us?"

"Sure, of course."

"The football team . . . they have this fucked-up tradition. That's why we broke up." My hands wring together anxiously in the middle of my lap. "It's a sort of game amongst the senior players. Every year, at the banquet, they try to switch dates. And . . . that's the only reason West invited me in the first place."

A range of emotions passes over her face as she processes my words. "Are you serious?"

"Yes," I say, voice small. "It's also why Cam invited you."

She stares at me in shock for a moment before whispering a breathless "Wow. So, they planned to just swap us for some random girls?"

"No, Shan," I shake my head, the truth tasting bitter on my tongue. "They planned to swap us for each other."

"Oh my God, Jade. Are you saying West wanted—"

"Yes, he was hoping he might get to spend the night with you," I awkwardly admit, unable to keep the tension from my voice. "But he told me that he called the whole thing off a long time ago. Actually, he ended things the night of the UFC fight. Before we were ever together."

A stunned whisper leaves her lips. "Damn. That's still . . . terrible. Every year, they just trade girls around like they're objects. That's so messed up."

"And West kept it from me until I practically begged him for the truth. The whole team was acting so fucking strange that night. Did you not pick up on it?"

"Not really." Her shoulders lift in a noncommittal shrug, a soft frown pulling at her lips. "I mean, I already know most of those guys. I guess I just thought they were being . . . friendly."

"Yeah, I guess I can see that."

"I'm so sorry you found out like this, though. West should've been up-front with you before things got serious."

A sad smile tugs at the corners of my mouth. "That's one of my biggest issues. I just . . . I thought my West was different. Knowing he chose to participate in all that bullshit just makes me see him in a different light."

She leans forward on the bed, patting my hand in a gentle, comforting touch. "Boys can be so thoughtless."

A reluctant chuckle escapes me. "You're telling me."

"I'm really sorry he hurt you. And I'm sorry that I somehow became tangled up in all this." She ducks her head, gaze dropping to our hands. "I can't even begin to imagine how complicated this makes things for you."

"Things are definitely a mess," I say. "But none of this is your fault. The blame lies solely with West."

"You mentioned you kissed him last night?"

"Yeah, another lapse in judgment."

She appraises me, her gaze thoughtful. "You don't think you'd ever want to try to work things out?"

"No, well . . . I don't know," I correct myself. With a sigh, I glance back at her. "Could you forgive your boyfriend if he did something like this?"

"That's not my call to make," she says softly. "You have every right to feel hurt and betrayed. If you don't think this is something you can forgive, then you don't have to."

"But before all of this, I was truly falling for him. Now, every time I think about him, about us, I feel torn. I want to be with him, but at the same time, I can't stand the sight of him."

"You're just not ready to let him go."

"Not yet." I press my lips together, biting the inside of my cheek. "I guess I'm waiting to see if he can somehow earn my forgiveness. If he sticks around once I'm done taking my space. Or if he just . . . lets it fade away."

"If he really cares, he won't let you go."

I toss myself back on her bed with a heavy sigh. "Maybe."

"Thank you for telling me." She gives me a gentle, genuine smile. "It means a lot that you could confide in me after everything."

I perch up onto my elbows. "How about we . . . I don't know, stay up and binge on junk food together?"

The laugh that escapes her is a warm, familiar sound, and I

realize just how much I've missed this in the last couple weeks. "I thought you'd never ask."

THE FOLLOWING MORNING, I'm rushing to make it to class on time and nearly trip over something on my doorstep. There, perched on the welcome mat, is an iced latte. I pick it up, noticing a small, folded note stuck to the bottom.

I crouch down to retrieve it, my fingers tracing over the hand-written letters. It's the first time I've ever seen West's handwriting, and the sight of it—so personal, so intimate—stirs a complex tangle of emotions in my chest. Part pain, part longing, it's an echo of our shared past and the uncertain future looming before us. With a deep breath, I unfold the note and carefully dissect the scribbled words:

> Jade—
> Our coffee deal was only fair play.
> And so is this—I'm not giving up on us, no matter what it takes.
> I'd do anything to earn your forgiveness.
> To show you how much I've changed since we first met.
> Let's start with something I should have done a long time ago.
> —Theo

Chapter Thirty-Three
WEST

THERE ARE two weeks left until this term ends, which means I have fourteen days to prove myself to Jade. To prove I deserve a second chance.

I have to make it through one last spring practice, Dayton's Spirit Night, and three grueling finals before summer hits. Before Jade leaves for Washington. Before training camp starts and I lose all sense of time.

But before all this can happen, there's one wrong I need to right.

I set up a meeting with both my team captains, Noah and Danny. While Noah was elected leader of the offense, my housemate spearheads the defensive team. If all else fails, I know I can count on them to have my back.

"What's this about?" Danny asks, settling into our living room couch.

"I want to put a lifetime ban on the Trade," I tell them, scrubbing a hand across my forehead. "I need your support bringing this to the team."

"Damn." Noah lets out a low whistle. "That's gonna be a hard sell."

I grit my teeth. "No shit."

"I'm fully behind that idea," Danny says, expression earnest. "Sofia thinks the whole thing is bullshit, anyway."

I arch a brow. "You told your girlfriend about it?"

"Of course." Danny gives me an affronted look. "I'm not gonna keep it a secret. Not when my teammates are making assholes of themselves right in front of her. Besides, she wouldn't tell anyone."

"Right." I purse my lips, stomach sinking. "The whole thing is fucked. We should have gotten rid of it a long time ago."

"I agree." Noah rubs the underside of his jaw. "But I think the team's gonna be pissed about breaking tradition. Especially all the rising underclassmen."

"Fuck that," I bite. "We'll make a new tradition. A competition that doesn't jeopardize our careers or make us look like total assholes."

"What do you propose?" Danny asks.

"Why don't we just let the team decide?"

"Okay, you have my support." Danny pushes off the couch, slinging his duffel over one shoulder. "We doing this after practice today?"

"That was the plan." I shift my gaze to Noah, awaiting his verdict. "You with us?"

"Fuck yeah, dude. Let's do this."

And so, after an exhausting final practice, we gather the team for a secret post-practice meeting, far from Coach's prying eyes. Noah, as our starting quarterback, takes the lead.

"Alright, guys, we have a new mandate for next year," he begins, cutting through the chatter. "We're getting rid of the Trade. We're here tonight to brainstorm other competition ideas for the banquet."

The room falls silent. So silent that the echo of a pin dropping would sound like a gong. The uncomfortable quiet only lasts for a moment before it's shattered by an objection.

"This is bullshit," McNair's voice cuts through the tension. "You doing this 'cause of Steph?"

"No," Noah says immediately, flicking a glance at me. I return his look with a silent nod of solidarity. "West proposed this idea. And both of your team captains are fully behind this decision."

The team explodes into a flurry of heated murmurs, a few enraged protests puncturing the charged atmosphere.

Miller, the absolute shithead, is the next to rise. "Of course you would fuck with the tradition," he bellows, his voice projecting over the crowd. "You'll all be graduating next year, and you all have girlfriends."

A wave of frustration sweeps over me. "It doesn't matter if we're single or not," I snap back. "It's some fucked-up shit, and we're not doing it anymore."

"We don't have to listen to you," McNair sneers, his voice dripping with contempt. "This is supposed to be our legacy for the underclassmen. It's tradition at Dayton, and you're not the one who gets to make decisions for the team."

A hot surge of determination burns through me. "Yeah, but you have to listen to your captains," I say, the words firm with conviction. "Noah and Danny agree with me on this."

Danny, always the mediator, jumps in. "He's right," he affirms, his tone leveled yet decisive. "Besides, if this is leaked, the women on this campus wouldn't touch you with a ten-foot pole."

McNair's response is a defiant cross of his arms. A silence drops over the room, heavy and expectant. I rake my gaze over each teammate, challenging them with a silent dare. Anyone else want to argue?

"If any of you decide to pull some shit next year, I'll personally ensure that Coach is made aware," I say, my voice slicing through the quiet. "I don't give a fuck if that incriminates me."

In the next moment, Noah steps up. "All in agreement, say aye."

The room pulses with energy as "Ayes" resound from every corner. I'm left stunned, a victorious grin threatening to break across my face. Satisfaction floods through me, washing away the tension that's been knotted in my gut for weeks now.

I know this was the right thing to do. And God, it was so much fucking easier than I could've ever imagined.

As the morning light filters in, I sit at my kitchen table, pen in hand, poring over a note for Jade. My phone lies nearby, having dictated my words via speech-to-text, and a small pile of discarded drafts gathers at my side. Each slipup results in another crumpled ball of paper, but I don't stop until my message is just right.

> Jade—
> Will you meet me at the batting cages for one more shot?
> Tomorrow morning—10:00am.
> I'll try my best not to strike out this time.
> —Theo

My palms are sweating, heart racing as I drop the coffee on her doorstep. It's a tricky balance, giving her the space she needs while subtly showing her I still care. Hell, I don't even know if she read the first note I left.

Maybe she tossed it in the trash. Maybe she'll toss this one as well.

If tomorrow comes without a word from her, I'll have to rethink my strategy. But time is against me. We're smack in the middle of Dead Week, the calm before the storm of finals, where procrastination runs the show.

The single highlight of this stressful week is Spirit Night, an event put together by the cheerleading team. It's meant to be a break in the chaos, a night where the entire campus comes together to let loose before diving headlong into the pressure of final exams. The event is filled with friendly competition, culminating in a bonfire under the stars.

Unfortunately, Coach Rodriguez has made it mandatory for our team to attend.

It's meant to be the last big blast before the end of the school year, and it's happening tonight. Under normal circumstances, I might be excited. But the thought of celebrating feels off, all things considered.

My phone buzzes, pulling me out of my thoughts, and an unexpected message lights up my screen.

JADE

I'll be there tomorrow, 10am

A rush of relief washes over me, followed by a strange fluttering of anticipation, a wishful longing for the girl who sets my world on fire.

I tuck my phone back in my pocket, a small grin tugging at my lips. On second thought, Spirit Night might not be so bad after all. Moreover, a night of friendly competition might be just what I need to keep me grounded until tomorrow.

A FEW HOURS LATER, I find myself smack-dab in the middle of a fierce game of tug-of-war. The cheerleaders herd us onto the field, placing the football and baseball guys against the ice hockey and men's soccer teams. You'd think it's a clean sweep for us, but the hockey guys pack a punch. Still, our linebackers come in clutch, pulling us to a last-minute victory.

Before I can even process the win, we're herded off to the next activity. I catch whispers of "balloon pop" and "relay race" threading through the crowd. Great. What kind of circus did I just volunteer for?

Suddenly, a familiar voice cuts through my internal groan. "Oh, hey. If it isn't my favorite scumbag."

"Hey, Shan." I heave a sigh, breaking away from the next lineup. "I'm assuming you had a chat with Jade."

"Yep," she says, arms defensively crossed over her chest. She looks away briefly to direct some stray players back to the field, but her accusing glare remains. "Your team's pretty fucked-up, huh?"

"Yeah, well, we're done with all that bullshit now."

"What do you mean?"

"I kind of wanted to tell Jade first," I say, awkwardly clearing my throat. "If that's okay?"

"Oh, yeah," she says, a knowing smile tugging at her lips. "You mean tomorrow, at the batting cages?"

A tiny sliver of hope pangs inside my chest. "Did she say anything else about it? Do you think I have another shot?"

She gives me a noncommittal shrug. "It's not my place to say."

"Right," I mutter, my brief hope deflating. "And hey, I'm sorry for involving you in all this. There was a harmless attraction there, but it faded as soon as I got to know Jade."

She waves me off, rolling her eyes. "It's fine. Just make it right with her, will you?"

"I'll try my best," I promise.

By the time the field games wrap up, I'm wiped out. My encounter with Shannon had jolted me, making the rest of the games seem like a breeze in comparison. That's the only reason I chose to stick around for the farewell bonfire.

There's no way I could've sat at home, struggling to study while my insides twist into a tight coil, my mind fraying at the edges.

Because tomorrow, my fate is sealed. One way or another, Jade is going to make a decision. I still have hope that she might give us another chance, but there's also a niggling doubt whispering that she won't.

For now, the only thing I can control is my actions and pray that they're enough for her.

As the bonfire roars an hour into the night, I distract myself with cold beer and small talk. Despite the emotional rollercoaster, it's a beautiful night, even if the heat from the fire feels like a physical manifestation of my anxiety.

Needing a breather, I excuse myself from the crowd, finding a quiet spot and an empty bench, attempting to clear the smoke from my head.

The moment I let my eyes drift closed, a warm weight plops down on my lap, yanking me from the brink of much-needed solitude. "So, did you finally get what you wanted?" a voice slurs slightly.

I jerk awake, jaw hardening. "Cass." My voice is as cold as ice. "I'm gonna give you two seconds to get the hell off me."

She rolls her eyes dramatically. "God, you're such a drama queen."

"Stop talking," I snap, my patience fraying.

"Fine." With a careless shrug, she slides off my lap, her unsteady movements causing her bottle to tip and spill its contents over my shoes. "Whoops."

The beer-soaked bottle lies forgotten on the ground between us. "You planning on picking that up?"

"Why?" Her smirk is all too familiar. "You want me down on my knees again?"

I resist the urge to grind my teeth. "Jesus, Cass," I growl, getting up to snatch the empty bottle from the ground. "Give me a break."

She feigns innocence, her hand finding its way onto my forearm. "I heard you and your little girlfriend broke up anyway."

I pull away from her. "That's none of your damn business."

A malicious glint sparks in her eyes. "What happened? Did she find out you actually just wanted to sleep with her roommate? God, West. History does have a way of repeating itself."

I can practically taste the anger on my tongue. "You don't know what you're talking about."

"Hmm," she hums, the smugness in her voice making my blood boil. "Really? Because I saw your ex earlier tonight."

My heart skips a beat. "Here?" I demand. "At the bonfire?"

She nods, confirming my worst fear. "If I remember right . . . she was all over Remi Miller."

I snap my mouth shut, shoving the bottle back into her hand with more force than necessary. "Why don't you stop trying to start shit?"

She just shrugs. "Fine, don't believe me, then."

"I won't," I spit, turning to walk away.

But the seeds of doubt she's planted are already sprouting, and my heart is pounding like a war drum in my chest. Should I try to find Jade? If she's actually here tonight, then maybe I should . . . go the fuck home. The knowledge of our meetup tomorrow urges me to stay away, to keep a clear head for the conversation we need to have.

But if Miller's actually after her, then maybe I have an actual reason to seek her out. The guy's a fucking dick, and right now, he's probably pissed at me.

Who knows what sort of stunt he might attempt?

Chapter Thirty-Four

JADE

TONIGHT, I'm having a surprisingly good time. It's a welcome reprieve, given how emotionally heavy this past week has been.

Since West left me that first note, declaring his intentions, I've been thinking about him nonstop. I've been toying with the idea of giving him another chance, wrestling with it, the pros and cons dancing in my mind like some twisted ballet.

To forgive him means setting aside all the white lies, swallowing down the jealousy, and stepping past the fear of being played again. And all of this needs to happen within a single week before summer. Seven days to unravel the tangled mess of insecurities and doubts that lay between us.

How could that ever be enough?

But maybe it's something we can navigate together tomorrow. Tonight, however, I plan to have some fun.

While Shannon's busy running the show, I steal away toward the coolers, tucked away in the shadow of an outdoor awning. It's quieter over here. But still, the bonfire's blazing, casting a glow over the enormous crowd, and I can feel the heat radiating from a distance.

"Hey, gorgeous." A familiar voice slides into my ears, the grin evident in his tone. I know without looking who it is. Miller has an uncanny knack for being in the same place as me, like a bee to honey. "We just keep finding each other, don't we?"

Turning from the cooler, I offer him a tired smile. This is our second "accidental" encounter tonight, the first being when he collided into me by the fire about an hour ago.

"You know what, Miller?" I say, pulling a cold bottle out of the ice. "You're giving me some creepy vibes tonight."

"It's Remi," he corrects, a playful glint in his eye. "But damnnn, my bad. Didn't mean to come on too strong."

"Just . . . tone that shit down."

"Hmm, thanks for the flirting advice." He chuckles, tugging at my hair. "You have any more tips?"

"Okay." I take a step back, creating some distance between us. "Rule number one: don't touch a girl without her permission."

"That's a good tip." He smirks. "What else you got for me?"

Pausing, I pop the top off my beer, taking a moment to draw in a deep gulp. "Don't flirt with a girl that's taken."

"So, you and West are still going strong, huh?"

"That's not your business," I say sharply. "And he's your team-mate. Don't you think you're crossing a line here?"

He just shrugs. "Teammates share all the time."

"Gross." I recoil, making a face. "One last tip, don't say shit like that."

"I don't see the problem with sharing, Jade." He licks his lower lip, eyes unabashedly roving over me. "You're hot. I'm hot. West is hot. We can all have some fun."

"Alright." I back away further. "Well, I'm gonna go vomit now."

"Oh, come on," he protests with a lazy drawl. "I'm just fucking around. You think I want West to kick my ass?"

"Honestly, I don't know what you're playing at," I snap, frustration bubbling in my voice. "But I'm leaving."

As I turn to go, he calls after me, his slimy parting words sending a shiver down my spine. "Come find me if you get bored."

Wending my way back to Shannon, I find her seated amidst a group of her fellow teammates. They're all immersed in lighthearted banter, their laughter echoing off into the night. A soft smile tugs at my lips as I approach.

"Hey." Shannon gives me a wide grin, patting the space next to her. I take a seat, allowing the comforting buzz of their conversation to wash over me. Emmy's here, too, and she gives me a sweet smile, her cheerful demeanor perking me right up.

Despite not being part of the team myself, the girls are all welcoming, and it helps me to relax, to feel a little bit more at home here.

But the moment is abruptly shattered when Cassidy strides up to us, her coy smile setting my teeth on edge.

"Hey, you," she drawls, the faux sweetness in her voice forcing a grimace. "I don't believe we've crossed paths tonight."

"No, we haven't," I say, trying to maintain my composure. Her presence is like an unwelcome gust of wind, disturbing my small sliver of peace.

She slowly sips on her drink, eyes narrowing slightly. "Seen West tonight?"

I shake my head with a wince. "No, I haven't. I didn't realize he was here."

"Oh, yeah, sorry." She smirks, the pretense of innocence doing nothing to mask her malicious intent. "I forgot you two broke up for a moment. It's a good thing, though. He just had me on my knees earlier."

The cheerfulness of the group evaporates instantly, replaced by a tense silence. Shannon's eyes flash with anger, while Emmy stiffens, her friendly demeanor hardening.

"Cassidy, that's enough," Shannon snaps, her protective instincts kicking in. "Stop trying to stir up drama. It's not welcome here."

"Seriously, Cass," Emmy chimes in, her voice tight with annoyance. "Enough with the mind games."

Caught in the middle of this unexpected storm, a familiar

discomfort creeps in. The night suddenly seems too long, the party too loud. A need to escape this situation claws at me.

"Shannon," I lean in to whisper, my voice barely audible over the sound of the bonfire. "I think I'm going to head home. I'm . . . tired."

Her gaze softens, and she gives my hand a reassuring squeeze. "I'll come with you."

I shake my head, not wanting her to abandon her post. She's been working hard to ensure everything goes smoothly tonight, and she deserves time to enjoy it. "No, you need to stay. I'll be fine."

"But—"

"Really, Shan. I'll see you tomorrow, okay?"

With that, I remove myself from the group, leaving behind the stunned silence and Cassidy's gloating smirk. Tonight was supposed to be a reprieve, a chance to forget about all my troubles, but it seems fate has a twisted sense of humor.

The party noise dwindles as I push through the crowd, the mansion receding behind me. I snake my way toward the front, finding myself on the main street. Under the dim, flickering street-lights, I unlock my phone, thumb hovering over the Uber app. That's when a familiar voice slices through the night.

"Jade," West calls out, the low timbre piercing my heart.

"Hi," I breathe out. "What are you doing out here?"

"I've been out here for a while now." He shifts on the balls of his feet, avoiding my gaze. "Just thinking about heading home."

"Why?"

"I was, uh, a little distracted. Just worried about you, actually." He runs a hand through his perfectly tousled hair. "I heard Miller was creeping on you, but I didn't know if you'd want me to intervene."

"Oh, right." Against my better judgment, I roll my eyes. "Well, I heard Cassidy gave you a blowjob tonight."

He takes a step forward, eyes flashing. "Are you fucking kidding me?"

"Nope, it came straight from the horse's mouth."

"Jade." He gives me a pleading look. "I swear to you, that did not fucking happen."

"I know it didn't."

He reels back. "You do?"

"Of course I know you'd never do something like that, especially not when you've been trying to win me back."

A sigh of relief escapes him. "I'm glad you at least believe that. Believe in me, I mean."

"Mm," I hum, distracted by my overworked brain.

His eyes search mine. "Were you . . . did you still plan on meeting me tomorrow?"

"I was planning on it, but maybe we should just talk now. Could I come over?"

"If that's what you'd like." He pulls out his phone, scrolling through the home screen. "I can call us an Uber."

"Okay."

The ride to his place is painfully silent, the tension winding tight around us. Even when we're tucked away in the safety of his bedroom, me perched on the edge of his bed and him sitting stiffly on a rolling chair, the discomfort persists.

"Baby," he breaks the silence, his voice taut. "There's so much I want to say to you."

"Can I go first?"

"Of course." He swallows thickly. "Whatever you want."

"There are a few things I figured out this week," I begin, scooting forward on the mattress, taking his hand. His palm is cold against mine, trembling ever so slightly. "First is that I do trust you. I believe you learned your lesson about keeping secrets, and I don't think you would do it again."

"I wouldn't," he says, soft and low, his fingers instinctively curling around mine.

"I also realized just how much I missed you," I continue, my gaze lingering on our intertwined hands before I slowly pull mine away, settling it on my lap. "I've been thinking about you so much."

"You're always on my mind." He drags his chair a few inches closer. "You should also know that I—"

"Wait," I cut in, squeezing my eyes shut for a moment, gathering my strength. "There's one more thing I need to say first."

"Okay?"

His gaze is fixed on me, eyes filled with a dizzying blend of confusion and hope. My heart races, adrenaline surging through my veins. I draw in a deep, shuddering breath, steeling myself for what I need to say.

"I think we should stay broken up."

Chapter Thirty-Five
WEST

My throat constricts, a harsh sensation running through me as I swallow down Jade's rejection. After every ounce of hope, every desperate apology and explanation, she still isn't ready to try again.

"You can't forgive me," I say, my voice a dejected whisper. The sting of defeat claws at me, lacing each word.

"That's not the reason," she says. Her voice is soft, almost comforting, in stark contrast to the situation. "I do forgive you, honestly. I see the growth in you since we first met."

"So, you trust me, you miss me, and you forgive me," I say, my confusion seeping into my voice. "Yet, you don't want to be with me?"

"It's not as simple as that." She leans forward, her warm palm stilling my nervously bouncing knee. "It's just—I don't think the timing is right for us."

"The timing," I echo, brows knitting together. My heart thrums in my chest as I process her words, each one a sharp jab to my senses.

"I'm leaving for the summer." She takes a deep, calming breath, her eyes dropping to her own fingers on my knee. "I'll be states away, and you'll be here working your ass off at camp. It doesn't make sense for us to jump back into this relationship. Think about it."

"I have been thinking about it," I say, a bitter chuckle escaping me as I run a frustrated hand through my hair. "I've been thinking about it every goddamn day for the past few weeks. I hear what you're saying . . . but Jade, I really don't give a shit about the timing."

"If we don't have a solid foundation now, then it doesn't make sense for us to try and work things out from a distance. I don't want us to just crumble again."

My hand snakes out, fingers finding hers. I trace the outline of her wrist, each stroke a silent promise. "I won't let that happen."

"You can't know that for sure."

"So, what?" My spine stiffens, the whiplash of emotions causing my muscles to coil. "You want to be together, but you just don't think the timing's right? I'll be honest with you; this seems like a cop-out."

"It's not," she says. "I was already worried about the summer, and now we've been broken up for weeks. How can we just come back from all that and then leave each other right away?"

"Because it's fucking worth it." I gently tip her chin, my thumb brushing against her soft skin. "Because I'll be thinking about you every day, regardless of whether or not we're actually together."

"And you don't think that's a problem?" She turns her head, my hand falling away from her face. "I don't want to make this summer any more difficult for you. For either of us. Don't we both deserve a summer free of drama?"

"Drama?" A muscle in my jaw twitches, my teeth grinding together. "That's what this is to you?"

"It's not . . . you're misunderstanding me." She stares at me, sincerity brimming in her eyes. "I'm talking about the insecurity, the jealousy, all the people who want to come between us. You know, like Cassidy and Miller."

"And Garrett?" I add, bitterness seeping through.

"Garrett's a complete nonissue."

"Then so are Cass and Miller," I insist, my voice laced with conviction. "Screw them. I've had absolutely nothing to do with that girl since last term. Miller is an asshole, but he's not even my friend."

"Then you should probably tell him you're not down for threesomes."

My muscles tense, gaze narrowing. "The fuck did he say to you?"

"He—no, you know what? It really doesn't matter." She shakes her head, waving it away. "I shouldn't have even brought that up."

"He better not have put his hands on you tonight. I don't know what the hell he's thinking, but—"

"See?" she cuts me off, flustered. "This is exactly what I mean, Theo. I don't want you to have to worry about this kind of stuff all summer long. Not when you should be focusing on making your dreams come true."

"I can focus on both," I plead, the denial fogging my brain as her words fully register.

Theo. She fucking called me Theo. It's like an electric jolt to my system, my pulse accelerating as she continues her point.

"You deserve to focus on yourself for the summer," she says, her resolve knocking the wind out of me. "Once we're both back at school, we can figure out where to go from there."

"So, what you're suggesting is a break, then, not a breakup."

"Well, we're not exactly together right now. So, if you want to get into semantics . . ."

A pit twists and turns in my stomach, gnawing at my insides. "This is really what you want?"

"I just think it's the best decision for both of us."

"And I disagree." My stare holds her captive, searching her face for any hint of doubt or second-guessing. "But if this is the decision you're making, then I guess I have to respect that."

"It just makes sense for us right now."

I rise from my chair, moving to settle beside her on the

mattress. The closeness is both soothing and torturous. "You know, there's something else I need to tell you. And this isn't a last-ditch effort to make you change your mind."

"Okay." Her brows pinch together. "Go ahead."

"We officially banned the Trade this week." I tilt my head back, avoiding her gaze. "I spoke with both our captains and got them on board. As a team, we decided to get rid of the tradition once and for all. It's over."

"Wow, seriously?" She nudges me in the shoulder, shifting my attention back to her. "You did that for me?"

"I did it because of you," I amend. "And because it's the right thing to do."

"I'm honestly shocked but really proud of you. Of your team," she adds. "That's . . . good."

"The team—*we*—should have never allowed it in the first place." I rake my hands through my hair. "It was a pointless, shitty competition."

"I'm glad you not only realized that, but you actually went out and did something to fix it."

"You helped give me the push I needed." I turn to face her, bumping our knees together. "So, thank you, Jade."

"I'm happy for you," she says quietly.

I stare back at her, gaze trailing across her beautiful features. That little dusting of freckles, that sweet birthmark, and those full, rosy lips. An overwhelming urge to kiss her washes over me.

"Fuck, baby." The words come out all weak and gravelly. "How am I supposed to spend a whole summer away from you?"

"I'll miss you, too." She gives me a sad half-smile. "But that's why I want you to forget about the breakup for a while. Just think about your training and work on yourself."

"If we're going to spend the whole summer apart, would you let me kiss you one last time?" I cup the side of her cheek, swiping a thumb across her birthmark. "As a goodbye?"

"Just one kiss," she whispers. "As a goodbye."

I lean forward, a faint brush of my lips against hers. "As a promise."

She pulls back. "Theo."

"Okay." I change course, heart hammering against my chest. "Just a goodbye, then. Or maybe a 'see you later.'"

She inches closer, her breath warm and sweet against my lips. My hand instinctively moves to the base of her neck, fingers weaving through her hair, pulling her against me and sealing the space between us.

The tenderness of the moment gives way to a raw, burning hunger. There's nothing sweet about this kiss. It's filled with heat, with hunger, with a desire to be consumed. It's filled with all the promises she doesn't want to voice.

And I only last about five seconds before my restraint completely snaps.

I draw her onto my lap, her body curling against mine, arms draped around my neck, legs straddling my waist. My grip tightens in her hair, tugging her lips back to mine in a punishing caress.

Teeth grazing her bottom lip, I pour every ounce of my pent-up longing into the tangle of our mouths. The air around us grows thick as she peels off her shirt, revealing the delicate lace of her bralette. The sight of her half-naked body, flushed with arousal, is pure, divine torture.

She's beautiful. She's perfect. But she's not mine.

"Wait." My chest heaves, breathless as I force out the words. "If I can't have you tonight, all of you, then we shouldn't do this."

"You're right." She places both hands on my shoulders, reeling back. "I'm sorry."

For a split second, I merely gaze at her, the ticking of my racing heart the only sound echoing through the charged silence.

"Oh, fuck it," I rasp.

My mouth finds hers again, then trails down to the sensitive hollow of her throat, my kiss drawing a breathy moan from her. My fingers dance across the small band of fabric holding her bralette together, unhooking it with ease. With a casual toss, the lace joins the growing pile of discarded clothes.

Our breaths come in sharp, ragged pants. As our eyes meet, there's an unspoken agreement, a silent acceptance of the illusion we've created and the inevitable heartbreak it might bring.

Both of us are pretending that this one night won't flip us inside out.

But right now, that looming heartache seems insignificant. I can't bring myself to care about anything but the woman beneath me. So, I carry on, flipping her onto her back, her legs splayed out in front of me.

"Tell me what you want," I demand, waiting as she shimmies out of her pants.

"*You.* I want you, Theo."

Her confession stokes the fire inside me, a roaring blaze that threatens to consume my every thought. Hastily, I shed the rest of my clothing, my erection straining for release. Her fingers move to discard her panties, but I stay her hand.

"Leave them," I command, my voice raspy with desire.

Her brows furrow, but the sight of my naked body seems to dispel any lingering doubt. I waste no time as I slip between her outstretched legs, my thumb brushing against her clit. The raw, primal desire to fully claim her overpowers my intention to savor the moment—to lick her, taste her, feel her climax on my mouth.

A shiver racks through her body, her back arching off the bed as she whimpers, "Please."

"Please what?"

Her gaze flits to the throbbing length of my arousal, leaving no doubt about what she desires.

Throwing caution to the wind, I fumble for a condom in the drawer of my nightstand, tearing open the foil package with a determined tug. The latex barrier in place, I position myself at her entrance, the fabric of her panties pushed aside.

With a slow, measured thrust, I push into her warmth. Her gasp is my reward, the sweet friction of her tight heat luring me deeper. The rhythm of our bodies synchronizes, timed to the beat of my thudding heart. I cup my hands around her breasts, squeezing and kneading as her hips roll against mine.

She's moaning, soft and breathless as I rock into her. It's a slow, torturous pace, but it feels so fucking good. Her nails dig into my biceps, and my balls tighten, an orgasm threatening to spill out of me.

Yet, I'm desperate to prolong this pleasure, to stretch out these precious moments before the inevitable end. But her hand wrapping around my throat dictates otherwise, choking the breath right out of me. The world blurs around the edges, my pulse pounding in my ears.

When my climax finally tears through me, I swear I see stars.

She follows soon after, her thighs clenching around me as she shudders in the throes of her own orgasm. Then we're locked together, sweaty and breathless, lost in the afterglow of our shared high.

The rest of the night is a hushed, delicate silence punctuated only by our soft breaths and the rustling of sheets. We clean up, curling against one another without a word, our bare bodies entangled under the soft blanket. And then, we drift off to a dreamless sleep.

I know I told her I would respect her decisions, but in this particular instance, her decisions are bullshit. She wants me to renounce our relationship for the summer. She thinks we can work on ourselves, live a drama-free summer without jealousy, insecurities, and doubts.

But that's not reality. Instead, I'll be spending the whole summer pining over her, wishing I would have done more to change her mind. Wishing I would have told her that I'm so fucking in love with her that it burns.

And that the idea of being apart feels like drowning.

But I guess my feelings are pointless. Because when I wake up the next morning, she's already gone.

Chapter Thirty-Six
JADE

IT'S BEEN a week since I landed at the SeaTac Airport. I'd completed my finals and then hastily booked the first flight home, yearning to put some distance between myself and the whirlwind of mistakes I left behind.

A huge part of me regrets that morning—the way I left West asleep in his bed, our bodies still carrying the warmth of our night together. A heated goodbye kiss that somehow crossed the line into something more . . . something that wasn't part of my plan.

Yet just because it happened doesn't mean I had a total change of heart. I still stand by the intentions I laid out from the start. Or, at least, that's what I'm telling myself.

A newly mended relationship facing nearly three months of separation . . . it's a recipe for heartbreak. West needs to focus on his training, and I can focus on my family.

My insecurities shouldn't be the distraction he has to deal with when he has so much at stake: his performance, the prospect of entering the draft after the season. I couldn't bear to be the one who screwed it up for him. And I know if we stayed together, he would only be thinking about how to make me happy all summer.

So yes, there will be girls swarming over him throughout our time apart. Cheerleaders, jersey chasers, summer school co-eds, and I'll be here, hundreds of miles away, wishing to trade places with any one of them.

That's a large part of the reason I slipped away from our warm bed that morning. Any longer and my defenses might've crumbled, and my insecurities would've gotten the best of me. Maybe if I were stronger, if I weren't so scared, I could handle the months apart without worrying that I'm an unnecessary distraction.

As it stands, he might decide that all this isn't worth it come September.

Because I messed up too. We had something good, something pure and real, and I pushed him away.

I have no doubt he's upset with me, probably thinks I'm not worth the trouble. After all, I haven't heard from him since I left. I don't know if he passed his courses, if he's taking summer credits, or if he even knows that I flew home.

For now, we're miles apart, each in our own worlds. I've made my choices, and now I have to live with them. Alone.

Despite understanding that I brought this upon myself, I've been moping around the house all week, prompting my parents to worry over my "mood." It's touching in a way but also a stark reminder of what it feels like to be constantly under their watchful gaze.

It's been thirteen days since I've heard from West. Thirteen days filled with self-pity, regret, and half-baked apologies that he'll never hear. However, that doesn't give my parents the right to invade my space. I'm an adult, capable of making my own decisions.

If I choose to relish in a steaming cup of coffee at eight o'clock at night, alone in complete silence, that's my prerogative.

Except, according to my dad, it's not.

My father strolls into the kitchen, a picture of feigned surprise as he spots me, using the clever ploy to cover the concern in his eyes. He guides his four-wheeled walker to my side, flipping its seat open before settling down next to me. "Hey, kiddo, you sure you're doin' okay?"

I manage to stretch my lips into a tight-lipped smile, the effort straining my already worn-out resolve. "Yeah, Dad," I reassure him, "I'm good."

"Well, you know you don't have to be," he reminds me gently, a hint of sadness lingering in his eyes. "Not around me, anyway."

"I know." My reply comes out as a mere whisper, my shoulders slumping under the weight of the truth. "And I'm sorry I've been so mopey lately. I really did miss you and Ma."

His response is a heartening grin. "Don't you worry. We know ya did, kiddo. But we have a little surprise for you out in the living room."

Confusion knits my brows. "What is it?"

A spark of mischief ignites in his eyes as he suggests, "Why don't you go on and find out? I'll catch up."

I peel myself off the kitchen stool and head down the twisted hallway. The sounds of hushed whispers float my way, slowly growing louder with each step. A familiar feminine voice tinged with a hint of anticipation—that's definitely my mom. But the next voice sends a jolt of surprise coursing through me—a deep, rich tone that unmistakably belongs to my brother.

I dash into the living room. "Ace!" I shout, tackling him into a forceful hug.

A warm chuckle rumbles from his chest. "Thank God we're back to this."

"You're home!" I stretch onto my toes to ruffle his perfectly styled hair. "You told me you'd be too busy this summer."

His smirk is all-knowing. "Then Ma called and said you've been down in the dumps. Had to make an exception for my little sis."

A flash of annoyance sweeps over me. "Mom! Can't you and Dad keep some things to yourself?"

"Sorry, angel," she murmurs, a soft, almost guilty smile playing on her lips. "I thought we might need some backup."

Despite my exasperation, I can't stop my own smile in return. "Nosy."

She rises from the couch, crossing the room to join my dad, who had slowly entered, the wheels of his walker clicking rhythmically against the threshold. "Well, your nosy father and I are going to sleep early tonight," she tells me. "Why don't you spend some time with Mica instead of drinking that awful coffee?"

I cast a glance toward the kitchen, where my coffee still sits, now untouched and forgotten. My dad follows my gaze and chuckles. "I already tossed it."

I mutter a soft "meddling parents" under my breath, just audible enough for them to hear.

Mica nudges me on the shoulder, a playful spark in his eyes. "Come on, Lil. Let's go out to our swing."

After hugging our parents good night, Mica and I make our way outside. The back patio is home to a large wooden porch swing, faintly illuminated by the soft glow of the outdoor lights. It might be a simple piece of furniture, but it's always been one of my favorite places in the world.

I claim the swing before Mica can react, sprawling out on the bench, feet kicked up in an exaggerated display of comfort. He scowls, a playful threat in his voice. "You better scoot your ass over, or I'm gonna crush you."

"Hey!" I feign indignation. "Aren't you here to cheer me up?"

His laugh is rich, a sound I've missed more than I realized. "That doesn't mean I can't threaten you with bodily harm."

In mock protest, I shift into a seated position. "You're the ass," I grumble, bumping my shoulder against his.

Unfazed by my jab, he plops down beside me, stretching his arms out leisurely across the backrest. "Lili, I'm gonna need you to fly out for at least five of my games this year."

"Five?" I scoff. "You realize that Garrett's finally letting me cover the Dayton games, right?"

"Are you trying to say that Dayton football is more important than your family?"

"I'm saying my potential career in sports journalism is just as important as you and your career."

A low whistle escapes his lips. "Damn. How about three games, then?"

"Sure." I huff out a laugh. "We'll make it happen."

There's a noticeable shift in his demeanor. "Are you ever gonna tell me what happened between you and West?"

"I would if it was any of your business."

His gaze hardens, his protective nature surfacing. "You're my sister. Everything about you is my business. And if he hurt you, I'll kill that little fucker."

Hastily, I attempt to dissolve his worry. "It's not like that," I insist. "He just made a careless mistake, and I ended things. He tried to mend it, but I thought it'd be better if we took a break for the summer. That's all."

He raises a questioning brow. "What kind of mistake are we talking about here?"

I shake my head, a clear dismissal. "It doesn't matter. It's all water under the bridge anyway. We're not together now, and it's probably for the best."

I'm still not entirely sure who I'm trying to fool here. But what I do know is that I wouldn't have made the decision to leave—to put this physical distance between us—if I didn't need to.

There's a reason I choose to spend my summers here instead of staying behind at Dayton. The same reason I always seek solace in the comforts of our childhood home, in the presence of our mom and dad.

"So, you're the one that ended it?"

I nod, mustering a tight smile. "You know I always look forward to spending my summers here, but I also *need* to be here, Ace. With family. With our dad, most of all. He's doing okay for now, but who knows how much longer he'll be in this condition?"

"And you didn't think West would wait for you?"

"No, I know he would. I just—I thought it was all too complicated. We're hundreds of miles apart. And I've never been in a serious relationship before, not like the one we had. Long distance just seems really tough, and especially for two people who don't quite have their shit together."

"And now that you're home, spending all this time without him, you still think you made the right decision?"

"I thought so," I confess, tears stinging at the back of my eyes. "But now, I'm not so sure I can handle it. I just . . . really miss him. I thought I was doing the right thing by keeping us apart, but I let fear take over, and maybe I pushed him away when I shouldn't have."

"It's not too late to change your mind."

"Maybe." I nervously twist a curl between my fingers. "But I'm not even going to see him again until September."

He rubs the scruff on his chin. "If you want to work things out, you don't have to wait."

"What do you mean?"

"You don't have to wait until September," he clarifies. "You can fly back to Dayton next weekend."

"Ace, I don't—"

"I'm gonna stop you right there." He places a heavy hand on my shoulder, gaze steady and serious. "I know what you're about to say—that you don't have money to spend on a ticket. But you already know what's mine is yours."

"You'll pay for my flight to go visit him?" I choke out, shocked by the suggestion. "My ex-boyfriend?"

"If it makes you happy, I'll pay for whatever you want. And I know West probably royally screwed things up, but you forgave

him. That's enough for me to know he's a good guy. Besides, I
kinda liked the kid."

"Are you still trying to suck up to me 'cause you slept with
Shan?"

"Jesus, Lili," he chokes out, clearing his throat before asking, "Is
it working?"

Laughter bubbles up from inside me. "Yeah, it's working."

"So, what do you think?" he asks, nudging me slightly. "You
heading back to Dayton for the weekend?"

The laughter dies down, and I'm left with a comforting silence.
My thoughts clear as I mull over his words. "Yeah." I finally nod.
"Yeah, I am."

It feels like an internal barrier just crumbled down. A decision
made not out of fear but out of a desire for something more, something real. I'm tired of thinking about what makes the most sense
on paper. I'm tired of thinking about what's rational and logical.

Because who wants a relationship based on cold, calculating
logic? That's not what drew me to West in the first place. That's
certainly not what kept me up for the last twelve nights, longing for
the comfort of his voice, waiting and wishing to hear from him
again.

So, it's time I take matters into my own hands now.

Chapter Thirty-Seven

WEST

Two weeks have passed since Jade took off in the dead of night, leaving me in a perpetual state of confusion.

At first, the sting was unbearable. Her abrupt departure was a reminder of how quickly happiness could be torn away. Together, we made a hasty decision, one driven by passion and longing, and then . . . she was fucking gone.

Couldn't bear the aftermath. Couldn't bear to face me in the morning.

Her words still echo in my mind, a bitter fucking lullaby: "I forgive you, and I'll miss you." It seemed so real, so sincere. And despite her resolution, her actions certainly made it seem like she wanted me, too.

But she warned me that first night at Lucky's when I kissed her in the hall. She might have craved my touch, my warmth, but that was it. Now, the sadness has been replaced by a hollow emptiness, a numbness that's more comforting than the continuous ache.

Jade's made it clear she wants me to focus on training this summer, and so I've been pouring every bit of my energy into it. The weight room has become my refuge, the field my battleground.

Today's practice ends with running skill patterns, again. By the time I'm done with the fifth set, which ends in another grueling forty-yard run, I'm running on fumes. Two of our wide receivers—and my least favorite assholes—are running their patterns alongside me.

"West, your girl still around this summer?" Miller's voice slices through the thick, humid air. His breathing is ragged. "We didn't get a chance to finish our last conversation."

My teeth grind together at his audacity. "That's real fucking funny, man."

"Yeah." McNair lets out a laugh that sounds more like a pig's grunt. "Just let us know when you're done with her, 'kay?"

My blood boils. "The hell did you just say?"

He snickers, clearly pleased with my reaction. "Just 'cause you don't like to share doesn't mean Mills and I have to play by your rules."

The red in my vision grows deeper. "I get that you two are pissed at me, but you really don't want to cross this line."

"Why?" Miller throws back, a smug smirk on his face. "Jade's a grown girl. Feisty, too. I'm sure she can handle herself."

An ominous calm descends over me. My voice drops dangerously low. "Say her name again and see what happens."

His smirk widens, unfazed by my threat. "And what if I moan her name in bed?"

He's baiting me, I know that. But I don't give a shit. In one swift motion, I lunge at him, my fist connecting solidly with his jaw. A gratifying crunch rings out, music to my fucking ears.

Miller stumbles backward, the force of my punch taking him by surprise. McNair jumps in but is quickly met with a shove that sends him sprawling.

I look down at the pair, a smirk tugging at my lips. I spit next to them. "Now will you keep your fuckin' mouths shut?"

Coach's booming voice echoes across the field. "Offense! What the hell's goin' on over there?"

"Nothing, Coach," I say as casually as I can manage. "We're just screwing around."

He barks back a warning. "You better get your shit together."

"You got it, sir!"

McNair scrambles to his feet, pulling Miller up with him. Their glares could bore holes into my head, but I just chuckle at the sight of them. Miller cradles his swollen jaw, eyes filled with unadulterated hatred.

"Fucking pathetic," I spit, my words as icy as the smile on my face. I turn my back on them and dive back into my training, channeling my anger into every move, every stride.

For now, this is the one and only place my focus lies. It has to be.

"DUDE, what the hell was that earlier?" Cam barges in, his duffel bag making a soft thud as he tosses it onto the couch next to me. His eyes bore into mine, demanding an answer. "I saw you throw that punch at Miller."

"He had it coming. McNair, too." I offer no further explanation, my gaze dropping to the floor. "Those fuckers wouldn't stop running their goddamn mouths."

"What's going on with you, man?" He sighs, crossing his arms over his chest as he steps closer. "You've been moping around the house for weeks, and now you're starting fights on the field. Is this all just because Jade left?"

"You wouldn't get it."

"Well, then why don't you explain it to me!" His voice is sharp, laced with frustration.

The words slip out before I can stop them. "I fucking loved her, okay?" I rake a hand through my hair, heart pounding. "But she clearly doesn't love me back. So, now I'm just . . . done. I have to be."

"Fuck, are you really?"

"I think so," I murmur, slinging one arm over the back of the couch and shutting my eyes. "Cam, she let me sleep with her, and then she left on the first flight out of here. Not even a word."

"But didn't she leave things open-ended?" His voice is gentle, hesitant.

My eyes fly open at that. "So, what?" Frustration surges again. "I'm supposed to continue to sit around waiting for her all summer? Wallow in self-pity and beat up my teammates in the process?"

"That's what I'm saying," he mutters. "Besides, you act like you only have two options here."

"What else is there?"

He gives a short chuckle. "You could actually try to enjoy yourself," he suggests. "Stop fucking thinking about Jade for two seconds and have some fun with your best friend."

Despite myself, I snort a laugh. "You had to make this all about you, huh?"

"No, you fucker." He playfully smacks me on the back of the head, his tone lightening. "This is about you. It's been about you for months."

A muscle in my jaw ticks. "The hell does that mean?"

"It means you've been torn up over this girl for a long-ass time. You've been ignoring your friends, staying in all the time, and acting like your world has ended when you're only twenty-one years old, for God's sake. Our lives have just fucking begun."

"I know I've been MIA, and I'm sorry for that," I say. "It's just been rough."

"So, what do you say? Let's go out tonight. You can try and forget about everything, even if it's just for the night."

His question hangs in the air between us, heavy and imposing. Do I want to forget Jade? Could I, even if I tried?

The thought makes my heart twinge with pain. Sure, moving on from my feelings for her in a span of two weeks isn't realistic. But constantly obsessing over her isn't healthy either. Especially when she's explicitly told me not to. I think it's about high time I let myself breathe.

"Maybe," I finally concede, meeting his gaze. "Maybe just for tonight."

A grin spreads across his face. "Then let's go get shitfaced at Lucky's." He gives my shoulder a firm pat. "We don't have practice until four o'clock tomorrow."

"Yeah, alright." The heaviness in my chest lifts slightly as I push off the couch. "I'm down."

It doesn't take long for Cam and me to turn our favorite bar into our personal playground. We go shot for shot like the old days, the alcohol burning my throat and dulling the edges of my heartache.

By the time we're six or seven drinks deep, we've roped in a couple of guys from the baseball team for a game of pool. We're swaying slightly, half-drunk already, but we're laughing and enjoying ourselves. It's the first time in weeks I've let myself genuinely smile.

Maybe Cam was right; maybe tonight I could forget, just a little.

As I'm lining up my last shot, two girls approach the table. "Hey, boys, can we play next round?" the taller of the two asks, interrupting my perfect line of sight.

"Sure, we're just about to bring it home anyway," Cam says with a chuckle. His cocky smile is as wide as the table. "After that, table's all yours."

The two girls exchange glances, a mixture of mischief and daring in their eyes. "Actually, we were hoping you two might show us the ropes." I allow my gaze to wander over my shoulder, taking in the sight of them cozying up to Cam like it's second nature.

"You cool with that, West?" Cam calls out, eyes glinting.

"Sure," I say absently, refocusing my gaze on the eight ball. With a flick of the wrist and a satisfying clunk, I pocket it. Victory.

Our win is met with a chorus of half-hearted cheers. The baseball guys retreat, leaving us with the two newcomers. One, a bottle blonde, seems more interested in Cam than the game. The other, a dark-haired girl with an edgy pixie cut, leans on the pool table, her eyes on me.

"So, West. Do you remember me?" Her question comes with a purposeful tilt of her head and a bat of her eyelashes. "We met here a while back."

I squint at her, my brain sifting through countless faces I've met at this bar before a spark of recognition hits me. "Uh . . ." I hesitate. "Zoë, right?"

She looks visibly taken aback, maybe even offended. "No? My name's Niah."

"Cool," I manage, nodding slightly.

She steps closer, biting her lip with a certain calculated charm. "Do you think you could show me how to shoot?"

Ah, classic move. "You've never played before?"

"Once or twice." She shrugs, a coy smile playing on her lips. "I might need a little refresher."

Taking my place beside her, I guide her through the sequence, adjusting her grip and stance. When she executes a flawless stroke, breaking the rack and sinking two stripes immediately, I can't help but be impressed.

"That wasn't just beginner's luck, was it?" I raise a brow, smirking as she shrugs casually, leaning her cue stick against the table.

"Sorry, no." She seems amused. "I guess I just wanted an excuse for you to touch me."

I blink at her. "You played me," I accuse, glancing around to find that Cam and his blonde companion have conveniently disappeared.

"I did," she confirms, unabashedly meeting my gaze. "You have a problem with that?"

"I guess I can appreciate a good hustle."

She grins, curling her fingers around my bicep. "Did you actually want to finish this game? Or would you rather just skip ahead and buy me a drink now?"

"I'm, uh . . ." I'm silent for a moment, caught in an internal crossfire. What is it that I think I am, exactly? Taken? Not anymore, and certainly not by choice. "Sure, Zoë. I'd be down for a drink."

"It's Niah," she corrects, fingers tightening around my arm.

"Right." I shake it off, gulping down the lump in my throat. "Sorry. Niah, let's go get that drink."

Chapter Thirty-Eight

JADE

IT'S SATURDAY MORNING, and my bags are packed.

I'm ticking away the last half hour before my ride to the airport arrives, seated at my kitchen table, nursing a lukewarm coffee. My eyelids are weighed down like bricks, the result of a sleepless night spent ruminating over my decisions.

With every minute that passes by, I weave another nightmare scenario in my head. What if I show up today and West looks right through me? What if I arrive at his house, bags in hand, and he's already decided he's over it, over me?

Lost in my thoughts, I hardly notice the sound of a car pulling into my driveway. I glance up, annoyed that my ride is here already, and hurry to the door. Gripping the handle, I swing it open, primed to step outside.

Except, it's not my Uber that's waiting for me. And the person standing there, now jogging up the path to my front door, has me shocked speechless.

"Uh, hey?"

"Oh my God!" I blink a few times, readjusting to the fog inside my brain. "Theo, how are you here right now?"

"Shan gave me your address." He chuckles, awkwardly scratching the back of his neck. "I told her I wanted to send you a surprise gift. Then I booked the first flight out here this morning."

"Wow, you're really here." My eyes widen, heart racing. "In Washington . . . at my house."

"I am." He gives me a guarded half-smile. "And look, I know you set some pretty firm boundaries. So, if you don't want to hear me out, I'll turn my ass around right now. I'm primed and ready to book the next flight home."

"No, of course I want you here." I grab his wrist, gently pulling him over the threshold. "Come in."

Once we're tucked inside, he glances around the entryway. "Are your parents home?"

"They went on a little trip for the weekend," I tell him, biting my tongue. "Just left this morning, actually."

He rakes a shaky hand through his hair. "Ah, okay."

"Don't get me wrong, I'm honestly so happy to see you." My brow crinkles. "But I'm really shocked right now."

"I'm here to get something off my chest." He swallows thickly. "I just—I needed to do this in person."

My heart stutters. "Alright?"

"I'm a little hungover from last night, so just bear with me."

I nod, guiding him over to the nearby bench. We both take a seat. He sighs, closing his eyes for a moment as his head drops back.

"Did you go out with the guys last night?" I ask. "To Lucky's?"

"Yes," he admits, avoiding my gaze. "And that's part of the reason why I'm here."

"Oh?"

"You know, I was so fucking upset when you snuck out on me." His jaw is firmly set. "Like it was just some meaningless one-night stand."

"I know," I murmur, shoulders slumped. "And I'm sorry, I should've never done that. I know we laid everything out on the table that night, but you deserved a proper goodbye before I left for the whole summer."

"Yeah, I won't lie, my feelings were really fucking hurt by that." He gulps low in his throat. "Then yesterday, I finally decided I was done being hurt. Or, at least, I tried to tell myself I was."

"What do you mean?"

"I just wanted to stop feeling so miserable, you know?" He reaches for my hand, pulling it onto his lap. "Cam convinced me to go out with him. We drank a bit, shot some pool, and then I got hit on by this girl."

"Yeah?"

"Yeah." He squeezes my hand. "I bought her a drink."

"West." I pull back, stomach dropping. "If this is going where I think it's going, I really don't need to hear it."

He shifts toward me, his strong fingers wrapping around my knee. "I need to say this to you."

I turn my head. "You went home with her, didn't you?"

His nostrils flare. "No, I didn't."

"Okay?"

"I've been in a fucked-up headspace since you left. So, I won't lie to you." A heavy puff of air escapes his lips. "The thought briefly crossed my mind. For just a split second . . . before I felt like puking."

My shoulders relax. "Oh."

"Nothing happened," he assures me. "I paid for her drink and then hightailed it out of there."

A flush of heat rises up my neck, colored by a mixture of relief and confusion. "Why are you telling me this?"

"Jade, I don't want to be with anyone that's not you. I realized this a long fucking time ago, but last night just solidified that fact."

His hand works its way around the back of my neck. "I know I begged to keep you. I basically asked you to break my heart. But then I just let you leave without laying all my cards on the table. And for that, I'm the one that's sorry."

"You don't owe me any apologies." I shake my head, his grip tightening around me. "Not anymore."

"I do, though," he argues. "Because I didn't fight for you the way I should have. Sure, I asked for your forgiveness. I tried, and clearly failed, to respect your decisions. But in the end, I still kept a piece of my heart from you."

"I'm the one that fucked up this time," I whisper. "I said I wanted a break because it'd be best for both of us. But now I know that I was just trying to protect myself, that I was just too scared to try again."

"And I don't blame you for that." He scoots closer, pressing his forehead against mine. "What I'm trying to say is that I love you, Jade."

My heart sputters, mouth running dry as I register those three little words.

"You what?" I finally manage to squeak out.

"I love you. I'm in love with you," he clarifies, sincerity reflected in his gaze. "And if I have to wait an entire summer for you to let your guard down, then so be it. The truth is, I'm so far from done with you."

A dull throb pulses behind my temples. There are so many words I want to say, but my mind is twisting, turning, catapulting off a cliff. "You flew all the way here just to tell me this in person?"

"I did." His thumb presses against my cheek, tilting my head until our gazes meet. There's a scorching heat behind those molten caramel eyes of his. "Actually, I also came to do this."

He draws me in, soft lips pressing against mine. Unlike the last kiss we shared, there's no longer a sense of urgency or desperate longing behind it. This time, his kiss is filled with certainty. It's purposeful, deliberate, and bolstered by unwavering confidence.

And when he finally pulls back, his eyes are shining.

"Turns out I passed English Lit." He swipes a thumb across my bottom lip. "Told you I'd come to collect."

Pride wells up inside my chest. "You passed?"

"Fuck yeah, I did." He beams. "Look, I know this sounds goofy, but I actually do need to take the next flight back. Coach will ream my ass if I miss our four-o'clock practice time."

I blink, shock coursing through my body. He actually woke up this morning, boarded a plane, and then flew hundreds of miles just for this one moment? "Oh, wow."

"I know." He winces. "I'm sorry to bail so soon. Honestly, I wasn't expecting you to . . . say anything back."

"Theo . . ."

"I'll just call myself another Uber," he awkwardly cuts in. "Unless you'd be willing to drive me to the airport."

"Actually, I think you're gonna need that Uber." His face falls, a stunned silence piercing through the stilted air. "Because I'm coming back with you."

"Wait, what?"

"My bag's already packed," I finally admit. "I was just heading to the airport when you showed up."

His brow furrows. "You're going back to Dayton?"

"I am."

"Why? I need you to spell it out for me." His hand, still around my neck, gently squeezes as he draws me closer. "Remember, I have a hard time reading context clues."

"I love you, Theo. I'm in love with you," I say, echoing his earlier confession. "And I don't want to wait an entire summer to let my guard down. I was going to tell you this in person, but the truth is . . . I'm so done with this breakup."

The fire in his eyes instantly reignites. "It was only a break."

"Okay," I relent, releasing a shaky breath of laughter. "Then I'm done with this break."

"You're serious." His fingers trail from the back of my neck down to my collarbone. He presses his palm flat against my chest, directly over my heart. "You really love me back?"

"I love you, period," I amend. "And I'm sorry I let my own fears and insecurities get in the way of that. I knew that if I stayed that night, if I woke up in your arms again, that I would've changed my mind right then and there. I didn't think I was strong enough to handle it, strong enough to let you go. But then, when I made it home, I realized just how miserable I was without you, and I knew I made the wrong decision."

"So, what does this mean?" he asks, wrapping me into his arms. "For us?"

"It means I'm gonna spend the weekend with you." I nuzzle my face into the crook of his neck, murmuring the words against his flushed skin. "And then we'll do long distance for the summer. I know it will be hard, but I have faith that we can make it work."

"Holy fuck."

I press a soft kiss to his jaw. "You good?"

"Oh, I'm more than good." His voice is light, raspy, choked with emotion. "You should probably say it one more time, though. Just for good measure."

"I love you, Theo."

"Goddamn," he drawls. "Those are some pretty words, baby."

I snort. "You're so corny."

"Yeah, but you love me anyway."

"I sure do."

"And I love you," he says, tone filled with unshaking sincerity. "So fucking much."

Chapter Thirty-Nine

JADE'S PERCHED on the edge of my bed, her bright eyes tracking my movements as I dart around the room, hastily pulling together the last pieces of my uniform.

The morning has been a fucking whirlwind, to say the least. Between our over-friendly Uber ride, the frenetic cross-country flight, and the white-knuckle speed I hit on the drive back in my truck, we've been flirting with the constraints of time.

"Anything I can do to help?" Jade's voice, soft and gentle, weaves through the chaos.

"No, thanks, babe." My words are clipped, lost in the rush as I toss my well-worn cleats, a couple of pairs of socks, and a crisp towel into my duffel bag. "I'm ready to go now."

"Could you drop me off at the Vault on your way to practice?" she asks. "It should only take an extra second."

Hoisting the bag over one shoulder, I pause to focus on her. "Wait, why?"

"I thought I'd grab a bite to eat." A simple shrug lifts her shoulders. "Besides, it's not like I can go back to my apartment right now."

As if I would've entertained that idea in the first place. She's already here—with me—exactly where she belongs. And fortunately, the girls are also subletting their place for the summer.

Shannon's tied up working at Sunshine Ranch, the camp where she first met Jade. She was offered a full-time counselor position this year, complete with a scholarship for her kid brother and on-site housing.

Of course, Jade was always planning on staying with her folks back in Washington. So, they'd found Emmy, a fellow cheerleader, to occupy their apartment for the next couple of months. Mica volunteered to cover their rent, just on the off chance they wanted to leave the place vacant, but Jade wouldn't allow it.

That woman has too much pride because Mica Jennings—one of the highest-paid cornerbacks in the NFL—could've easily covered that shit. Five thousand dollars of summer rent is basically equivalent to fifty bucks for that man.

"I thought you'd just stay here," I tell her, my voice soft.

"You want me to stay here while you're gone?"

"Of course I do." I tug at my brow, surprised at her question. "But if you're hungry, I can always order you something before I head out."

She tilts her head. "Why?"

"I just like knowing that you'll be here waiting for me," I say. "In my house, preferably in my bed."

"Is that so?"

"Yeah, you could even take your clothes off if you wanted."

Her eye roll is punctuated by sweet, soft laughter. "Wow, so generous."

"I'm serious, though." Bending down, I plant a soft kiss on her forehead. "Stay here while I'm gone?"

"Your wish is my command."

A chuckle breaks free. "I gotta say, I like the sound of that."

"Get outta here, you perv." Her playful shove sends me off with a grin. "You're gonna be late for practice."

She shifts from the edge of my bed toward the middle, stretching her legs out across my mattress. I linger in the doorway, just for a minute or two, unable to take my eyes off her.

She's beautiful. She's perfect. And now, she's all mine.

"I love you," I murmur, the words hanging heavy in the air.

"And I love you."

Ah, there it is. Now I can finally tear myself away and head off to practice. The familiar aching in my chest, the one I've barely tolerated over the past month, has officially settled.

THE MOMENT I touch down on the practice field, I spot the defensive team huddled together, my housemates lingering among them. When they see me headed their way, their faces flush with relief. I know they must've been sweating my absence—ill-prepared to cover my back and invent some half-assed excuse for Coach.

So, I throw a quick nod to the offense before moving to greet them.

"Shit, West." Danny cocks a brow. "We thought you wouldn't make it back in time."

Strapping my helmet on, I chuckle. "Almost didn't. But believe me, it was worth every second."

"Oh?"

A wide, bragging grin spreads across my face. "Jade came back with me. She'll be staying over for a few nights. Hope that's alright?"

He gives me a knowing smile. "All good, man. I'll be at Sofia's anyway."

"Awesome." I turn to Cam next. "Thanks for covering the ticket fare, man. You know I'm good for it."

"As long as you're happy." He jerks his head toward our coach. "You better go join the offense before you piss off Coach, though."

With a hefty pat on his shoulder, I spin on my heel to join the rest of my crew. Despite the knowledge that I'm in for a brutal practice—both hungover and love drunk—I still feel fucking fantastic. Now that Jade's back in my life, it's unlikely anything could knock me off this pedestal.

Emerging from practice three hours later, I'm flushed, soaked in sweat, and running on an adrenaline high from the workout. The lure of the locker room shower is strong, but my eagerness to see Jade is stronger.

We only have this short slice of time together—two and a half days—and I'm not wasting another second of it.

Once I'm home, my bedroom door gives way under the slight pressure of my impatient hand. Jade's sitting there, cross-legged on my bed with a book in hand, and she glances up as soon I walk in.

"Hey there." I stride toward her, swooping down to peck her lips. "This is certainly a sight for sore eyes."

Her answering smile makes my heart stutter. "How was practice?"

"Practice was practice." I toss her a smirk, peeling off my jersey and the layers of padding beneath. "Come shower with me."

"Wait." She blatantly stares at my half-naked body, eyes trailing down to the lace-up fly on my pants—the nylon-and-mesh combo clinging tightly to my thighs. "Your housemates could come home any minute."

"Danny's staying at Sofia's tonight." I grin, fingers fumbling with the lace ties. "And Cam knows you're here."

Her eyes darken. "Still . . ."

"Trust me." I pause my movements. "Even if Cam comes home early, he wouldn't care. You should've heard the noises coming from his room last night."

Her brows shoot up. "Wait, really?"

"Yeah," I say awkwardly. "He ended up bringing home that girl from Lucky's."

"The one who was flirting with you?"

"Nah." I brush away her concern with a wince. "He hooked up with her friend."

"You know it's okay, right?"

"What's okay?" I mutter darkly. "That I entertained the idea of picking up some random girl last night when less than a day later, you were already planning to visit . . . It still doesn't sit right."

As she twists to face me, her legs gently sway over the side of the bed. "Baby, we weren't together," she says softly.

"I'm still insisting it was only a break."

"Okay, Rachel." A small, knowing smile graces her features as she shakes her head. "Let's just agree to keep the past in the past. I want to move forward from now on."

I thread our fingers together. "I want that, too."

"Then it's a deal."

"Deal," I echo. "You know, I thought we agreed that you'd be naked when I got back."

She lets out a humorless snort. "No, you agreed on that."

"Well, lucky for us, I quite enjoy undressing you." I give her a playful tug, pulling her toward me. "Stand up."

She complies without hesitation, gently lifting herself up to meet me. My hands, as if guided by muscle memory, navigate their way to her slim waist, fingers gently bunching up the flimsy fabric of her shirt. In one swift motion, I lift it over her head.

"Theo, you're all sweaty."

"Is that so?" I ask, my hands already tugging at her shorts. "Does that gross you out?"

"I—uh, no." Her breath hitches as I press against her. "It's a good thing you're so hot."

"Mm," I hum, my hands slipping beneath her shorts, tracing the elastic band of her panties. "But I'm still filthy, baby. Will you help me get cleaned up?"

"Uh-huh."

"Fuck," I groan out. "I missed—"

Before I can finish, a loud, authoritative knock interrupts us. I reluctantly pull away from my girlfriend and trudge my way over to the door. Swinging it open just enough to peek out, I'm greeted by the disgruntled face of my best friend.

"Hey, man. Sorry to interrupt," he says, forcing a tight smile. "Just came by to let you know Danny scheduled an emergency practice for tomorrow. Defense wasn't on their game, apparently. Elliot plans to do the same for y'all."

The news crushes me. "Fuck, seriously?"

"Yeah, just thought I'd let you know before you made any solid plans."

"Thanks, Cam. Are you sticking around or . . .?"

"I can take a hint, dude." He snorts a laugh. "I'll head out. Just need to grab my stuff, and I'll be gone."

"We'll hang out next weekend, alright?"

"Whatever you say, man."

With that, I close the door, heaving a deep sigh. Our little bubble of bliss has been burst by reality, the promise of more uninterrupted time with Jade now marred by the unexpected practice.

And before Cam's intrusion, I was mere seconds away from dipping my fingers inside her—from touching places I haven't felt in weeks. Even the last time, it was only one stolen night we shared. Before that, it'd been nearly a month since everything was right between us.

Or, *fuck*, since I created the illusion that everything was right.

But now, we are right—pure—so fucking real that it fills the once-empty pit inside my chest. And I was hoping to spend the next two days reveling in it all.

"I know you're upset, but it'll be fine," Jade rushes to assure me. "I entertained myself just fine today, and I can do the same tomorrow."

"I'm not upset," I mutter, running a ragged hand through my hair. "I'm pissed off. We barely have any time together as it is."

She steps closer, pulling me back in. "Then why don't you take your anger out on me instead?"

"What?"

"Be angry at me," she amends. "Remember how I snuck out on you? Left you here all alone in the middle of the night."

My heart pounds. "You—"

"Don't you think I've been a bad girl?" Her fingertips trace the lace on my pants. "Maybe I should be punished."

My dick twitches. "Oh—fuck."

"Tell me what you want, Theo." She gazes up at me through thick lashes, fingers poised and ready to unwrap me like a fucking present.

Am I dreaming?

"Get on your knees, baby." She listens, sinking down in front of me, her hands still clutching at my pants. "I want you to wrap your pretty little mouth around my cock."

She smirks up at me, carefully undoing the laces before sliding the fabric off my hips. Her eyes flash at the sight of my erection. I rake my fingers through her curls and fist a tight handful at the base of her neck.

Her tongue darts out to moisten her lips—once, twice, before her jaw drops open, and she leans in. A groan forms in my throat as the heat of her mouth engulfs the head of my cock. My balls pull up tight, and the skin at the base pulls taut.

One of her small hands wraps around me, moving in rhythm with her mouth, sucking the tip between her lips.

"No," I breathe out, gripping her wrist with my free hand. "I want you to take all of me."

Her eyes meet mine, hooded and promising. She nods, and I tighten my grip on her curls, guiding her down further. My cock pulses as her tongue massages me, almost suctioning me to the roof of her mouth.

"Open your throat, baby."

She complies, taking the last inch of me, choking slightly as I bottom out. A tear slides down her cheek, and I swipe it away with my thumb.

"There's my good girl," I rasp.

I swear I see a smirk in her eyes. She pulls back, bobbing her mouth a few times on my dick. Then she grabs my free hand and guides it to the back of her head. Oh, fuck. Does she want me to—

Her lips slide off me with a wet smack. "Fuck my face."

She doesn't have to tell me twice. I press my palm flat against the back of her head, yanking her into place. Her arms rest gently on her knees as I fuck into her mouth, setting a rough rhythm.

My head falls back. "Fuck—Jade—I—Goddamn."

My legs tremble, my cock straining and on the brink of release. She pulls back, jerking me off with one hand as she hastily unbuttons her top with the other. Then, with a strangled moan, I come, painting her chest with thick stripes of my release.

The world spins as I grab her shoulders, my breath coming in ragged gasps. I exhale deeply, working to regain my composure.

"I feel like I invented you in a fucking lab," I murmur.

Her eyes twinkle as she kneels in front of me. "Sugar, spice, and everything nice?"

"Hell yeah." I smirk. "Sorry you have to deal with my snips and snails, baby."

"I love your snips." She laughs, and it's a rough, throaty sound that sends another twitch of excitement to my dick. Her voice is officially wrecked.

I pull her to her feet. "God, I love you."

"Will you show me?"

Oh, sweet Christ. This fucking girl of mine.

I guide us over to the bed, grabbing a clean shirt from the nightstand. We sit, thigh to thigh, as I clean the remnants of my release off her chest. After discarding the shirt, I gently lay her back on my bed.

As I reach for a condom, she stops me. "Do you think we

could go without one this time? I have an IUD, and I'm clean. Also, I haven't . . . I mean—I haven't been with anyone since you."

My heart jumps into my throat. "You haven't."

"Of course not."

"Of course not," I echo in a low voice. "I mean—me too."

"So, you want to?"

My grin breaks free. "Fuck yeah, I want to."

"I've never—"

"Same," I reassure her, threading our fingers together. "You're my first."

Her lips curve upward at the corners, her smile sweet and shy —such a sharp contrast from the fiery girl who, just moments ago, demanded that I fuck her face.

"Kiss me," she hums.

Eager to obey, I cradle her face, pulling her into a slow, tender kiss. She quickly wriggles out of her shorts and panties, and the contact of her bare skin against mine racks a shiver through my body.

Our hips brush together, and the slickness of her desire warms my thigh. I grab for her waist, dragging my fingertips across the softness of her stomach before dipping down further. My thumb smooths over her pulsing clit.

"You want my hands?" I manage to gasp out.

She shakes her head, her trembling fingers encircling me and guiding me to her entrance. I close my eyes, surrendering myself to the feeling of her wet core pressed against my tip.

With one last ragged breath, I slide my bare cock, inch by gratifying inch, inside her tight pussy. Holy—fucking—shit. I've never felt anything this good before. I rock against her, overwhelmed by the untimely need to explode.

She moans my name, her inner walls clenching as she moves. "Baby—don't—I'm gonna lose it way too early if you keep that up."

"I don't care," she murmurs, hips snapping rhythmically against mine. "Come, Theo."

Theo. Theo. Theo.

I release a deep groan, losing myself completely as I slide in and out of the woman I love. It doesn't take long for us to tumble over the edge, climaxing together. Then, I pull her into my arms and murmur sweet nothings against the top of her head.

I love you. I'll never let you go. You're it for me.

Because this is it. This is everything I've been missing for the last twenty-one years of my life. Not just great sex. Not just sugar, and spice, and everything so fucking nice. But a girl who starts a fire in my heart—one that I'm never willing to let dim.

Chapter Forty

JADE

FORTY IS my new hard limit.

Forty rain-washed summer days and forty long, lonely nights spent away from West. He's been kicking ass at training since my last visit, gearing up for his final collegiate season and next year's draft. Every day, I remind myself why I've chosen to spend this time at home.

Dad's doing okay these days. Even still, his MS is progressive and unpredictable. For now, he's mostly independent with daily life activities, yet his health continues to decline. It could be months from now, years even, but someday he'll need more assistance than our mom alone can offer.

That's why I'll never regret spending my summers in northern Washington—even if that equates to a few disjointed months of long distance.

Family comes first for me. Although someday—perhaps in the not-so-distant future—West could become my family, too. In a way, he already has.

Even when we're hundreds of miles apart, our connection is undeniable. Raw and magnetic, to the point where my parents can't keep their comments about it to themselves. Always mooning about how brightly their little angel's been shining.

So, when Ace offered to pay for our trip to Baltimore, it didn't take much pleading to con him into an extra set of tickets. NFL preseason is about to kick off, and to our shared delight, the star cornerback is scheduled for his first away game.

It's Bobcats versus Nighthawks.

Or, on a more personal note, it's West versus Jade—competing in an impromptu battle over who can provide the most orgasms in a single weekend getaway.

Of course, West is winning. He's always winning.

With less than two hours to kickoff, I find myself perched on the bathroom counter of our hotel room, my legs wrapped around West's shoulders while his lips tease my clit.

"Theo—that—ohh," I murmur, bracing myself on the counter's edge.

My fingers absent-mindedly thread through his thick head of hair. While he sucks and licks like his life depends on it, I resist the urge to grab those silky strands and yank his face even closer, burying that perfect tongue inside me.

"Please," I beg through trembling lips.

He lifts his head from between my legs, replacing his mouth with one thick finger. I gasp as he pushes it slowly inside of me, filling me as the rough pads of his fingers tighten around my hip.

"Please what, baby?"

One fingertip curls against my front wall, and I nearly lose control. "Just fuck me," I finally manage to squeak out.

His lips curve into a smug smile. "No."

"No?" I demand, outraged even as I continue to grind against his hand.

"No." He grins wider. "You're gonna come on my fingers again. Then you're gonna come on my tongue. And then maybe, if you're lucky, I'll let you come on my dick."

A knot of pleasure tightens in my lower belly. "I . . . hate . . . you."

A low, throaty chuckle escapes him, the vibrations against my thigh making my breath hitch. His thumb draws slow, deliberate circles over my clit, and with one last calculated stroke, I come undone.

"There you go, baby." He continues to trace his fingers over my sensitive folds. "Such a good fucking girl."

The following moments are a blur. West's smug smile, his fingers slick with my arousal sliding into his mouth, my hasty attempt to gather my composure. When I finally find my footing, I tell him in a huff, "That doesn't count."

"Like hell it doesn't."

"It was going to be a mutual orgasm, and you sabotaged me! Cheaters never win, West."

"So, I'm West now, huh?" he asks with a teasing smirk. "That's not what you were moaning when I had my tongue—"

"Fine, then you win," I cut him off, folding my arms over my chest. "Game's over. I guess there's no more orgasms for either of us this weekend."

With a chuckle, he pulls me close, wrapping an arm around my shoulders, "And you call me dramatic."

Pettiness fuels me to pull away. "Can you just get out of the bathroom so I can finish getting ready?"

"Sure, Jade." He bumps me with his forearm and flips on the faucet to wash his hands. "If it helps even the score, I'll let you suck me off after the game."

"Theodore Westman-Cooke." I gasp, swatting at his shoulder. "You're an actual heathen."

"Good thing I've already tricked you into falling in love with me."

Before I can formulate a response, he cups my chin between two strong hands, leans in, and kisses me. It's brief but intoxicating. Then he pulls back with a wet, sloppy smack of his lips, saunters out of the bathroom, and flops onto our king-sized bed.

"I still hate you," I call out, cheeks tightening with a smile.

"And I still love you," he lazily calls back.

It takes me nearly twenty minutes to comb through the rough tangles in my curls, scrub away the mascara streaks under my eyelids, and fix up my smudged lipstick. By the time I'm finished, we're chasing the clock.

"Ready to go, love?" I ask as I slip on a pair of sneakers.

"Mhm, don't forget your phone." He nods toward the night-stand. "Uh, Garrett may have texted while you were in there."

"Oh? Did you see what he wanted?"

"I, uh—I swear I didn't intend to read it." He gives me a sheepish look. "I heard the notification, picked up your phone, and just saw the message."

I fight a grin. "Babe, it's fine."

"Well, he wants you to call him."

"Probably just wants to talk about the paper." I swipe my phone off the nightstand, hovering over Garrett's unopened message. "Fall term starts in two weeks, so we might need to start hammering things out."

"Yeah." He gives a humorless snort. "I'm sure that man would love to hammer things out with you."

"Ew, stop." I stifle a gag. West already knows that nothing happened between us—past, present, and certainly not future. "I told you he's in a relationship. He has a partner, whom he *lives* with."

"Yeah, yeah," he says dismissively.

I tuck my credit card, some Carmex, and our hotel key into a transparent bag. Phone in hand, we head out the door.

"Should I call him on our way to the game or just wait until tomorrow?"

"How about you just wait until school starts?" he grumbles. "I'm sure Garrett would love if you did his job for him, just like the end of last term."

"That's not how it was." I thread our fingers together. "We were a team."

We enter the elevator at the end of the hall, and he punches the lobby button, perhaps just a tad too forcefully. "Yeah, a team where he's the editor in chief and you're doing the grunt work without an official title or rank."

"When you put it that way." I stiffen as his thumb presses into my palm, a silent sign of reassurance. "Um, maybe I'll just call him now—see what he wants."

"Sure." He pats his back pocket. "Should I order the Uber?"

"I forgot to tell you Ace sent a car for us. They should be here to pick us up—" I pause for a moment, double-checking the time. "—about five minutes ago."

"God damn it." His grip tightens around my fingers. "I owe him enough for this trip already."

"You don't owe him anything. He's glad to do it."

The elevator dings open, effectively cutting off his continued grumbling. We hustle through the lobby hand in hand, and he tugs me close as we slide through the revolving doors.

Once we make it outside, there's a black SUV waiting for us at the portico, engine idling. West hastily pulls open the back door, and we both rush to slip inside.

This whole thing, from the driver in the tailored suit to the heated leather interior, is some Mica Jennings luxury bullshit. I'm certainly not accustomed to it, but I'm also not complaining.

I nudge West's thigh with my knee. "I'm gonna call him now."

"Go ahead, baby."

I slide one finger over Garrett's contact with a sense of resignation. As expected, he picks up on the first ring. "Warner speaking."

"Hi, you wanted me to call?"

His voice booms through the speaker, businesslike, curt. "Yeah, I need you back on campus next week."

"What?" My brow crinkles. "I'm not planning on coming back until the Saturday before term starts."

"As co-editor in chief this year, I need you here for planning purposes."

A stunned silence falls over me. "As what now?"

"Co-editor."

I can't help but shake my head, although I know he can't see me. "No, I heard you the first time, but I'm a little confused. Since when am I co-editor?"

Beside me, West comes alive, his eyes darting in my direction, searching my face for answers I can't give. I shrug, lost in the same confusion he must be feeling.

Garrett's voice returns, methodical and plain. "I thought it was intuited after all our teaming last term."

"Garrett, no," I say, my tone a mixture of amusement and disbelief. "You don't just *intuit* something like that."

"Okay, so you're declining?"

"No, I'm not. Just hold on one second." I push the heel of my palm against West's knee, seeking his grounding presence, his silent support. "What would this entail?"

"You'd be doing a lot of the same work you helped me with last spring. You'd also need to head up a few sections. I've put you down for feature, student life, maybe news. Of course, I assume you'll want the sports section."

"No."

"No, what?" His voice has an edge, a tiny crack in his composed façade. "So, you are turning down the position?"

"No, I want to be co-editor, but I want nothing to do with student life." With West's knee as my anchor, I push back. "You should take that section."

"Done," he fires back, leaving me blinking in surprise.

"Done? Really, it's that easy?"

"You're a valuable asset, Jennings. I'm not afraid to make compromises so that I can keep you."

"Uh, thank you," I manage, glancing at West, my face burning. "I'm glad we'll be official partners."

"Agreed. I'm sure you'll be most happy to divvy up the football coverage however you see fit."

"It's funny you say that, considering I'm still gonna have to trade off with Liam this year."

"Why's that?" His question hangs in the air, just long enough to make me squirm.

"Uh—I promised my brother I'd go to more Bobcats games. I'm actually on my way to one now."

"You two big fans or something?"

I pause awkwardly, then plunge right ahead. "Actually . . . my brother is Mica Jennings."

"Nice. Am I—supposed to know him?"

I laugh then, a choked sound that has me leaning against West's shoulder for support. "No, Garrett. No, you're not."

"Alright, then." He clears his throat, regrouping. "So, I'll see you on campus next week?"

"That actually won't work for me. How about the Thursday before term?"

His negotiation is swift. "Make it Wednesday and you've got yourself a deal."

"Great." I deflate, dragging my hands over my face to hide my beaming smile. "See you on the twenty-sixth."

"Have a good evening. I hope you and your brother enjoy the game."

"Thank you." My voice is raw, strained. And then the call ends.

Silence stretches on between me and West, thick and heavy, until it snaps with my laughter. Unrestrained, I double over, shaking with the force of it. Through watery eyes, I find West grinning back at me.

He presses a kiss to my head, his voice brimming with pride and affection. "That man is still a certified dipshit. But my God, Jade—I'm so fucking proud of you."

Chapter Forty-One

WHOEVER FABRICATED ALL that nasty shit about long distance—how it's undeniably stressful, how it's taxing on your relationship, how every damn day is a fight to stay connected—well, they must not have felt the way I feel.

Of course I've missed Jade over these last few months, but it's only her physical presence that's been absent. I still get to hear the sounds of her sweet laughter, see the pretty smile on her face, and listen to those witty little quips I've grown to love.

Although I don't get to feel her, touch her, taste her as often as I'd like . . . I sure do spend plenty of time thinking about it. Actually, I think about Jade pretty much nonstop—on the field, in the locker rooms, and late at night from the safety of my own bedroom.

That's when I get so fucking lost in the memories of her, in the sweet sounds of her moaning my name.

Theo. Theo. Theo.

I wish I could bottle that sound and drink it before every big game. I'd definitely be a shoo-in for the first draft pick.

Honestly, my prospects are pretty fucking ace anyway.

Coach has positioned me in a solid spot for scouting this season. He's been pushing me toward the feature back title. He also put me on a two-week speed challenge to shave time off my forty-yard dash.

It's the best chance I have of making the draft. We've been developing my highlights reel, and now we're cutting down on my run time. In the past week and a half, I went from a 4.49 to a 4.44. For now, my time beats the average, but I know I can still do better.

I just need to keep my eyes on the fucking prize.

In reality, I need to shut off my brain for a few minutes and stop daydreaming about my gorgeous girlfriend. The same one who's headed back to campus as we speak.

I scrub a towel across my still-damp hair, lightly gelling the strands while I stare down my reflection. My lips curve into a full-out grin as I recite my daily mantra: "My name's Theo, and I'm smart as hell."

Jade was right—that silly affirmation has helped me manifest all the best shit in my life. This last year, I passed all my classes. I kept my scholarship. And most importantly, I got my fucking girl back.

I think I owe it to the mantra now.

Once I spot Jade's familiar curls bobbing in the crowded terminal, my heart starts pumping wildly against my chest, my stomach filling with that same giddiness I felt on our first date.

She perches onto her tiptoes, scanning the sea of unfamiliar faces until our eyes catch. Then she breaks into a clumsy sprint as I fling my arms out. A moment later, her body collides with mine.

"I missed you so much, baby." I tuck my nose against the crown of her head, breathing in that sweet, floral scent.

"It's only been ten days," she murmurs, capturing my lips in a chaste kiss.

"Mhm, and I thought about you every second."

A light flush of pink colors her cheeks. "I'm sure you thought about me while Coach was kicking your ass out there."

"Hell yeah, I did." I pull back, threading our fingers together. "Especially afterward . . . you know, while I showered in the locker rooms."

Her head drops back with a teasing groan. "You're relentless."

"And? You love that about me."

"You know, if you do end up sharing the field with my brother, then you're gonna need to keep that shit on lockdown."

She's right. After watching Mica play in Baltimore, I've been itching for a spot on his team. Not only does he love his job, but the Bobcats have been killing it their last few seasons. Mica also promised to put in a good word for me.

Apparently, he'd love for us to be teammates, although his reasons might be selfish. Before I flew back to Dayton, he cornered me and said, "If you're on my team, then it'll just be easier to kick your ass if you hurt my baby sister."

Fortunately for both of us, that's never gonna happen. Not again, anyway.

I bring our joined hands to my mouth, lips pressing against her skin. "Jade."

"Mhm?"

"You know, I've been thinking . . . we still have a few days before term starts. I'll have some time off. What do you think about a road trip? We could drive up the coast, hit up Amber Isle, maybe."

She blinks in surprise before a slow smile curls the edges of her lips. "You want to take me to the beach?"

"Yeah," I say, squeezing her hand gently. "Maybe it could be our thing. Every year, no matter where life takes us, we take a long weekend and head to the coast. Just you and me."

"That sounds perfect."

"Then it's a deal." I pull her in for another kiss. "Our annual tradition, no matter what."

"I'm excited." She shifts on the balls of her feet, eyes shining. "I've actually never been there before."

"I'd be happy to pop your cherry, babe."

She snorts a laugh, swatting me on the arm. "Of course you would."

"You know, I also heard that Amber Isle's a good place to get married."

Her eyes go wide. "Let's not get ahead of ourselves."

"No, I know." I flash her a warm smile, my heart clenching. "But don't worry, in a few years, I'll find the most perfect way to propose to you. And when I finally get that ring on your finger, it's gonna be because I deserve it."

She pulls back, blinking up at me with those pretty brown eyes. "You think so?"

"Yes," I say. "And don't think I won't come to collect."

THE END

Epilogue

JADE

TODAY'S THE DAY. It's my boyfriend's first official NFL game.

I'm all geared up in my Bobcats jersey with West's last name proudly displayed across the back. Last April, he was selected by the Bobcats as the nineteenth draft pick. We always knew he was a shoo-in for the first round, but Carolina was a toss-up until the very end.

Needless to say, my brother and I went absolutely feral when we heard the news.

Now, nearly four months later, I'm prepping for a trip to the stadium, yanking a few wayward curls from my ponytail. The two of us are running late again, as per usual. But just as soon as I pop that last flyaway into place, the front door of my apartment smacks open.

"Jesus Christ, Cam," I chide, tossing a throw pillow directly at his head. "Did I not tell you to stop barging in here?"

Cam was given a key to our apartment last June, just on the off chance that I'd need his help checking in. With West constantly training and traveling, he wanted me to have a backup, a failsafe in case anything was to happen.

Honestly, he's similar to my brother in that respect. Protective, cautious, and overbearing at times.

Sure, I'm often left alone in our city apartment, but I honestly crave the solitude when West's away. It's my time to breathe, relax, and rejuvenate from the busy lifestyle that we both lead. Besides, I'm mostly cooped up studying anyway.

My master's in Sports Journalism is grueling work, and the Hussmann School is a full-time commitment.

"Yeah, well, this is an emergency," Cam says, jutting out his chin. "We're about to be late as fuck."

I sigh, tucking my cell phone into my back pocket. My eyes dart to the clock above our stove, indicating that we are, indeed, about to be late as fuck.

"Sorry, I was trying to see if I could fit my lucky sweatshirt under this jersey, but it's gonna be too fucking hot."

"No shit. It's still summer." He gestures toward my open doorway with a wild flourish of his arm. My stomach's in knots as we rush from the apartment together, practically running toward the back parking lot.

We both skid to a stop when I spot his familiar SUV. Cam's parked sidelong in a space marked for WC & J Residence Only. I quirk a brow in his direction, hands flattened against my knees as I catch my breath.

"You know, there's visitor parking here."

"Just get in the damn car, Jennings."

The ride to the stadium is a whirlwind of nerves and excitement, punctuated by Cam's erratic driving and an unending stream of music blasting through the speakers. The nerves in my stomach tie themselves in knots, one over another, a tangible manifestation of the excitement I've been trying to keep at bay.

"I think your heart's about to jump out of your damn chest," Cam points out, a teasing lilt to his voice.

I let out a small laugh, my fingers unconsciously tracing the hemline of my jersey. "You're not doing any better. Don't even try to hide it."

The retort earns me a smirk and an exaggerated eye roll. But all conversation stops as the stadium finally comes into view. The transition from nervous anticipation to pure, unabashed joy is almost surreal.

And now, it's been hours since we parked and found our seats, hours since the initial excitement gave way to a colossal tidal wave of pride.

In fact, I don't think I've ever been prouder of West than I am in this moment.

Well, except for that time when he passed his English Lit course. Or when he graduated from Dayton with a degree in Social Sciences, subverting the low expectations he set for himself. But this is definitely a close third.

Both my boys are killing it on the field tonight. West is rushing the ball like his life depends on it, while Mica dominates the defensive line. At the end of the fourth quarter, West lines himself up, takes two steps toward the line of scrimmage, and throws a quick pass to their team's tight end.

The completion lands him his first regular-season pass for a touchdown. The sounds of celebration are ear-piercing, nearly drowning out the announcer's voice. "And that's the game, folks. The Carolina Bobcats take home the win, with a score of—"

It's complete chaos in the family box. Cam and I are losing our minds, cheering and screaming alongside the ear-piercing crowd. When I glance over, West's mom, Aileen, has tears streaming down her face. I wrap my arms around her, embracing her small frame as she cries into my hair.

Aileen is not only one of the kindest women I know, but she's also filled to the brim with adoration for her one and only son. Although my parents couldn't make it to today's game, they're watching it live and incessantly texting us all in the group chat. I swear my phone hasn't stopped buzzing since the start of the game.

Aileen tilts back, fingers braced around my body while she holds me at arm's length. "I'm so proud of our boy," she says, projecting her voice through quiet sniffles.

"He's really something, isn't he?"

She finally releases me, turning to embrace Cam with similar vigor. My eyes drift around the crowded box, latching onto the faces of dozens of team spouses and significant others.

They're all cheering for their partners in equal measure. And although it's endearing to see their smiles, there's a pang in my chest at the thought of what's missing.

I'm the only person here to represent my brother, for what feels like the hundredth time. No wife and no semblance of a girlfriend, not even the promise of one. Because Mica Jennings is still . . . himself. Jumping from girl to girl, partying after away games, and having his name plastered in the tabloids.

No plans for settling down anytime soon.

He says it doesn't bother him, but I know, deep down, he wishes he had someone to come home to at the end of the day. I can see it every time he looks at West and me—happily in love and moving through the next chapters of our lives together.

And when we're all around Shannon, he barely even glances in her direction. I know he doesn't want to upset me, but we've all moved on except for him. It's like he can't even stand the sight of her now.

As for Shannon's feelings on the matter, well, it's clear she's no longer impressed by my brother. She's happily partnered up with someone else and has been for the last six months. Regardless, I wish Mica could find his own version of a happy ending, and sooner rather than later.

By the time the team filters into the box, I'm a giddy ball of anticipation. Player after player saunters through, each with a well-deserved swag to their step. They hug and kiss their partners, happily chattering away about the game.

And it's not long before I catch West's eye.

His face carries the brightest smile I've ever seen from him, gaze laser focused on mine. He takes a few long, purposeful strides toward me, pushing through the crowd with one mission in mind.

It's obvious from the look in his eye—West is about to kiss the shit out of me.

I pop up from my seat to meet him halfway, our lips crashing together. This isn't just a game-winning kiss or a simple victory peck. It's a pride-filled declaration of love for the person I can't live without.

When he pulls back, his hands are still cupped around my face.

"You were incredible out there," I murmur.

He kisses me again, this time a gentle press of his lips to my forehead. "God, I fucking love you," he says.

I return the sentiment, nodding to his mother on my right. He takes a moment to collect himself, as if he just remembered that he's in a room filled with his teammates and their family members. It's not just the two of us here, existing in our own little world.

He embraces his mom, then his best friend, then it's right back to me. "Where's Ace?" I ask, eyes darting around the box.

"He said he'll catch up with us later. He needed to have a word with his agent, I guess." He wraps an arm around my shoulder, turning his attention to our company. "As for me, I think I need a quick detour to the restroom. I'm gonna have Jade walk with me if that's cool?"

Cam playfully rolls his eyes, shooting us both a shit-eating grin. His mother, on the other hand, appears blissfully unaware. "Sure, honey, just don't be gone too long," she says, shaking her phone toward us. "I want to get some good pictures of all of us."

"Of course, Mom."

His fingers thread through mine, tugging me behind him as we bob and weave around the crowd. He guides me toward a private bathroom in the upper-level suites, single-minded and sure-footed.

As soon as we're shut inside together, his hands are glued to my hips.

"Sorry." He ducks his head, murmuring the words against my neck. "I just needed a moment alone with you."

"Don't be sorry."

"That was incredible." He shakes his head, damp hair tickling below my ears before he pulls back. "And you—fucking hell, you look so damn good in my jersey. Mica's never gonna get to see you wearing his number again."

"You know he'd kill both of us for that. I promised him I'd rotate."

"Whatever." His lips curve into a full-out grin. "I can't even care about that right now. Just—I need to kiss you."

He snakes a hand around the nape of my neck, tugging me closer as our lips meet.

"You did so great today," I mumble against him. "When you made that final pass to Fischer, I almost lost my mind."

"I know, right?" He moves to place soft kisses against my cheeks, my chin, my forehead. "That was fucking wild—my first touchdown pass in the League. I'm still so wired."

"I bet you are. I know I am." In fact, I doubt that I've ever felt more alive than I do in this moment. There's nothing like watching the love of your life finally achieve his dreams. "I'm so proud of you, though."

"Say that again," he groans.

"I'm proud of you?"

"Yeah, that." His head tilts back, a pleased smile on his face.

"Okay, well, I am." I run my fingertips along his muscled arms, trailing up until I'm cupping the underside of his jaw. "Proud of you, that is. I also love you. So. Damn. Much."

"I love you . . . and I need you." His fingers slide up my neck, thumbs circling the soft spot under my ears. "Can I please fuck you?"

"Here?" I gasp his name, squirming as he shifts our hips together. "My brother, your mom, and your best friend are all out there waiting for us."

His head dips as our lips brush. "I don't see your point."

"My point is—" Another gasp leaves me as his teeth nip at the shell of my ear. "—we can do this later. You know, when we head back to our apartment tonight."

"Always so logical," he grumbles.

"If I get on my knees, will that tide you over for a few hours?"

He pulls back, swallowing past the lump in his throat. "I—you . . . Christ. Really?"

"Shh." I press my index finger to his lips, trailing it down his chest as I drop to my knees. "Let me show you how proud I am of you. Just for a minute."

My fingers make quick work on the fly of his pants, sliding inside to grasp the length of him. He's painfully hard already. His cock sits heavy in the palm of my hand, warm and throbbing as I pump him over once. Twice. I pitch forward, lips primed to—

And then, there's a pounding on the door, an unwelcome interruption to West's game-winning prize.

"Get the fuck out here, you two!" The sound of Mica's voice hits us like a cold bucket of water, dashing both our hopes for a little post-game fun.

"Shit," West grumbles, hastily tucking himself back inside his pants, dick rapidly deflating at the thought of being caught by my brother.

"Give us a second," I call back, voice dripping with irritation.

Mica pounds on the door again, three times before he finally relents. I listen for the sound of his footsteps trailing away. Then, with one tiny shred of regret, I finally get off my knees.

"I guess we should head back out there," West mutters, a warm flush to his cheeks.

"I think that would be wise. Later, though, I promise."

His laughter is warm, soft, a sweet melody that wraps around me like a familiar blanket. "You know, I can't wait to come home to you . . . every day for the rest of my life."

My heart clenches. "Pretty sure you have to ask me first."

"Don't you worry that pretty little head." He gently flicks the end of my nose, a playful smile on his lips. "It's coming."

"I love you, Theo."

"And I love you," he promises with one final kiss to my crown. "More than anything."

Acknowledgments

Thank you to all my wonderful OG readers who've been waiting for this book for over two years now. This was one of the first full-length novels I ever completed, and it's been a blast to see how far it's come.

Thank you, as always, to my beautiful baby girl and to my husband for their support.

Very huge thank you to my beta readers, Ale, Megan, and Nikki, for helping me refine this story! Without you, The Trade wouldn't be where it is today.

Thank you to my forever friends, Becka, Erin, and Hannah, for sticking around with me all this time.

Thank you to my bestie, Shannon, for lending me the use of her name.

Thank you to my editor, Sandra, for being so sweet and flexible, and for helping me put the final touches on my last three novels.

And one final thank you to every person reading this. I'm endlessly humbled by all of your support.

About the Author

Ki Stephens is a romance enthusiast who finds comfort in the happily-ever-after . . . with just a little bit of angst along the way. She has a special interest in works that include neurodivergent characters like herself. When she's not daydreaming about books, Ki enjoys working with kids, creating art in her backyard studio, and spending loads of time with her baby girl, her husband, and their three pets.

She released her debut novel, Spring Tide—Book 1 in the Coastal University Series, in December of 2022.

www.kistephens.com

Made in the USA
Coppell, TX
13 January 2024

27633279R00208